HIS CINDERELLA HOUSEGUEST

CHARLOTTE HAWKES

MENDING THE ER DOC'S HEART

SUSAN CARLISLE

MILLS & BOON

First published in Great Britain 2022
by Mills & Boon, an imprint of HarperCollins*Publishers* Ltd,
1 London Bridge Street, London, SE1 9GF

www.harpercollins.co.uk

HarperCollins*Publishers*
1st Floor, Watermarque Building,
Ringsend Road, Dublin 4, Ireland

His Cinderella Houseguest © 2022 Charlotte Hawkes

Mending the ER Doc's Heart © 2022 Susan Carlisle

ISBN: 978-0-263-30135-9

08/22

...them, and ...or ...ting—or building with blocks—she is company director for a small Anglo/French construction firm. Charlotte loves to hear from readers, and you can contact her at her website: charlotte-hawkes.com.

Susan Carlisle's love affair with books began when she made a bad grade in mathematics. Not allowed to watch TV until the grade had improved, she filled her time with books. Turning her love of reading into a love for writing romance, she pens hot Medicals. She loves castles, travelling, afternoon tea, reading voraciously and hearing from her readers. Join her newsletter at SusanCarlisle.com.

Also by Charlotte Hawkes

Tempted by Her Convenient Husband

Billionaire Twin Surgeons miniseries

Shock Baby for the Doctor
Forbidden Nights with the Surgeon

Also by Susan Carlisle

The Single Dad's Holiday Wish
Reunited with Her Daredevil Doc
Taming the Hot-Shot Doc
From Florida Fling to Forever

Discover more at millsandboon.co.uk.

HIS CINDERELLA HOUSEGUEST

CHARLOTTE HAWKES

MILLS & BOON

CHAPTER ONE

THE MUSCULAR MOTORBIKE hugged the bend tightly and skilfully hurtled along the quiet A roads as Dr Lincoln Oakes—Lord Oakes to those who knew his family—raced to work on time.

He was never late. *Never.*

Strictly speaking, he supposed he wasn't late now. The crew weren't due on the air ambulance base until seven o'clock and it was still only six-forty. But that didn't make him feel any less agitated; it was a full ten minutes past the time he usually liked to be in work—always the first one in.

As if timings—not never-ending nightmares of that hellish night in the last war zone he'd been in—were the sole cause of his agitation.

Shifting on his motorbike, Linc accelerated harder and drew down from the sense of satisfaction that slid through him as the sleek machine emitted another throaty roar as it surged smoothly along the road.

As if that would change anything.

As though tearing along these country lanes meant he could somehow outpace the ghosts that haunted him, or silence the voices that whispered their accusations to him in the witching hours. The nightmares were turning his head into a battle zone so that every time he jerked awake he could practically hear the gunfire, smell the acrid smoke, and feel the scorching Afghanistan sun.

Anniversaries of that terrible night were always painful, but this one—the fifth one—was hitting him harder than usual. No doubt because it had only been a month since the funeral of the old Duke of Stoneywell—the man who had been not only his father but his guide for the first two decades of Linc's life, but who had been more like a stranger these latter fifteen years, and not just because of the cruel disease that was Alzheimer's.

Without warning, memories closed in on Linc, making the scraping inside him all the more intense, and raw. He pushed them forcefully away; the last thing he needed was to be late for his job as an air ambulance doctor and miss a shout. How many more people could he fail to help?

Rolling the throttle as he leaned his bike, Linc powered around another tight bend—as if he could somehow escape his demons. As if he didn't know by now that it was impossible. But if he could just get through the next few days, after that they would grow weaker, and he'd be able to stuff them down for another year.

Finally, the roof of the Helimed hangar pulled into view. The glint of the morning sun off the harsh metal coverings. Down this straight, and a left into the entrance road, and he'd be there—into yet another shift that could mercifully occupy his thoughts for the next twelve hours.

Skidding his rear tyre as he drew to an abrupt halt, Linc threw his leg over the seat and yanked his helmet off as he moved. Another few strides and he was hurrying into the building where the close-knit team relaxed in between shouts, and he waited for familiar sounds to chase his ghosts away; letting them slink off at the door the way they always did when he was around his crew.

But today, instead of everyone being gathered in the

kitchen, the usual mouth-watering breakfast cooking smells filling the air, his attention was drawn to the rec room—their recreation space—where there seemed to be something of a meeting going on.

Spinning sharply, he strode down the corridor and slipped into the room alongside Tom, one of the two paramedics on his crew.

'What's the story?' he asked, jerking his head towards the air ambulance charity's regional coordinator. 'What's he doing here?'

'You just got here?' Tom craned his neck around in surprise. 'You're always the first one in.'

'First time for everything.' Linc tried to shrug it off, even as he hated to do so. 'So, what's going on?'

'It seems Albert and Jenny were in a car accident on their way home last night.'

'Hell.' Something walloped into Linc, hard and low. 'What happened?'

Albert had been their Helimed crew's pilot for as long as anyone could remember and was like a father figure to the rest of them. They had a standing joke that the older guy had been installed along with the oldest parts of the rec room's ratty furniture.

Even Jenny, Albert's real-life daughter, had started as second paramedic on the team on the very same day that Linc himself had begun, four years ago. So, in a tight crew like this they weren't just colleagues, they were also like family.

'Not sure exactly what happened.' Tom shook his head. 'But apparently it's serious but not life threatening.'

'Well, that's something at least.' Linc blew out a deep breath.

'Yeah. We're just waiting on more news.'

'And that's what the chief came to say?'

'That and the fact that he's managed to get hold of an outside pilot for today's shift.'

'Why an outside pilot?' Linc frowned. 'Echo team's pilot is our go-to standby. What about a second paramedic?'

'We haven't got echo team's pilot—not unless he's turned into one of the hottest females I reckon I've ever seen.'

Linc snorted. 'Playboy Paramedic Tom's on heat again.'

Though to be fair, Tom's flirting always came second when he was a shout. Playboy or not, Tom was a damned good paramedic.

'Yeah, yeah.' The other man laughed now. 'I can't help it if women love me. They love you too, only you're too damned prickly to ever notice. As for our second paramedic, it's Probie.'

Linc eyed the lad across the room. In an air ambulance unit like theirs, they almost always had a trainee with them, whether it was a trainee doctor, or a trainee paramedic, and they almost always got the nickname Probie. This particular lad had been a land ambulance paramedic for years before he'd joined their Helimed crew. Making him up to a full-blown second paramedic to cover Jenny seemed like the good decision.

The new pilot, on the other hand, was a different matter.

'Fair enough re Probie,' Linc muttered. 'But I still don't see why they don't just bring in echo team's pilot. At least we'd all know how this particular crew works.'

'You know that Albert had started to talk to the powers that be about retirement, right?'

'Damn, I knew he was thinking about it,' Linc conceded. 'I didn't realise he'd actually spoken to anyone outside our team, though.'

'Apparently HQ already had feelers out for a new permanent pilot.'

'Yeah, well, they've got big shoes to fill replacing Albert. He was a top-notch RAF pilot with countless missions under his belt.'

'And apparently this new pilot is Army Air Corps. Plus she has over a decade's experience.'

Something slammed into Linc before he had time to think. A memory that punctured his chest and then bounced around, rattling at his ribcage, and evading his attempts to capture it.

'Army Air Corps?' he echoed, more sharply than he'd intended.

'Yeah. HQ were desperate when the call came in about Albert so they ended up phoning the regiment up the road to see if the military could lend us a pilot even for the day.'

'It's about eighty miles away,' Linc pointed out jerkily. 'Hardly *up the road.*'

'You know what I mean.' Tom brushed it off. 'Anyway, from what I can gather, the AAC told HQ that they could lend us a pilot, and that she's even getting ready to leave the military for Civvy Street. Regional have been falling over themselves all morning at the idea of securing her as a permanent replacement for Albert.'

The memory rattled harder in Linc's chest. There was no rational explanation for it, yet it was there all the same.

A feeling.

An image.

Piper.

He hadn't thought of her in years. No, scratch that—he hadn't *allowed* himself to think of her in years. Which was a slightly different thing.

An Apache pilot within the Army Air Corps, Piper had served on several tours of duty with him—including that last one. Her skill and passion for her career had made her a guardian angel of the skies, and a glorious light illuminating the darkness of that hellhole.

And if it hadn't been for Piper's fast thinking and even faster flying, then those enemy leakers would have slipped the lines and managed to get into the hospital where he and his team had been holed up with the civilian patients. Which would have simply meant more numbers added to the body count that final hellish day.

But more than her skill and dedication to her career, the two of them had grown close on that tour, seeking each other out during downtime, sharing war stories, or simply trying to make sense of the events of a particular day or week.

Not to mention the *almost-kiss* the two of them hadn't quite shared.

If his responsibilities to his brother—the acting Duke of Stoneywell—hadn't left him no choice but to leave his beloved army a matter of weeks later, Linc had often wondered what might have happened between him and Piper.

Linc shoved the memories away, the way he had on those few occasions when she'd sprung, unbidden, to mind over the past few years. Whoever the new female pilot was, it wouldn't be Piper. The woman had always been married to her career above all else—there'd be no way Piper would be leaving the AAC for Civvy Street. She'd always joked that they'd probably have to carry her out of that job in a wooden box.

'Linc?' Tom's voice dragged him back to the present and he forced himself to focus on his colleague.

The last thing he needed was another haunting by his past right now.

'Yeah? Oh, right?' His voice sounded scratchy, but that couldn't be helped. 'Well, I guess an ex-AAC pilot wouldn't be a bad stand-in for the crew.'

'And if Albert's finally ready to enjoy a bit of retirement, then we can't exactly begrudge him that, can we?'

'Right,' Linc grated, his mind still racing despite his attempts to calm it.

It was almost a small mercy when a flurry of movement in the corridor negated the need for him to add more, as the charity's regional co-ordinator bustled cheerfully back in, a figure at his back.

'Okay, team, I'm delighted to introduce you to your new pilot. This is Piper Green.'

Linc's entire world—his entire being—went suddenly, somehow…liquid, and yet granite hard, all at the same time. It was a miracle his diaphragm could even move enough to allow him to keep breathing.

For a moment, he had to wonder if he was seeing things…if she'd been conjured up by the fact that he'd just been thinking about her. And the morning sun shining at her back like some kind of prophetic halo only made it seem all the more as though the image from his head had somehow slid out into the real world.

But slowly, *slowly*, his brain began to process what his eyes were seeing.

'Legs?'

Linc was hardly aware of uttering her name—well, nickname, anyway. He certainly didn't recognise his own voice, and the fact that he hadn't uttered it loudly meant that she oughtn't to have heard him from her position across the room. But he didn't think it was his imagination that she turned her head slowly and she looked straight at him, those familiar, all too expressive rich amber depths seeming to pierce right through him.

The five years fell away in an instant. It might as well have been yesterday that they'd last seen each other. There was no denying that…*thing* that still coursed between them, as powerful, and greedy, and urgent, as it had once been. For several long moments, Linc simply drank her in. As if he were back in that parched, bone-brittle desert, and she were his only source of crystal-clear water. He might have known it couldn't last long.

Abruptly, something followed the attraction; something that was far more potent—and unwelcome—than mere chemistry. It punched through Linc in that split second before he quashed it, and it was all he could do to stay standing in the doorway—affecting a casual air—as he folded his arms across his chest. As though that could somehow protect him from the emotions charging through him.

Attraction. History. But worst of all, *guilt.* For leaving at the end of that last tour without even a word. Because he didn't let people get close and he didn't get attached.

And Piper had threatened to do both.

Dimly, Linc became aware of his crewmate talking, but it was impossible to process anything over the roar in his head.

'Say again?' he murmured.

He wasn't sure he could have dragged his gaze from Piper, even if he'd tried. And by the way she was staring back at him—slightly wide-eyed and just as dazed—he thought perhaps she was finding it just as surreal. But if he didn't get a grip quickly, the entire crew was going to know that something was up and that might lead to questions he wasn't prepared to answer.

Even to himself.

With a concerted effort, Linc forced a more neutral expression onto his face, and lifted his voice to something approaching a normal tone.

'Hello, Piper, it's been a long time. Welcome to Heathston Helimed, otherwise known as Helimed hotel one-niner.'

Linc was here?

Somehow Piper resisted the compulsion to shake her

head. As if that could somehow dislodge the apparition that stood in front of her.

'*Doc?* Major Lincoln Oakes?' she heard herself say. Casually. Teasingly. Somehow conveying the impression that she was in total control, when the reality was that her legs thought they might buckle under her at any moment. 'It can't be.'

This was the man who had haunted her across time, and the planet, for the past five years? Even as she eyed him, it felt as though their history was unrolling between them— as rich as any eleventh-century tapestry—for the entire Helimed base to see, if she wasn't careful.

For the better part of six months, on the worst tour of duty she'd ever been on, he'd been her go-to. The person she'd most looked forward to seeing—in the mess hall, in the officers' tent, or even just on the sandy perimeter line that made for a makeshift running track in that godforsaken camp—to offload the events of the day.

In an environment like a theatre of war, bonds could be forged quickly. Tightly. It was entirely possible for a colleague to know and understand you better than your own family. And it had been like that with Linc. They'd somehow…*clicked*.

Until their *almost-kiss* had nearly ruined it all.

They'd agreed it was a mistake—a line they would never again risk crossing—and still, a month later he'd left the armed services altogether, leaving her feeling vulnerable, and foolish.

If she'd known he was part of this crew, she would never have taken the post—emergency or not.

Okay, that wasn't precisely true. But she would surely have been better prepared for the inevitable encounter. A strong pep talk maybe—that reminded her just how she could resist Lincoln Oakes's particular brand of all things male. Thank goodness she'd already changed into the armour of her heavy-duty flight suit.

Not that it seemed to matter. Somehow, she still felt half naked and completely exposed in front of him.

'You two know each other?'

Piper blinked, startled. She turned her attention to the paramedic standing next to Linc, with his practised smile and easy charm. The guy was clearly accustomed to women falling at his feet, and he was certainly good-looking. But she hadn't even noticed him, standing next to Linc. From the instant that Linc had spoken, her entire world had zoomed in on just the two of them—like the narrow shot of one of those photographs she'd taken out in that bleak war zone.

She didn't care to analyse what that said about her. Or her unresolved feelings for a man she hadn't seen in half a decade, and hadn't really expected to ever see again. No matter what little fantasies her subconscious had conjured up sometimes, in the dead of night.

But now wasn't the time to dwell on that. Piper dredged up a bright smile and tried to remember what the guy had even said. Nothing came to mind, and it was a relief when Linc's rich, steady voice answered instead.

'Piper was an Apache pilot back when I served. We did a couple of tours together.'

'Apaches?' The other guy nodded with another practised grin. 'Sweet.'

And Piper couldn't help noticing the way Linc's jaw tightened. Was he remembering the undeniable chemistry that they'd once shared? Even if they'd deemed it too inappropriate for their respective military roles? Or was that purely in her own head?

Even now, as she watched him smooth his chin with his forefinger and thumb, a delicious shiver rippled over her back. How insane was it that she could still recall precisely how it had felt when that calloused thumb had once skated over her cheek to brush away the desert dust that seemed to get into absolutely everything? The way her breath had caught as his head had dipped, ever so slightly, towards hers.

And then the camp's shrill sniper alarm that had ripped them apart.

Piper tried telling herself that it was that particular all too vivid, adrenalin-pumping memory that made her blood pound through her body right now. A physiological reaction to that alarm call, rather than to the man standing right in front of her.

Maybe she would have believed the lie, had regret not still rippled through those nights when the ghosts of that almost-kiss would tiptoe through her dreams. A muted sorrow that the single moment five years ago had been shattered, their one chance gone.

No, she'd certainly never expected to see Linc again. Yet suddenly, here he was. Here *she* was.

It didn't matter how hard the logical, practical side of her brain told her that it was merely coincidence, it didn't silence the low, deep hum inside her. A hum that told her it wasn't just chance—it was something more. Something she didn't dare put a name to, but if she had dared, she might have called it…*fate*.

'So she's a good pilot, then?'

The colleague's question brought her crashing back to reality—to the here and now. She watched as Linc did that thing with his head that wasn't a shrug, precisely, but was just as non-committal. Standard, unreadable Major Lincoln Oakes.

'Yeah, Piper's a good pilot, and what we called army barmy,' he confirmed evenly to his colleague before turning back to her. 'So you can't seriously be thinking of jacking it in and heading to Civvy Street?'

There was something strangely comforting in his words, although his question set off the pounding in her chest again. Though this time for a different reason. He was right, the Army Air Corps had been her life—*flying* had been her life—but the army had its own drum beat, and it was her time to move on from Captain and get her Majority. But a Captain flying helis was appropriate—a Major flying them was not. And you couldn't exactly tell the Army that you didn't want a promotion.

Besides, running a flight-training wing would have taken her further from her mother and brother, for longer. And they both needed her; now as much as ever.

Still, Linc didn't need to know any of this.

'Not thinking of.' She wasn't sure where the nonchalant laugh came from, but at least it sounded a lot more natural than it felt. 'Already done. Paperwork went in three months ago and I'm officially out the door within this next month, hence why they were happy to loan me out to your air ambulance when they got the emergency call this morning.'

'You drove down this morning? It's a ninety-minute drive.'

'One of my colleagues flew me in,' she explained, awkwardly. Though she couldn't have said why.

It was almost a relief when the paramedic inadvertently rescued her.

'Who cares whether she drove, or flew in?' he clucked, making her smile despite everything. 'Allow me to be more welcoming than my colleague here. I'm Tom, Heathston Helimed's most eligible bachelor—August edition. It's great to meet you, Piper.'

There was such an easy likeability to the guy that she

couldn't help grinning. At least it was easier than all the sizzling tension between her and Linc.

'Hi, Tom. Nice to meet you.' She grinned, shaking the paramedic's outstretched hand. 'Sorry about your crew-mate, Albert. I hope he makes a speedy recovery.'

'We all do,' Tom agreed. 'Though, in the meantime, it looks as though you're the newest member of Helimed hotel one-niner—*Legs*, was it?'

'Old army nicknames,' Linc dismissed smoothly. 'Shared tours of duty. That's it.'

Tom looked greedily from one to the other. 'Nah, there's a story here, right? I can feel it in my bones.'

'Your bones are just going to have to wait, then.'

Piper whirled around as another crewman, who she'd seen manning the air desk in the room across the hall, now stepped through the doorway. 'Nine-nine-nine call just came in; not a lot of info, just that there's a kid on a bike somewhere near Roughston Lake. He's gone over and it sounds like there's an arterial injury; he's bleeding from his groin.'

'Piper,' the regional coordinator followed the crewman. 'I appreciate we haven't finished your briefing yet but...'

'No problem, I'll get the heli started.' Piper nodded grimly, heading rapidly out of the room and to the hangar. At least she'd already prepped the bird earlier that morn-ing, and taken it out to the tarmac.

She didn't need to wait for anyone to tell her that they needed to get up into the air. She could practically hear Linc's voice in her head, reminding her that every second mattered. Here, as much as on the battlefield.

Which was exactly what she needed to also remind her of the other rules they'd had out there, in that war zone. Namely, steering clear of whatever it was that still arced between them. Because the truth was that they would never act on it.

They couldn't.

It wouldn't be professional. Which was why nothing had ever *really* been going to happen whilst they served together, and nothing would happen now. Better to eject all unsolicited thoughts about Lincoln Oakes out of her head, and try instead to reinstate the banter, and the old rapport they'd once shared.

Anything to protect her mother and brother and stop questions about why she'd turned her back on her army career—the career that had always meant so very much to her.

CHAPTER TWO

'THIS IS HELIMED hotel one-niner,' Piper confirmed to the region's air traffic control a few minutes later. 'We have four on board and we're ready for lift; heading for Roughston Lake, just a few minutes up the road.'

None of them were dwelling on the fact that if it was an arterial injury then the kid could bleed out before they even arrived.

A moment later, the radio crackled and her flying permission was granted. Lifting the helicopter into the sky, she circled it around and headed off into the skies.

'Do you know where you're heading?' Linc's voice came over the internal helicopter intercom, from his seat in the cockpit beside her.

As she understood it, he would usually travel in the rear of the craft, being the critical care doctor, and one of the paramedics would sit up front with her as the navigational pilot, but she wasn't surprised he was up here now. Assessing her on this first run. Typical Major Oakes-style. By the easy acceptance of the rest of the crew, they didn't seem to be finding it all that startling, either.

'Yeah, with the barracks just up the road, I've flown around this region for years. Besides, I was going to head for Roughston Lake until more info comes through.'

She saw, rather than heard, Linc's nodded grunt of agreement.

They didn't have to wait long for their update. A couple of minutes later, the air desk crewman's voice came over the system from back at the base.

'Helimed hotel one-niner, this is hotel zero seven, we have an update on the casualty, over.'

'Go ahead, hotel zero seven.' Piper automatically flipped her comms to respond, her years of training kicking in despite the unsettling feeling of having Linc back on the scene.

'Seems the patient was taking part in some unofficial dirt-bike races in the woods to the north side of the lake when a collision occurred. They're quite deep in and the land crew are having trouble reaching them. The patient was propelled approximately six feet up into the air, along with his bike, and when he landed the handlebars of the bike fell onto him. He was bleeding profusely, but the other racers have allegedly managed to staunch it.'

Without even realising what she was doing, Piper cast Linc a look. They both knew that the injury was serious. The patient could bleed out in a matter of minutes, so it was up to them to find a way to get to them. Fast.

'Message received, hotel zero seven,' Linc acknowledged. 'We're about two minutes out but the area to the north is quite densely wooded. Can you get someone to step into a clearing and try to signal to us, over?'

'Roger that, Helimed hotel one-niner. Will ask now. Out.'

'Best landing area?' Piper asked over her headset as the air desk clicked out.

'There are only a couple of possibilities.' Linc's voice was tight, but it was the expression on his face that told her a fuller story.

Evidently, if she wanted to land close then she was going to have to do some pretty nifty flying.

Sure enough, Tom's voice crackled over the headset from his seat in the rear, next to a probationary paramedic lad who had only been introduced to her as Probie.

'No, you can't land on the north side. We've been here before and the main race humps are deep into the woods. It's too dense to land so Albert had to ground us close to the lake and we had to trek in. It takes about ten minutes.'

'The lad likely doesn't have ten minutes,' Linc noted grimly. 'Can you get us any closer, Piper?'

Focussing on the woods, she looked for anything that might work.

'Look for a track or a clearing,' Piper urged, nosing her helicopter forward.

'Like I said, it's too dense and—'

'There's a track at nine o'clock position,' Linc interrupted Tom's caution as Piper brought the heli around.

'I have visual,' she confirmed, dropping slightly to get a better look. 'It's narrow, and the ground is bumpy.'

'But you can land it?' Linc urged.

Piper took another look. There looked to be a marginally wider section about fifty metres further up. The pylons were still there, but they dipped a little further into the tree line. It wouldn't be the easiest landing…but then again, it wouldn't be the hardest she'd ever managed either.

'I can land it,' she agreed. 'Probie, you're going to have to watch my tail. Tom, check the rotors on the right side. Linc…'

'I've got the left,' he said immediately, reading her thoughts. 'You just focus on the wires and the landing.'

Edging forward, angling her heli as they went, Piper dropped lower. Lower.

'Tail might be a bit low,' Probie's nervous voice suddenly piped up. 'I'm not sure… I can't…'

'Can you go forward another metre?' Linc asked, his calm voice taking over.

Piper eyed the track ahead of her. Another metre forward could be too close on the nose. But perhaps she could land on the hump a little further again, clearing both the nose and tail. She cast a critical eye over the power lines. Further forward would be moving out of the widest part, but she was fairly sure there could be enough room if she angled the heli a little more.

'How are the rotors looking on the left if I move forward about ten metres, Linc?'

He craned his neck for a better view. Tom and Probie were silent, clearly out of their depths. But she could deal with that. She absolutely trusted Linc's assessment anyway.

How unexpectedly easy it was to fall back into being a team with him. As it once was.

'Yeah,' he answered after a moment. 'It'll be tight but there's room.'

'Keep visual.'

'Understood.'

Carefully, she edged forward, constantly reassessing the wires, the rotors, the tail, confident that Linc was doing the same on the left side. And then, finally, they were down safely. Less than eight minutes since the emergency call had first come in.

'Nice flying.'

And it was ridiculous how good the compliment—however gruffly uttered—made her feel. But Linc was straight back onto the task.

'Okay, Probie.' He leapt out of the aircraft and grabbed his bags, with Tom following suit. 'Stay with Piper to help shut the heli down, then bring bloods and additional kit as fast as you can.'

And the next moment he was gone, racing along the track towards the waiting rider. Disappearing over a ridge exactly the way he'd done the last time she'd seen him, five years ago almost to the week.

'All right, fella, I'm Linc. I'm the air ambulance doctor. I'm here to help. Can I get in there, lads?'

Slipping through the cluster of dirt-bike riders—their bikes strewn around the area like machines at an abandoned scrapyard—Linc crouched down next to a couple of lads as they pressed some sort of coat to the fallen rider's wound.

By the lad's pallid countenance and the amount of blood on the ground around him, the injury was going to be severe, but the kid was alive.

'Well done, lads,' he praised. 'You've done a good job here, a really good job. Can you talk us through what happened whilst I take a look at your buddy? What's his name?'

'Kev,' one of them choked out, dazedly wiping his blood-stained hands on his padded trousers. 'He was near the front of the pack when he came off going over the mound. I don't know if he landed on the bike or the bike landed on him, but by the time the rest of us came up the rise, the bike was there, and there was blood, like, pouring out of him. We didn't know what to do except try to stop it somehow.'

'You did really well,' Linc reassured him. 'Did Kev lose consciousness at any time that you know of?'

'Don't think so.' The other lad shook his head wildly. 'Don't know, but he was groaning and crying out by the time we got on scene.'

'Okay, great,' Linc assured again before turning to the kid lying on the ground in front of him. 'Okay, Kev, mate, I'm going to need to take a closer look.'

As Tom slipped the mask over the rider's face to help him breathe, Linc removed the coat and carefully inspected the wound, the young lad's groans getting louder.

'Punctured the femoral,' Linc murmured the confirmation to the paramedic before adopting a deliberately breezy tone as he addressed his patient, all the while packing stuff into the wound to try to staunch the flow. 'You've got good mates here, they've kept you going. I just need to get the bleeding stopped, and then we can give you some pain relief. Yeah, I know that hurts, mate, but you're doing great. Your mates did a really good job.'

More than that, if it hadn't been for the other riders applying pressure, the likelihood was that their friend would have bled to death before the air ambulance crew had arrived.

And even with everything those kids had managed, if it hadn't been for Piper's unparalleled flying skills, then his crew would have had to put down a mile up the track and by the time they'd raced to the scene, it could have already been too late.

Maybe having Piper around didn't need to be so...*unsettling*, after all. She was a great pilot, and hadn't they always agreed that their professional lives came first—above everything else? It was the way they'd managed to keep that distance between them during that last tour, anyway.

So why would that be any different now?

Thrusting the jumble of thoughts out of his mind, Linc focussed on his patient, packing the wound, and applying a tourniquet, all the while talking to the groaning lad. It was a good sign that Kev could answer some of his questions, even through the pain, and it made their job faster. Finally, Linc turned back to his paramedic.

'The kid's going to need a transfusion. Can you get more

info out of the group, and find out where Probie is with the other kit?'

At least the aircraft carried some blood and they could give him a transfusion. In the meantime, now that the bleeding was stemmed properly he could offer Kev some pain relief. The kid might not be able to feel his lower leg, but he was clearly in pain.

Linc worked quickly and efficiently on his patient as Probie raced up within moments with the second kit bag. The sooner they could get him to hospital, and to the vascular surgeons whom he needed, the better.

Linc's primary concerns now were about stabilising his patient and dealing with haemorrhagic shock.

'Blood pressure is one-twenty over ninety,' Tom advised him after a moment.

'SATS?'

'Ninety-five.'

Linc nodded, running through a final head-to-toe examination.

'Okay, let's get him onto the scoop.'

Within minutes, the team—assisted by a couple of other riders recruited by Linc—were carrying the kit and the patient as quickly yet smoothly as they could over the undulating terrain, back to the helicopter. Time was still of the essence, of course.

Linc cast another glance at the monitors attached to his patient. The kid was a fighter, that was for sure, alert and responsive so far, and his blood pressure seemed to be holding fairly steady. Now Linc just needed to keep him that way right up to reaching the hospital.

And who better to get them there quickly than Piper?

As if to prove his point, by the time the stretcher reached the landing spot, Piper was out and opening up the door for them to load the patient, slotting into her role and working with them as quickly and harmoniously as if she'd been a part of the crew for decades, rather than not even a day.

As if she fitted.

So maybe he should just get over his own personal feelings and take comfort from the fact that, of all the pilots that Regional could have got to cover Albert's sick leave, Piper was one of the best.

And he'd just have to find some way to live with his own sense of guilt.

'Talk about a baptism of fire,' Tom was gushing as Linc sauntered into the Helimed's rec room, an hour or so later. 'That landing was the most awesome thing I've ever seen. I don't know if even Albert could have made it. And then whipping the heli around that fast for that second shout…? Man, you're one helluva pilot, Piper Green.'

'Thanks.' Piper smiled, but it wasn't the bright, life-loving smile Linc recognised from five years ago.

It was just a little bit dimmer. A little sadder.

'So, you were saying that you flew Apaches,' the paramedic pressed obliviously, the admiration unmistakeable in his tone. 'Aren't there, like, two or three female Apache pilots?'

And it didn't matter how many times Linc told himself that Piper was a crewmate and nothing more, he couldn't stop his gut from tightening at the dark cloud that skittered over her lovely features before she deftly concealed it.

What was she hiding?

'There are only a few of us, yes,' Piper admitted after a moment, before seemingly reluctantly correcting herself. 'A few of *them*.'

Did she miss her Apache? Linc couldn't help wondering. It wouldn't have surprised him. Piper had always seemed committed to her career in the military—surely something had to have happened to make her leave?

And then, in the next thought, he reminded himself it was none of his business. She didn't need anyone nosing into her life any more than he would want anyone looking into his life. Into his secrets.

'I've got paperwork to finish up,' he muttered, making his excuses and leaving the room.

Anything to get away from Piper, and questions about what she'd been up to in the five years since he'd last seen her.

Slamming the door to his room, he sank down in the tattered wingback that he'd salvaged from some skip a couple of years earlier, and propped his feet up on the battered coffee table opposite.

There was no paperwork to finish, he'd already completed that well before he'd headed for the rec room, but perhaps a quick nap might help him to catch up on the last couple of weeks' worth of broken sleep.

It was certainly easier to switch off here, with the lull of noise down the hallway, than it was back in the oppressive silence of his own apartment. Thrusting his hands behind his neck, Linc closed his eyes and tried to nod off.

The sharp rap on the door had him springing to his feet—all the evidence he needed of how wound up he clearly was.

'Yep?'

The door swung open, but he didn't need to see Piper step through to know it was her. Every fibre of his body already told him that.

'Is this a bad time?'

'No,' he ground out. 'It's fine. I was just finishing the case reports.'

She cast a glance at his desk, then at the wingback.

'Trouble sleeping?'

He frowned.

'Not at all.' He might have got away with it, had he left it at that. But curiosity got the better of him. 'What makes you ask?'

She blinked at him, then squared her shoulders. A gesture so Piper-like that he couldn't believe he'd forgotten it. Or her characteristic bluntness.

'I always have trouble sleeping this time of year. The anniversary of that day, you know?'

He folded his arms over his chest before he could stop himself. Even just her words made the ringing louder in his ears. They made the screams that much more real. And they made his guilt that much more unbearable.

'Yes,' he rasped. 'I know.'

She scuffed her boot against the worn carpet, then seemed to get a grip of herself again.

'It was a bad night.'

Which didn't come close to describing just what hell the fifteen-some hours of that firefight had been.

'It was,' he agreed simply.

Another moment of silence stretched, long and taut, between them.

She wrinkled her nose.

'Do you want me to go?'

He opened his mouth to tell her it would be for the best. But the truth was that her leaving was suddenly the last thing he wanted.

'Stay if you want,' he heard himself say carefully instead.

She eyed him for a moment, then nodded.

For a moment, they each edged around the room, yet always keeping a piece of furniture between them. First a chair, then his desk. Eventually, he settled into his office chair whilst she perched on the edge of his couch.

'You look…well, by the way,' he offered, after a moment.

'Thanks.' She raked her hand over her hair, even as it was tied up in its usual tight bun.

But he could remember exactly what it looked like when she released it from the confines of that net. How soft it had felt that one time, beneath his fingers. That pleasantly light, vaguely coconut scent.

Angry with himself for his sudden weakness, he slammed the memories away. And then she started to speak.

'I never feel particularly great at this time of year.' She bit each word out, as though she wasn't even sure she'd intended to say them. 'I find it hard to sleep. Hard to keep my mind straight, you know?'

He did know. All too well. But that sense of guilt was threatening to suffocate him.

'I like my own company a lot of the time,' she continued. 'But just around this week, I find the solitude a little too…'

'Claustrophobic?' he answered, before he even realised he meant to speak.

'Exactly.' She nodded, with evident relief. 'I just like the company. Even if it's inane chatter in the background, it's comforting to hear it there.'

'Maybe you should talk to someone,' he managed. 'Do you still see some of the other guys from that tour?'

'A few.' She shrugged. 'And we used to get together the first couple of years. But, you know how it is, people get posted off here and there, and we end up losing touch. What about you?'

'This place keeps me busy.' He deliberately sidestepped the question.

'Which isn't exactly an answer.' Piper eyed him ruefully. And when she spoke after another silence, there was a new quiver to her voice.

'I always hoped I'd see you again. To apologise.'

'Apologise?' Linc frowned as he watched her suck in a lungful of air, as she clearly tried to steady herself.

But it didn't make her voice any less shaky. Nor did it clear that glassy look from her eyes.

'For not doing more. I should have caught those leakers before they got to their weapons stash.'

Linc stared at her for a moment, then, before he realised he was even moving, he found himself walking around the desk and crossing the floor, pushing any last obstacles between them out of the way.

Like the spell that only this woman had ever seemed to be able to cast over him.

He didn't know if that made it easier to accept, or harder to. And he had no idea what he'd intended to say to her. But before he could speak, the shrill alarm signalling a new shout blasted through the base.

Habit and training had them both on their feet and lunging for the door handle in an instant but, for a split second, they stopped and looked at each other.

'Perhaps we ought to talk,' he said gruffly, without knowing he'd intended to say anything at all. 'After this shift. And not here.'

Piper stared for a second, then jerked her head into a semblance of a nod.

'To clear the air?'

'In a manner of speaking,' he bit out.

The truth was, he didn't know what he thought it would do. He only knew that Piper was the last person who should feel they owed him any kind of apology, though he had no idea how he was supposed to articulate the guilt racing through his head at that moment.

'Are you heading back to barracks tonight?'

'No.' She shook her head. 'I'm booked into a hotel in town.'

Linc frowned.

'I thought they flew you here in a hurry this morning? You won't have a car.'

'No, but I can get a cab. In two days' time we have a couple of days' downtime, don't we? I'll head back to barracks and pick up my car then, depending on how Albert's doing.'

'Fine.' He gritted his teeth, his mind still galloping away without him. It wasn't the cool, collected self he was accustomed to. 'I've a spare helmet, I'll give you a ride to your hotel tonight, and maybe we can get a drink and talk?'

Amber eyes locked with his.

'I'd like that.' She pulled a face. 'But I don't particularly want to be the topic of gossip around here.'

'No one else needs to know anything,' he assured her. 'In fact, it's better that they don't. It's just one former colleague giving another a ride into town. Nothing more to read into it.'

Was he convincing her, or himself?

'Besides,' he pressed on firmly, 'no one is even likely to see that much. Albert and I were always the last to leave at the end of a shift anyway, by the time he'd put the heli away and I finished any paperwork.'

It was odd, the way he could see the very moment when her last reservation fell away, and she nodded at him.

'That would be…great, then,' she confirmed. 'Thanks.'

And, just for a fraction of a beat, he paused a moment to nod at her, before pulling the door open and racing down the corridor to the air desk whilst she ran to start the heli.

'What have we got, Hugo?'

'A middle-aged female marathon runner has collapsed

whilst training. Husband says she usually trains around fifty miles per week. Suspected cardiac arrest.'

'Send the details through,' Linc shouted, hurrying back into the corridor just as his paramedics were dashing past him. 'We'll get air-bound.'

Because, knowing Piper, she was already ahead of them and had called it in to the local air traffic control. Just another reason why she was the perfect fit for this team in Albert's absence.

CHAPTER THREE

THIS IS A MISTAKE, Linc told himself some nine hours later as he sat in the hotel bar opposite the unsettling Piper, and tried not to stare broodingly at the drinks that stood, both still untouched, between them.

He certainly shouldn't have offered her that lift on his motorbike.

His body was still sizzling from the feel of Piper's arms wrapped so tightly around his waist as she'd pressed her body against his back—making him react as if he were a seventeen-year-old kid all over again, taking the devilish Missy Jackson out on his bike the very day he'd passed his test.

Only, to be fair, back then, having his bike had been more of a thrill than the feel of Missy hugging herself to him. The same could most definitely not be said of Piper, right now. He could still feel Piper's warmth, and smell that vague coconut scent of hers that he'd recognised in an instant. Like a long, slow lick down the length of his sex.

Thoughts that had no business invading his mind did so, all the same, whilst the secluded booth and atmospheric lighting weren't helping, either.

'I think perhaps I should leave you to it, after all,' he muttered. 'It must have been a long day for you.'

It was those amber depths that snared him. Keeping him

rooted to his seat despite needling him to leave. Before he did something they might both regret.

'I thought you wanted to clear the air?'

He'd thought so too. Now, he wasn't so sure. He couldn't quite fathom what he thought he was doing here with Piper.

Was he here to clear the air? Or had a secret, traitorous part of his dark soul hoped that one night with this woman might finally slake this inconvenient attraction that had never quite abated between them?

Even now, seated across the low table from him in their quiet, tucked-away corner of the room, Piper was captivating. Simple jeans encased her long, elegant legs, which were stretched out in front of her in a way that exposed tantalising flashes of midriff.

His palms itched with the effort of not reaching out to see if her tanned skin was even half as smooth as he remembered it to be. No other woman had ever made him feel so out of control. Not before Piper, and certainly not since.

'Perhaps I should go first,' she rasped suddenly, snagging him back to the present. 'That apology I owe you—'

'You don't owe me any apology.' He cut her off far more abruptly than he'd intended. 'If anyone owes an apology right here, it's me. I let those leakers get out of the hospital. I afforded them the opportunity to get to their weapons cache.'

'And how were you to have stopped them?' she demanded softly. Too softly. It slid under his skin and he couldn't do a thing to stop it. 'You were the one trapped inside that hospital, Linc, trying to save all those women and kids. I was the one safe up in the skies.'

Linc shook his head incredulously. He thought of the surface-to-air missile that had blasted past her cockpit, leaving her Apache reeling in the air. Another metre and she wouldn't be here now.

Whether he'd realised it or not, it was yet another fact that had haunted him the past five years. Yet another reason why he couldn't seem to find peace.

'You can't seriously think you owe me anything,' he growled. 'If you hadn't stayed—if you'd done as ordered and returned to base—all those innocent people would have died. You saved a hundred or so lives that day.'

She eyed him intently. Too intently.

'Is that what your nightmares are about?' she challenged him, in that same soft, all too perceptive tone. 'Some misplaced sense of guilt?'

'It isn't misplaced. You can't have forgotten how many lives were lost that day. Our guys, and all those innocent civilians besides.'

'Of course I haven't,' Piper choked out. 'You think you're the only one tormented some nights? I wake up hearing those screams, so vividly. Especially at this time of year... around the anniversary. You're not the only one who feels guilty, Linc.'

'What do you have to feel guilty about?' Each word punched its way out of him. The black truth that he hated to recall, let alone voice. 'You stayed, and went on to do more tours, protect more people. You did everything you could. I was the one who quit the military after that tour.'

She didn't answer immediately, watching him, instead. With anyone else, he would have changed the subject instantly—with anybody else, the subject would never have got this far. But he didn't. He simply waited for her to say whatever it was that was clearly racing around her mind.

As though he *needed* to know what she thought of him, after all that had happened.

'I guess, if I'm to be honest, that's the bit I never really understood. I watched you run into burning, bombed-out hospital buildings—quite literally, Patch—and emerge with a woman or a kid over your shoulders. You never seemed afraid of what might happen. In fact, a few times during that last tour, I thought you were almost daring anyone to shoot you. Like you wouldn't have cared if they had.'

Linc couldn't breathe. It was as if all the air had been sucked instantly from his lungs. Her assessment of him was so spot on, and so damning, that he wasn't sure he could even think.

Abruptly, he lifted his tumbler and downed it in one—something he never did. He didn't even taste it. Still, he stood up and walked to the bar, ordered another and returned to Piper.

It had been three years since he'd drunk enough so that his skull hurt, so that he'd forget everything, but tonight, he thought he might just sink back into that old self. It was that, or grab the woman sitting in front of him, and let them both make the mistake that their bodies clearly still wanted to make.

Drinking the memories away seemed like the lesser of the two evils—even if it was the one his body screamed against the most. At least his penthouse was within walking distance of this place so he didn't have to worry about getting caught on his motorbike and dragging the family name into his night of self-indulgence.

'Talk to me, Linc,' Piper pressed, by the looks of it taking herself by surprise as much as him. 'Why did you leave? It wasn't because of us…was it?'

'No, Legs, it wasn't because of us.' He laughed—a low, hollow sound. But still, he wasn't prepared for the admission that dropped, unbidden, from his lips. 'It was because of my father.'

Or, more accurately, the man he'd believed to be his father…right up until that deliberately cruel bombshell from his mother years earlier again.

But Piper certainly didn't need to know that. Any more than she needed to know that the man had been a duke, or that he himself was a lord.

'What happened to your father?' Piper asked, her tone instantly empathetic as she wrinkled her nose, clearly trying to remember things. 'Did something happen to him? I remember you saying that you and he had been incredibly close before you'd left to be a doctor in the army.'

'It was a long time ago since we were close,' Linc ground out, torn.

Half of him—the logical half—wanted to shut the conversation down the way that he would have done any other time, with any other person. But then there was an irrational part of his brain that seemed ready to spill any number of inconvenient truths to Piper, just because she was asking.

The way he never did.

It had to be the lack of sleep. And the alcohol.

He was terribly afraid it was neither. And then, as if to prove a point, his mouth started moving, apparently of its own volition.

'When I got back from that last tour my head was all over the place—just like everyone else who actually made it out of there, I guess,' he added hastily.

'That doesn't lessen the impact on any one of us, trust me,' she assured him quietly. 'What happened, Linc?'

And even though every practical fibre of his body told him to shut the conversation down, he found himself not only continuing it, but actively answering Piper's question.

'My...father had been fighting Alzheimer's for years. But when I got home that last time, I got a call from my brother, Raf, to say that he'd really gone into decline during my last tour. My brother needed me to come home. The family business needed both of us.'

The family business, in point of fact, being the dukedom

of Stoneywell, as well as Oakenfeld Industries—named after their Oakes family name. With their father mentally incapacitated but still alive, the position of CEO of the board hadn't passed automatically to Raf, and with Linc away with the military, it had seemed that various powerful members of the board, whose plans for Oakenfeld definitely didn't align with those of his family, were attempting a coup against Raf taking over as the interim CEO.

Another few points of detail that Linc didn't feel he could share with Piper. He had already blurted out too much.

'Basically, I didn't feel I had much choice but to leave,' he concluded tightly. 'Though, faced with the same set of circumstances, I'd make the same choice all over again. Raf needed me. So did our sister, Sara.'

'And that's what's driven the guilt,' Piper noted quietly. 'You aren't alone, Linc. I promise you. I stayed, but I feel just as guilty. So many buddies who didn't make it out of there because of that one night, yet I did. You did. There doesn't seem to be any rhyme or reason.'

'None,' he echoed, his voice too thick.

'So you put your family first. You had obligations to them. That's nothing to feel guilty about. In fact, it's admirable. And you and your brother managed to resolve things?'

'We did,' Linc confirmed. 'In time.'

Though it had taken a lot of blood, and sweat from them all, and a few private tears from their usually stoic sister.

'And your father is still…'

'He died.' Linc shook his head. 'Last month, in fact.'

'Oh, Linc, I… I'm so sorry.'

'Thank you,' he bit out automatically. Perfunctorily. 'But the truth is that, in many ways, he was gone a decade and a half ago.'

'It doesn't mean you don't feel the loss.'

And there was something so profoundly sad about her in that instance—a shadow that he thought he'd seen only once before, years ago—that reached inside Linc and tugged—implausibly—at his hardened heart. The one he'd thought he'd locked away years ago.

'You sound as though you're speaking from experience,' he rasped out, suddenly finding he wanted to know more about the enigmatic woman sitting across from him.

He wanted to finally hear some of those secrets he'd always felt she'd held so close—the secrets he'd always made himself respect when they had been serving together.

But they weren't serving together any more—working on the same Helimed team wasn't the same, and, anyway, it was temporary. And tonight had been a first in so many ways, not least the fact that he'd told Piper things he'd never voiced to anyone else—not even Raf or Sara.

What was it about Piper that made it so easy for him to talk to her? What was it that made their connection so... real?

Well, whatever it was, he needed to get a grip, Linc decided firmly, or else he might find himself unburdening himself to her with everything.

And nobody wanted that.

'So, *are* you speaking from experience?' Linc asked again, as though Piper hadn't noted the exact moment that he'd started shuttering himself down to her.

She tried not to lament the loss—in some ways, she was surprised it had taken him so long and that he'd already shared so much with her.

It was more than he'd ever told her back in the army. More than he'd ever told anyone, as far as she was aware. She'd always found him something of a closed book, guarding his personal life as if it was nobody else's business—exactly the way she'd always done.

In a theatre of war, like they'd been in, it had felt like the safest thing to do. *Compartmentalising*, some of the guys called it. It probably explained how they'd kept each other at arm's length despite the attraction that crackled and fizzed inside her every time she was with Linc. Zipping through her body, straight to that ache in her chest. And, if she was going to be absolutely honest, at the apex of her legs.

She'd never been in any doubt that it was something Linc felt too, even if rules and regulations—and their own ranks—had helped them keep things strictly professional, at least for the most part.

But they weren't out there any more. They weren't even in the military any more—or she wouldn't be in a matter of weeks. There was no safety net. Now, here they were, in her hotel bar, with him sharing secrets that she suspected he'd never told anyone else before.

And she found she suddenly wanted to do the same.

It was a terrifying, heady realisation.

'My father died when I was seventeen,' she confessed, before she thought she'd even meant to. 'I found his death… confusing.'

'How so?'

A hundred things rattled through Piper's brain. Though none of them anything she wanted to say—least of all the way he'd died, or the fact that he'd gone from being a kind, loving father and husband to a violent alcoholic, in those final years. That wasn't just her secret, that was her mother's secret, too, and one Piper didn't feel she had a right to share.

'I was conflicted. He was also…ill in the years before he died,' she settled on at last—because, to her mind, alcoholism was a form of illness. At least, thinking that way made it easier to deal with what had happened. 'He hadn't exactly been the greatest father before his death.'

'That must have been hard,' Linc murmured, and she was grateful that he didn't point out how she'd always told everyone in the army that she'd come from a close, loving family.

'It wasn't pleasant,' she admitted. 'Part of me was glad he was gone. Another part of me felt guilty about not feeling sad enough.'

Linc dipped his head, and even though it was just a gesture, she felt as though he really understood. It was strange, how they hadn't seen each other for five years, yet one night had almost restored that closeness they'd once shared.

She'd missed it—*him*—more than she'd realised.

'Is that why you joined the army?' he pressed.

She hesitated. He'd asked her that once before, way back when. She hadn't answered then. She'd been afraid it would lead to more questions that she hadn't been ready to face.

She still wasn't sure she was ready to face them, even now.

'Sort of…it's complicated.'

'That's a cop-out,' he replied. But the faint tug of his lips assured her he wasn't about to press her further on the matter.

She offered a rueful smile of her own.

'My point was simply that I understand how difficult it can be when someone you love dies, even though a part of you feels as though you lost them years ago.'

'Something like that,' he muttered almost to himself, before turning his attention back on her. 'So, why are you leaving? I thought you were a lifer.'

Another question she wasn't ready to answer. Another situation over which she felt she had no control. Her mother and brother needed her. What more was there to it than that?

'Family obligations,' she said eventually. 'Like you said before, I guess.'

'Right.' He raked his hand through his hair in a gesture that was heart-wrenchingly familiar to her.

'At least you have more hair now.' She made herself tease him instead. 'Not so regulation short.'

It was still short, but thicker somehow, and soft-looking.

Without warning, an X-rated image slipped into her mind, and even as Piper tried to slam it away she found herself shifting in her chair. The air between them as taut as ever, an almost delicious friction sliding between them, as though Linc could read her racy thoughts.

'I didn't mean...' She shifted again, trying to get comfortable. A feat that was impossible when the jostling feeling was coming from within. 'I just—'

'It's fine.' He cut her off in a tone that made it seem as if it was anything but fine.

A tone that was too heavy, and loaded, and full of all the things they always avoided saying.

'Linc...'

She wanted too much, that was her problem. She might have fought it five years ago, but it had been there, all the same. And now, she was here and the lines that they'd drawn were faded, and weak.

And this week, of all weeks, she hated being alone. Hated being trapped with memories of that night.

'What are we doing here, Linc?' she whispered, her throat scratchy and dry.

'We're...talking,' he ground out. 'Just like we used to do.'

And never mind if keeping himself from crossing that short space from his chair, to where Piper sat, cost him far more than it had any right to.

'Just talking?' she pressed, and he thought the naked desire in her tone might be his undoing.

'Just talking.' He barely recognised his own voice. 'Easy, and comfortable, the way it always was.'

'Except it isn't like that, is it?' rasped Piper. 'Things are different. It's...fraught.'

She paused, but he didn't trust himself to answer.

'Or are you going to tell me that I'm reading something into it?' she asked, eventually. 'Are things just simply awkward between us because I'm about the last person you would want to work with?'

'Piper,' he growled.

And he didn't know when he'd closed that gap, or when he'd taken her shoulders in his hands. But he couldn't bring himself to say anything more, and no more than he could bring himself to drop the contact.

He was trapped—in some kind of painfully exquisite limbo.

'Is it the memories of that day?' She swallowed. 'Only we used to get along well, the two of us, and...oh, I don't know.'

And he could have said it was that—the memories. He could have left it at something they both would have accepted. But he couldn't. He had to push that little bit further.

'It isn't the memories of that day,' he rasped.

At least, not entirely.

And he wasn't sure when he'd inched closer to her. Lowered his head a fraction to hers.

He told himself to back away. That he didn't need the ghosts of their attraction spiralling through him on top of everything else. But he couldn't seem to move.

'Linc...' She barely whispered his name, but it was enough. That longing he recalled all too vividly from that night in his tent. The one where he'd almost kissed her, before they'd remembered where they were, and the job they'd each had to do.

But hell, the need to kiss her again, *now*, was burning through him; so brightly that he thought it might sear him from the inside out.

Her mouth was scant millimetres away, and the closer he dipped his head, the more her eyes seemed to flutter closed. And when his lips finally brushed hers, it was like a kind of song that poured through him.

A celebration.

A symphony.

A glorious sound that he'd heard once before, but then had been forced to shut out for good.

And now, he could hear it again. He could revel in it. As her lips moved slickly with his, and her tongue moved to dance with his, it felt to Linc as though he'd been waiting for this for a whole lifetime. Maybe longer.

Hauling her to him, he revelled in the feel of her arms looping around his neck, the feel of her breasts pressed to his chest. He let his hand caress her cheek, indulging in the feel of her silken-soft skin under his fingers, he raked a thumb over her plump, lower lip, feeling her sharp sigh roll through him, right to his sex.

And he wanted more. So much more, that he was beginning to lose all sense of where he was, and what they were supposed to be doing.

It was only the background hub of the rest of the hotel bar that finally pierced through the fog in his brain and yanked him unceremoniously back to reality.

He pulled his head from Piper, and eyed her for a long moment as he struggled to refocus.

'We can't do this,' he managed.

By the expression on her face, she was fighting the same battle.

'No,' she breathed raggedly. 'We can't. This is…a distraction. Nothing more.'

She didn't sound remotely convincing, but he grasped at it all the same.

'A distraction, yes,' he agreed. 'It's the shock of seeing each other again.'

'The stress of the anniversary.' Piper nodded, too quickly. Too fervently.

As if she was trying to make herself believe it.

'It would be a pleasant diversion, but we still have to work together so ultimately it would be unprofessional.'

'Unacceptable,' she offered with a hollow laugh.

The sound echoed everything he felt himself. Desperately, Linc pretended the tightening around his ribcage wasn't so painful. Walking away from her—again—was the right decision, but that didn't mean he had to like it.

'So this never happened?' she whispered.

And it told him all he needed to know, that he hated the sound of it so very much.

'This never happened,' he rasped. 'We go back to normal.'

Whatever their version of normal had ever been.

CHAPTER FOUR

FROM HER VANTAGE point at the top of the hill, Piper peered down into the valley and wondered how the team were faring.

Another shout, this time a road traffic collision involving a car and a pick-up truck allegedly overtaking vehicles when oncoming traffic had appeared around a bend.

From the information patched through by Hugo, the main casualty for the air ambulance was the fifty-year-old male of the oncoming car, who'd had nowhere to go when he'd seen the pick-up hurtling towards him.

The man's wife had been in a more stable condition, and had already been taken to the local hospital by road ambulance, but Piper could see the fire crews working to release the husband from his crushed vehicle.

It looked less than hopeful, but she'd seen Linc perform enough near miracles out in hellish war zones to know that if anybody was going to achieve it, then it was likely to be Linc. However, getting the patient up the hill to her location could well be an issue.

Checking out the scene as best she could without leaving her machine, Piper looked for a suitable site to land in the event that they needed her closer. Her radio crackled but she wasn't about to disturb her team whilst they were working, as long as she could be ready to move once they called for her.

By the looks of the terrain, the most feasible site was going to be the tarmac of the country lane itself, but the trees lining either side weren't going to make it easy.

Still, she was determined to spot a good LZ if it meant shaving a precious few minutes off her team getting their patient to hospital. Minutes that could, as both she and Linc knew from personal experience, save lives.

'Who pinched the last jam doughnut?' Linc demanded in good-natured disgust a couple of days later, as he crossed the rec room to find an empty pastries box. 'Was it you, Legs?'

It hadn't surprised him how well Piper had slotted into the team so easily—years of being an army pilot in a similarly close-knit team meant that she'd slipped seamlessly into the role of Helimed pilot.

However, it had surprised him that the two of them had somehow managed to fall back into their old roles of pretending the chemistry between them didn't exist. As if the other night in the hotel hadn't happened—another *almost-kiss* to add to the one from five years ago.

His libido could do without making a habit of not quite kissing Piper Green—not to mention that insistent thrumming in his soul, whenever she was around.

He ought to be elated it had been so easy to relegate their attraction to the outer limits of his consciousness. So why wasn't he?

Tearing his thoughts back to the present, Linc watched as their air desk operator poured out five steaming mugs from the coffee machine. He reached for one gratefully before turning to face the room to fully take in the sight of three shattered crew members sprawled over the various pieces of battered furniture.

'You snooze, you lose, Patch. You know the rules.'

In the corner, Piper threw her legs over the arm of her raggedy easy chair and licked her fingers unapologetically—not helping his wayward libido one bit. The thrumming in his ribcage shifted decidedly lower.

He fought to ignore that, too.

It was remarkable how a morning of intense shouts—one of the most demanding mornings Linc thought he'd experienced in the four years since he'd been with Helimed—bonded a new team. Even given the circumstances of Albert's absence. And if his libido didn't kick up into overdrive every time he spoke to Piper, Linc thought he might actually start to enjoy having her stand in.

As it was, pretending that he wasn't acutely aware of the damnable woman every time she entered a room, or left the room, or even shifted position in said room, was becoming exhausting.

Almost as exhausting as having to fight off some irrational urge to cross the floor, sweep her into one of the bunk rooms, and do devastatingly naughty things with her in the way he was certain they both should have done years ago.

It took an absurd amount of effort to eject the thoughts—and the deliciously erotic accompanying images—from his brain.

'I wasn't snoozing.' One-handedly, Linc balled up the empty doughnut box and launched it expertly across the room to the rubbish net—an old kids' basketball hoop—above the bin. 'I was restocking the medical supplies after the last shout. It's part of my job, go figure.'

As if that could convince anyone who might be watching closely enough that he wasn't remotely affected by this particular woman's presence.

'Whilst we were in here with the doughnuts.' Piper laughed, and the sound rippled through him far too easily. 'So I refer you to my earlier comment. You snooze, you lose.'

'Isn't there another box in the kitchen?' ventured the probationary paramedic as Piper rolled her eyes comically.

Sexily.

'Ugh, Probie. Don't tell him yet.'

'Thank you, Probie.' Linc forced himself to laugh before striding to the hatch and reaching right across for the other glossy white box.

Anything to occupy his hands. And his mind.

'Muppet,' he heard Hugo say. 'You should have let them squabble it out for a little longer before you reveal that. It's better than a TV soap.'

'Oh. Sorry.'

'You'll learn.' Hugo laughed. 'I reckon you're best off staying out of it where these two are concerned. I've a feeling they're going to be like an old married couple.'

'You two are married?' Probie gaped, eyes wide as Piper spluttered into her coffee. 'Aw, man, how come I didn't realise that before now?'

Linc grinned again, taking advantage of Piper's coughing fit to enlighten the poor kid.

'Yeah, happily married. Ten years now. We've got five kids and Legs is a complete slob. Our house is a tip.'

'You're kidding?' breathed Probie, his eyes flickering from one to the other.

'We are *not* married,' countered Piper, still spluttering. 'I wouldn't go near Patch if he was the last man on earth. And I'm not a slob.'

'Sure you are.' Linc was thoroughly enjoying himself as she narrowed her eyes at him.

And, just for a fraction of a heartbeat, their gazes held.

That split-second memory of the one time when something almost had happened between them. The kiss that still haunted his deepest dreams to this day. And as Piper half lifted her hands, as though she'd been about to brush her fingers over her lips, he knew that she too was thinking of that night.

But then, abruptly, she gave a toss of her head as if to shake the unwanted memory aside, and offered a snort of derision.

'My tent was always tidy, even out in Camp Harton. But anyone would look messy next to neat-freak Patch here. Or so the colonel said. Even the battlefield hospital area seemed that bit more ordered when Linc was around.'

'Wait.' The young paramedic looked from one to the other. 'So, you aren't really married?'

'We aren't really married, Probie,' Linc managed, determined not to let anyone see his internal struggle to regroup.

'But Hugo said…?'

'I simply meant that I reckoned, since they'd served together, that they were going to *act* like an old married couple.' The air desk operator chuckled.

'Is that why he's called Patch?' Probie asked suddenly. 'Because he has OCD and likes a clean patch.'

'Nope.' Swinging around, Piper brushed the sugary crumbs off her cargo trousers. 'He's called Patch because he used to patch soldiers up.'

'Oh, I get it. And you're called Legs because you flew a helicopter instead of marching?'

'Nope.' Linc snorted. 'She's called Legs because she ran like a gazelle every time the alarms went off. She was always the first to her heli in a shout.'

Although, privately, he could think of other reasons why her nickname was so damned fitting for her.

'Yeah, I get it.' Probie nodded eagerly. 'Patch and Legs.'

'For the record, Probie,' added Hugo kindly, 'I don't recommend you call either of them by those names. I've a feeling those are nicknames the pair of them earned serving together out in some war zone. We didn't earn that right.'

'It's cool.' Piper shrugged, but her smile was overbright.

Linc said nothing. Hugo was right, it would be anything but *cool* if anyone who hadn't been on that tour of duty with them used those nicknames. And by the way Piper was carefully avoiding meeting the new kid's eye, Linc knew she felt the same, however welcoming she was trying to act.

'Oh.' Probie sniffed. ''Cause I was gonna say that I couldn't understand why you were complaining the other day about bridezilla, if you already had a wife.'

'Say again?' Piper's voice cut in a little too quickly, and a little too sharply, at least to Linc's trained ears. 'Patch is getting married?'

As though maybe she was…jealous?

No, not *jealous* exactly, he corrected hastily. But…*something*. It mattered to her more than it ought to. Enough to make something pull tight in him.

He eyed her with amusement.

'My sister is getting married,' he clarified.

'Oh.' She squirmed under his direct stare, but to her credit, she didn't back down. 'Sara? Hmm, she's your younger sister, isn't she?'

'Good memory.' Was it arrogant of him to think it proved how interested she still was in him? 'She keeps trying to pair me off for the wedding.'

'Why?'

It was Piper's characteristic bluntness that made him grin the most.

'Optics,' he lied. 'Long story.'

'Ah.'

It was one simple word, one tiny syllable, but it was

loaded with so much meaning, and Linc hated that the very sound of it made it feel as though he'd just pushed her away again.

Then again, wasn't that what he did?

As tightly knit as he liked to think the crew was, he didn't want to share his biggest secrets with them any more than he'd wanted to share them with his buddies back in the army. The men and women in whom he entrusted his life.

He found he couldn't tear his eyes from Piper's as they watched each other without saying another word. If there was ever anyone he would trust with his secrets, then it would probably be this woman.

But not the fact that he was a lord. Or, more to the point, that he wasn't really a lord at all; at least, not by blood— his mother had made that clear, in her own gleefully cruel way. And perhaps it was that which hurt the most. He'd not only lost the decent, moral old duke as his 'father', but the man had also been his compass. And his anchor. Without the duke claiming him as his son, by blood or not, was he really part of the Oakes family anymore?

And Raf and Sara could claim that it didn't matter to them one bit, and that he was their brother no matter what— but he didn't feel the same. He felt like more of an imposter than ever. Was it any wonder he'd joined the army the week his mother had so gleefully dropped her bombshell on the family—in all its brazen ugliness?

And was it any wonder that even now, over a decade later, he still couldn't bring himself to go...*home*?

'So just take someone with you to keep your sister happy, if it's just optics,' Probie interjected suddenly, causing Piper to finally break eye contact and look at the young lad.

Linc felt the loss far too acutely.

'He can't do that,' Tom scoffed. 'You don't take a casual date to a wedding and not expect them to read too much into it.'

'Humble as ever, Tom?' Hugo laughed, as he prepared to head back out to man the phones.

'You can mock, but you know I'm right. Linc knows it, too.' The paramedic grinned, calling after him. 'That's why he keeps refusing dates, even if it risks incurring the wrath of a kid sister. Which, trust me, isn't something you want to take lightly.'

'You have to have some female friends who don't want to sleep with you, don't you?' Probie turned to Linc.

'Men and women can't be platonic friends,' countered Tom before Linc could answer. 'Not really. At least one of them wants more. Possibly both.'

'I'm sure they can.' Probie frowned. 'Look at Linc and Piper.'

And suddenly, both pairs of eyes swivelled to consider the pair speculatively, and Linc didn't need to see Piper's reaction to know that she would be tensing up.

'Well, they're just odd,' Tom snorted.

'I know,' the young Probie exhaled abruptly. 'Since you're just good friends, maybe you ought to go to the wedding together.'

'I think not,' Piper objected, her voice tight.

And even though the logical part of Linc agreed, it didn't stop another part of him—a decidedly more primitive part—from wishing that maybe that could have been an option.

'Probie, I'm looking to convince my sister to stop setting me up with dates, not encourage her. All Piper and I do is quibble.'

'Yeah, like an old married couple.' Probie frowned, clearly not following. 'Just like Hugo said.'

'No,' Piper managed, just as the air desk jockey sauntered back in.

'Forgot my favourite pen.' Hugo paused mid-reach.
'Wait, what did I say before?'

Before Linc could change the subject, Probie had set it all
out. But that didn't explain why Linc paused long enough
for his old crewmate to answer, instead of shutting it down
there and then.

'Might be a plan,' Hugo offered thoughtfully, before
grabbing his pen and hurrying back out.

'No,' Piper repeated. *Stiffly,* Linc thought.

'I mean, you want your sister to back right off, don't
you?' the crewman continued. 'And you two *do* act like
you've got that something-something going on.'

'We most certainly do not.'

'Maybe not consciously.' Probie shrugged, refusing to
back down. 'But it's there, all the same.'

'We've worked together before,' Piper repeated. 'Nothing more.'

And even though he knew the truth, Linc found he didn't
want to actually hear her denying there had ever been anything between them.

'Enough, guys.' He thumped a coin onto the worktop as
a distraction. 'Pool tournament. Who's taking me on first?
Only ten pence a wager.'

'No chance. I lost a fiver to you last week, and we were
only betting ten pence then,' Hugo scoffed. 'Besides, I have
to get back to the phones.'

'I'll give you a game.' Tom stood with a dramatic sigh.
'If only to shut the pair of you up.'

'Suits me.' Throwing the rest of his coffee down his neck
and snagging a second doughnut, Linc strode over to the
pool table. Racking the balls, he shook his head as though

to empty it of thoughts of Piper, and picked up a coin. He definitely needed the distraction.

'Call it,' he told Tom.

'Heads.'

Linc dutifully tossed the coin up and caught it.

'Heads it is. Your break.'

'No one's break, sorry, guys.' The door swung back open as Hugo hurried in. 'A man's fallen off a ladder whilst trimming a hedge. The electric trimmers have made a partial cut through his upper arm. He's conscious but losing a fair amount of blood.'

CHAPTER FIVE

LINC THRUST OPEN the door of the heli HQ with a sharp kick; the darned thing was sticking again. He made a mental note to repair it at some point in the day, but deep down he knew his sour mood was more to do with the text he'd just received than the door itself.

What was it about his usually fair-minded kid sister that was really pushing his buttons these days? That mile-wide obstinate streak that both amused and infuriated him, though not in equal measure. If he weren't so fond of her, he might have warned her fiancé that Sara was turning into the ultimate bridezilla, and to run for the proverbial hills.

But, for all her faults, he loved his sister to distraction. And his older brother for that matter. And if they were more concerned than he himself was with matters of appearance, and stature, then they were entitled to be. All he'd ever wanted in life was to be in the army, and to be a doctor, and he'd done both.

Ranulph—Raf—had been the one lumbered with the responsibility of primogeniture, as well as all the crushing responsibilities of their father whilst the old duke had been losing his mind to the cruel disease that was Alzheimer's.

Even Sara had played her part as the obedient daughter of a duke and duchess—despite the way their mother had undermined her own daughter, and scorned Sara's every choice her entire life. All because their mother had been jealous of her daughter's youth, and sharp intellect.

And none of that even came close to the horribly cruel bombshell their mother had dropped on Linc himself—from practically her death bed, as if she couldn't have been more dramatic. Finding out that his father was not the loving, kind-but-firm duke, but some playboy jockey who was as notorious for his women as he was for his racing wins, hadn't been the most grounding moment of Linc's life.

It had sent him hurtling from the family seat at Stoneywell for a start, joining the army and throwing himself into tours of duty as if he didn't care if he lived or died.

Back then, he *hadn't* cared.

But things were different now. His life felt more stable in the air ambulance. Still, returning to Oakenfeld for his sister's wedding wasn't something he was looking forward to.

Linc drew in a deep breath. Being the second male heir—if he could legitimately call himself that—unquestionably had its advantages, like ditching his title as Lord Lincoln Oakes, for a start. No one here knew who he really was, just as no one in the military ever had.

Not even Piper.

He was so caught up in his thoughts that the sound of a thump in the rec room caught him off guard.

'Who's there?' he barked out instantly, dropping his bag where he stood and striding down the hall, fists at the ready. 'You'd better give yourself up. I'll give you one chance.'

'Linc?'

The familiar, feminine voice punched straight through Linc. He lowered his fists and turned to retrieve his bag, and to catch his breath. It was one thing to act normally around Piper when the rest of the crew were there as a safety net…but the knowledge that it was just the two of them here now made things shift. Even the air seemed to grow thicker.

He pushed the thought away and strode into the room, frowning.

'You're here early. How did you get in? The door was still sticking when I unlocked it just now.'

'I came through the hangar.' She shrugged—slightly awkwardly, he thought. Or was that just his imagination? 'I wanted to just check on the heli. So, are you putting the coffee machine on?'

He eyed her briefly, but whatever he thought he'd seen was gone. It was definitely his imagination. He needed to get a grip. Piper had a way of slipping all too easily under his skin. He gritted his teeth and held up the shopping bag.

'I picked up a few ingredients from the local store on the way in.'

'Breakfast?'

And again, he wondered if he was reading things that weren't there when he thought that she perked up a little too much at the idea of food. As if she hadn't eaten recently... He knew the signs from the army—those lads who hadn't had a decent meal for days.

'Next time, it's your turn,' he said with a laugh, even as he watched her closely.

'Of course.' She dipped her head but though she did a good job of disguising it, there was something she was hiding.

'You want to start the mushrooms if I start the bacon?'

'Actually, I can't really...cook.' She wrinkled her nose.

'I didn't know that.' He eyed her in surprise. 'Then no time like the present to learn.'

And, under the threat of another wave of that thing he kept pretending didn't exist between them, Linc ducked into the kitchen just as there was another slam against the wall, signalling the arrival of more of their crew arriving early.

He really needed to remember to sort that door out, too. Something about Piper's appearance this morning still bugged him.

'We've got an eighteen-year-old who has taken a tumble from height unknown at one of the waterfalls near Heathston Heights. He's responsive and breathing, but nothing else known for now. We need to get airborne now,' Linc declared, reaching for his helmet along with the rest of his team. 'We can be on our way to the grid until the exact location details come through.'

Racing out onto the tarmac, he wasn't surprised to see Piper already in the heli and starting her up.

'Strong winds today, guys,' Piper announced as she prepped to get the all-clear from the region's air traffic control. 'Good chance we'll be taking off sideways, so just keep alert for me, okay?'

Waiting long enough to ensure she was airborne and happy, Linc patched through to their HQ's air desk.

'Helimed hotel zero seven, any updates, over?'

'Negative, Helimed hotel one-niner, there are no land crews on scene yet, and the initial caller doesn't have much info, over.'

'We're going to need a better location,' Tom grumbled over the headset. 'Or we aren't going to know where to head to.'

'I could take a pass over the most popular waterfalls,' Piper suggested.

'Nothing to lose,' Linc agreed. 'I take it the original caller is a kid who doesn't know which one they're at? Time's trauma and all that, so has to be worth a try.'

He peered out of the window as Piper dutifully took her first pass over.

'Anyone got visual?' she asked.

'Nothing yet,' Hugo denied.

'Nor here,' noted Linc. 'Wait, about two o'clock? Looks like something down there.'

Piper duly nosed the heli in the direction.

'Yeah, that looks like it. Nice spot.'

'A couple of kids are waving us down,' Tom added.

'There are power lines running just up from the river,' Piper noted grimly. 'But I can land in that field to the other side. Looks like a low wall for you to hop over, then a bit of a sprint, but nothing more.'

'Good call,' Linc agreed as Piper was already circling the heli around.

Quickly, smoothly, she landed it.

'Clear to go,' she confirmed as Linc and his two paramedics grabbed their gear and started moving.

It was a good call by Piper to try the pass over, Linc considered. He really ought to tell her that when they got back to base.

'All right, lads.' He turned his attention to the kids as they moved to greet the crew. 'I take it this is Bobbi? Can you tell me what happened, son?'

Squatting down next to the casualty, Linc began his preliminary observations. Although the lad was moving and making sound in response to Linc's questions, he wasn't making coherent replies.

It was going to be down to the kid's friends to piece together what they'd seen.

'He was climbing on that ridge.'

'No, he wasn't, he hadn't reached that ridge.'

'Wait, which ridge are we talking about?

Quickly, methodically, Linc worked with the group, until

the land ambulance crew arrived on foot—their vehicle stuck a few hundred metres away in the car park.

'This is Bobbi, seventeen. About twenty-five minutes ago he took a tumble whilst climbing around the waterfall. He lost his grip and fell around twelve feet onto these jagged rocks down here.

'According to one of his mates, Bobbi was unconscious for around a minute, but he was awake and responsive by the time we arrived. He cites general pain around his lower back, towards his right-hand side, and some pins and needles in his right hand. Suspect spinal injuries, possibly T-Twelve fracture, and ideally I want to evacuate with the assistance of mountain rescue, using an inflatable mattress scoop. Bobbi's initially had morphine, but is still complaining of significant pain. We're about to administer ketamine.'

'You got here fast.' One of the land crew paramedics smiled grimly as she cast her eye over Linc's team. 'We couldn't even be sure which waterfall it was.'

'Yeah, it's definitely not easily accessible by road. You did well to get here,' Linc noted. 'We were lucky we got in scene within ten minutes of the call. Our pilot took a fly-by, and we happened to spot him.'

Linc thought of Piper and was surprised at the sensation that punched through him.

'You're taking him back with you guys?' the paramedic surmised.

Linc nodded at her.

'Affirmative. Once we get him on the scoop and into the heli, we'll alert the hospital that we're a few minutes out, and they can have a spinal team on standby. The sooner we get him into their hands, the better chance they've got of mending his broken back. But getting him out of here smoothly is going to be the biggest hurdle.'

The paramedic nodded. 'Should be easier with the six of us. You just tell us where you want us, and we'll do it.'

'That's the idea,' Linc agreed, returning to his patient for the last checks. 'Right, let's get things moving.'

Piper took her time last parading the heli, giving everyone time to leave. Almost getting caught by Linc that morning had been too close; she needed to find somewhere else to stay. Time for another Internet search tonight.

If it hadn't been for Linc, she might have confided in the rest of crew hoping that one of them might know somewhere. But she didn't want to look weak...vulnerable in front of Linc. She wanted him to be as impressed with her as a Helimed pilot as he had been when she'd been an Apache pilot.

And it didn't matter how much she pretended not to know the reason for her pride, she was terribly afraid she knew precisely why it mattered to her.

Despite her bravado that it would be easy to set their attraction aside again, it was still there, sizzling between them. Only this time, now that they didn't have the rules and regulations of the army to shore up their defences, the pull was stronger than ever, and she had no idea how to snuff it out. She wasn't sure she even wanted to.

But she had to—there was nothing else for it.

Finally thinking she'd waited long enough, Piper poked her head through the door that connected the hangar with the crew area.

Blissful silence, and dark but for a small light someone had left on in one of the side rooms, spilling enough warm light into the corridor that she wouldn't stub her toe in the darkness, the way that she had done the night before.

Padding quietly down the hall, she slipped into the kitchen and flicked the radio on—the place was too deadly silent otherwise. Then she pulled the pot of ready-to-boil noodles from her bag. Hardly the most nourishing dinner, but it would have to do. It was better than the last couple of nights anyway, when she hadn't had anything. Reaching out, she flipped the switch on the boiling water tap.

'What exactly are you doing?'

Piper was fairly sure she leapt several feet into the air. She spun around, careful to stay in front of the offending pot of noodles, and her hand pressed to her chest as though that could somehow slow her racing heart.

Worse, she wasn't entirely sure it was purely down to the shock.

'Linc? I thought everyone had gone home.'

'Everyone else has,' he drawled. 'I had the last case report to complete. What's your excuse?'

She should have realised he was still here when she saw that light on down the hall.

'I was last parading the heli.'

Not entirely untrue, though she wasn't surprised when his eyebrows twitched sceptically.

'Just like you were checking it over before I arrived this morning?'

'You aren't the only one to take their job seriously.' She jutted her chin out defiantly.

His eyes narrowed.

'Are you sleeping here?'

'Of course not,' she blustered.

'You can't stay here overnight, Piper. This place isn't insured for that.'

'Good job I'm not, then.' She hadn't realised that. Oh, Lord, what was she to do now? Well, whatever it was, there was no need for Linc to know her predicament. 'Like I said, I was last parading the heli. Now I'm leaving.'

He leaned slightly to the side.

'So what are you trying to hide?'

'Not sure I'm following?'

'You've never been a great liar, Legs.'

Funny, but coming from Linc it sounded more like a criticism than a compliment. She frowned but suddenly, he was right in front of her, reaching around her for the packet. But she couldn't breathe, she certainly couldn't think. But then they were kissing, and she had no idea who had moved first but she was terribly afraid it had been her.

And he tasted every bit as magic as he had the last time. Every bit as addictive. Every bit as thrilling.

It was more than a shock when he tore his mouth from hers and set her away from him.

'Is this your idea of distracting me?' he growled. 'I must say, it's quite effective, you almost had me. Almost.'

She could admit that it wasn't a distraction at all, and that the kiss had caught her off guard just as it had done with him.

Somehow, she didn't think Linc would believe her.

'Can't blame a girl for trying,' she made herself quip instead.

But it only earned her a narrowed gaze.

'You're eating here, and you're sleeping here,' he bit out. 'Why? What happened to the hotel?'

Piper dug her fingernails into her palm, silently praying for one last distraction to save her from having to admit her failings to Lincoln Oakes, of all people.

'Turns out it was just for those first few days,' she ground out eventually, 'because of the lack of notice. But once they flew me back to barracks for those couple of days' downtime, they expected me to drive down from there.'

'Every day?' he scoffed. 'It's a one-hundred-and-sixty-mile round trip.'

'It's just over an hour each way on the motorway at that

time of day.' She shrugged. 'Plenty of people have to do that kind of commute in the non-army world, so I understand.'

'That's ridiculous. You couldn't just stay in the hotel?'

'Did you see the rates of that place?' She forced a laugh, hating the way he was looking at her.

As if she couldn't organise herself.

Or perhaps she was just projecting.

'Somewhere else, then?' he demanded. 'It might not be the biggest town but there are at least a couple of other places I can think of that are still decent.'

'I tried them both,' she admitted. 'Apparently there's some kind of expo going on at the moment and they're both booked out. So are the affordable but decent places further afield.'

'Oh, right.' He thought for a moment. 'Local B & Bs? There are some good ones.'

'Again, booked out, or astronomically priced.'

'There have to be some inexpensive but decent places a little further afield.'

'Only if I go about an hour out, and if I'm doing that then I might as well drive back to barracks. Otherwise, just whilst the expo is on, they're all outside my budget.'

'Your budget? You're a pilot, you can't exactly be hard up for cash.'

Piper fought down a rumble of emotion. Frustration, guilt, and a couple of others that she didn't care to admit.

'The Air Corps don't exactly pay commercial pilot rates. You know that.'

'Still, it's good pay.'

It was, she had to admit that. Reluctantly, Piper nodded.

'Yeah, okay, it's good enough. But it…isn't all mine.'

He narrowed his eyes at her again.

'You send it home, don't you? To your mother? That's

why you joined the army when your father died, so that you could look after her?'

How could he possibly read her so easily? She hated it.

And, at the same time, it was something of a relief.

'My brother was a baby at the time,' she blurted out. 'Mum couldn't possibly cover the mortgage, and the household bills, and the cost of a baby on her own, though she'd always worked.'

'I'm not criticising her, Piper,' Linc said quietly. 'Or you.'

She swallowed. No, he hadn't been criticising anyone. And yet she'd taken it as such all the same—which probably revealed a good deal too much about her more than it did about Linc.

'Right. I know that.'

His expression shifted.

'Your brother was about seven when we last served together, right? He'd be about twelve now?'

'Yes, twelve,' she confirmed, marvelling that he'd remembered such a small detail. 'He's at secondary school.'

'And your mum doesn't work?'

'She does,' Piper countered. 'She took a job years ago as a dinner lady in his old primary school so that she could be there for him before and after school, but it doesn't pay that much and there's no work in the holidays.'

If it weren't for the fact that they needed to protect the young kid from the truth about his dad's death for as long as possible, maybe her mother could have got a better job and paid for afterschool care. He might only have been a baby when his father had attacked their mother, but who knew what a baby remembered, or later tried to process?

Little wonder that her mother had always wanted to be there for her brother, to make sure he stayed on the right path, and didn't fall in with a poor crowd. The kid was completely innocent and he deserved a normal childhood—

and that was what she and her mother had always tried to give him.

Besides, none of that was what took the bulk of her money. But there was absolutely no way that she was going to tell the former Major Lincoln Oakes that in those final months before his death, her father had managed to rack up over-six-figure debt—borrowing more and more each month from a loan shark, just so that he didn't have to admit to anyone that he'd lost his job and couldn't get another one.

She and her mother had been paying him back for over a decade now, and they were almost clear. Almost free. She could practically taste it.

The moment they were released from that dark cloud would be the moment her entire family could finally start afresh.

But every penny she had to pay for some overpriced hotel was a penny they didn't have for the debt collectors. And that was something she couldn't just accept.

'So you're sleeping here because the journey back to barracks is ridiculously long, and you can't afford a hotel,' he summarised.

Her cheeks burned hotter, but what other option was there than to tell the truth? It wasn't as though she could bluff it—he was too sharp to believe any excuses. She splayed her hands out in front of her.

'Only because prices are high whilst this conference is on. I can't eat into what little they have. My brother's a nearly teenager, and aside from the household bills, there are all kinds of school bills now. Uniform, sports kit, field trips. Not to mention the fact that, as a boy, he could easily eat us out of house and home. He eats more than I've ever eaten—by a mile.'

'Yeah.' Linc grinned abruptly. 'I remember what my brother and I were like at that age. Still are now, to be fair.

We'd inhale in one day what Sara would have eaten in a week. I remember after one full-on rugby tournament, we came home and ate a box of cereal each, and each with a litre of milk. Then a roast chicken and a loaf of bread between the two of us. Then we started on the cake that the cook had been baking for our father's birthday.'

'You had a cook?' Piper's eyebrows shot up to her hairline, and Linc could have kicked himself.

'My mother was terrible in the kitchen,' he covered as smoothly as he could.

It wasn't a complete lie, but it wasn't exactly the truth, either. Oakenfeld Hall had three cooks—the formidable Mrs Marlston, and her two very capable assistant cooks. But the woman had been more of a mother figure to him and to Raf, especially, than their own mother ever had.

Still, Linc kept all that information firmly to himself.

'So what are you going to do now you're leaving the Air Corps?'

'Hopefully I can get a steady gig. Otherwise I'll be a freelance pilot.'

'Meaning if you don't fly then you don't earn,' he noted. She didn't answer.

'So are you going for Albert's job permanently? You know he's leaving, don't you?'

Linc wasn't sure what he thought about that. The idea of Piper being around permanently wasn't exactly an unpleasant one—far from it. But it would mean that those lines they'd drawn would have to stay in place for good.

Which, he told himself firmly, was absolutely fine by him.

'Actually, I was going for the position of pilot for the Helimed across the border in the county over.'

'Which one?' he asked, curious despite himself.

She wrinkled her nose at him, as though weighing up whether to answer. It was almost comical. *Almost.*

'West Nessleton Helimed,' she admitted at last. 'It's closer to my mum, and my brother. This temporary placement here kind of fell into my lap. A good hearts and minds role between the AAC and the community, plus it's hardly worth sending me on a training exercise when I'm leaving.'

'And you still need to keep your flying hours up,' Linc realised. 'I fully empathise, truly. But you can't stay here, Piper. Like I said, the insurance simply doesn't cover it and I can't risk this entire base just for one person. Even for you.'

'I know.' She nodded furiously. 'I'll pack my things.'

There was a beat of hesitation.

'Where will you go?'

She squeezed her eyes closed, trying not to think of her mother or her brother. Or the fact that the boiler still needed replacing before winter set in. And of course the newer models meant that it couldn't be swapped like for like, so it would need to be sited somewhere else in the house; which meant floors lifted, new piping laid, and ceilings torn down.

It never seemed to be an easy job, and it always seemed to cost far more than it should.

Carefully, determinedly, she schooled her features so that none of this showed, and instead shot Linc her breeziest smile.

'Like you said, there are some inexpensive B & Bs a little further afield. I'll try them.'

For all his sternness, he looked back at her with concern.

'And your mother?'

'She'll understand.'

And she would. Her mother was always worrying whether she could afford to be sending them so much, as well as paying the mortgage, and most of the bills. It was one of the main reasons why Piper wished she didn't have to worry her at all.

Hastily, she began stuffing all her belongings back into her rucksack. Maybe she could sleep in her car instead. At least that way, she wouldn't have to let her family down. Shrugging her leather jacket on and throwing her bag over her shoulder, Piper headed out to look for Linc.

'Okay, I'm going.' She ducked her head around the door to the office, but he wasn't there.

He probably didn't want to hear anything more from her tonight anyway. She'd be better slipping out quietly, and in the morning they didn't have to discuss it at all.

She was halfway along the corridor when Linc appeared at the door of the kitchen, her noodles dinner in his hand and a distinctly unimpressed expression tugging at his features.

'Are you forgetting something? This was what you were going to eat?'

'Oh, thanks,' she muttered, not bothering to answer the question itself—what would be the point?

She stretched out her hand to take it, but he dropped it unceremoniously in the bin beside him.

'You aren't serious? You can't live on that.'

'Don't...' Piper gaped at the bin in dismay. 'That's all I've got. And I don't live on it. You made a full breakfast this morning, for a start.'

She hesitated, torn between needing the unopened pot, and not wanted to let him see her take it out of the bin. He skewered her with a look.

'You aren't honestly debating whether or not to go dumpster-diving, are you?'

Heat bloomed in her cheeks anew.

'Of course not.'

'And you're still a bad liar.'

'Fine.' She snorted. 'But it's hardly a dumpster. It's the kitchen bin, and I know for a fact that it was cleaned out at the end of the shift so there'll be nothing in there but my unopened pot.'

'Stop.' He shook his head, slamming the light off and stepping out in the hall so decisively that she almost stumbled in her effort to back up. 'I don't need to hear any more. You can come home with me.'

'What?' It felt as if all the air had been sucked out of her lungs in a single instant. 'No. That's ridiculous.'

'No more ridiculous than what I've heard tonight,' Linc growled. 'You're camping on the couch and living off packet noodles, meanwhile I have a two-bed apartment, and a fridge full of fresh food.'

'I'm not staying with you.' She shook her head, horrified. 'I can't.'

Though whether at the idea of it, or at the way her body was reacting so entirely inappropriately, she couldn't be sure.

'Don't be a martyr, Piper,' he rasped. 'You can't stay here, and you clearly don't have much money if you're trying to support your mother and brother. The bedrooms at my place are opposite ends of the apartment, and we'll be here much of the time. You can stay just until the landlord has sorted your own place.'

She wanted to object, to politely decline. The idea of being in such close proximity to Linc seemed like a terrible one. Not to mention the wound it inflicted on her pride, having to rely on him like this.

But pride was no match for the crushing weight of responsibility. There was no doubt that even if she paid Linc something towards her stay, a week with him would be a lot cheaper than a week in a hotel. Especially around here.

Without doubt, her mother could use that money a hand-ful of times over.

'Okay.' She nodded at last, stuffing back her unwanted sense of pride. 'Thank you. It would really help my family.'

And she pretended to herself that there wasn't a single part of her that was being tempted by entirely un-practical motives.

Not one single part of her, at all.

CHAPTER SIX

LINC HAD NO idea what he was doing. He'd invited her to his apartment...to *live* with him. Temporary or not, it had to be the most insane suggestion he'd ever made. The veneer of professionalism had well and truly slipped.

He could dress it up in the excuse that he was doing a good turn for a colleague in need, but the reality was that he found the idea of her actually being here...*thrilling*.

And wasn't that a concern all in itself?

He watched from the kitchen as she made her way around the living area, taking in his apartment's open-plan layout, double-height ceilings, and full-height windows on three sides, and he found he actually cared what she thought of it.

Not that he was going to tell her that he'd designed it himself—or that his family business had built several of the striking, sleek, glass and steel tower blocks in this area of the city. Yet still, he couldn't help wondering whether it was something that she liked.

He couldn't explain why her opinion mattered.

'When you said apartment, you didn't say it was a penthouse that covered the entire floor,' she muttered, after a long moment.

'Does it matter?'

She turned to look at him, wrinkling her nose, but she didn't answer.

'Some warning might have been nice.'

'Why? What would it have changed?' he asked easily. 'You needed a place to stay, and I have a spare room.'

She glowered at him but still didn't answer. It was crazy how much of a kick her little show of defiance caused in him. A return to the confident, fiery Piper he'd once known, instead of this smaller version of herself that he'd been beginning to see around the heli base.

'Why does it bother you so much, Legs?' he asked her, without warning. As if the nickname could ground them again.

She cast him a dark look.

'It doesn't.'

'That's clearly a lie.'

Piper chewed on the inside of her lip for a moment. Then shrugged.

'Do any of the crew know you live like some kind of millionaire?'

'Hardly,' he replied tightly. 'But no, the subject has never come up.'

'Just as it never did in the army?' she challenged. 'I think you deliberately hide this side of your life.'

'Like you hiding the fact that you've been supporting your family all this time?' He tried turning the tables, but all she did was lift one delicate shoulder.

'Something like that.'

A simple admission that reminded him there was more to Piper that he didn't know—and that roused his curiosity far more than it had any right to. They eyed each other, almost warily.

Still, now wasn't the time.

'Perhaps I should show you to your room?' he suggested instead.

She spun around a little too quickly, a telltale ragged pulse beating at her throat. He tried not to notice the way her pupils dilated, turning her amber eyes a much darker shade, or the slight flaring of her nostrils that betrayed her.

Responses that were all so deliciously…base—despite all their drawing lines in the sand. And Linc knew he shouldn't feel that punch of triumph—but it reverberated through him all the same.

But that didn't mean he was about to give in to such temptation.

Without waiting for her to catch up to him, he stepped from the open area to the hallway and strode along the plush corridor to the left. Dutifully, Piper followed him.

'Guest suite is down that way.'

'And…your master suite.'

'Back up on the other side of the living area,' he assured her. 'Just like I promised.'

'Right,' she managed, clearly a little shocked. 'This place is incredible.'

Something pulled in his chest at the unexpected note of self-censure in her voice. As though she felt she'd failed in some way.

'I've been here a while.'

'Whilst I can't even afford a hotel room right now.' She shook her head.

Guilt stabbed through him. Clearly their very different circumstances were some sort of deep-seated issue for Piper that he'd never quite appreciated before now.

'It's no failing, Piper. For a start, doctors get paid more than pilots in the military, we both know that,' he noted. 'At least at our respective levels.'

'I understand that…' She bit her lip again. And he hated that she somehow thought less of herself.

But he could hardly tell her who he really was. Linc cleared his throat, searching for an easy way to explain it away.

'I've also made money by dabbling in the stock markets. It's a bit of a hobby.'

Which was true enough. He was good at it too; it was a hobby the duke had taught him as a child on his knee.

'I wouldn't even know where to start with stock markets.' She shook her head. 'I never realised how very… different we are.'

And he knew as soon as she said it that she hadn't meant for that to come out, even if he couldn't fathom why this all seemed to matter so much to her. Why, at least in her mind, she was drawing a division between them. Why she was highlighting the differences between them, and using that as an excuse to keep their distance from each other.

He found that it was his *not understanding* that rankled so much, and it occurred to him that distance was the last thing he wanted from this woman.

What the hell was wrong with him?

'Not so different.' Linc shrugged, deliberately playing it down. 'You learned to fly helis as a seventeen-year-old, around your family estate, did you not?' Although come to think of it, if that was the case, what had happened to that estate?

She eyed him oddly, and he had the distinct impression that there was a war going on in her head.

'No, I didn't, actually.'

'Oh?' He frowned. 'I thought I heard it mentioned back on that last tour of duty.'

'The two other female pilots on that tour had learned that way. And, given how every other pilot in the entire corps were men, they assumed I'd learned that way too. I stood out enough without telling them I wasn't a product of boarding school or super-rich parents, so it was easier just to let them think that I was like the other two females.'

'It was about fitting in?'

Even as he said it, a few other pieces of the puzzle he hadn't realised he'd started began to fall into place.

The way she'd always kept herself to herself; the way she'd never quite looked comfortable socialising with some of her peer group.

Had the military been an escape for Piper the way it had been for him—albeit for different reasons? She'd been running away from who she was, whilst he'd been running away from who he wasn't. As ironic as that was.

After his mother had pulled the proverbial rug from under him, he'd lost his identity. Joining the military as a doctor had given him back a sense of purpose, and a sense of worth. If it had somehow done the same for Piper, then no wonder they'd always felt that pull towards each other.

But wasn't that all the more reason to keep that proverbial line between them?

'Go and settle in,' he advised, not quite recognising the rasp in his own voice. 'Freshen up, get some sleep, whatever you need. Help yourself to anything in the kitchen. Tomorrow night I'll cook for us.'

And maybe they could finally find a way to be more comfortable around each other. Before the entire crew began to think there was more going on than there actually was.

Piper closed the door behind her and leaned against it, her hand moving instinctively to her ribcage as though she could slow down her racing heart. It felt as though it was going at about Mach 10, and she knew it couldn't handle the G-forces.

She'd never been able to handle her attraction to Linc; it was one of the reasons she'd been so firm about drawing that professional line between them, five years ago.

Yet it had been easier to do back then, on a tour of duty, with all the military rules and protocols. Now, by contrast, the only rules, the only boundaries, were self-imposed. And it was getting harder and harder to enforce them. She was terribly afraid that here, in such close proximity with no colleagues as buffers, that invisible line was going to disappear altogether.

Worse, she wanted it to.

Pushing back off the door, Piper took a step into the space. Belatedly, she realised that she wasn't standing in a bedroom, she was standing in a private living room. A generous space with a couch, and an antique study desk, and a breathtaking view of the city below occupying one wall. Solid doors occupied the other three walls, the double set she'd entered through, and opposite was another double set. Carefully—as if she were afraid she might intrude on a stranger in the space—she padded around.

The two single doors opened up on a bathroom and a dressing room that were each probably the size of the main bedroom in the terraced house she'd bought for her mother. She doubted her entire wardrobe would have filled even one of the bespoke cabinets in the dressing room, whilst the travertine-tiled bathroom was like something out of a high-end, glossy hotel brochure.

She eyed the enormous bathtub—clearly designed for couples—and wondered whoever had the time for a bath. Growing up in her childhood home, and then in the military, showers had been de rigueur, and she'd never really missed the long soak that so many other women seemed to enjoy.

Now, however, the bath seemed to call to her. Piper moved falteringly forward, flipping the taps and watching a stream of hot, inviting water flow out. A peek into a small basket on the honed, polished counter top revealed a selection of spa products, and she selected one at random and dropped it almost nervously into the bath. The scent was instantly relaxing.

Feeling a little more confident, she made her way back through the room, piling her hair onto her head and snagging it into place. And then she allowed herself a little flourish as she pushed open the set of double doors that surely had to lead to the bedroom.

Her breath actually caught in her throat.

The room itself was the size of an entire floor of her house. It had walls, a floor and a ceiling, but the similarities ended there. A huge bank of windows flooded the room with light, making it feel even more spacious and inviting. It took her a moment to realise that a set of patio doors led onto a wide balcony with gleaming oak wood decking, and a sleek metal and glass balustrade that offered tantalising views of the city beyond.

Piper stepped outside on autopilot, drawn to the spectacular sight. Like a carpet of land right at her feet. It made her feel free and powerful being up here and looking down on the city. As if she could do anything, conquer anything.

No wonder Linc loved it up here.

More than that, it allowed her to feel so far removed from her ordinary life that she could almost imagine she was a different person. Not herself. Without thinking, she followed the balustrade as it ran around the outside, lured by the sights as well as by the warm afternoon sun.

Then, tilting her face up towards it, the brightness making up for the lack of summer heat, Piper spread her hands out on the smooth wooden balcony rail and inhaled deeply.

Perfect relaxation.

'I assume you do know that you're outside my bedroom?'

The dry voice had her spinning around in an instant, fumbling for her words.

'What? Oh…no.'

Piper stopped dead. Linc was wearing nothing more than a pristine white towel around his waist, and his hair was slick, evidently from a shower. And everything become a hundred times worse. That hypersonic boom in her chest reverberating loudly—too loudly—in her head.

She couldn't seem to peel her eyes from the solid wall of his body, no matter how fiercely her brain screamed at her that she should. She'd always known he was muscled, the way his clothes had always clung so lovingly to him— from his army combats to his flight suit—had made that clear, but to see him in the flesh, naked, was a whole different ball game.

Like staring at the model for one of the great classical sculptures. A study in sheer masculinity.

Piper swallowed hard, desperately scrambling for something, anything, to say.

'You got a shower,' she managed to choke out at length.

Well, *accuse*, really. As though he didn't have the right to do what he liked in his own home.

'I did,' Linc agreed. 'I'd imagine you'd want to do the same, after a day like today.'

'I do.' She nodded, a little emphatically. 'That is, I usually do. But I saw that bath and I thought… I mean, it's clearly a bath for two.'

If the balcony had crashed under her feet and plummeted her down to ground level, she didn't think she'd have minded. In fact, she would probably have welcomed it. Wincing, she chanced a glance at Linc. Sure enough, he looked stony-faced.

'I mean… I didn't…' She felt more flustered than she thought she'd ever felt in her life. 'That wasn't supposed to sound like…'

'An invitation for me to join you?' he finished for her— grimly, she thought. 'No, I didn't imagine that it was.'

'Of course not,' she managed.

Liar, whispered that traitorous part of her body that was already starting to go molten at the mere suggestion.

'I don't normally indulge in baths, you understand.' Her mouth kept talking and she couldn't seem to stop it. 'I know it's probably not environmentally friendly…and sharing a bath is probably better in that sense…'

She tailed off awkwardly as Linc looked all the more pained.

'I think…perhaps…' She struggled to work her jaw. 'I think I should go to bed. It has been a long day, and the past few nights haven't been the most restful.'

'Then I hope you enjoy a relaxing bath,' he managed tightly. Gruffly.

'Yes. I…ought to get back to it.'

Evidently, this proximity to a practically naked Linc was frying her brain in a way that was more than a little embarrassing.

'I think that's for the best,' he rumbled as Piper grasped at the excuse to leave.

It was crazy how out of control she felt here, alone with him. With no military and no Helimed to act as a buffer, she felt fairly certain she was perilously close to losing her mind.

Either that, or she would lose every shred of her dignity, throwing herself at Linc the way she didn't seem to be able to stop herself.

Even as she scurried along the balcony, his low, rumbling voice seemed to chase her all the way back into her suite. And it didn't matter how firmly she slid the glass doors closed, it couldn't keep out that heavy ache in her chest. And lower, if she was going to be honest.

Swinging the bathroom door closed, then locking it, Piper hauled off her clothes and proceeded to drop them unceremoniously into the woven basket she always used as a laundry bag. The one that her mother had made for her before her first ever tour of duty. The one that, no matter where Piper was, always made her feel like home. Then, at last, she turned off the taps, stepped into the oversized tub and slid blissfully beneath the water, lying back and finally closing her eyes.

Slowly, slowly, the water lapped soothingly over her skin as the heat eased away the tensions of the day. Without warning, images of Linc exploring her body flew into her brain.

With a start, she lurched forward in the bath, making the water slosh precariously up the sloped sides. She ought to be embarrassed, having such sinful thoughts about the man.

Instead, she couldn't seem to stop them.

Reaching for the loofah she'd already set out on the side, she began to scrub crossly at her skin.

Linc was spoiling everything. Being alone with him was definitely very different from working with him, and coming here had been a mistake, she told herself furiously.

So why didn't the rest of her body seem to believe that one bit?

CHAPTER SEVEN

PIPER WAS RUNNING through her pre-flight checklist the next morning and flushing the engine compressor section with de-ionised water, when Linc entered the hangar. And before she could stop it, her chest leapt in some kind of misplaced anticipation.

'I feel perhaps that I owe you an apology,' he declared without preamble. 'For last night.'

'Shh.' Automatically she glanced around the empty space before taking a step towards him.

A mistake, she realised instantly.

That stony look threatened his face again, and she tried not to take it as a kind of unspoken rejection.

'There's no one here, Piper. They're all in the crew room, or rec room, I checked.'

'Of course you did.' She scrunched up her nose.

'Listen, I offered you a place to stay because I wanted to help. I apologise if I made you feel awkward, or uncomfortable in any way.'

'You didn't,' she replied quickly.

She'd done that all by herself—by having such wholly inappropriate thoughts about him.

'Well, I hope that's true.' He inclined his head. 'I want you to feel you can relax. And stay as long as you need to.'

'Thank you,' Piper managed, fighting the urge to run her tongue all over her suddenly parched mouth.

No doubt Linc intended to be kind. Chivalrous. But, crazily, that only made him all the more appealing to her. Somehow it was easier to resist Linc when he was being a devilish playboy, rather than this solicitous, softer man.

Easier to resist? a voice mocked in her head. And that fraught knot in her stomach pulled tighter.

'I also wanted you to know that I'm going out tonight. So you'll have the place to yourself, just in case that makes things easier.'

It didn't. Not at all. Something sliced through Piper and she told herself it couldn't possibly be jealousy.

Definitely not.

'Thank you for letting me know,' she managed stiffly, instead. 'Should I…?'

She stopped abruptly, hating herself for caring where he was going. Or who with.

Linc frowned at her.

'Should you…?'

It would be better to shake it off and make some kind of joke. But Piper found she couldn't. She needed to know.

'Should I make myself scarce? In the morning? In case they think we're…'

He eyed her incredulously.

'I'm not going on a date, if that's what you think.'

'Oh.' She forced herself to sound casual. 'Well, okay, but, for the record, I don't expect you to curtail your private life. It isn't any of my business, and I don't care either way.'

He skewered her with the intensity of his gaze, and she forgot how to breathe.

And then, without warning, he took a step towards her.

'Do you really not care?' he murmured, moving his face closer to hers.

So close that she could feel his warm breath caressing her cheek, and it was all she could do to fight some ridiculous impulse to lean forwards and press her lips to his.

'Not at all.'

Maybe she would have sounded more convincing if her voice hadn't cracked, right at that moment. Fire burned in her cheeks, then spread over every inch of her skin. And still, she couldn't move.

'You lie like a cheap NAAFI watch,' he muttered suddenly.

'I'm not lying,' she croaked before snapping her mouth shut.

She feared she revealed more and more of herself with every unguarded thing she uttered.

'For what it's worth,' Linc drawled slowly, 'I'm meeting my sister. She's flying in tonight and we're having dinner to talk about what she expects of me for her wedding. So, no date. Not that that matters to you, I know.'

'I see,' she managed, and she hated herself for the way her heart soared at his words. 'But it still isn't my business.'

'True, but still, now you know,' he murmured before turning to head for the doors. 'I'll get back before anyone comes looking for me and finds me here.'

'Thank you,' she gritted out.

'Unless you want me to be your second for the two-person checks?'

There was another kick in her ribcage.

As the critical care doctor, Linc wasn't the designated data pilot, and therefore no one could reasonably expect him to run through the checks with her. Offering to be the stand-in now would certainly give them a legitimate excuse to be in here together for a little longer. But she really shouldn't read into the fact that he was offering to do so.

Was it a test? If she really didn't care where he went or

who he dated, should she say she'd wait for the data pilot and tell him to leave?

'Well, you do happen to be here now,' she heard herself reply instead. 'And the sooner this thing is first paraded, the sooner she's ready for any shout.'

She could pretend it was about practicality all she liked, she suspected they both knew the truth. Still, picking up the digital notepad, Piper cast her eye over the stats for the heli.

'It won't hurt to just give a final check to the bowsers outside, either,' she told him. 'With the charity day coming up, and several longer-distance flights to get to events, we should ensure they have enough fuel of their own if we can't access the airport's main supply for any reason.'

'Good plan,' he agreed. 'Then we should probably also check the medical supplies, since we're both here.'

'Probably.'

And what did it say that the idea of being alone with Linc, with the safety net of work, seemed more than a little appealing?

For the next half-hour or so, they worked quickly and efficiently together, prepping the supplies and kit for the shift ahead. The easy banter between them seeping back in as the work tasks diluted the tension that had been building around them. It was a welcome breather.

They were about five minutes from the official shift start, and about to head over for a mug of tea, when the red phone sounded across the base. Hugo raced over a few moments later to pass on the details.

A twelve-year-old who had been thrown from her horse on a stretch of narrow country lane.

'We're good to go,' Piper acknowledged, grabbing her helmet and heading out onto the tarmac to get her heli started.

Within moments Tom had joined her, pulling up the map

and punching in the grid reference, passing on the location details that had initially been transmitted.

'You're all clear for lift, Helimed hotel one-niner,' the ATC voice crackled over the headset.

'Thanks,' Piper acknowledged as she got her bird into the sky before banking sharply.

'I'd suggest following the main A road up to the supermarket roundabout, then follow the country land from there,' Linc's voice came over through her headset. 'This is the third accident in the same location this year—usually the drivers were morning commuters taking a short cut to bypass traffic on the motorway. They hurtle along the country road, don't observe the speed limit drop from sixty to twenty on this particular section where there are several sets of stables and a dairy farm, and end up screeching their tyres trying to stop when they round the bend to find a herd of cows crossing the road, or horses just coming off the end of the bridleway.'

'That's going to spook the animals,' Piper noted grimly, duly turning the nose to follow the A road. 'You know the best place to land, too?'

'Yeah, there's a field just to the left as we head to location. Albert usually lands there, and there's a decent gap in the wall, so it's easy enough to get out, as well as bring the patient back through.'

'Sold,' she confirmed, concentrating on getting them there quickly as the radio crackled again.

'This is hotel zero seven, we have an update on the casualty,' Hugo's voice told them. 'Twelve-year-old female was thrown from her horse. Landed on the undergrowth and was unconscious for about a minute. She has been confused ever since. No other injuries reported.'

'Update received, out,' Linc acknowledged, addressing his team as Hugo ended the update. 'We'll check her over head-to-toe anyway, of course, but it seems we're looking at assessing whether she's suffering from simple concussion or extradural haematoma.'

'I'll get the heli as close as possible,' Piper assured him. 'In case you need to get the casualty to a major trauma unit as quickly as possible. We're coming up on the location now.'

Bringing the heli around, she looked for the field Linc had mentioned.

Damn.

'It's a no-go for the landing,' she told him. 'There are livestock in the field.'

'Hell. They're usually in the area on the other side of the road.'

Piper cast her eye over in that direction.

'Well, one of those fields is clear, but the overhead wires on that side of the road are going to push us to the back corner.'

'Anyone see an exit point?' Linc asked quickly.

'Nothing on the left,' Tom advised after a moment. 'What about you, Probie?'

'I think there's a gate at the bottom corner of the field,' Probie advised carefully. 'Yes… I'm sure there is.'

'Good eye, Probie,' Linc's voice agreed after a moment. 'There's a gate leading to a dirt track which joins the country lane itself. Wait a moment…yeah, there's someone running over that way now, waving. Land here, Piper. You're clear on the tail.'

'Left is good,' Tom agreed, as Probie chimed in that the right side was also clear.

Slowly bringing the heli down, Piper nosed down the field before finally letting the skids touch the ground.

'You're as close as I can get,' she told them, as the team

all started to move. 'But if you need me to move, just let me know.'

Then they were gone, and all she could do was sit. And wait.

Linc's mind was still on that last shout as he pulled on his shirt later that evening.

By the nature of what the air ambulance did, they were usually only called to serious cases, and his time with the army had exposed him to any number of horrific injuries. But cases involving kids were always worse.

Seeing such young patients— whose whole lives should be ahead of them—suffering life-changing injuries could be almost unbearable sometimes. Especially when, like that last shout, there had actually been nothing more for his team to do than to load the girl onto the heli and get her to hospital for the right scans.

The kid might not have had any external injuries that he and his team could patch up and help to heal, but it had been clear from her constant confusion that she'd suffered some kind of brain injury despite her riding helmet. And his team could do nothing about a head injury except get her to a major trauma unit as quickly as they could.

He hated that sense of helplessness. That feeling of not being able to *do* something to change the situation.

And now he was supposed to go out and enjoy an evening with his sister, albeit also endure her inevitable reprimands, as though everything were fine. Yet tonight was one of those nights when all he really wanted to do was stay here and maybe hit his home gym. Anything to expend the fraught feeling—the sense of frustration—that was slamming around inside him like a ball on a squash court.

But he had to go. He'd already delayed it to try to get his head back to reality, but he had to go. It was part of his responsibility to his family, to his sister. Hauling open his door, he stalked down the hall, picking up his mobile from the hall stand where he'd dropped it, and had his hand on the penthouse door when Piper emerged from her end of the hallway.

Linc dropped his hand without even meaning to.

Clad only in a short dressing gown that revealed acres of mouthwatering skin and offered yet more proof of why the nickname *Legs* was perfect for her, she sauntered up the corridor, her nose so buried in a book that she hadn't even noticed him.

His body reacted instantly. Viscerally.

As though it were traitorously exempt from whatever practical, cerebral agreement he and Piper had come to concerning not crossing any professional boundaries. Surely no red-blooded male could have failed to respond to the glorious sight of Piper? Though perhaps he would have fought his body's instinct a little harder had a part of him not welcomed the fact that it distracted from the sense of frustration he'd been feeling after the shout.

Piper was closer now, and still she hadn't noticed him. Dimly, he thought he ought to say something, or make a noise to alert her to his presence. But when he did, he barely recognised his own voice.

'Piper?'

She stopped short, the shock evident in her expression.

Her hair still wet and slick from the shower, her bare feet with the delicately painted pink toenails that he would never have believed if he weren't seeing them now.

The last thing Piper had ever seemed to him was soft, or pink—he found he rather liked seeing this unexpected softer side of her.

'I thought you were out,' she accused tightly, visibly swallowing.

He moved and her eyes dropped instantly to the small

open V at the top of his shirt, and her tongue flicked out wickedly over her plump lips.

Rather as if she couldn't stop herself.

He felt a kick somewhere in his gut, revelling in the way she seemed to have to fight herself to lift her gaze back to his face.

'You're supposed to be at dinner by now,' she continued, in a strangled voice.

And he revelled in that, too.

'Not for about an hour. After the last shout, I called Sara and pushed the time back.'

Her expression grew pained, but her darkening pupils betrayed her. He knew women well enough to know that look. Moreover, he knew Piper well enough to know that look.

'You didn't tell me,' she accused. But hoarsely.

He couldn't help teasing her.

'And miss the show?' he rasped, his eyes sweeping slowly over her before he could stop himself.

He was rewarded instantly when her nipples tightened visibly beneath the soft fabric of the dressing gown, like a scorching lick of heat over the hardest part of himself. Even as his brain bellowed at him to back away—to maintain that divide between them—a far more base, more carnal sound roared through his body. And the longer he sinfully indulged in her, the more that fraught knot in his gut began to slip undone.

The devil on his shoulder whispered how easy it would be to call his sister and cancel their meeting altogether just to stay here with Piper so they could make their own entertainment.

His head filled all too easily with images of her wrapped around his body. Not to mention those tantalising glimpses of soft skin that kept peeking out from beneath the collar of her silky dressing gown.

As if reading his mind, she clutched it a little closer to preserve her modesty. But those darkening eyes, that ragged breathing, told a different story.

'I was planning on getting something to eat and going to bed early.' She managed to sound prim yet sexy all at the same time.

A true skill, Linc rather thought. He took a step towards her, and watched that pulse flutter manically at the base of her neck.

Crying out to him.

'That sounds like a wise idea,' he ground out. 'I would do the same if I could.'

'You're going out.' Piper's voice was hoarse.

'I am,' he acknowledged, battling the urge to take another step towards her.

He succeeded. But that didn't mean he was ready to take a step towards the door.

'It was a difficult day,' she murmured, after a moment.

'It was.'

'Do you think the kid will be okay?'

'I hope so,' he muttered. 'I hope she regains her memory quickly.'

'Sometimes, it's easy to forget how short life can be.'

'And get caught up in the rules?' His gaze held hers. 'The idea of what's right, or what's appropriate?'

'I guess…that's what I'm saying.' She hesitated, and he tried to quash the sense of victory that rolled towards him.

'Do you want me to stay?' he demanded, the rasp in his tone seeming to echo around the room.

Her eyes darkened and she moved one single step in his direction before seeming to stop herself.

'I…your sister is waiting.'

And he tried to cling onto the logical, practical argument that said they should keep their distance, but there was no quashing his triumph this time. It punched through him. Loud, and vibrant.

'How tempted are you?' he heard himself demand.

'Who says I'm tempted?' she replied on a choppy whisper—wholly undermined by the way her body leaned towards him.

'That isn't precisely an answer,' he managed, his voice raw, his body jolting at the way her breath caught audibly. 'Are you as tempted as I am? More?'

Linc couldn't have said who moved first, but abruptly the gap between them closed, and her body was against his, and fighting temptation was no longer a question. Something else was in control of them now: the attraction, the lust, that they'd been staving off for weeks—for years, if they included back in the army.

Finally, *finally*, he slid his fingers through her damp hair and set his mouth to hers, glorying in the way she lifted her hands and seemed to simply…cling on, and the fire licked at him in an instant.

It moved through him, getting higher and hotter as she let him angle her head for a better fit, testing first this way and then that way, seeming to melt against him that little bit more with every delicious slide of his tongue against hers.

Dully, he was aware of a mobile phone ringing in the background, but he didn't care. Scooping her up, his hands cupping that perfectly toned backside, he carried her over to the kitchen countertop and sat her down. Was it him, or her, who wrapped her legs around his waist to pull him in, just a few layers of fabric separating her soft, wet heat from the very hardest part of his body, just like in every dirty dream he'd ever had about her?

And he liked that carnal sound she made, low in her throat, when he told her as much.

And still, he wasn't even sure she meant to move and yet her hands lifted up between them until her palms were spread gloriously over his chest. So that the pulse in her thumb was right over the drumming of his heart.

He shifted and she moaned against his mouth, pressing her breasts to him, so tightly that he could feel how proud and pert her nipples were. His mouth watered. The need to take her, to claim her, was almost painful. This thing they'd shared had been arcing between them for so long. But he was determined not to rush. To take it slow.

Slowly, with painstaking deliberation, he slid his hand down to cup the base of her head, tipping it back so that he could feast on the long, elegant line of her neck, relishing the way she shivered in response and leaned back further to grant him better access.

He couldn't have said what it was about the scrabbling outside—perhaps the unusualness of the sound, perhaps his subconscious had been expecting something the moment his phone had started its incessant ringing—that alerted him something was wrong moments before the door to his apartment swung open.

And all he could do was shove Piper behind him, his first thought preserving whatever he could of her modesty.

CHAPTER EIGHT

PIPER HAD BARELY registered what was going on as Linc pulled her down from the countertop and set her firmly behind him just as a woman—a stunning woman, to be precise—strode into the room.

Linc's sister, presumably.

The woman stopped abruptly when she saw them. But rather than looking embarrassed or shocked, she looked angry. With an odd undercurrent of...curiosity.

By contrast, Piper found all the self-confidence she'd had to finally kiss Linc seeped out of her in an instant. She wasn't even certain she could remember how to breathe.

'What the hell do you think you're doing, Sara?' Linc growled, clearly not suffering from the same lack of confidence.

Any other woman—any other person—would have cowed at the unmistakeably dangerous edge to his tone. Even Piper found herself desperate to move, but unable to budge. Embarrassment and anger were waging their own little war inside her head, and she wasn't yet certain which was going to win.

Sara, however, barely even flinched.

'You weren't answering your phone,' she continued, her focus on Linc. 'I didn't think you were home.'

'So you just let yourself in?'

He advanced on her, clearly furious, but the woman just jerked her chin up at him as only a sister could.

'You gave me a key.' She lifted her immaculately tailored shoulders in a gesture too elegant to be considered as unsophisticated as a shrug.

'For emergencies,' Linc growled, but his sister seemed to ignore that, too.

'We were supposed to be meeting for dinner earlier.'

'I called you to tell you I was running late from our last shout.'

'By which time I was already in the air,' his sister noted disdainfully. 'Coming here seemed like the logical solution. Was I supposed to divine the fact that the reason you pushed our meal back an hour was because you're…otherwise engaged.'

Sara scrunched up her nose, evidently unimpressed, and despite her best efforts Piper couldn't stop the heat from flooding her cheeks at the loaded accusation. But in the war between shame and anger, the latter was beginning to win out.

'We didn't…that is… I'm not the reason…' Piper began in a clipped voice before Linc took over for her.

'Piper had nothing to do with me pushing the meeting time back tonight.'

And Piper wondered if she was the only one to notice that slightly thicker note to his tone. Whether she was the only one who understood the reason behind it, that sense of helplessness as they'd flown that confused twelve-year-old kid—who couldn't even remember her name, or that it was her birthday that very day—to the hospital.

'I think I ought to leave,' Piper managed.

'Good idea,' Linc's sister agreed coldly.

But as Piper began to move out from around Linc—her

state of undress be damned—Linc snaked his hand around to protect her.

'I'll walk with you,' he murmured reassuringly, before turning his attention back to his sister. 'This is my home, Sara, you don't speak to my guests like that. And you certainly don't send her scuttling back to her bedroom like some chastened child.'

'Her bedroom?' his sister echoed in disbelief. 'She's living here?'

'Staying temporarily.' There was no hint of apology in Linc's voice. 'Not that it's your business, but for Piper's sake I'm telling you that she's our emergency pilot since our usual one was in an accident. Since she's from out of the area, she found herself without accommodation.'

'Of course she did.' The sarcasm was unmistakeable. 'And I can see the attraction, I can, Lincoln. But moving her in with you? You aren't pregnant, are you?'

This last bit was patently directed at her, but Piper didn't get chance to respond before Linc had dropped his arm from around her waist, and advanced on his sister.

This time, he didn't think there was any way he was reining in his anger.

'Too far, Sara,' he growled, as he took his sister firmly, though not harshly, by the shoulders, and began to propel her swiftly to the exit. And Piper thought the woman must have realised she'd overstepped because, this time, she didn't argue.

But, at the last moment, another man appeared in the doorway.

'Is there a problem?'

His low voice rumbled through the penthouse, sounding so achingly familiar that Piper had to twist her head around to check that it hadn't come from Linc himself.

In an instant, every line of Linc's body changed. He

stopped ejecting his sister as she thrust out her hand to the door jamb and spun herself around, whilst Linc folded his arms over his body.

'I didn't know you were coming,' he told the other man, and Piper thought it was interesting how his attitude had changed.

Clearly this was someone who mattered to Linc, who he cared about—his older brother, Raf, perhaps? The man certainly had an air of quiet authority about him that was so similar to Linc. Plus, even though she'd never met him, the way Linc had always talked about him, it had been clear that he respected and loved his brother. She'd always known when he'd managed a video call with his brother from out there, in that theatre of war. Linc had always seemed to be much more settled and grounded for weeks afterwards.

Though she'd never really bothered to ask herself why Linc's state of mind had always been so important to her.

'I told you what I need to discuss with you is important,' Sara announced now, triumphant as her glance encompassed the other man. 'Why else would Raf have come?'

So it *was* Linc's brother, Raf.

At least her own presence here had been apparently forgotten, for the moment. Piper wondered if she could slip away unnoticed.

'About the optics of your wedding,' Linc was saying to his sister as Piper inched towards the hallway to her suite— not that she dared break cover from behind the countertop. 'Isn't it always, these days?'

Despite the circumstances, Piper winced on Sara's behalf at the evident disdain in Linc's voice. Linc didn't mean to, that much was clear, but his dismissal of his sister's wedding clearly hurt her, though she rallied impressively. And even though Piper knew it probably wasn't her place to comment, nonetheless, she made a mental note to mention it to him when they were alone again.

'It's about more than just me, Linc,' Sara pleaded.

'I know what it's about,' he scoffed. 'It's always the same.'

And this time, when Sara bit back, Piper could almost understand it.

'No, you don't, because you never listen, and you never bother to come home. Tonight is a prime example. Apparently, Raf—' she spun again, this time to look at her other brother '—the reason Linc decided to make us wait this evening is because he was otherwise occupied with his new…houseguest. *Piper.*'

And as easy as that, the woman was back to a barely concealed contempt that cut right through Piper.

'That's enough, Sara,' Linc bit out, with audible fury in his tone. 'That's your last warning.'

And though she appreciated him defending her, Piper could only wish the ground would open up and swallow her whole. Anything to get away from the scrutiny—and the disdain.

For all the confidence she had in her career, and on the battlefield, she'd never found it easy to deal with strangers. Especially those who were clearly monied, and accustomed to throwing their wealth around. Like this woman.

Now, as much as it galled Piper to admit it, Linc's siblings were making her feel smaller and smaller with each passing moment. She certainly wasn't prepared for the brother's reaction.

'Wait… Piper?' he mused, as though the name meant something to him.

A dull drumbeat started up in Piper's chest, though she told herself that she shouldn't read too much into it. She mustn't.

'You served with Lincoln, didn't you?' the brother pondered. 'A few years ago?'

'Just around five years,' Piper forced herself to answer.

'Is that right?' Sara interjected. 'And now you're here and living with my brother, though we've never been formally introduced.'

Her tone was pointed, but Linc wasn't having any of it.

'Nor will you be now,' he gritted out, moving back to be closer to Piper. Half shielding her, half lending her strength.

'It would be good to remedy it, though,' his brother stated evenly. 'Perhaps Piper would like to get changed and accompany us to dinner.'

'I don't think so.' Linc didn't even hesitate, meanwhile Sara was gasping with obvious dismay.

'Raf...this is family business.'

'Sara, you've been rude enough already,' her older brother chastised. 'Linc and Piper have both been more than patient and I think we can all agree that these aren't the circumstances under which any of us would have chosen to meet. I think going for a meal together would help to remedy that. Would you not agree?'

And even though Raf was looking at both of them, Piper could tell that his focus was on his brother.

This was a test. Raf was using the invitation to gauge his brother's feelings towards her.

And even though a part of her wanted to jump in and tell both siblings that she and Linc were just friends, she found herself waiting for Linc to speak. Steeling herself—though she didn't care to examine why—for the moment he told them that she had no place joining them.

Slowly, she dragged her eyes from Raf, and Sara, to rest on Linc. Preparing herself for the inevitable. And, at last, he responded.

'The choice is yours, Piper,' he told her slowly. Thoughtfully. 'Would you care to join us?'

Shock walloped into her. She didn't need to look at Linc's brother to know what he was reading into the moment—not that she could have dragged her gaze from Linc even if she'd tried—and she could certainly hear the sharp intake of breath from his sister.

What was Linc even playing at? He might as well have announced some intention to commit himself to her. It was certainly what it sounded like. She couldn't explain it. Certainly couldn't understand it.

She opened her mouth to tell him that she would be spending the night here, with her bath and early night as planned.

'Give me a few minutes to change,' she heard herself say instead.

And then, with a confidence that she hadn't known she'd had before—at least outside a helicopter cockpit, she stepped out from behind the counter, and strode as casually as she could across the hallway and down to her guest suite.

Let them make of that whatever they would.

It only took her a few moments to push herself off the closed door, where she'd been leaning and trying to catch her breath. She didn't have long to get ready if she didn't want to irk Linc's siblings—notably his sister—any more than she already had.

There was no pretending that she hadn't noticed the critical way that Sara had eyed her up and down, leaving her feeling as if she were a dog, or a horse, rather than a human. Only Sara probably would have shown more interest and care if she *were* of the four-legged variety.

She still didn't know what had possessed Linc to invite her; less still why she'd accepted, but at least she was grateful that she'd already showered. There might not be enough to time to blow-dry her hair the way she might have preferred, but she was accustomed to deftly twisting it up into an elegant chignon, and brushing on a quick hint of make-up.

As for her clothes, she didn't have much choice. Her go-to evening wear was a pair of flowing black trousers—her only non-work pair, in fact, but she liked that they seemed to make her more glamorous, less gangly—and a pretty top that she'd brought on the off-chance of going out for an evening.

And she told herself that Linc definitely hadn't been in her mind when she'd been standing in front of her locker in barracks, taking that particular top off its hanger.

It would have to do. Nothing that she had would come anywhere close to the exquisite creation that Linc's sister had appeared to be wearing, but at least she would feel sufficiently dressed-up to hold her own at whatever restaurant they seemed to be booked into.

Linc was still trying to work out why the heck he hadn't shut his brother down when he'd invited Piper to join them for the evening.

He'd known it had been a test. Clearly, he'd failed it. By allowing the situation to play out he'd left his siblings with the impression that there was something going on between him and Piper.

Isn't there? a voice taunted in his head, before he could shut it down.

The fact remained that he'd needlessly opened Piper up to more scrutiny, and he only had himself to blame.

'I still don't understand what she's even doing here.' Sara flounced across the room and threw herself into one of the pristine dove-grey leather chairs in the living area.

'I told you, it's about practicality,' he repeated, though

he was beginning to doubt that, even of himself. 'We're old friends, so when she needed somewhere to stay for a week or two, I was happy to oblige.'

'Yes, I can see how happy you are.'

If it hadn't been for Raf's presence, he wasn't sure he would have continued to indulge his sister. For all her prickliness he loved her intently but, had his brother not shown up, he would have happily ejected her from his penthouse the first time she'd been rude to Piper.

Even now, her snort of derision wound him up even tighter than before.

'You looked like a pair of guilty, libido-ridden teenagers standing there when I walked in. And, frankly, you were never that guilty as a teenager, Lincoln.'

'You're sailing close to the wind, Sara,' Linc growled.

A wiser person would have heeded the warning. His sister, however, actually waved her hand in the air even more derisively.

'You might not be a monk, dear brother, but I can count the number of dates you've had with the same woman on one hand. Now you're telling me that you've actually moved this *Piper* into your apartment?'

'I told you out of courtesy,' Linc replied coldly, 'but ultimately it isn't really any of your concern. Yours or Raf's.'

'It's entirely of our concern. Which you'd know if you'd take your head out of your backside long enough to listen to us. To come back and be the part of the family you've always been—'

'That will do, Sara,' Linc ground out, just as Raf uttered something along similar lines.

Sara spun around instantly.

'The point of this evening is to talk family matters with Linc. *Private* family matters. How can we do that with his "houseguest" in there?'

'Sara.' This time it was Raf who cut her off first. 'I know you're worried about the family company, but I've never known you to be so catty before. I can't say I care for it.'

Raf's tone was the perfect balance between commanding and caring. It was a skill that his brother had always known just how to execute, and one that Linc had long envied.

'I'm also worried about you,' she added stubbornly, before swinging back around to Linc, her eyes flashing. 'You do realise that two of the board members have been trying to topple Raf by secretly buying up shares and now have forty per cent. They're weeks away from organising a coup.'

'What does it matter?' Linc growled, his eye on the door to Piper's suite, beginning to regret his earlier decision. This was definitely not a conversation he wanted her to overhear. It would mean having to explain too much. 'So long as you, Raf and I stick together, they can never out-vote us; we still hold the controlling interest.'

'Except that the devious bastards have managed to dig up some of the truth about you. About Mum. They've got a whiff of the fact that…well, you know…and he's going to use that against Raf.'

It was as if the world froze—his siblings, his penthouse, time itself.

'This isn't the place, Sara.' Linc was aware of Raf's censure, but it was too late.

It was said. The box was open. The thing the three of them never, *never* discussed swirled around the room.

'They know that the old duke isn't my father.' Linc wasn't sure how he managed to sound so calm. So in control. He felt anything but. 'Say the words, Sara.'

'They know,' she choked out. 'And they're using that to claim that your shares were never yours to inherit. They're trying to have you thrown off the board. The board votes next week.'

His tongue felt too big for his mouth. Too unwieldy. Yet somehow, he didn't know how, he spoke.

'Then let them. If that's the weapon he's using to unseat Raf, let him use it. If the board votes me out, and claims I'm not a proper Oakes, then let them. They aren't wrong. The duke wasn't my biological father. I'm just your half-brother.'

It was as if every fear he'd ever had—the very reason for him leaving Stoneywell and not returning—was suddenly coming to pass. His past was rushing up on him, threatening to swallow him whole, and there was nothing he could do to hold it back.

'You *are* our brother.' Sara pushed herself up from her seat and flung herself at him furiously for a moment. 'I don't care what anyone else says or thinks.'

And it was ridiculous how touched he was at her unfailing love. The way she'd always been, even that first night their mother had so gleefully announced the truth about her infidelity. As loving and supportive as Raf, as their father, had been—even when she'd produced a DNA test to prove it, driven by some vicious compulsion to hurt the old duke that little bit more.

But somehow, that had only made it all the harder to accept. Because the more they had closed around him, the three of them in a protective ring around him—the more he'd felt as if he wasn't one of them. Like a cuckoo in their nest.

Ultimately, it had been their love that had pushed him to join the army to get away from them. Irony at its worst.

'He was our father. To all three of us,' Raf rasped out as Sara moved back to her own seat. 'I will not hear otherwise.'

'But if the argument is accepted, it will make things easier for you. My shares would just revert to you two.

Those old cronies win nothing by getting rid of me, so let them do it.'

'That isn't the point,' Sara cried.

'I think it is,' argued Linc, as though his heart weren't cracking, right there in his soul.

'No,' Raf disagreed quietly. 'Besides, even if it were the point, there's more to it.'

'Meaning?'

'Meaning that they also know Daddy knew about the infidelity,' Sara revealed. 'And that you couldn't be his… biological son. So they're contesting his state of mind at the time his will was drawn up.'

'Say again?' Linc thundered, his head swirling with the revelations.

'They're saying that the Alzheimer's started earlier, and that decisions he made during the later years—the direction that the company took—might not have been taken had he been in his right mind.'

'He was in his right mind.' Linc frowned. 'He knew exactly what he was doing with the company, right up until those last few years. It's the same direction Raf has been taking the company—'

He stopped abruptly, his mind beginning to work through the noise.

'Which is precisely why they're using it as a means to get Raf out, too,' Sara bit out.

Linc turned to his brother.

'You can't let them get away with it.'

'I'm dealing with it,' Raf rumbled softly. Steadfastly.

Looking from one brother to the other, Sara threw her hands up in frustration.

'But it would be a whole lot easier if you came home and helped. Raf, will you please tell him that he needs to come home?'

Linc didn't know why he looked at his brother. Raf couldn't possibly need his help. His older brother was always so in control, so strong. And still, he watched, certainty turning to shock when Raf didn't instantly refute Sara's claim.

'It would…help,' his brother acknowledged after a moment.

There was little need to say anything more. For Raf to even say that much meant that they were in trouble. It was almost unconscionable.

'Most of the board members don't want a coup,' Sara pressed after a moment. 'They want the problem to just go away. And maybe it would, if you were home. If you were part of the business, just like you were always meant to be. Like we were all always meant to be.'

'I don't see what my presence would change,' Linc growled, feeling even more of an imposter than ever.

'It would show your commitment to Stoneywell. To the family name, and the family business, just as Daddy always believed we would be.' His sister's voice trembled, somewhere between grief and ferocity.

Still, Linc shook his head.

'That won't change the facts. I'm still…who I am.'

Not his father's biological son.

'It would change things if you came back home and settled down. Maybe took on the role as Chief of the Stoneywell Medical Centre,' Sara pointed out. 'There are plenty of old-guard board members who supported Daddy, and who would like nothing better than for him to be proved right by the three of us running Oakenfeld Industries together, the way he had always envisaged.'

'I'm not a private practice doctor.' Linc hated that she was suggesting such a move. And hating himself even more for refusing to help. 'I'm a former army doctor. I'm an air ambulance doctor. I go where I'm needed, not where cash-splashing celebrities want me to be.'

'Then reconsider,' Sara snapped. 'For Raf, if not for yourself.'

'Raf doesn't need me. He can resolve this issue without my help,' Linc argued, even as several pieces began to topple into place. 'Is that what all your phone calls have been about? All this pressure to bring a plus one to your wedding rehearsal next week? To your wedding? You want me to pretend to the board that I'm finally settling down and thinking of coming back to the fold, a changed man?'

'It couldn't hurt,' his sister blasted.

He begged to differ. He'd never known a problem his older brother couldn't fix.

'It's fine, Linc.' His brother dipped his head, as though reading his mind. As in control as ever. 'I'll think of something. I still have a few plays in motion before next week.'

'Right,' Linc agreed.

But guilt still moved through him. If it was that easy, then Raf wouldn't be here in the first instance.

The glittering, shimmering tears in his sister's eyes didn't help, either.

'Since when did you get so selfish, Lincoln Oakes?' she choked out. 'All these years we've supported your choices, from the army to the air ambulance. But now we need you and...'

The click of the door down the hallway silenced whatever else his sister had been going to say, and he and his brother stood automatically as the surprising sound of high heels clicked down the marble flooring towards them.

And then it was his turn for the words to pile up in his chest. Caught in the vacuum, every breath in him was sucked out.

Piper looked stunning. No, more than that, she looked

positively majestic, standing in front of them like some kind of goddess, with the most dazzling smile falling from her lovely face.

And he thought only he could read the tiniest of tension marks around the normally smooth edges.

Mine, the shockingly primitive thought bellowed in his head. In his soul. *All mine.*

Then his remarkable Piper stepped towards his sister, her arm outstretched.

'Shall we try this again?' she asked lightly, almost breezily. 'I'm Piper. It's lovely to meet you, Sara. I've heard so much about you over the years, it's great to finally put a face to—'

'Lady Sara,' his sister cut across her with a smile of her own that was bright but sharp.

Instinct made him step forward.

'For God's sake, Sara,' he growled, moving to stand next to Piper, but it was too late. His gut pulled taut as Piper twisted to him, blinking in shock.

'Lady Sara?' she asked tightly.

'Just as my brother here is Lord Lincoln.' Sara's voice sounded muffled as he held Piper's gaze. 'Surely you understand that's how titles work?'

Tearing himself from Piper, he moved to his penthouse door and yanked it back open.

'Leave now, Sara,' Linc gritted out.

How had he not realised that his secret would be revealed if Piper spent any time with his siblings? Had he been so caught up with what had happened between them in the moments before his sister had walked in?

Regrettably, he realised the answer was *yes*.

'Titles?' Piper was still echoing, evidently stunned.

'Of course.' Sara was eying her curiously now. 'You'll

understand my surprise that you're apparently living with my brother but claim not to even know that.'

'She didn't know.' Linc stepped in. 'And it really is time you left.'

'What about dinner?' Sara demanded.

'Goodbye, Sara,' Linc managed icily, his eyes on a reeling Piper. 'Go home. Go to dinner. But you will leave my home.'

'I have a better idea.' Raf stepped in calmly. 'Linc, you and Piper go to the restaurant, and talk on neutral ground. Clearly we've overstepped the mark here. I apologise. Sara, you and I are leaving.'

'No, but—'

'Now, Sara.' Raf ushered her to the door in much the way that Linc himself had before.

Linc was grateful. For all his own usual self-control, looking at Piper's ashen face at this moment, he could happily have kicked his sister out on her designer-clad backside.

'I'm glad to have met you.' Raf shook Piper's hand smoothly, even as he kept propelling Sara towards the door. 'I regret that it wasn't under better circumstances. Perhaps next time.'

And with those words hanging in the air like some kind of simultaneously unspoken criticism and assurance, Raf removed the two of them from the penthouse leaving Linc to finally be alone with the only woman he realised he could ever have imagined knowing his most guarded secret.

CHAPTER NINE

PIPER WAS STILL processing the revelations of the previous evening as she first paraded the helicopter the following morning. Hardly surprising, since she'd also been thinking about it all night; barely able to sleep.

They'd eaten at the finest restaurant Piper thought she'd ever been to. A ten-course tasting menu fit for the lords and lady that Linc and his siblings were.

But between the glazed scallop with salt-baked parsnips, nasturtium, and crisp pork belly starter, and the rich, mirror-glazed cocoa delight with edible gold leaf flecks for dessert, they'd also talked.

Linc, the man she'd known for years—the army doctor she'd served alongside on multiple tours—was a lord? It still seemed too crazy to be true.

He'd talked to her about his family's Oakenfeld Industries, and shared inheritances, he'd explained to her about Raf being the new Duke of Stoneywell, and given her a brief outline of the board members who were trying to topple his brother, but she still wasn't entirely sure that she understood all the facts, even now.

She hated his guilt that his abandonment of the family business had led to such instability, and a part of her could now begin to understand what his sister meant by using the optics of her wedding to make it appear that Linc was finally ready to settle down and return to the family fold.

But Piper couldn't shake the feeling that he was leaving out something more to the story. She couldn't escape the idea that there was a vital piece that he wasn't sharing.

Perhaps it was to do with the way his siblings had seemed much more open and receptive towards Linc than he had to them. As though there were a sheet of one-way glass between them, and Linc were on the protected side of it.

Five years ago, he'd given her the impression he would have moved heaven and earth for his brother and his sister. Now, she wasn't so sure. Part of her felt as though he wanted to…it was simply as though there was a wall stopping him. A wall that only Linc himself had built. She wished she understood it.

It all made her wonder if she'd ever really known him at all.

She'd been about to sleep with him—well, perhaps not *sleep,* precisely—and she hadn't even known the truth. Worse, she wasn't even sure a part of her cared. She, who had always told herself that she would never give herself to a man she couldn't be completely honest with.

Yet here she was, still wondering whether she was imagining something between herself and Linc, or whether it really existed. Even lying in that luxurious guest bed last night, still reeling from the revelations, it had been like some form of exquisite torture—knowing that Linc had been only metres away, at the other end of the penthouse.

How could it be that he was sending her out of her mind on so many different levels?

It felt as though the more time she spent at his home, the more she wasn't sure she understood herself at all.

How was it he could leave her feeling so gloriously desirable, yet at the same time so damned easy to resist? No wonder the more time she spent in his penthouse, the more sexually frustrated she seemed to be feeling. She, who had never really considered herself to have a particularly high libido in general.

Which was surely why spending time with Linc intimately, even for pretend, was the last thing she should do?

'Hey, Piper, grub's up. My famous chilli.' Linc interrupted her thoughts, appearing at the door of the base just as she was finishing pulling the trailer back to the hangar. 'You okay?'

'Sure.' She regrouped quickly. 'I didn't know you were cooking.'

Because if he could pretend that everything was normal between them, then so could she.

No matter that it cost her dearly to do so.

But then he stayed by the door, as if there was something else on his mind.

'Something else you wanted to say?' she managed, impressing herself with how nonchalant she actually sounded.

Surely he couldn't hear that slight quiver in her voice?

'Have you heard the news about Albert?' he asked abruptly.

And there was no reason for her heart to plummet, but it did.

'What news?'

'Albert and Jenny are being discharged tomorrow. Jenny suffered a couple of fractured ribs from the steering wheel but nothing critical so she'll be laid up for a little while, but Albert got off with only a few minor injuries so he should be back within a fortnight.'

'That's great.' Guilt sliced through Piper at how hard it was to keep her smile bright.

'You could be back at barracks, away from here before you know it.'

'Even better,' she acknowledged, her smile so wide she feared her face might actually fracture.

She was pleased for the crew, obviously. The idea of any of them being injured wasn't one she would wish on anyone. At the same time, a part of her would have welcomed a little more time with Heathston Helimed.

With Helimed, or with Linc? that insidious little voice challenged. And even as she told herself the idea of leaving was only hard because the steady income was just what she needed to help her family—not any other reason, of course—she knew she didn't believe it.

For a moment, they seemed caught in time. Watching each other without a word. And then Linc spoke. Quietly, catching them both off guard.

'Is it, though?' he asked, making a move to close the gap between them.

She held her hands out palms up. Neither trying to stop him, nor caution him.

'Isn't it?'

Before he could answer, the alarm sounded for another shout. Wordlessly, they each sprang into action, as if the moment had never happened. But even as she leapt into the cockpit, she couldn't quite evict the thick feeling that squatted heavily on her chest.

By the sounds of it, she had a handful of shifts left here and then she would be gone. From Heathston Helimed... and from Linc's life.

'What's the call?' Piper demanded as the crew raced over the tarmac and to her heli.

'Road traffic collision on the main A road, up near Farm Mere. High-impact collision between bus and motorcycle;

potential head injury. Police are already on scene controlling the site.'

If the police had cleared the area, she might even be able to land on the road. Running through her checks, Piper started the heli up.

'Everybody ready?'

Quickly, the crew ran through their own checks before Piper adjusted her headset and contacted the local air traffic control.

'Heathston Tower, this is Helimed hotel one-niner,' she identified herself. 'We have four on board and we're ready for lift. We're heading about thirty miles north to Farm Mere, following the line of main A road, over.'

And it was strange how, if these were to be her last two weeks for shouts with this crew, she already felt as though she was going to miss it.

'I think the best bet is going to be to RSI him,' Linc decided, less than twenty minutes later as he and his team finished their assessment of the casualty.

It had turned out to be a twenty-five-year-old male who had been heading down the main road when the bus driver, blinded by the sun at the rider's back, had pulled out in front of him.

The young man's body seemed to have borne the brunt of impact, with a broken rib and an open fracture to his lower limb, but it was the potential head injury that was concerning Linc the most.

'Gary was heading to his girlfriend's to propose,' the young man's mother sobbed, having arrived on scene a few minutes earlier, along with the land ambulance crew. 'He said when you know, you know, right?'

'Of course.' Linc nodded empathetically, not prepared for the image of Piper that flashed, unbidden, in his brain.

He thrust it aside.

'So, we've carried out a physical examination, and, along with Gary's agitation and lack of awareness, we're concerned he may have a brain bleed,' Linc informed her, as simply as he could. 'We want to put him into an induced coma to help protect his brain until we can get him to hospital, okay?'

He didn't add that the decision to RSI the woman's son hadn't been taken lightly. His crew knew that timings would be critical, first administering a strong induction agent to sedate him, and swiftly following it up with a rapid-acting paralytic agent in order to both induce unconsciousness and allow them to intubate.

'What do you think he weighs?' Linc asked Tom. 'About eighty kilos?'

'Yeah, I'd say eighty, maybe eighty-five,' Tom agreed as they considered the levels of drugs they needed to administer.

'Okay, Probie, let's run through the checklist,' Linc instructed. 'Then, Tom, you sedate, and we'll bag him for a minute to let that take effect, before administering the next.'

The team worked systematically, running through the list, and taking advantage of the road ambulance crew who were now also on the ground.

Ten minutes later the team were loading the patient into the heli, with Tom calling it in to the hospital before they set off on the flight. They'd dealt with the lad's other injuries as quickly as they could, but the main focus was still on the brain bleed and trying to stop Gary's brain from swelling.

For the duration of the flight, Linc knew he was going to have to focus primarily on keeping his patient's oxygen and carbon dioxide levels stable.

And still, the mother's comment was floating around Linc's head. *When you know, you know, right?*

Linc wondered if that was true.

Then he wondered why he cared if it was or wasn't.

He was still wondering about it several hours later as his own motorbike hugged the lanes, taking him home after the shift. And most of the evening, as he paced his unexpectedly quiet penthouse. Which felt ridiculously quiet and empty, without Piper's soft voice, or her laugh, which reminded him of a hundred twinkling Christmas lights.

Before Linc realised what he was doing, he picked up his phone and flicked the screen to her number, his thumb hovering over the call button before reason got control of him.

What was he even doing? Had he really been about to call her to find out where she was and if she was okay? Like the kind of boyfriend he definitely wasn't, had *never* been. What had got into him?

It had to be the unexpected news that Albert was on the mend and would be returning sooner, rather than later. News that should delight him. In one way, it did. He was unquestionably relieved for his old buddy that the accident had turned out to be less serious than first imagined, and pleased for Albert that he would be ready to return to the field so relatively quickly.

But at the same time, his thoughts had leapt straight to Piper, and something in his ribcage kicked hard at the idea of her leaving. At never seeing her again. It didn't seem to matter how many times he told himself that she was simply an old friend, or that her leaving his life again had been inevitable.

Even welcome.

It didn't feel very welcome now, knowing that once she returned to barracks, it could be another five years—another fifteen—before he saw her again.

Most likely, it would be a lifetime. And he ought to be

fine with that. So why wasn't he? Why did his body feel as though it were going to implode with the things he was keeping inside?

Piper had been the only person outside his siblings who he'd ever told so much about himself. And even then, it was all he could do not to share the darkest, most damaging secrets of all.

If he wasn't careful, this pent-up sensation was going to swallow him whole. He needed to expend it in some way— he didn't care how.

Stalking down the hallway to his home gym, and hauling off his T-shirt as he went, Linc flicked on the music, letting the low reverb of the bass fill his head. Maybe it could drown out any unwanted voices, needling otherwise.

He had no idea how long he stayed. At least long enough until his hand ached despite the gloves, the sweat was running rivers down his back, and his lungs burned with the effort of breathing.

He was nearing the end of the boxing session when Piper walked in unexpectedly, and, though there was nothing overtly sexual in her attire, his gaze went almost of its own volition to admire the way her jeans clung so lovingly to her backside. He promptly felt like a jerk as she launched into conversation without preamble.

With a low growl of frustration, he turned his attention fully back to the leather bag that had already been bearing the brunt of his confusion—and imagined himself. As though he thought he could wallop some sense into his own head.

'I didn't realise you were home already.' Piper faltered. 'I've been waiting for you in the living room ever since I got back.'

Jab.

'I came straight here.'

Jab, hook.

'I wanted to talk about Albert's return,' she began, before adding hastily, 'Which is great news, of course.'

Abandoning the punchbag, Linc moved quickly to the speed ball. Anything to distract his head and his heart. The rhythm was almost hypnotic, the familiar *thwack-thunk* quickly gathering pace and helping to keep some distance between him and Piper.

His personal best had long been about three hundred and five hits in a minute, but right now he was fairly sure he could easily smash that.

It wasn't something he thought he ought to feel proud about.

'Linc, please,' she blurted out abruptly. 'Stop. Just talk to me.'

The worst of it was that he simply obeyed. Catching the ball with one hand, he turned slowly to face her.

'What do you want to hear, Legs?' he ground out. 'That's it's okay to be upset about your job without anyone accusing you of not being happy Albert's recovering well?'

And he hated himself for the guilt that skittered over her face.

'Of course I'm happy for Albert.'

'As am I.'

When you know, you know, right?

He shook his head free of the echoes.

'I...have a proposal for you,' Piper bit out, on an awkward breath.

And Linc told himself there was no reason that his body should react to that, at all.

'I'm listening,' he told her solemnly instead.

'You remember that I told you I was going for a role at the air ambulance over the border in the next county?'

'West Nessleton Helimed,' he agreed. 'I remember.'

'I understand they already have their go-to list for pilots but what if I agreed to play the part of your date, in exchange for you putting in a good word up there for me? Just to get me an interview, nothing more.'

'You're negotiating with me?' Linc asked, and it was on the tip of his tongue to tell her that he'd already mentioned her name when the regional coordinator had called him a couple of weekends earlier—but something stopped him.

He suspected he knew exactly what that *something* was.

'Yes.' She bobbed her head. 'You need someone for your sister's wedding, and I need someone to give me a recommendation.'

He ought to say *no*. He ought to walk away. But he found that he couldn't. Faking a date might have seemed like a bad idea when his sister had suggested it but now that Piper was offering to be that date, he found he was suddenly considering it. As insane as it was.

'It isn't a game, Piper,' he growled. 'We'd be staging a relationship, a new side of me.'

'Which you told me last night would buy your brother enough time to convince the wavering board members that the direction he wanted to take the company in is the right one.'

'It would,' Linc confirmed. 'He has several lucrative contracts lined up—they're with the solicitors now but Raf won't rush them. He wants to dot the proverbial "i"s and cross the "t"s. He's thorough—it's what makes him so good at what he does.'

'But the board votes before that, yes?' she pressed. 'So you give the board something to think about and that buys him enough time.'

'In a nutshell,' Linc agreed. 'But using you to convince them I'm ready to change my life? Do I need to remind you of what happened between us the other night?'

Piper twisted her hands in front of her body.

'That was the other night. We were caught off guard and we let things get away from us,' she muttered. And he wondered which of them she was trying to convince more. 'But we've dealt with that now. It's no longer an issue.'

'Isn't it?' he muttered, fighting the pressing urge to take a step forward and reach out his hand to roll a lock of her hair between his fingers.

And when that delicious heat bloomed across her silken skin, he actually *ached* to press his mouth to it.

'It isn't. Like you said, this is a negotiation, nothing more. We both have something the other needs and if we handle it right, then we can both win. West Nessleton is near my family, I couldn't land a better role. But that job opportunity won't be out there for me for ever. So please think about it, Linc. Just don't think too long.'

And then she disappeared through the door and down the hall to her suite. But only because she didn't trust herself with him if she'd stayed in the gym.

He knew, because he didn't trust himself with her either. Not when he suspected that he only had to pull her to him and begin kissing her again for them both to go up in flames.

And *that*, he told himself firmly, would not be a good idea for anyone.

CHAPTER TEN

WHEN HE'D SAID the family home, Piper realised a few days later as they were flown over the countryside in the family's private helicopter, what he'd really meant was *ancestral* home.

With hindsight, she shouldn't have expected anything less than the vast, sprawling country pile with land surrounding it in all directions.

'This is where you grew up?' Piper couldn't help but gape as she shifted in one of the oversized, butter-soft seats. 'How far does it extend?'

Without warning, Linc leaned closer to her, to place his eyeline approximately around hers. The effect on Piper was instantaneous, making her hot and jittery. And her skin seemed to pull so tight, almost as if it were suddenly too small for her own body.

'See that treeline over there, by the stone church?'

She wasn't sure how long it took her to remember to breathe.

'I...yes.'

'To the shoreline down there?' He swept his arm across the other way, where Piper could see the sea in the near distance.

'Right.' She swallowed. Hard.

'And then from that winding country lane that bisects the county up there, down to the golf course over there.'

'I guess it's some people's dream to live next to a golf course,' she managed, her voice sounding thicker than usual.

'In the interests of full disclosure, the golf course belongs to us. Stoneywell Golf Course—it hosts some of the top annual gold tournaments.'

'Of course,' she choked out, but that could hardly be helped.

Just another thing to add to the fact that the area he'd indicated had to be hundreds upon hundreds of hectares. The entire housing estate where she'd grown up could have fitted into his mere back garden, several times over. Linc came from an entirely different world from the one she'd come from, and that gap between the two of them couldn't have been more striking.

Or humiliating.

For the first time, something slid down her back. Perhaps it was apprehension, more likely it was resignation. Just another place she didn't really fit in—no matter how much she might try to tell herself otherwise. Pretending to be Linc's fiancé in exchange for his good word was one thing. But what if someone got curious about her? Or worse, recognised her?

'It is,' Linc's voice came back over the headset as he dipped his head in acknowledgement. It left her scrambling to remember what her question had even been.

And still, she couldn't seem to stop her tongue from moving.

'Say again?'

'You asked if this was where I grew up,' he reminded her. 'And it is. It's where Raf and I climbed trees and built forest dens. It's where we learned to shoot clay pigeons, and fish, and ride.'

'You ride?'

Of course he would do, coming from a place like this, she realised belatedly.

'Not as much as I'd like to, any more. Though I used to love it. Raf and I often took our horses down to the beach and then galloped on the sand. You've never ridden?'

'Never.' She shook her head.

'Not even on holiday?'

'Not even donkey rides on the beach.' Her smile was rueful.

A part of her had dreamed of it, as a kid. But when she was growing up, her family had never had that kind of money. Not even before all the financial worries.

'I'll teach you. It's easy enough.'

She seriously doubted that, though she didn't say as much. What was Linc doing anyway, suggesting things like that? They both knew she was only here for the wedding rehearsal dinner, definitely not long enough for her to do anything like learning to ride a horse.

For the next few moments, she sat in silence, drinking it all in as the pilot brought their luxury heli down onto the estate's bespoke helipad. Just like another parking bay, to a place like this.

What she wasn't particularly expecting was the welcoming party that appeared to be waiting for them near what had to be an imposing eight-foot-high wooden front door. Linc's sister, of course, along with who was likely her fiancé. And Raf—as tall, dark, and brooding as before. Today the fraternal resemblance seemed all the more striking.

Then, before she knew what was happening, the heli was down, the engine off and the blades stopped, and Linc was out of the aircraft and reaching back to help her down.

Under other circumstances, she felt she would have brushed away his unnecessarily chivalrous offer, but now it was all Piper could do to release his hand once her feet were firmly on land.

The welcoming party swept forward, and she noted that Sara's fiancé appeared to have slipped away as they'd landed.

'Lincoln.' Sara smiled, hugging him quickly before turning to her. 'And... Piper. It's nice to meet you again.'

The steely smile was still there...just decidedly more polished. Presumably under threat from either Linc, or Raf. Possibly both. Even so, Piper felt her mind go blank and just as she was about to wish she'd never agreed to do this she felt Linc's warm hand brush the small of her back, silently lending her strength.

She discreetly drew in as steadying a breath as she could and turned to Linc's sister.

'Lady Sara,' she managed politely, before turning to Linc's brother. 'Lord Ranulph.'

'Sara and Raf will be fine,' Linc stopped her tightly. 'Isn't that right, Sara?'

'As you're our brother's guest, we don't stand on formality,' Raf's rich, deep, familiar-sounding voice agreed smoothly. 'It's very good to meet you again, Piper. We're grateful to you for persuading my brother here to finally return home.'

Raf held out his hand to shake hers, and the severe expression on his face gave way to that surprisingly warm, equally familiar smile. And once again Piper was struck by the connection between the two brothers. That kind of easiness; a bond. A trust.

It made Piper want to trust Raf, too.

'Isn't that so, Sara?'

'Raf...' This time the interjection earned her a withering look from her older brother.

'Would you care to address Linc's guest as Captain Green for the duration of her stay?' the older brother asked quietly. Firmly.

'She isn't serving any more,' Linc's sister objected for a moment, before appearing to bite her tongue. 'Fine.' She flashed a tight smile, though it was clear she didn't like it.

'Piper acting as my fiancée was your idea, after all.' Linc finally deigned to speak but made no attempt to conceal the amusement in his tone.

'You having a date was my idea,' his sister snapped. 'This engagement twist was all your idea. Be it on your heads when people ask you all about your relationship and you can't answer.'

'And therein lies the fun.'

Sara cast him a withering glower.

'That's always been your problem, Lincoln, you treat everything like a game.'

Linc slung his bag over his shoulder, his hand returning to the small of Piper's back. 'Shall we find our rooms?'

Strong, comforting, and more than a little welcome.

'Linc, if you have a moment.' His brother moved to walk beside them, his hands clasped behind his back, back to serious mode again. 'There have been a couple of recent developments with the board.'

'You want to talk about them now?' Linc asked, his deep voice matching the calm gravity of his brother's.

'Not this moment, but as soon as you get chance.'

'You ought to know about them,' Sara noted pointedly. 'The sooner the better. I can show your guest to the suite.'

'I think not,' he declined, moving to walk with her.

And she could accept it gratefully or do what she was supposed to be here to do.

'I'll be fine,' Piper told him quickly, before she could bottle out.

'I thought we could take a walk together.' He leaned in so that only she could hear, the soft sweep of his breath at her neck making her shiver with delight before she could stop herself. 'Perhaps escape this place.'

'I'd like that,' she murmured back. 'As soon as you're finished with Raf and Sara.'

'Piper...'

'Truly,' she managed firmly.

Linc eyed her wordlessly, then he looked at his brother. Finally he dipped his head and fell in beside his brother, the two of them walking with their heads bowed together. And Piper couldn't help but notice Sara staring wistfully after them as they went. The younger sister who might have spent her whole life racing to catch up with her two, bigger brothers.

Piper couldn't explain why she had to fight back the wealth of emotions rioting through her at that moment. Perhaps because it made her think of her own family—her own sister—and the ugliness that had marred their relationship ever since before their father had died.

Seeing Linc's interplay with his family—both the other night, and now—had been unexpected...and unsettling. In an instant, she'd been able to imagine exactly what the trio must have been like as kids. A tight little band of three, growing up in a place like Oakenfeld Hall.

It had her revisiting all her military memories of Linc, seeing them in a new light. Raf the older one, always trying to be responsible and keep the peace. Sara was the baby of the group, the daughter torn between living up to her title as a lady, and wanting to tomboy it around with big brothers who she clearly idolised.

As for Linc, he was the middle kid. The second brother

who would neither be the heir to the dukedom, nor the much-vaunted daughter. No wonder he'd carved out his own place in the world by joining the army, and becoming a doctor.

Could it be that his enigmatic personality was less about keeping others out, and more about protecting himself? Piper stared at Linc for a moment, her mind reeling.

'Can I ask you something?'

Piper swivelled around in surprise as Sara fell in beside her. And even though it was phrased as a question, there was a peremptory tone to Sara's voice that brooked little argument. The customs of being a lady who commanded attention, Piper presumed.

Still, she forced another smile, for Linc's sake.

'Of course. I'll try to answer if I can.'

'Why are you doing this?'

She didn't need to elaborate for Piper to know what she meant. For a moment, she wondered whether she should stick with the old army buddies connection, but there was something too practical about Sara for that to satisfy her. In the end, Piper plumped for the truth.

Or a part-truth, at least.

'I'm leaving the Army Air Corps. We agreed that if I attend this weekend's rehearsal dinner and next week's wedding as his fiancée, then he'll recommend me as pilot for one of the other air ambulance bases.'

'One of the other air ambulance bases?'

'In the next county.'

Sara cast her an assessing glance.

'Why not the one where you both are now?'

'Heathston already has Albert.' No need to tell Sara that he was retiring. 'Besides, my mother and brother live a county over. The other base will let me be nearer to them.'

'You're moving to be closer to your family?' Sara eyed her even more intently. 'How old is your brother?'

'He's twelve,' Piper couldn't help but smile. 'Sometimes twelve going on forty, other times twelve going on about seven.'

'So family is important to you?' Linc's sister didn't even crack a smile, but there was an earnest note to her voice that hadn't been there before.

'It is,' Piper answered after a moment. 'Even when I was away, I used to speak to them as often as I could. They're all I have.'

'Just like Raf and Linc are all I have now. And my future husband, of course.'

'Of course.' Piper kept her voice light.

'It's why I want Linc to come home. We need him here. He belongs back here.'

'He doesn't belong in a clinic.' The words tumbled softly from Piper's lips before she could stop herself. Before her brain could engage. 'He's an army doctor, or an air ambulance doctor, getting out there to the patient and saving lives in the field. I don't think Linc would ever be a good wait-for-them-to-come-to-him kind of doctor.'

Instantly, she realised her mistake. She braced herself, waiting for some cold dismissal from Linc's fierce sister. Sara might have engaged in this conversation with her, but, for Linc's sake, she should have thought twice about saying something that would agitate the bride-to-be.

'That's pretty much what Linc said the other night.' The sad admission shocked Piper.

And even though she knew she shouldn't press her luck, she heard herself speaking again.

'For what it's worth, it's always been evident that Linc loves you and your brother very much. I think a part of him would even want to return home. I just think...there's a barrier there, and I don't know why but he can't seem to overcome it.'

Slamming her mouth shut, Piper braced again. There was no question this time that Sara would think she had overstepped her boundaries.

Yet, once again, Linc's sister shocked her.

'Do you…?' She tailed off, shaking her head. And then, 'Do you think he wants to, though? Overcome that barrier, I mean?'

'I don't know,' Piper told her truthfully. 'I don't know the full story, clearly—Linc has never shared that. But… I think so.'

Sara nodded. And then, as if she hadn't shocked Piper enough already, she drew in a deep breath.

'I think, perhaps, I have misjudged you,' she managed, awkwardly. As if she wasn't accustomed to having to make such admissions. 'Perhaps you're not such a poor decision by my brother, after all. We shall see.'

Then, as though putting an end to the exchange, Sara lifted her head and picked up the pace as they hurried to the great staircase. All Piper could do was follow.

'Is this walk so that I can escape this place?' Piper asked wryly as she followed him through a door off the long, elegant hallway. 'Or so that you can?'

'Perhaps a little of both,' he admitted grudgingly, leading her down a tight, winding staircase, and through a low door. 'I have a confession to make, Piper. You don't need to be here.'

'I don't?'

'I talked to Regional about you weeks ago—the moment I heard about the pilot opening at West Nessleton. So you don't need to be here.'

'I don't understand.' Her brow furrowed in confusion. 'You don't *want* me here?'

'I'm saying you don't *have* to be. I know how overbearing Sara can be, not to mention the people who'll be watching us this weekend, scrutinising us, and looking for any weakness.'

'Did your brother say something?' she asked, without thinking.

Still, she wasn't prepared for Linc to look so sheepish.

'He may have reminded me what I was about to subject you to between extended family and the board. I wanted to give you one last chance to back out.'

And Piper thought it was that moment that made her all the more determined to stay and help him out. Smiling to herself, she glanced around at the scenery, then pulled up short.

'Wait, are these the kitchen gardens? They're beautiful.'

She stopped to take a better look around, pleased when Linc moved to stand next to her.

'They were designed by my great-great-great-grandmother in eighteen seventy, and re-imagined by my father and grandfather before Raf was even born. Over there, you can see fig trees and apple trees, and over that way are grapevines.'

She followed his hand, taking in the rich display.

'And if you look this way—' he placed his hands on her shoulders to turn her as she pretended not to notice the shiver of pleasure that danced along her spine '—you can find prickly cucumbers and even liquorice.'

'Is this where you spent time with your father?'

He turned back sharply.

'What made you ask that?'

Piper shrugged. The question had been out before she'd even realised she'd intended to ask it.

'I don't know, you just love cooking and you're so passionate about the ingredients you use…' She tailed off.

But just as she thought Linc was going to ignore her and start walking again, he surprised her.

'Yeah, I guess it is where my father and I bonded most. Here, pottering around the gardens in the precious little time he got to spend here, or riding across the fields.'

'But here was more special?' she guessed. 'Because riding was with your siblings, and the garden was just you and him?'

Another pause.

'The garden was just for the two of us,' Linc agreed at length. 'And a couple of gardeners, of course. Now it's just the gardeners, and we run culinary courses from the estate; the guests get to choose their ingredients from everything that we grow.'

They stood, quietly watching, for a few more moments before Linc seemed to take in a deep breath, and strode forward.

'Come on, there's plenty more to show you.'

For the next couple of hours, Piper let Linc take her around his childhood home, showing her everywhere from the formal gardens where the public were allowed to admire the house, to the private grove of trees where he and his siblings first learned to climb.

She walked the light trail with him, imagining how pretty the stone bridge must look at night, strewn with colourful lights that twinkled and shimmered in the reflection of the water beneath.

And then, suddenly, they were down by the sea; on the private stretch of beach that belonged to the family.

'I don't understand why Sara doesn't just get married in some private ceremony here on the beach, instead of some spectacle with a couple of hundred guests we barely even know, let alone like.'

Piper blinked, and she despaired of herself for the butterflies that were now fluttering madly—unfittingly—around her stomach.

Grimly, she attempted to quash them.

'Is that why you're so against your brother-in-law? Because he's agreeing to what you'd call a *spectacle* of a wedding?'

'I'd rather he asked her to scale everything back. I think that might take some of this unnecessary pressure off her. Duke's daughter or not, there's no need for all the fanfare. I can't help wondering if he's encouraging Sara because of how good it could make *him* look.'

'Have you asked your sister?'

Linc didn't answer immediately, instead choosing to glower out to sea—and at the bright sunlight as it glanced off the cold waves.

Piper wrinkled her nose and tried again.

'Sara doesn't seem the type to let herself get pushed into something she doesn't want.'

'You'd be surprised,' Linc replied darkly. 'She has always demanded more of herself than anyone else ever did. I suspect she might think a lavish wedding is her way of supporting Raf.'

'Why?'

'I don't know. As a reminder of how much weight the Stoneywell name holds?'

It was so far removed from Piper's own reality that she was almost frightened to answer and show herself up.

'The point is,' he continued, when she didn't answer, 'that it isn't just about me not seeing why she needs all this fuss or fanfare. It's more that I don't even understand why she's getting married at all.'

'Perhaps because she loves her fiancé?'

Piper tried to keep her voice upbeat but there was no mistaking the strain in her voice. After the way her father had treated her mother, she wasn't sure she believed in love either.

Wasn't it just a way to get away with treating another person as if they were dirt?

'You don't believe in real love any more than I do, Legs.' Linc snorted humourlessly, as if reading her mind. 'You act happy for couples, but I know how much we both wonder what the hell they're thinking of, tying themselves to another person for life.'

'I don't think that,' Piper objected. Weakly.

He shook his head.

'You might fool others, but you forget how long we've known each other. I've seen your expression when buddies gave up their military careers for their new spouse, the disbelief. Something you couldn't quite understand because you never would have done that. Neither would I. You and I are the same.'

'I gave up flying army helicopters for the love of my family,' she pointed out, but the nose wrinkle gave her away.

'Did you?' he challenged. 'Or was your reason more practical? Did you actually have much of a choice?'

She didn't answer him. She didn't need to.

'The same as I did,' he carried on after a moment. 'The only reason I gave up my army medical career was because of that final ambush. Because I have responsibilities within this family, and because my father's ill health meant that Raf was fighting avaricious board members. At that time, he couldn't have held them off whilst Sara and I were living the lives we were living.

'You were an army doctor.' Piper frowned. 'What's so damaging about that?'

'Nothing, in itself.'

But the dark look that stole across his taut expression told a different story. Furious yet lost, all at the same time. The two emotions seemed to war across his features, then stole inside her ribcage like a fist, and squeezed. And then squeezed some more.

'Linc?' she prompted, unable to help herself.

'It's a story you don't want to hear, Piper.'

She didn't understand what made her close the gap between them. Or what made her reach up and place her palms to his chest. But suddenly, there she was. More than that, he wasn't pulling away.

'Try me,' she whispered. 'Why do you seem to be carrying such guilt around with you, Linc? What is it that you feel you owe your siblings?'

And she wasn't sure how long they stood there—perhaps whole lifetimes—and Piper pulled her lips into a tight, nervous line as she tried to will him not to shut her out, the way he always seemed to shut everyone out.

But even as she knew that was exactly what he was doing, preparing to push her away, a movement across the landscape caught her attention. A figure swaying oddly.

She watched in horror as the man suddenly buckled, then collapsed to the floor.

'Linc…' she cried instinctively. 'Over there.'

CHAPTER ELEVEN

VAULTING THE WALL, not needing to look to know that Piper would be following, Linc raced across the fairway and to the men.

He was almost grateful for the distraction. There was no way he had been prepared to answer Piper's questions.

Even as he ran he noted the two figures hunched over a third. It certainly looked as if they were attempting chest compressions but the rhythm was wrong. Too slow. And the closer he got, the more he could see it looked like two guys in their twenties over a likely fifty-something bloke.

'Is he okay? Can I help?'

The two men cranked their heads to him in evident relief.

'It's our dad. We think he's had a heart attack,' one of them—the older-looking one who was attempting chest compressions—managed in a strangled voice.

'Can you do that CPR thing?' The other looked up at them helplessly.

'I can. I'm a doctor,' Linc assured them as he dropped beside the collapsed man and checked for breathing or a pulse. The man had neither. 'Can you tell me what happened?'

The two sons eyed him, somewhat stunned, before the older one spoke again.

'He said he was feeling a little bit faint, and then he just…collapsed.'

'Any history of illness?' Linc pressed.

'No.' The two men looked at each other before shaking their heads. 'Nothing.'

'Have you called emergency services?'

Again the two men looked blankly at each other.

'We were more concerned with doing CPR. I mean, that was the right thing to do, wasn't it?'

'Exactly right,' Linc assured them. 'You did well, and now we're here to help. Piper, can you—?'

'Already on it,' she confirmed as her mobile connected to the emergency services, stepping to one side to deal with them whilst Linc continued the chest compressions.

They both knew the odds on a person surviving a heart attack outside a hospital were low—around ten per cent, according to heart charity figures. But it didn't mean he wasn't about to do his damnedest to make this the *one*. It was what he was programmed to do.

'Right, I'll do the compressions.' He looked at the calmer of the two brothers, then indicated to the ground on the other side of their father. 'You can kneel here and ensure his airway remains clear.'

'The clubhouse has a defib,' the other brother remembered suddenly. 'Should I call them?'

Linc nodded.

'Yes, call them. Tell them that your father is in cardiac arrest, and to bring any other kit they have.'

'I'll help.' Piper stepped back to the group. 'The land ambulance is on its way.'

'Acknowledged.'

With one ear to the boys, and the rest of his focus on the man on the ground in front of him, Linc realised it was good to realise that one person he wasn't worried about was

Piper. If anything, her presence could only make the entire scenario that much easier.

It was more than he could say for any other date he might have chosen to bring to this damned wedding.

For the next few minutes Linc worked with one of the sons to keep the blood and oxygen flowing around their father's body, surprised when Piper returned so quickly with the medical kit.

'They were already on their way,' Piper told him quickly. 'Another player had seen him collapse and alerted the club-house.'

'Right, can you take over chest compressions whilst I set it out?'

She hurried around to drop by his side, already in place to minimise time off the chest, as Linc made way for her, counting out her rhythm before he'd even got to his feet.

Quickly, he took a pair of scissors from the kit and cut the man's clothing away to give them better access.

'Okay, machine is charging.' He announced his warning a minute or so later, having set everything up. 'And stand clear.'

As the machine gave its warning sounds, Piper lifted her hands off the man's chest, moving backwards.

'Rhythm check,' Linc announced, bending down to check for a pulse. There was nothing.

'No.' Piper shook her head, also checking the femoral, as the defib machine reported its own automatic results.

'No output PEA,' Linc confirmed. 'Continue CPR.'

Wordlessly, Piper resumed compressions. Another couple of minutes and they could try shocking the patient again. The bleeping and automatic instruction from the defib machine rolled around them, but it was Linc's presence that was giving her the most confidence.

'Machine charging,' he warned again, a few moments later as the defib bleeped. 'Off the chest, and clear.'

Another shock. Another check.

'Rhythm check?' He had nothing.

Piper began to shake her head, then hesitated.

'I think they can feel a beat.'

Linc moved to her position and made a check of his own. It was faint, but there was something there.

'Let's continue CPR,' he said. 'Do you want a break?'

'Okay for now,' she confirmed, bracing her arms and beginning another strong set, leaving him free to carry out his other checks.

By the time the land ambulance turned up about five minutes later, the man's heart was beating again.

'He's making some respiratory effort,' Linc told them as he handed over. 'You'll want to intubate to minimise damage to the brain, as well as give him some medication to help blow off the carbon dioxide build-up.'

With both teams working together, it wasn't too long before the man was on a scoop and in the ambulance, his chances looking far more promising than they had done less than half an hour earlier.

And as they watched the ambulance roll off the fairway and back to the main road, Linc couldn't help thinking how easy everything was with Piper around. Not just the way she had slotted in to help, even though she was usually the pilot, not the paramedic, but the way she'd slotted in here with his family. Into his life.

It was the same way she'd been out on tour all those years ago. That same quiet confidence that had attracted him to her back then.

But that still didn't explain why he'd almost decided to open himself up to her the way he had done, down on the beach earlier. Why he was ready to reveal secrets to her that he had never even shared with his sister. Or fully explored with Raf.

What was it about Piper Green that had him turning inside out? Worse, he wasn't even sure that he minded.

Piper watched the land ambulance roll carefully off the fairway, hoping that everything they'd just done would be enough to save their impromptu patient's life.

But her mind was already shifting back to the man beside her. The man who, if she wasn't very much mistaken, had been about to shut her down the way she was beginning to realise he always did. Only now, he was looking at her with a different expression on his face. One that was familiar, and unfamiliar, all at the same time.

'You asked me what is it that I feel I owe my siblings,' he repeated without warning, and when his gaze slid to hers she refused to look away.

'I did,' she agreed softly. 'Anyone who watches the three of you together can see the love and respect you all share, so why have you built this wall between them and you? Do you begrudge your sister's wedding so much?'

It wasn't even a guess. It was more words that flitted through her head and out of her mouth, trying to find some button, some trigger, that might help him to talk to her.

'I don't begrudge my sister anything,' he bit out defensively.

It wasn't the button she'd been looking for, but it was something. The tiniest wedge, a fraction of a millimetre in an almost non-existent gap. All she had to do was nudge it in that little bit further.

'Then what is it, Linc? Because there's something going on here, and if I'm going to play this part for you all this weekend, then I ought to understand it, at least.'

'There is no *ought* about it,' Linc clipped out. 'But since you're suddenly so damned interested, I'll tell you. My parents never had what you might call a good marriage—no great shock there, plenty of couples don't—but as the Duke and Duchess of Stoneywell, divorce was never on the cards. Lady Oakes, the Duchess of Stoneywell, you surely know the name, Piper?'

Even as she shook her head to deny it, something shifted in the recesses of her brain. An old story she hadn't heard since she was a kid.

'The Duchess of Stoneywell... Lady Oakes.' Piper's brow furrowed deeply. 'I think I know those names.'

'I imagine you do.' It was all he could do to keep his mouth from twisting up in disgust. 'She was nothing if not attention-hungry, our mother. If she wasn't centre of attention then she wasn't happy, and if she wasn't happy then no one else could be, either.'

Piper wanted to answer. She wanted to say something to help, but nothing would. So she stayed silent, and simply listened.

'No matter that our father was trying to be the duke and run a demanding estate, and keep a business afloat in a harsh economic climate so that hundreds of employees didn't lose their jobs—my mother wanted more of his time. His attention. Not because she loved him, you understand, but because she was a narcissist and couldn't stand the idea that not everything revolved around her.

'And when she didn't get the duke's attention—she looked elsewhere for her fun. Worse, she made sure everyone knew how overlooked and unappreciated she was, and how her husband didn't make time for her. She told anyone who would listen how unkind he was to her. Emotional cruelty, I believe she told one paper.'

So that was why Linc had never courted attention, Piper realised suddenly. It was why he didn't want publicity, and had never told anyone in the army, or in the air ambulance, who he really was. It was beginning to make sense now. And crazily—dangerously—it made Piper feel special that she was the one he was confiding in.

'My father was always blinded by my mother. She was his downfall from the start. She wanted money, and to live the life of a duchess, but she didn't want any of the responsibility. She hated my father for being so upright, and moral, and boring.'

'I don't understand.'

'My mother brought scandal after scandal to the family—in fact, she was a scandal all to herself. The revelation that I was a bastard son was just her final coup de grâce. Raf and I only realised recently how much our father protected our family from her indiscretions—even up until her death. The papers had run stories about her from time to time, over the years—from deeply unflattering stories, to downright disgusting rumours. I'm surprised you didn't read any of them. She certainly did her best to get them into every media outlet going if it increased her exposure—in more ways than one.'

Piper squinted, fervently trying to recollect vague memories. She'd never really been one for gossip columns, or glossy mag tell-alls. Now that Linc had put it into her head, she did think she recalled a few less than pleasant things.

'That was her?'

'That was her.' Linc dipped his head curtly. 'You understand now why I never wanted to bring anyone back here. I didn't want to subject them to this, but also, I didn't want the gossip or the attention. Raf can do well without my name being associated with his.'

She shook her head vehemently.

'You didn't give them anything. Your father knew the truth and he didn't care.'

'Our mother did our best to drag our family through the mud, whilst our father was fierce about protecting the three of us from all of it.'

'Your father sounds like a decent, upstanding gentleman.'

'He was,' Linc managed fiercely. 'He stood up for what he believed in, and what he thought was right, and damn the rest of it. I'll never match him. Not like Raf does. I'm my mother's son, but I'm not his son.'

The roaring started in her brain in an instant, at the mention of scandal. As though she feared her own life might seep into his. She thrust it aside. That wasn't going to happen. Here she was telling Linc not to let his past and his mother's sins ruin his relationship with his siblings, and she was about to let her own past, and her father's sins, ruin this moment with Linc.

It was too much for either of them to have to bear.

'These aren't your sins to bear, Linc,' Piper said softly, realising that her words were as much for herself as for him. 'Your father never thought they were, and your siblings certainly don't. Raf and Sara are asking for your help because it's their excuse to get you back home. They aren't holding you accountable, you must see that.'

'They don't need to hold me accountable, Legs. I hold myself accountable.'

'Is that why you've built this invisible wall between them and you? Is that why you keep them at arm's length? Why you joined the army? The only reason your sister keeps pushing you towards the Stoneywell Medical Centre is because it's the only thing she can think of to bring you back home.'

'It isn't for me,' Linc growled, but it wasn't as fierce as before.

She was getting through to him, and for some reason that made her feel good. More than good.

'And she knows that, but she tries anyway because she wants her brother back in her life. They both do.'

'Our lives aren't compatible.' Linc refused to agree, as Piper splayed her hand over his ribcage as though that could help her to reach him faster.

'Only if you don't want them to be. There are a hundred things you could do back here, with your medical skill, and as Lord Lincoln, if you wanted to. Like setting up a Stoneywell air ambulance for a start—look at what might have happened today if you and I hadn't been passing that golf course right at that moment.'

'You can pretend scandal goes away all you want to, Piper. But take it from someone who knows, the truth is that it never does. It follows a person, and rears its head at the worst times. No one can escape it. No one ever will.

And later, much later, when the roar had died down in her brain and her heart had stopped hammering around her ribcage, Piper would think it was that precise moment—those precise words—that had felled her at the knees.

Because he'd brought her to the table as a way to help douse any vicious rumours. But if anyone decided to look into her, and expose her own set of sordid truths, then she could do Linc and his family far, far more harm than good.

Her stomach heaved, and lurched. She'd spent so many years trying to bury this truth, from herself as much as anyone else. But now, there was nothing else for it; she needed to tell him the truth. Not now. Not when the rehearsal dinner was this evening.

But after that, perhaps when they left Oakenfeld Hall and went back to his penthouse. Certainly before the wedding next week.

Before someone else lit the match and it all went up in flames.

Taking both of them with it.

CHAPTER TWELVE

THE WOMAN WAS a damned enchantress.

Linc watched Piper shimmer and charm her way around the room—just as he'd known that she would. Just as she'd always been able to handle herself around brigadiers and generals, and charm their respective spouses.

Just as she'd always charmed him.

It ought to concern him just how easily he felt she slotted into the role as his fiancée—*pretend* fiancée—but he found he was more spellbound than disquieted. And didn't that say something in itself?

Even Raf had remarked how happy he looked, earlier that evening when his brother had walked in to find him retrieving his grandmother's jewels from the study safe to lend to Piper. And when he'd pre-empted Raf's objection to lending out their grandmother's ruby necklace, reminding his brother—and possibly himself—that it was all just a ploy, he thought it was telling that Raf's only response had been, 'At least one of us should be happy.'

As though it were real.

It didn't help that Piper's words were still stalking around his brain. Could she be right about why he'd stayed away all this time—with the army, and now as a Helimed doctor? She made him question whether he had really been helping his family the way he'd once told himself he was doing.

Not that he was about to give up being a doctor. But perhaps moving a little closer to home might not be the worst idea, after all.

And Piper?

Ignoring the question, Linc set down his brandy tumbler onto the bar top, so loudly that the ice cubes rattled, and swung around so that his back was completely to the woman who seemed to occupy more of his thoughts than ever.

It didn't work.

Moments later, Linc found himself striding across the floor and towards her, before he even realised what he intended.

'Dance?' he bit out, less a suggestion and more an order, as he held his hand out.

And he had to fight to pretend not to notice the current of electricity that jolted through him, when she reached out obligingly, and slipped her smaller hand into his.

Without a word, he led her to the floor, before sweeping her into his arms for a simple waltz. And, just like that, the rest of the room—the rest of the world—fell away, and Piper was all he could see. All he could smell—from the pleasant citrus notes of her shampoo to that delicate note of her perfume.

His entire body prickled with awareness—and not just the more obvious, baser parts of his anatomy. Had any woman before ever affected him the way that Piper did? Pretend relationship or not, he was terribly afraid he knew the answer to that.

'Was my role not to mingle whilst you talked to board members and let them think you were ready to return home to the family fold?' she murmured up at him.

Though he noticed even as they danced that she seemed

as incapable of tearing her gaze from him as he was of looking away from her. Linc took that as a positive.

'It was indeed.' He lowered his mouth closer to her ear, telling himself it was so that no one could possibly overhear their conversation. 'I understand we've already given them a great deal to mull over.'

'Oh?'

'I'm told that those who were arguing for my shares to be stripped from me, and who were using this evening as an opportunity to put forward their case, are now beginning to lose their collective voice.'

'That's good news, isn't it?'

Was he only fooling himself to think that the faint quiver in her voice intensified the closer his lips came to her skin?

'It's very good news,' he agreed. 'What's more, Raf tells me that he has already been approached by several board members who had been wavering before, but who are now ready to throw their full weight behind him. And I'm beginning to wonder if returning home might be a good idea, after all.'

She stiffened in his arms, her feet momentarily faltering. But he held her to him and kept them moving gracefully around the dance floor.

'You're thinking about really leaving Heathston? Not to run a medical centre, surely?'

This time, he knew he didn't imagine the shiver that rippled through Piper.

'And what happens when you don't have a fiancée after all? When you don't get married, or have kids, or all those things they believe a true Oakes lord should do?'

And the odd thing was that Linc couldn't explain why. He had never, not once, imagined himself getting married and having a family. Now, suddenly, he could. The image was distant, and somewhat hazy, but for the first time in his life, it was actually there. The only thing he could make out clearly was Oakenfeld Hall in the background.

Had Piper been right, that being an army doc had been his way of escaping the life to which he'd never quite reconciled himself? And had she also had a point that the day he would find peace would be the day he accepted that he was part of this family whether the duke was his biological father or not?

'What you said today about it being time this region had a Helimed to service it, that made sense to me.'

Piper blinked at him.

'Well, yes. It would certainly have helped that man today.'

'Perhaps Oakenfeld Hall could sponsor a Helimed team up here. It would be something that would fit with my father's vision for Oakenfeld Industries—giving back to the community.'

'It makes sense,' she agreed, though her unexpectedly taut body was at odds with the sentiment.

'It does. That way I could also attend board meetings. Perhaps it's time I actually supported Raf and Sara and be present at these things.'

What made it so strange was the fact that he actually wanted to. Ten years ago, being back here he'd felt like a cuckoo in the nest. Even five years ago, he hadn't quite...*fitted*. But now, with Piper by his side, it felt somehow...*right*.

Except that Piper wasn't part of the equation. He shouldn't have to keep reminding himself of that fact.

Whatever the hell that was supposed to mean.

'That's great,' she managed, forcing a bright smile that was entirely at odds with the way her body was tensing so strangely in his arms.

Though he told himself he had no intention of saying

anything, Linc heard the next suggestion slipping out of his mouth.

'The place would need a pilot. Should you decide West Nessleton Helimed isn't for you.'

'I can't move anywhere.' Piper laughed, though it sounded hollow to his ears. Or perhaps he was merely imagining it. 'My mother and my brother need me.'

He wanted to ask what it was that Piper herself needed. But he stopped himself.

'Of course.' He nodded curtly.

'If it wasn't for them, then maybe…' Her voice sounded thick. Unfamiliar.

But he could hardly process it for the racket going on in his head.

'You don't need to explain yourself,' he growled.

And he assured himself that the uninvited feeling in his chest—which felt altogether too much like regret—was purely because it would be a shame for his new Helimed operation to lose out on a pilot of Piper's calibre.

'Linc, there's something…' The tortured words caught in her throat as she stared at him miserably. A haunted note that reached inside his chest and squeezed. 'There's something I need to tell you.'

'You don't need to say a thing,' he made himself bite back, telling himself he was grateful for the reality check.

He even thought he might believe it himself.

'I do need to.'

And he couldn't tell whether it was the most honest truth she'd ever told him, or a complete lie. Before he realised what he was doing, Linc lowered his head to Piper's ear.

'You should never feel as though you have to do anything.'

'Right,' she muttered, turning her head.

And as their lips brushed each other's, the contact shot through him, demanding more, and making him greedy.

'I think we can do better than that,' he murmured.

Wordlessly, Piper pressed her body tighter against his, and perhaps it was the way her body seemed to mould itself to his, or maybe it was the incredible soft, sweet groan of pleasure she made as he fitted his lips to hers, but an intense heat seared through Linc.

White-hot and gloriously electric—unlike anything he had ever known before.

Because Piper's unlike any woman you've ever known before.

He beat the voice back, but there was no denying the truth in the words.

Piper was perfection. She tasted of longing, and need, and all manner of sinful things that he'd spent the better part of a decade telling himself he didn't imagine every time he'd looked at this woman. From the swell of her breasts pressing against his chest, to the scrape of her tongue against his.

As if they'd both been waiting for this moment for a lifetime. Even two. Linc forgot that this was all meant to be a show, pretend. He only knew that he didn't want to stop. Didn't think he *could* stop.

He found himself pouring himself into the kiss. Confessing a thousand truths to her that he couldn't say with words—not even in the privacy of his own head.

But they were in that kiss, and he couldn't seem to stem them.

This was the excuse he'd been looking for. The moment to allow them both to cross that invisible line they'd drawn between them in the desert sand, all those years ago. And her presence at this dinner no longer felt pretend, or staged, perhaps it never really had done. It felt right, as though she belonged here, by his side, every bit as much as he did.

The kiss stretched on for ever, glorious and exultant. But when they finally pulled apart, coming up for air and remembering where they were, he knew he wasn't ready to let the evening end with just that.

By the glazed expression in Piper's stunning eyes, and her telltale rapid pulse at her throat—the one that begged him to cover it with his mouth—she felt exactly the same way.

Suddenly the ballroom felt too crowded. Too suffocating. Abruptly, he dropped his arms from around his fake fiancée's luscious body while keeping hold of her hand, then turned her round and ushered them both off the dance floor.

'Where are we going?' she asked breathlessly as they weaved their way through the crowd.

Linc couldn't bring himself to answer. He couldn't bring himself to do anything to break the moment; to give him pause to rethink what he was about to do. What he'd wanted to do with this one woman from the first time he'd ever laid eyes on her, before they'd thrown up obstacles such as *professional behaviour*, and *duty*.

But now none of those obstacles existed any more and finally, *finally*, they could be honest with each other about who they really were. And what they wanted from the other.

Piper allowed Linc to guide her out of the ballroom without another word.

After that earth-shattering kiss, she was finding it hard enough to remember to breathe, let alone talk.

That kiss...

It took everything she had not to lift her fingers to her lips in wonder—just to check that she hadn't been dreaming it.

He'd turned her inside out. In one single kiss, he'd wiped away all the fears that had been racing around her head that evening. Even now, her mind grappled for them but came up empty-handed.

All she could think about was Linc. The kiss had erased every apprehensive notion she'd ever felt. It had been perfect. They'd fitted together perfectly.

As if they'd been hand-crafted for each other, something inside her whispered.

If he could do that with just one simple kiss, what could he do to her with something more intimate? If she continued walking with him along that corridor and upstairs to the bedroom—where he was patently taking them—then she was certainly about to find out.

Piper told herself to stop. Instead, she kept walking—and she didn't falter for even a step. As if she'd been waiting for the moment her entire life.

Aching for this moment.

Right up to the moment when her heel snapped off the high heels she'd never quite got used to wearing, and would have sent her tumbling to the ground, if not for Linc catching her fall.

'I can't walk like this,' she muttered, not sure if it was embarrassment or frustration that she felt the most potently.

'Hold on,' he gritted, and placed her arms around his neck.

And then, before she could ask him what he was doing, he simply lifted her up as if she were as light as air to him. Any thoughts began to seep out of Piper's brain. All she could think about were his strong arms around her; and how solid, how unyielding, his chest felt against her body.

She ran her tongue around her suddenly parched mouth. Not that it made it any easier to speak in anything approaching her usual voice.

'What…do you think you're doing, Patch?'

As if using his nickname could shift this…*thing* vibrating inside her. As if it could remind her of that nagging voice that was now shoved to the back of her brain; and she couldn't quite hear what it was trying to say, even if she'd wanted to.

But all Linc did was offer a wordless smile—a dark, utterly masculine curve of his mouth—before striding across the room to shoulder open a discreet door that she hadn't even noticed existed.

Craning her neck, she peered down the long, quiet, spine of a corridor that was presumably the servants' route through the house. A way of getting around quicky and easily, without cluttering up the main hallways where the gentry would be.

As if proving her theory, Linc made straight for a narrow, spiral staircase, and there was something so thrilling about the focussed look in his gaze, and the effortless way that he was carrying her, that made her feel ridiculously feminine, and…obedient. And made her forget everything else.

And then, finally, they were back in their suite. Alone.

'Should we really be doing this, Linc?' she whispered.

'I want you,' he answered simply, his deep voice grazing deliciously over her as surely as if he'd used his teeth.

'Here?' she whispered. 'Now?'

'Here,' he growled in confirmation. 'Now.'

He unzipped her dress, the deliciously naughty sound of it filling the room. Then he slid her dress off her shoulders, stripping her. But it wasn't a race—oh, no—instead, Linc worked painstakingly carefully, pressing his mouth to taste each newly exposed part of her, lavishing attention on every single inch of her bare skin, and taking his time as if he could have feasted on her for ever.

It was a dizzying, glorious notion.

Piper gave herself up to the feel of his lips, his mouth, his tongue inching his way over her flesh as though they had a lifetime to indulge. Maybe two. He tasted her and teased her, tracing exquisite patterns down the long line of her neck, and over her shoulders, his fingers brushing up and down her arms, and she gave herself up to the dazzling sensations that were ricocheting around her body.

It was as though he intended to learn every bit of her, from her forehead to her chin, and from her jawline to her collarbone, he kissed her. Soft, hot brushes of his mouth that sent shock waves through her every single time. And if a century or more had passed them by, then Piper wouldn't have cared.

Then, at last, he turned her round. Inch by stirring inch whilst he slid her dress lower to expose her spine, and then spent perhaps another entire century pressing his lips to the skin there and lavishing attention as he made his way carefully down.

And all she could do was obey. And feel. And marvel.

Never in her life had she known that the mere act of undressing a person could be so electrifying. So indulgent. This bit was the means to the end. The rushed bit of foreplay that was over and gone before she could even blink.

But Linc made it an art form all on its own.

A teasing, thrilling, stirring show that stoked the already smouldering fires in her higher and higher. She wanted more. So much more, and so very badly, that as his mouth moved lower, her dress pooling at her feet as he turned her back around to face him, she feared she would start shaking with desire.

She was sure that she shook with need, and still Linc took his sweet time, giving the removal of those lacy scraps of underwear as much painstaking time as when he removed her gown.

And then, when she was finally naked in front of him, he lifted one leg, kissing down her thigh, and her shin, before moving his mouth to inside and making his way back up again. Closer and closer to where she was aching, *actually aching*, for him the most. But he skimmed past it and when Piper heard a muffled sound, it took her a moment to realise that it was her own voice.

As he repeated the exploration down her other leg, all she could do was grip her shoulders with her hands and wait, just wait, for him to make his way back up again. And if she'd stopped breathing somewhere along the line, then there was nothing she could do about that.

Then, at long last, he was there. His lips inching their way up the inside of her thigh. Higher. Higher. And suddenly, his mouth was right there, at the apex of her legs, where she was molten, and sweet, and yearning for him—and finally, he slid her leg over his shoulder, pressed his mouth to her core, and he feasted on her.

Piper wasn't sure how she stayed standing. She heard her own rasped breathing as his wicked tongue did things to her that she had only ever dreamed of. And not even in such incredible detail. He was toying with her body in ways she hadn't even known were possible, and she wasn't sure she would ever be the same again.

She didn't want to be.

She only wanted this. *Him*. And if everything else simply faded out of existence, then Piper couldn't have cared less. And still, he played with her, driving her on faster, harder.

Her raspy breaths turned to gasps, and cries. At some point she must have slid her fingers into his hair as if that could somehow offer her purchase, as he finally toppled her, high and fast, into blissful oblivion.

* * *

By the time Piper came back to herself, she realised he must have carried her across the room to the bed, and he'd laid her down, and rid himself of his suit.

She watched, almost hungrily, as he moved to the end of the bed. Naked, and proud, and every bit as magnificent as she'd pretended not to imagine him to be.

'Are you ready for this, Piper?' he gritted out, and it occurred to her that he was only just managing to control himself.

The realisation was a liberating one. Pushing herself up onto her elbows, Piper reached out with one arm and hooked him around the neck to pull him down onto the bed.

He was all hers, if only for this one night; she would never get this chance again.

She might as well make the most of it.

CHAPTER THIRTEEN

'COME BACK TO BED.'

Piper jumped guiltily as Linc's hoarse voice floated through the dark. Still, she didn't move, keeping her eyes trained on the blackness of the gardens beyond the window, and her arms wrapped tightly around her body.

As if she could somehow ward off the cold guilt that crept through her.

'That should never have happened,' she muttered quietly.

There was no need to say anything more than that; they both knew she was referring to the fact they'd just slept together. Well, not so much *slept*… But the truth was that she wouldn't have changed it even if she could have gone back in time. Just to have that one, perfect night with Linc had to be worth it.

So what did that say about her moral fibre?

Piper heard the rustle of bedsheets, and the soft padding of his feet as Linc crossed the room to her. She still didn't turn around, but then she didn't try to stop him either.

'What's going on, Piper?'

She shook her head, searching for the right words.

'I just…' She steeled her shoulders, hating herself more than ever. 'I haven't been honest with you. I never thought things would get this far. I should never have let them get this far.'

'So be honest with me now.'

His easy tone took her breath away. As if he thought that whatever it was, they could get through it together.

More likely she was just projecting.

'I lied to you about my family,' she blurted out, hating herself. 'That is, not lied exactly; more, omitted.'

He didn't answer, but his hands moved to her shoulders. As though *he* wanted to soothe *her*. It was an odd notion, though not an unpleasant one, though she was too accustomed to being the one taking care of others to really appreciate someone else taking care of her.

Or give herself up to the temptation.

Carefully, she moved to the side and away, trying to put a little distance between them. All the same, when he didn't close the gap again, she felt strangely…bereft.

'I'm all wrong for you. We come from different worlds.'

Linc shook his head.

'No, we come from the same world, you and I. First the military world, now the Helimed world.'

'You're the son of a duke, Lincoln,' she burst out.

'Accepting that I'm his son and not just my mother's unwanted kid, then I'm the second son of a duke, which, to all intents and purposes, means very little. I'll never become the duke—that's my brother's role, not that he wants it either. But he has no choice.'

'You're still a lord. And I'm…'

'You're what? A bright, intelligent woman? A skilled pilot? A beautiful human being, inside and out? Take your pick, Piper; just don't start any nonsense about not being good enough for a lord because, trust me, titles don't mean anything.'

'Nonetheless…' Her teeth were worrying at her lower lip so hard it was beginning to chafe. She forced herself to stop. 'I'm not the person you think I am.'

'That doesn't even make sense, Legs. You're overthinking things.'

'No, I'm not.' She shook her head, trying to stop the shaking from overtaking her entire body.

She had to do this, no matter how unpalatable it was.

'I once told you that my father died.'

'You did,' he agreed after a moment's thought.

'What I didn't mention was that my mother was accused of killing him,' she confessed heavily, resenting every word that was coming out of her mouth.

'Say that again?'

She found the barely concealed horror in his tone disheartening. Or was she just imagining it would be there? And then, as suddenly as her moment of boldness had come, it disappeared again. Without warning, she swayed, and stumbled, and just as she felt herself about to crash to the floor she felt two strong arms catch her and carry her to the wingback chairs that overlooked the expansive gardens.

It was surely the height of irony that staring at them through the bars of the lead-paned windows was as though she were staring at them from behind the bars of her very own prison.

Piper gritted her teeth and forced herself to speak.

'It wasn't true, of course,' she managed. 'It didn't take much for the police to realise that my mother would never have hurt my father. Though I wouldn't have blamed her if she had.'

'You're going too fast, Piper,' Linc rumbled. 'Back up a few steps and tell me from the start.'

But she couldn't. Her mind was spiralling and her mouth seemed hell-bent on blurting out whichever details popped into her head first.

'The point is that I should never have come here and pretended to be your fiancée,' she rushed on. 'And when we were on the beach and you told me about your mother and how bad a scandal would be for your family, I should have told you then. At the very least, I should never have slept with you. That was wrong and I'm…sorry.'

Or at least, she really ought to be. She shouldn't be neatly wrapping up what had just happened between them into some perfect memory she could open up in the future and replay. Relive.

'Piper, stop. Breathe.'

Linc's voice cut into her thoughts and she realised she'd been speaking faster and faster, as though putting it all out there as fast as possible could get this whole ordeal over with sooner.

As if Linc wouldn't have a mine of questions.

'Sorry,' she muttered, struggling to catch her breath.

'Just take your time, Piper. Start from the beginning and explain it to me. All of it.'

And it was the quiet empathy in his tone that struck her more than anything. Very much as though he cared.

Ridiculous notion.

'I don't know where to start,' she admitted, after a moment, splaying out her hands helplessly. 'I'm sorry, I just…'

'It's fine, let me help,' he soothed, and she wondered how he could be so calm after what she'd just said. 'You once told me that you had a good childhood. You said that there was a lot of love, if not a lot of money.'

'I did,' Piper managed miserably, though the words felt strange in her mouth. Thick, and heavy, and gloopy. 'And that was true, for the most part.'

She lifted her shoulders helplessly. It wasn't that she didn't *want* to tell him the truth—for the first time in her life she'd found someone she actually felt she could explain it to—it was more that she had no idea *how* she was supposed to tell him. How she was even to begin to explain.

Words swirled around her head, but she couldn't seem to make any of them come out of her mouth.

'I actually have a sister as well as my brother. She's three years older than me but we don't get on any longer. She and I grew up with my parents in a small terraced house on a housing estate. My sister was the pretty one, the bold one, the funny one, she charmed everyone she met within moments, and I adored her. Everyone adored her. But my father was the one she loved most—a daddy's girl from the start—whilst I was closer to my mother. I was quieter, more reserved, like my mother. He loved us all, of course, but not the same way.'

She paused, trying to slow her racing pulse and order her thoughts. All the while, Linc knelt quietly opposite her, his hands at her elbows as though he wasn't appalled by the very sight of her. She wondered what must be going through his head.

'I was fifteen when my father was in an industrial accident. He lost part of his right hand and his job. He'd been a manual labourer all his life, and without his hand, he'd now lost his job, and couldn't provide for his family.'

'What about compensation?' Linc asked. 'If it was an industrial accident, surely he should have got a payout?'

'The company couldn't afford it and so they declared bankruptcy. There was nothing my father could do. He'd always been a proud man, but then he found himself thirty-eight, unable to work.'

'What happened, Piper?'

She took a breath, beating back the memories that she'd pushed away for so long. Carefully locked behind a thick door in her mind, where they couldn't get to her. Couldn't hurt her.

'We didn't have much money. My brother hadn't even been born but my mum worked a waitressing job already, and she got a second one cleaning an office block in the evenings. I got a job in a local corner shop.'

'And your sister?'

'She'd moved out when she was eighteen, just before Dad's accident. She'd met a boy, fallen for him, got pregnant, and got married. He'd landed a job at an oil refinery across the country, so they'd moved away.'

'So she couldn't help,' Linc noted.

'No, but I don't think anyone could have given that he didn't tell them. He didn't even tell my mum. He pretended that he'd got a job but borrowed money from a loan shark,' she bit out. 'I can only imagine that he thought it would tide him over until he really did find something. But then the next month came and he borrowed more. And the month after that. I think that was when he started drinking.'

'Your father became an alcoholic,' Linc guessed.

Piper jerked her head stiffly, hating that she had to confirm it.

'He'd never really been a drinker, but I guess he found it numbed his brain and helped him to forget his situation. But he was a mean drunk.'

'By *mean*, I'm guessing you mean violent? Abusive?' Linc gritted his teeth, as though he was angry on her behalf.

It was…unexpectedly endearing, Piper thought dimly.

'Not to my brother or to me, but to Mum.' She didn't care to go into too much detail, but that didn't mean the memories weren't there. The screams, the sight of him, the fear for her mother. 'It didn't help that she just kept making excuses for him, and practically killed herself doing everything he demanded to keep him happy. She fell pregnant at the age of forty-two with my younger brother.'

Piper didn't elaborate, the look on Linc's face—reflected in the moonlight—assured her that he understood.

'I tried to get her to leave so many times, but she just kept saying she'd taken a marriage vow with him. *In sickness and in health*, and that he was sick. Even when he broke her arm, she just said that he was sick and that it was her role to take care of him.'

'I'm so sorry, Legs,' Linc growled. And she found herself smiling—albeit weakly—at the nickname, just as she suspected he'd intended that she would.

It was a moment of levity that she'd needed. Sucking in a deep breath, she pressed on.

'I think it would have been different if he'd ever tried to hurt me, or my brother,' Piper mused. 'I think she'd have left straight away. I'd like to think so, anyway.'

'So he never touched either of you kids?'

'Never.' Not that it lessened what he'd done to her mother. 'One night when he had put her in the hospital for the umpteenth time, I decided enough was enough. The hospital recognised the type of injury and they sent in a social worker as they always did, but this time I refused to cover for him. I told them what was happening, then I contacted our sister and I told her too.'

There was no way that Piper could keep the sorrow out of her voice, nor the tinge of anger, no matter how she tried.

'She said I was lying. That I was mistaken. She argued that if Dad was going through a hard time, then it was because he'd been through such a traumatic accident, and Mum ought to take better care of him and have more empathy.'

'She can't have really believed that.'

'I don't know.' Piper shrugged. 'Maybe she did. She never personally saw that side of him. To her, he was a quiet, gentle man who wouldn't even kill a spider in the bathtub. He used to take them outside and release them into the garden.'

'Events can change people, Piper. Not always for the better.'

Piper pulled her lips into a tight line, as though that could somehow ward off the sadness of the memories.

'I know that. I suppose my sister simply didn't want to see the truth. So she said it wasn't possible.'

'Your mum didn't collaborate your story to the social worker either,' he growled. 'Did she?'

Slowly, Piper moved her head from side to side.

'No, she refused to back me up. She claimed she'd been in the house alone, vacuuming the stairs, when she'd tangled her feet up in the hose and fallen. We all knew she was lying, but without her speaking out against my father, no one could do anything about it.'

'So you all went back home together.'

'We did. Mum didn't talk to me, except to say that she would never forgive me. She could barely even look at me. But, for a while, it was okay. I think maybe me telling the truth had scared him. Even if no one could act without my mum admitting it, he knew I wasn't going to be complicit.'

'It didn't last though, did it?' Linc demanded. 'It couldn't. He wasn't going to change.'

And the bleak expression on his face reminded her that, in her own way, Linc's mother had been just as cruel and abusive. It was just that hers was mental abuse rather than physical.

They each had their demons, her and Linc. How had it taken all these years to realise that?

'Eventually, he couldn't keep it up and the cycle started again. I was seventeen and desperate to join the army as soon as I could, but I was afraid what he'd do if I left him alone with her. Or with my baby brother. I tried to get her to leave again. To say something. To do something, but she wouldn't. Then, one night, when I was out at work, he came in steaming drunk as usual, but he'd run out of money.'

She squeezed her eyes shut as the memory slammed into her, and a wave of nausea threatened to overwhelm her.

'It was bad, wasn't it?' Linc growled, though his hand didn't stop caressing hers.

It was an unexpected comfort.

'The worst it had ever been,' she admitted, swallowing hard. 'I…'

'You don't need to go into details if you aren't ready.'

She nodded, grateful.

'I threw the money I'd earned that day at him, and grabbed the baby, then I got Mum out of there. I didn't really have a plan, I just thought we could go to a halfway house or a shelter, or something. We were just leaving the front gate when we heard the smash. I don't know what possessed me to go back inside. I think it was the eeriness of the silence that followed. Just…nothing. But when I peered around the doorway, I saw he'd fallen into the coffee table and as it had smashed, a shard of glass penetrated his femoral, a little like that motocross kid on the first shout we did, really.'

'He bled out?'

'We tried to stem it. We got some tea towels and tried to apply pressure, but neither of us really knew what to do back then. By the time the police and ambulance arrived, he was dead.'

'There was nothing more you could have done with that kind of injury,' Linc managed gruffly.

Piper didn't answer. Logically, she knew that was true, but it didn't always help.

'How could they possibly have accused your mother of killing him, though?' Linc frowned.

And perhaps this was the worst of it all. Piper inhaled deeply.

'They didn't. My sister did.'

'Your sister wasn't even there.' Linc sounded infuriated.

'No, but she couldn't accept it had been an accident. She insisted we must have done something to him. Even when two different neighbours concurred that they'd heard him still shouting in the house when we were on the driveway, and then the crash, she refused to let it go. She has always blamed my mother for living when my father died, and she has never accepted the truth.'

She'd even tried to win custody of their baby brother, claiming that their mother was unfit for the role. But Linc didn't need to know that additional sordid secret. He already had enough gory truths to disgust him about her family.

'I'm only telling you all of this so that you understand why I should go. Why I have to leave now. Before any of this comes to bite your family.' She shifted on her chair, but Linc didn't move. He caged her, without even touching it.

Or perhaps it was simply that a traitorous part of her wanted to pretend that he was stopping her from going.

Oh, she never should have come.

'I'm so sorry that happened to you.' Linc lifted his hand to her chin, cupping it.

Piper twisted her mouth awkwardly and stayed silent.

What else was there to say?

He dropped his hand. 'I promise you, as soon as we get back to Heathston, I'll help you find a place for your mother and your brother to move to, so they can be closer to you now.'

'No,' she bit out. Loudly. 'I don't need your help. I can

look after my family myself. If this job in West Nessleton comes through, we'll be fine.'

'You don't need to leave,' he argued softly.

And dammit if all she wanted to do was believe him. She stamped the urge out viciously.

'Of course I do. I'm a landmine in your family just waiting for someone to detonate it. And you said it yourself today. The last thing your family needs right now is more scandals to make the board topple Raf. I'll head back to Heathston tonight and I'll find somewhere else to live. You need to stay here and come up with some plausible reason as to why I can't come to the wedding next week.'

'Legs...'

She shook her head, refusing to listen.

'The sooner we go our own ways, the better. And I think your plan of moving back here to be closer to your family and set up a new Helimed for the region is a great idea.'

'Piper.' His voice was still quiet, but this time it was firmer.

Enough to silence her.

But she still didn't look at him until he hooked his fingers under her chin and lifted it up.

'I don't care about your past,' he told her. 'I certainly don't care about dragging up a horrid past that no one should ever have had to go through, least of all a mother you've always said was kind, and generous, and good.'

'That's admirable.' She tried to pull her face away but found she couldn't. For all her attempt to resist him, she couldn't bring herself to break that contact. 'But you know what they say: mud sticks, and all that.'

'Then turn it into a cleansing mud treatment.' Linc shrugged. 'My sister claims they're all the rage.'

'It isn't a joke.' Piper blinked at him.

'Perhaps not. But nor is it the end of the world, the way

you're telling yourself it is. I want you. I like you. And you like me, too.'

'But you said it yourself, your family have endured enough scandal with everything your mother did. If they should dig up my past, then everything we did here to try to help your brother will have been for nothing.'

'I highly doubt anyone will delve into your past, Piper.'

'They might.' She jutted out her chin. 'You can't risk it. You said it yourself, there are people looking to discredit you just so they can get your shares.'

'And Raf and I have talked and come up with a way to deal with them. Me being here with you has gone a long way to helping that. So come back to bed, Piper. No one will care about me by tomorrow, or who I date. And no one will care about your secret. You're safe with me.'

And it was tempting, oh, so tempting, to just obey. To put the ugliness behind her and simply be with Linc. Be herself. Because it was true, she did feel safe with Linc.

She just wasn't sure he was entirely safe with her.

'I can't…' she forced herself to say.

He slid his hands down her legs, straightening them out so that he could help her to her feet. As though he could help her to move on.

God, she should have told him the whole truth. Everything. Even that last part about her sister. If she ever discovered that Piper was dating someone like Linc—that she was happy—Piper didn't think there was anything her sister wouldn't stoop to in order to take away that happiness.

It had never before occurred to her that her sister was acting out of her own sense of guilt.

'Linc, wait.' She faltered, hating this bit more than anything. 'There's something else.'

'I don't want to hear more.' He stopped her with his

mouth. His tongue dipping so enticingly into her mouth. 'It's your past, Piper. Let it stay there.'

'But…'

'Just enjoy this for what it is,' he growled, dropping kisses from her mouth to move lower, to that sweet spot just on the column of her neck. 'For however long it lasts.'

And later she would think it was that last remark that convinced her to stay quiet. Even though a part of her wanted to tell him the truth, he was making her brain go fuzzy. Her thoughts dissolving into sheer sensation.

And, as he said, there was no need for everything to be laid out there. They were having fun for now. It wasn't as if this relationship could ever really go anywhere.

She ought to be grateful to him for reminding her of that fact.

And even though she wasn't convinced Linc was entirely thinking things through—even though she knew the moral thing to do would be to walk away, the way she should have done two weeks ago—she let him lower his mouth down to hers.

She let him, and she surrendered to him.

Because she might have wanted to listen to her head… but right now, her traitorous heart was the one in control.

CHAPTER FOURTEEN

'ANYONE SEE ANYTHING?'

Piper brought the heli around as all four members of the team scanned the ground below them for signs of their new patient. Not helped by the hazy mist that was beginning to roll in over these mountains.

'Nothing this side,' Probie answered over the headset.

'Nor this side,' added Tom.

'Can you take us back up a little higher?' Linc's voice rumbled. 'I might have something, though it's a little further south-east than the caller said it was.'

Piper duly took the bird up, her eyes still expertly scanning the ground even as she considered how well they were working together these days. Better than ever, she might even say.

It had been almost a week since she and Linc had returned from Oakenfeld Hall, and neither of them had raised the subject of her family since then. Instead, they'd spent their days pretending to their colleagues they were still nothing more than friends, but their nights exploring every inch of each other.

Piper thought that Linc had probably learned every line and every contour of her body, first with his wicked hands, then with his even more wicked tongue. Not that it made each night any less of a revelation. Another journey of exploration. And she couldn't imagine ever tiring of such adventures.

Still, she didn't know what it meant. Linc hadn't mentioned his idea of him returning to his home since the evening of the wedding rehearsal. Had he changed his mind since things between the two of them had shifted? Or was he simply waiting for whatever this...*thing* was between them to peter out?

Sometimes Piper thought she didn't want to know. Other times, she thought the uncertainty could drive her insane.

Or perhaps that was just the guilt, eating away at her no matter how many times she tried to stuff it back down. Ultimately, it would ruin everything, she knew that. And still, she couldn't bring herself to do anything about it. As if gorging on her time with Linc could somehow save her from when it all fell apart.

And it would.

'See better now?' Piper asked, having taken the heli up to a better height. Not so high that it made things too small to see, but enough to give them a clearer, longer view. 'The caller said she wasn't familiar with this range. If her walking partner fell the opposite side to the one she thought, she could have given us the wrong info.'

Linc leaned forward, peering closer.

'Yeah, pretty sure I saw a flash of blue over there, two o'clock position.'

Piper followed his direction. It certainly looked as if someone might be down there, behind a mid-sized outcrop. Probably hoping to take shelter from the downdraught of the rotors, without realising they didn't actually know where their casualty was.

'Can you take a fly around?' Linc asked. 'Or is it too close to that rock face?'

'I wouldn't like to go all the way around. There might

be loose rocks. But I can certainly bring her round a little more.'

'It isn't the best place to land down here,' noted Linc. 'If that blue *is* them, we might have a bit of a trek in.'

She'd been thinking the same thing. Down at this level the ground was too uneven for the heli. The only flat area she'd seen was too close to the sharp mountain face, which meant there was a good chance she would have to take the heli back to the top and let the crew either make their way down the long, winding path, or abseil.

Usually, it was mountain rescue heli that operated in these parts, but they'd been called to a shout just out to sea with a man overboard.

'Let's see if we've got the right people.' Piper grimaced as she manoeuvred her heli into a better position. 'Anyone got a clear view?'

'Yeah, that's our guy,' Linc confirmed after a moment as he called it in, whilst Piper backed the heli away and looked more earnestly for somewhere to land. 'Hotel zero seven, this is Helimed hotel one-niner, over, ready with an update, over.'

'Go ahead, hotel one-niner.'

'We've located the casualty but the ground is too rocky to land close by. Confirm a land mountain rescue crew is on their way, over?'

'Yeah, that's confirmed, Helimed hotel one-niner, they should be with you within the next fifteen to twenty minutes, over.'

Piper waited for Linc to conclude the call.

'I want to head down this valley a way,' she told him. 'I think I saw a flatter area on the way in, which wouldn't make it any faster for you guys to get to the casualty, but it would make evacuation a lot easier if you don't have to get them back up the mountainside.'

'How long?'

'Not long,' she assured him. 'I know time is of the essence.'

Turning the nose in the direction she wanted, Piper flew as efficiently as she could. Sure enough, the flat area she hoped for came into view quickly.

'Here okay?'

'Yeah, great. Well spotted,' Linc agreed. 'Take us down.'

She didn't need to be told twice. Quickly, skilfully, she turned her heli until it was on the granite plateau.

'You make that look a damned sight easier than it is,' Linc complimented as he opened the door and bundled out with his bag.

And Piper tried not to flush like the kind of giggly schoolgirl she couldn't remember ever having been, as he cast her a wink that only the two of them shared.

She might have known it couldn't last.

It was late by the time Linc arrived home—and wasn't the truth of it now that it really did feel like a home, not just a penthouse, since Piper had moved in?

But his anticipation was short-lived when he walked through the door to see Piper looking ashen, and Sara glaring at her as if she were something not even the stable cat would deign to drag in. He had a feeling it was only Raf's presence that was keeping things from degenerating further.

And it should have concerned him—that dark sensation that pierced straight through his body at the thought that someone had hurt Piper.

He wanted to wring them out for their audacity, no matter who they were. Even his sister.

'Care to tell me what's going on?'

His voice might be silky smooth, but surely no one could

have missed the warning note that threaded through it. Not even bull-headed Sara.

'This…woman—' Sara spat the word out as though it were poison in her mouth '—could destroy our family.'

'I suggest you're a little more careful concerning what you say about my guests in my home,' he managed, the warning note even clearer.

But it seemed that his sister was even more obstinate than he'd anticipated.

'You should steer clear, Linc. She isn't who she pretends to be. Her name isn't even Piper Green. Did you know that?'

'I did not,' Linc acknowledged as casually as he could whilst he turned to Piper. 'You took your mother's name after his death, presumably?'

She blinked at him, and he realised she'd been expecting accusations.

'I did.' Her voice cracked.

He took a step closer as if to lend her his support, but she refused to even look his way. It didn't matter, he could read the shame in every line of her body, and he balled his fists into his pockets as though that could somehow contain his anger.

He loathed the sight of the scarlet stain that stole cruelly over Piper's cheeks. He knew how it felt. He'd felt the same way when his mother had announced with such delight that he wasn't even his father's biological son.

'So that explains the name,' he turned to his sister coolly. 'And I'm also aware of her father's death. After all, that was going to be your next question, was it not?'

'What do you mean, you're aware?' Sara's voice pitched higher.

'I already know what you're going to say,' Linc clipped out. 'Piper told me herself. The question is why were you nosing in her private business?'

'Because unlike you, I believe it's prudent to know about the people trying to insinuate themselves into our lives. And if you know, then you should have told me. And Raf.'

'I wholly disagree.' He forced a casual note into his voice, knowing it would lodge itself under his sister's skin with far more effect than raising his voice to her. 'I know Piper's past because she chose to tell me herself. And I didn't choose to share it because I determined that it wasn't our business. Though I'm surprised at you, Raf.'

'No.' Raf shook his head, taking a step away. 'Not me. I just wanted to be sure you knew about it. If you do, and you're happy you know the truth, then I am too. I trust you.'

Any remaining words Linc had for his brother died on his lips as Raf turned to Piper and offered her an equally dignified apology before turning to Sara.

'We should leave now. Linc knows, we have our answer. Piper, you have my apologies.'

'Well, you don't have mine,' Sara snapped. 'I'm not going anywhere until Lincoln realises exactly how this... phony has played him.'

'Then you're doing it alone,' Raf growled, taking his leave with only a final nod of his head to Piper, causing Sara to turn back on her.

'I trusted you. I told you that I was *happy* you were in my brother's life.'

Linc blinked in surprise.

'Did she really say that to you?'

And, finally, his beautiful Piper lifted her head and met his sister's glower head-on.

'You told me that maybe you had misjudged me, and that perhaps I wasn't such a poor decision for your brother, after all,' Piper managed, every word like glass in her mouth. 'And I didn't have the decency to tell you that you hadn't misjudged me at all. I should never have gone to your wedding rehearsal, and for that, I truly am sorry.'

'You don't owe anyone an apology,' Linc growled, his ribcage tightening at the misery in her expressive eyes.

'I do. I told you my past could damage your family, and I was right.'

'It hasn't damaged anything. What was it you told me, Piper—that I didn't carry anyone else's sins but my own?'

'It isn't the same thing,' Sara blasted out furiously. 'She helped to kill her own father.'

Beside him, he heard Piper's sharp intake of breath, her anguished gurgle. He wasn't sure how he manged not to bodily eject his sister from his penthouse, there and then.

They both knew there was only one person Sara could have got that information from. But surely even his sister wouldn't have gone that far.

'You have no idea what you're talking about,' he ground out coldly.

'I know she and her excuse of a mother covered up what they did.'

'Since when do we blame victims of abuse, Sara?' he managed icily. 'And, for the record, Piper wasn't even there when it all happened.'

And right now, he could only imagine what had to be going through Piper's head.

His Piper.

The realisation walloped through him, leaving him almost light-headed. He needed to talk to Piper alone. Sara needed to go. Striding across the room, he flung open his penthouse door.

He was throwing his sister out twice in as many weeks, but there was nothing else for it.

'I also suggest you follow Raf's lead, and leave.'

It was the most controlled thing he could think of to

say. Moving back across the room, he put his arms around Piper, his entire body feeling it when she stiffened against his touch, as though she was barely stopping herself from ducking away.

And all he wanted was his sister gone so that he could make Piper talk to him. Make him understand that his sister had no right to do what she was doing.

'You're choosing her over us?' Sara pulled a disgusted face. 'You can't do that.'

'Then I suggest you don't make me,' he warned her. 'Get out, before either of us say or do something which we might regret.'

'You can't do this, Linc, I won't let you.'

'Leave. Now.'

She opened her mouth as though ready to respond, before appearing to think better of it. And then, at length, she snatched up her bag and stormed to the door.

'You'll regret choosing her over family.'

'I think not.'

'I don't want her at my wedding.'

'That is regrettable, but it's your wedding. But know that if Piper isn't welcome, then neither am I.'

'Of course you are. You have to be there, you're my brother.'

'If Piper isn't welcome, then neither am I,' he repeated. 'Your choice.'

And he waited, his chest pounding, as his sister finally got the message and left, leaving him and Piper alone.

'You shouldn't have done that,' Piper managed as aftershock wave after aftershock wave slammed through her.

It twisted her tongue, preventing her from answering. She wasn't even sure she could still breathe.

'I had to,' Linc bit out after what felt like an age. 'You

were letting her talk to you as if she had a right to say those things.'

'I can't stop her.' Piper pressed her hand to her forehead as if trying to stave off a headache.

Hardly surprising.

'You could have told her the truth. Everything you told me.'

'You aren't serious?' Piper breathed incredulously. 'I told you because I trust you, Linc. I don't want to talk to Sara. It's humiliating enough without having to tell everyone.'

'Sara should never have spoken to you that way, but you could have told her what really happened. Not let your sister keep spreading lies about you and your mother, going unchecked every time.'

Did he know how much he was asking of her? He couldn't possibly. And what did it matter, anyway? What had just happened had been avoidable, if only she'd stayed away from Linc the way that every fibre of her had screamed to do from the start.

Even before he'd told her how far from scandal his family needed to be. Even before he'd told her about his fame-hungry mother.

A bomb like this had always been inevitable, the fall-out predictable. And still she'd gone ahead and let herself be with him.

She'd brought it on herself. And she told him as much.

'You did not bring anything on yourself,' Linc declared instantly. 'If anything, my sister brought it on herself. But you should have trusted me to have your back.'

'Why, Linc? Why should I ever have trusted you?'

He stared at her as though she had two heads.

'We're supposed to be a couple.'

Piper snorted derisively, if shakily.

'Fake couple, Linc,' she managed—giving the impression that the words tasted acrid in her mouth. 'There's nothing real about what's between us.'

'I disagree.'

So simple. So certain. It caught her off guard, and for a moment she only stared at him.

Then she offered the faintest shake of her head.

'You're confusing love, and lust, and yearning, I fear,' she managed, with a coldness of her own.

And if he didn't know her as well as he did then he wouldn't have realised that her heart was being ripped out, just as his was.

'Whatever has been between us was sexual attraction, Linc. That was *all* it was. Sex. There was nothing real— nothing substantial. We don't even really know each other.'

'I think we both know that's a lie.' His tone changed.

And as easily as that, all the heat slid out of the situation. Piper stared at him miserably.

'Maybe it was,' she admitted, so quietly that he almost missed it. 'Maybe we did have a chance at something more than just *pretend*. But that's gone now. This was meant to be Sara's wedding week, from her rehearsal last weekend to her wedding this weekend. Now it will be tainted with my squalid past for ever.'

'Trust me.' Linc moved towards her. 'There's nothing my sister will relish more than a meaty story to make her wedding more memorable than any of her friends'.'

'You're wrong.' Piper shook her head. 'We were meant to be a couple to make things go more smoothly, now it will only cause more gossip and upset. If the board members use this to help their coup, do you really think either Sara or Raf will ever relish such a *meaty story*?'

And he hated that she had a point.

'I'll deal with it,' he promised her grimly. 'I think it's clear to her that if you aren't welcome, then neither am I.'

'So you're issuing ultimatums?' Piper challenged sadly. 'That's how you want to handle the wedding of your only sister? By backing her into a corner?'

A dull bellow started in his chest. Was that how it would look to his sister?

'I'm not backing her into any corner.'

'We both know that isn't how Sara will see it.' Piper shook her head. 'And for what it's worth, I think I'd feel the same, in her position.'

The bellowing got louder.

Piper was right, he couldn't force Sara to accept Piper at her wedding. But if he attended alone, then he might as well be giving Sara licence to investigate anyone he ever chose to date.

Can there be anyone else after Piper?

He stuffed the thought away quickly.

But still, she deserved better than this. Better than accusations that neither she nor her mother—both victims in different ways—would ever deserve. And Piper was right, now wasn't the time to punish his sister for trying to look out for him in her own, slightly twisted way. But given the way their mother had always treated her—jealous of her daughter's youth, and acuity, and looks—was it any wonder that Sara had never known quite how to communicate with other women?

Still, right now, his main concern was Piper. If he wanted his family to accept her at all—though if it came down to a choice between the two of them, he knew now that there would only ever be one winner—then he needed to wait until after Sara's honeymoon.

He would attend the wedding alone, avoiding a scene, because it was what Piper wanted. And because he had long since known how to pick his battles.

'This isn't about anyone else,' he ground out. 'This is about you, and it's about me.'

'We both know things aren't that simple,' Piper denied, as the resignation in her tone made his very soul ache.

'Nonetheless, I'll go to the wedding,' he confirmed after a moment, watching the relief chase across Piper's face. 'But only because I won't allow your name to ever become the reason for any distance between my siblings and me.'

'Linc…'

'However, this isn't the end of our conversation, Piper.' He gently lifted her chin so that she could see the promise in his eyes. 'We'll talk when I get back.'

'Yes,' she whispered.

And later, much later, he would wonder if she'd really meant it, or if he'd abjectly failed to read the lie behind that one, simple word that had fallen so easily from her lips.

CHAPTER FIFTEEN

'LET'S GET TO our patient.' Linc leapt out of the heli as soon as Albert landed at the new shout.

Without waiting for a response, he raced across the field and vaulted the drystone wall at the end, and into the residential street, following the direction pointed out by various bystanders.

It had been just over two weeks since his sister's wedding. Over two weeks since he'd returned home to find that his penthouse was empty and Piper had left. The place hadn't felt like home ever since.

Even now, he didn't know whether she'd gone the moment he'd walked out of the door, or whether she'd left the next day, when the story her sister had sold to the press about the undeserving Piper bagging herself a lord had hit the gutter press.

But the question that really ate away at him was why she hadn't taken any of his calls, even when she'd realised that the story hadn't gone anywhere—especially when the few desperate journalists who *had* tried to follow up on the piece had realised that both he and Piper had served together in theatres of war.

The potentially 'juicy scandal' had faded into obscurity as quickly as it had appeared. No one had cared, least of all his brother, or the Oakenfeld board. In fact, if anything, it had made the old cronies review him in a different light—a military hero who could be an asset to Oakenfeld Industries. Linc couldn't say he cared for the image change but if it meant Piper would be free of any hounding—and Raf would be given a boost—then he was prepared not to argue.

But what had really come home to Linc was that he wouldn't have cared what anyone had said. The only person he'd realised he truly cared about was Piper. She had gazed into that dark void in his soul, but instead of fearing it she had flooded it with light, with warmth, with *Piper*. Without her, he wasn't even sure he felt whole.

So tonight, at last, he was determined to find her in person—no more unanswered phone calls—and tell her. He'd given Piper long enough to come around to his way of thinking, to come back to him on her own. Now it was finally time to go out and bring her home. It was likely the only thing that would make him feel he could breathe again.

Even the return of Albert had only just taken the edge off his sense of disquiet   the old pilot slipping back into his role with obvious relief.

Rounding the corner, Linc hurried to where a paramedic—one of the land crew already on scene—was signalling to him. He could already see the patient over her shoulder as the man lay groaning on the ground.

'This is Jez?' Linc surmised.

'Yes,' the paramedic confirmed as she led Linc over. 'Jez is a normally fit and well forty-year-old male. Approximately thirty minutes ago he was on the roof of his home repairing the mortar around the chimney stack when he slipped and fell around ten metres onto the flower bed below.'

'Loss of consciousness?'

'None reported.' The paramedic shook her head. 'He's talked us through events and there doesn't appear to be any loss of memory. He's complaining of mild back pain. He is able to breathe deeply and there is good bilateral air flow. I'm concerned about a laceration to the back of his head, but he isn't complaining of any head pain.'

Linc glanced over to the patient, who was still lying on his side.

'No collar?'

'I didn't want to move him until you got here, in case he had a spinal injury.'

'Okay, thanks.' Linc nodded, indicating to Tom and Probie to approach the patient. 'Hello, Jez, I'm Linc, the air ambulance doctor. Mind if we take a quick look at you?'

He crouched down on the opposite side of the patient to Tom, and the two of them began their assessment.

'Can you tell me what happened, Jez?'

The man talked them through the accident with surprising accuracy and calmness.

'And on a scale of one to ten, Jez, if one is mild, and ten is the worst pain you can imagine, can you tell me what your pain level is?'

'I dunno, Doc,' the man pondered slowly. 'It isn't bad actually. It's more of a dull ache around my back. About one. Not much more.'

Linc and Tom exchanged a glance but didn't speak. Given the height of his fall, and the way the man had landed, if his pain wasn't acute then he was either miraculously lucky, or he'd done some serious damage that was preventing him from feeling the pain.

'I'd like to get him out of this narrow passageway so that we can examine him more easily,' Linc told the crew. 'Best thing is going to be to get him on a scoop and to a level part of the garden. Tom, can you hold the neck whilst we turn him and then we'll get a collar on as soon as we can?'

The team worked quickly and efficiently, working together to get the patient onto the scoop without causing any further injury to what was potentially a serious neck problem. Soon, they had Jez on the flatter part of the lawn with better access around him, and began a more thorough examination. The most concerning discovery was that the man seemed to have damaged his C-Four and C-Five neck vertebrae, which was impairing his body's ability to transmit the pain.

A false move, and there was a chance their patient could end up being paralysed.

'Okay, Jez.' Linc moved over his patient until the man could see him. 'We're concerned you may have injured your neck, so we're going to keep your head stable with some tape, as well as the collar.'

'Okay, Doc.'

'We're going to get you in the air ambulance now, and get you straight to Heathston Royal Infirmary, okay?'

For the moment, despite the laceration on the back of Jez's head, the man's good cognitive function didn't suggest any major head injury. But without full scans and X-rays at the major trauma unit, Linc couldn't rule out the possibility of a brain bleed.

The sooner they got their patient to hospital, the better.

Piper huddled down in the seat of her car as she watched Linc and Albert in the distance, whilst they pulled the helicopter back in after their shift.

It had been a little over a fortnight since she'd last seen him—as if she didn't know it right down to the days and hours. Possibly the worst time of her life, if she was going to be honest—which was saying something. And every day she'd had a moment of weakness when she'd almost, *almost*, taken his phone calls, or picked up the phone herself.

Somehow she'd resisted. Until now. Until the letter—

the job offer—that had arrived in her barracks' post box this morning. Not just any offer, but the offer of a job at Stoneywell air ambulance—with Linc as the critical care doctor, just as he'd once suggested.

Her heart rattled against her ribs with nervous anticipation. She needed to know if he just wanted a pilot, or if he wanted something more from her as well.

Piper shifted again in her seat, and eyed the car clock as Linc dropped the handle to the trailer and headed inside to complete his paperwork whilst the old pilot completed the last of the post-shift checks.

The rest of the crew would be leaving within the next half-hour or so, leaving Linc alone in the base. And then she was determined to go and speak to him—despite her jangling nerves.

Because the truth was that she'd had plenty of time to think these past couple of weeks. Plenty of time to realise that sneaking out of Linc's penthouse the day after his sister's wedding—the day that first venomous piece from her sister had come out—hadn't been her finest hour.

In truth, she felt it had been the biggest mistake of her life, not least because every inch of her had missed that maddening, thrilling, gorgeous man, every second since she'd done it. It had taken her more steel than she'd ever known—even flying her Apaches in war zones—to ignore her phone every time his ringtone had shattered the semblance of peace that she'd pulled around herself.

Only, perhaps he hadn't missed her the same way. Perhaps he'd been calling to detail exactly the damage that her sister's story had done to him. And to his family's name. Little wonder that she was ashamed at herself for lacking the moral fibre to take his calls and find out, and even less surprise that, after a while, he'd stopped calling altogether.

Clearly he must have realised that his life was far less complicated—far less messy—without her in it.

At least, if there was such a thing as a silver lining, the press didn't seem to have published anything more than that one single story. She'd scoured the newspapers every day since yet, to her shock, nothing new seemed to have been written.

And finally, *finally*, Piper had started to try to breathe once again. Enough to regret running from the man who had stood by her even against his own family that last night. But the more time had passed, the more it had felt as if it was too late to change it.

Until now.

Instinctively, Piper's fingers felt for the letter in her pocket. Linc might not have sent it personally but it felt like an olive branch, all the same. A last chance. And what did it say about her feelings for Linc that she had jumped into her car and travelled all the way back to Heathston to speak to him, instead of simply picking up a phone?

Piper started as the door to the base burst open and Probie sauntered out, followed by Hugo. She hunkered down in her seat hoping they wouldn't spot her car, nestled as it was between an old airport minivan and the fence line. But they were too caught up in their own conversations to look her way, and within minutes they were gone.

A short while later, both Tom and then Albert followed.

Which only left Linc.

Her heart lodged somewhere between her chest and her throat, Piper folded her legs out of her car and hurried towards the base door. She was halfway across the tarmac when she spotted him. Lolling on his muscular motorbike and waiting as though he had all the time in the world.

For her.

The others might not have spotted her, but Linc hadn't missed her.

A part of her wanted to turn around and run in the opposite direction. Another part of her wanted to run to him. In the end, she merely hesitated and then walked slowly over, pretending that her entire body didn't notice when he stood up, feet apart and arms folded over a simple black tee that only served to enhance that utterly male body and remind her of the last time she'd explored every inch of it.

But her palms didn't itch—she wouldn't allow them to. She refused to remember just how it had felt, running her hands all over this man's body, again and again, as though she had a thirst that only he could sate.

And she told herself that, for all her apprehension, she hadn't imagined this moment—seeing him again—a hundred times. A thousand.

He looked so casual, so easy, standing there. But she knew only too well the dangerous edge which lay, barely concealed, beneath the surface. The one that judged her and made her feel lacking.

'You changed crews,' he stated simply. Evenly. That low voice doing things to her insides even now. Even under the cloud she could feel hanging above her, pressing in on her. 'Even before Albert returned to Heathston.'

'The schedule suited me better,' she lied.

She should have known better. Linc quirked one eyebrow upwards, though there was no amusement in it.

'Let us be honest, shall we? You wanted to avoid me.'

'No... I...okay, yes.' Her eyes slipped away from his in shame. 'I did. But can you blame me? After what that tabloid story said about you?'

'This is your apology?' He arched his eyebrows even as the corners of his mouth quirked up.

Remorse flooded instantly through her.

'You're right. I'm sorry. My sister had no right to sell such a story to a paper. It was filled with lies and vitriol—'

'I don't care about your sister, Piper,' he cut her off easily. 'And I certainly don't expect you to have to apologise for the choices *she* made. If anything, she couldn't have sold any story had Sara not alerted her to the fact that you and I were together. So let us not waste our time with any pointless blame game, shall we?'

She frowned at him.

'You understand that Sara was just trying to protect you all.' Piper lifted her shoulders defeatedly. The action revealed far too much of how she really felt, but she couldn't stop herself. 'I know how your sister feels about the importance of family.'

'Then it is unfortunate that she chose to go about it in a way that resulted in more negative attention for us all. But that isn't the apology I am looking for, Piper.'

'It isn't?' She eyed him incredulously as dark things began to fill her up inside.

Could it be the hint of possibility?

'I'm talking about an apology from you,' he clarified, as if he could read every one of the questions that had been flying around her brain up until a few minutes ago. 'For simply leaving like that. For not waiting for me.'

It hit her squarely in the chest. She opened her mouth, closed it again, then drew in a breath.

'You're right. The way I left was cowardly but I couldn't bear the idea of hearing you say to my face how disgusted you were…*are* with me. How I'm the reason for a scandal that you all wanted so badly to avoid. I don't think I want to even imagine the things your sister is calling me right now.'

'I can deal with my sister,' Linc told her ominously. 'Just like I told you I could do that night.'

She wasn't sure it made her feel any better. It was all

she could do not to let her shoulders sag suddenly, in defeat. And still that steady gaze held hers, threading through and making her feel hot yet unsettled, all at the same time.

'Why are you here, Piper?'

And this was it. She could bottle it, or she could do what she came here to do.

'I came to talk to you,' she told him simply. 'To ask you a question.'

'Fire away,' he invited.

Reaching into her pocket, she retrieved the letter but, though she held it out towards him, he made no move to take it. Clearly, he was expecting her to talk instead.

'Did you send me a job offer to join you at Stoneywell air ambulance when it's up and running next month?'

And she found she was actually holding her breath, waiting for him to answer.

'I did not.'

It took her a moment to realise that the crashing sound was only in her head.

She should have realised that it had only been her imagination that Linc would still want her. Miss her.

Regret sliced through her.

'Of course you didn't,' she stumbled on, wishing she were anywhere but here, making an even bigger spectacle of herself.

But at least she knew now. She could put that ghost to rest.

'I should… I'll go now.'

'But I knew it about it,' he announced, halting her in her retreat. 'And you aren't asking the right question.'

'The right question?'

He pushed himself off the motorbike and sauntered, too casually, towards her. She could only watch, paralysed. Her throat feeling suddenly parched.

'How does a letter like that get sent out without board approval? Without every member of the board knowing about it?'

Hope jolted in her chest. Kickstarting like an old engine with a faltering battery, but starting all the same.

'How does a job offer like that get sent out without board approval?' she rasped.

'It doesn't.' Linc shrugged.

The silence was almost crushing as it wound around Piper's brain.

'It doesn't? So, you knew? And your brother knew? And…'

'And Sara knew. She sends her apologies, by the way. Grudging and sheepish though they may be, she has finally accepted that her meddling caused this latest debacle.'

'I can't see your sister apologising for anything.' Piper shook her head. 'If anyone knows her own mind, it's Lady Sara—'

'Sara is acutely aware that we all have our secrets,' Linc cut her off, and there was something in the way he said it that made Piper stop. 'She just forgot that salient fact for a while. Call it the noise of her impending nuptials, but she is far more herself now it's all over. She will tell you that in person, if and when you decide you're ready to meet her again.'

'Right.' Piper pursed her lips, not sure she could quite believe that. 'Nevertheless, I know you don't want to hear it again, but I really am sorry about what my sister did.'

'You should have stuck around to tell me that at the time.'

'I was going to,' she admitted, before she could censure herself. Another detail she hadn't intended to just blurt out.

But the intent look that overtook his angular features stole any other words from her mouth.

'Were you, Piper? You didn't leave the moment I walked out of the door to the wedding?'

'Of course not,' she cried, though perhaps she should have, had she been a more honourable woman. 'I wanted to stay and talk to you. But then the newspapers came out the next morning, and my sister's story splashed all over them…'

'I would hardly call a half-story buried in a middle page *splashed all over them.*'

'No.' She flicked her tongue out over her suddenly dry lips. 'Right. But still, I was ashamed. I didn't think you'd believe I had nothing to do with the piece.'

'Is that really how little you think of me?' he challenged her, a dark frown clouding his maddening, beautiful face.

Something—she didn't care to name what it was— sloshed around inside her.

Had she really thought he wouldn't even hear her out? Or was that just the excuse she'd told herself? The only thing that helped her to push away from her true feelings—the fact that she was in love with Linc.

After all, the only reason she had even been at the wedding rehearsal dinner had been to play at being his fake girlfriend because settling down was the last thing Linc wanted to do.

'I was supposed to be there to make people think you were ready to settle down and return to Oakenfeld. The idea was to get the board members on side. I knew that story could only hurt and there would be no coming back from it.'

'Do you really think Raf and I didn't have a back-up plan?' Linc stepped forward abruptly.

Before she could react, or step back, his palm was cupping her cheek, and moving away wasn't an option. If the entire world had just rocked on its foundations, she wouldn't have been more shocked.

'Linc…'

'You were there because I wanted you there.' His husky voice scraped over her. 'I wanted them to meet you, whatever excuses I may have told you—told myself—at the beginning.'

'You don't mean that,' she managed, but she wasn't sure how.

'I know what I mean, Legs.'

It wasn't just his words that swirled within her chest, making her feel…lighter, and more hopeful, than she thought she'd felt in a long time—perhaps ever. No, more than what he was saying, it was the way that he was looking at her. The intensity of the expression in his gunmetal-grey eyes.

The same expression he'd worn that last night they'd shared, when he'd lifted himself wordlessly above her in bed, their gazes locked as though nothing could tear them apart, and then he'd buried himself so deep inside her that she hadn't known where she'd ended and he'd begun.

Her heart slammed into her chest wall as every fibre of her screamed out to listen. To stop being so hell-bent on protecting herself that she turned her back on something this incredible.

But it wasn't that easy.

'You can't,' she rasped out, finally finding the strength to step back. Away.

But the space didn't make Piper feel better. It just left her feeling empty. Bereft.

'Why can't I?'

And he actually sounded…amused. But how could that be right?

'We're from two entirely different worlds. It wouldn't work. *We* wouldn't work.'

'We're from the same world, you and I.'

'Hardly.' She snorted. 'You're the son of a duke, and I'm the daughter of a woman who was once accused of killing her husband. No matter how false it is, it's one of those things that I don't think will ever go away. You said it yourself.'

'Then we'll find a way to turn it around to our advantage.'

'You can't. Your family don't need the scandal. You told me that, too.'

'My family can handle it. Or *would have* had it been necessary. As it was, the couple of journalists who visited Oakenfeld looking to follow up on your sister's story ended up digging up the fact that you and I used to serve together.'

'Oh.'

'Indeed.' Linc pulled a grim expression. 'They started talking about us as war heroes, which made the board prick up its collective ears. Apparently, they'd never considered using me in that way to enhance the Oakenfeld name.'

'I see,' she managed, not sure whether she really saw at all.

'But even if they hadn't felt that way, it would have been a sorry state if standing up for an abuse survivor like your mother—like you—brought my family scandal,' Linc growled. 'And if it had done, it wouldn't matter because it's the right thing to do.'

'Actually, I spoke to my mother after that newspaper story came out.' Piper almost giggled at the shock of what she was about to say. 'She told me that she was tired of hiding away. Sick of still feeling like she was my father's victim after all these years.'

'Is that so?' Linc arched an eyebrow.

'She said it was almost a relief that my sister had finally done something. That she'd been waiting for some kind of attack all these years and now it had finally come, but no one who knows her seems to care. Some don't even realise it's our family, and those who do have told her how brave and inspirational they think she is.'

'So your mother is happy?' Linc pressed. 'I ask because there's one of the old estate keeper's cottages available, which Sara said she would be more than happy to renovate for your mother and brother. Her way of trying to prove she's sorry.'

'That's…surprisingly sweet of her,' Piper managed. 'Thank you. But my mother is happy where she is. She feels she has people around her who genuinely care for her, and for my brother. She told me that if the story has done anything, it has shown her the kind of good people her friends are—and that she hoped I have the same.'

'So your sister's plan has backfired on all fronts,' Linc mused.

Piper nodded jerkily.

'So it would seem.'

'Yet, even if it hadn't, I would have still been there for you, Piper. I would have stood side by side with you, because I care about you.'

'You care about me.' She heard the torture in her own voice, but that couldn't be helped.

She wanted to hear more. *Needed to.*

'I…care for you, too, Linc.'

Except that wasn't the word she meant to use. Not at all. 'Linc…'

'As for our different backgrounds, which you seem so hung up about, it doesn't matter. You and I are more alike than you seem to want to admit; we both chose an army life because we thought we could make a difference. We each chose Helimed for the same reason. We're more right for each other than anyone else I know—our different backgrounds don't change that fact.'

'I know,' she muttered, not sure what else to say.

'I hope you do.'

Without warning, he smoothly closed the remainder of the gap between them again. Piper held her breath, waiting for him to reach his palm out to her cheek as before but he didn't. Instead, she found her own hands had crept up and were lying on his chest, though she didn't recall moving.

Clearly her body knew things her head was still denying.

'I love you, Piper Green,' he told her soberly. 'I think I've loved you from the first moment I met you.'

'That was lust,' she croaked, but he shook his head.

'It was love. You were strong, and fearless, and I loved your dry sense of humour from the get-go. Though I'm not denying there was a healthy dose of lust in there, too. Denying it these past few years hasn't helped.'

'You're mistaken,' Piper whispered. But it was crazy how badly she wanted to believe him. 'It was just some silly attraction fuelled by that interrupted kiss. If we'd slept together that night, then it would have all fizzled away years ago and last week would never have happened.'

'You and I both know that's a lie. Nothing would have fizzled away, no matter how many times we slept with each other. Though we weren't the same people back then that we are now. We each had our pasts to deal with, and we needed to come to terms with that in our own time.'

And, for some reason, it was that that made Piper smile the most.

'You're saying we were too immature back then, *Patch*?'

'I would never say that out loud,' he replied dryly.

'I love you, Linc.'

The words were out before she could stop them. But then she repeated them because it felt better than she could ever have imagined to finally be able to admit it. To him, to herself, out loud.

'I love you, too,' he growled, cupping her face in his hands. 'You make me a better man. The man I think I always thought I couldn't be. You make me want the life I have tried to shun, because, with you at my side, I know I can still make a difference.'

He lowered his mouth to hers and finally, *finally*, as he kissed her for what felt like entire, glorious lifetimes, they found their way back to each other.

And when they surfaced at last, with Piper clinging to her lord as they stared at each other in wonder, he reached out and took something from the rucksack at his feet.

'Marry me, Piper.'

She wasn't sure she kept breathing.

For a long moment, she gazed at the stunning ring that seemed to wink at her from its antique box.

'You had that in your bag?'

'I was coming on my way to see you tonight, when I spotted your car hiding over in that corner.'

It took everything she had to try to think straight.

'It's too soon...your family,' she murmured. 'We should wait to see if everything dies down for your brother.'

'Raf can handle himself,' Linc growled. 'He told me so himself. As for waiting, you and I have waited for years.'

It was as if he was echoing the thoughts in her head.

'I want you now, Piper. As my wife, my partner, the mother of my children.'

'I want that too,' she breathed.

'Then marry me.'

'Yes.' She nodded. 'Yes, of course I'll marry you.'

And she watched wordlessly as he slipped the magnificent ring out of the box and onto her finger.

'We can have it resized if it doesn't fit.'

'It fits perfectly,' Piper whispered. 'Like it was meant to be. It's stunning.'

'It's a three-and-a-half-carat marquise-cut diamond that belonged to my great-grandmother. Now it's yours.'

'And now you're mine.' She laughed, as a sort of frothy, fizzy happiness seemed to bubble up inside her, filling her with joy.

It was a revelation. It made her feel as if she was finally home.

* * * * *

MENDING THE ER DOC'S HEART

SUSAN CARLISLE

MILLS & BOON

To Josie, the granddaughter of my heart. I love you!

CHAPTER ONE

A CHILD'S SHRIEK ripped through the air at the other end of the grocery store aisle. Izzy Lane's heart jumped. The box of tea she'd touched fell to the floor, bringing down five others. Her head whipped toward the sound. What was going on? Was the child hurt?

As a pediatric nurse, that was always her first thought. Prepared to help, she looked down the aisle to see what the difficulty might be. No problem there. All she saw was a young boy of about three sitting in a cart, flailing his hands and kicking his feet until the cart rocked. As her heart rate returned to a regular pace, her concern turned to worry over the boy toppling the cart.

A tall solid-shouldered man wearing a knit golf shirt had his head down, talking to the child. "Shush, Henry. We talked about this before we came in."

The boy wailed, "I want Sugar Loops."

"You need to pick out another cereal." The man glanced at her, concern on his face, his mouth drawn into a tight line. Picking up a box, he showed the child. "What about these?"

"Sugar Loops!" the boy demanded at the top of his voice.

Izzy shook her head with a wry smile. It wasn't going well for the dad. She'd had her fair share of those moments in her line of work. Sometimes there were behavioral issues that weren't immediately obvious to others. Maybe that was the case here.

Her chest squeezed. She had to admit the boy was cute. With his cotton-white hair, full cheeks and big eyes. Despite his tantrum, Izzy wished she had a child who could give her a hard time. She'd believed that would happen with Richard until he'd cheated on her. For years he'd led her on, getting her to pay for his school by telling her he loved her. He had her believing he wanted to marry her and then start a family. Instead she'd just been used. Now that dream had been shattered.

Her attention returned to the jumble on the floor. The corner of her mouth lifted in exasperation. She had a mess to clean up. Setting her armload of items down, Izzy went to her knees and picked up the tea-bag boxes replacing them on the shelf.

Another yell vibrated around her. Izzy shuttered and watched with a quirk to her mouth as the man handed the sugary cereal to the child. She muttered, "Frustrated parents will do anything to survive."

While she'd been busy, the man and boy had started toward the front of the building. They moved alongside her. Her head jerked up to meet startling silver eyes.

Izzy cleared her throat. Had the man heard what she'd said?

He continued to watch her as if he knew she'd been focused on them. "Sorry we were so loud."

Izzy remained snared in his look, embarrassed that he might think she was judging him. "Not a problem."

Relief filled her as he moved on. She turned and watched him go. Tall, with a hint of gray at his temples, he looked as if he'd carried a burden on his shoulders for too long. Izzy shook her head. Tired from moving to a new town and learning a new job, she was ready to get home. Such as it was, being just a hotel room. Her own issues were enough without being concerned about a stranger and his problems. The current challenge consisted of cleaning up around her and paying for her groceries. She gathered her items into her arms again.

Making it to the checkout lanes, she went through the self-checkout while the man and the boy were in a line for a person at the cash register. A loud complaint came from behind her, and she didn't have to turn around to know it was the same little boy, Henry. "Candy."

She glanced over her shoulder to see the man patiently listening to the demand. If he were her child… Sadness swamped her. But he wasn't.

Izzy sent her items through the self-checkout and bagged them. The man and his child headed out to the parking lot. The noise level lowered by a half. She could have sworn a collective sigh came from everyone. It hadn't taken much to put the late afternoon Atlanta crowd on edge.

Finished with her business, she started toward her car. She'd chosen the first grocery store she'd come to on her way to and from Atlanta Children's Hospital from the efficiency hotel.

A giggle and an expletive drew her attention to the parking row one over from where her car sat. The man from earlier was picking up apples rolling across the asphalt. Henry sat in the buggy parked against the late model SUV.

The man really was struggling. Her heart went out to him. He needed help. Izzy hurried between the cars toward him, bending down to pick up apples.

He looked up from where he crouched, trying to pull an apple out from under a car tire. The man had the most beautiful eyes. They were like looking at quicksilver with a serving of intelligence in the depths. It was as if he could see more of her than she wanted him to. She blinked, registering the weary look on his face.

"Here you go." With a smile, she handed him a couple of apples.

He looked at her as he opened a bag with gratitude. She dropped the apples in. Henry squealed.

"I'll stand with him while you finish up here." She walked over to the boy. "Hi, Henry."

He settled and watched her with wide eyes.

"Do you have a dog?" Izzy asked.

The boy shook his head.

"How about a cat?" Izzy made sure to keep a hand on the cart so it wouldn't move.

Henry shook his head fast enough to make his eyes wobble.

Izzy couldn't help but grin.

The father joined them and put the bag of fruit in the vehicle. "Thanks for your help." He ruffled Henry's hair and took him out of the cart, giving him a hug. "Next time I'm going to make sure the bag is tied before I let you hold the apples."

Henry looked at the man with simple adoration.

A sweet sadness filled Izzy. There was obvious love between the two. She'd hoped to experience that with Richard and their child. Instead Richard had used her, thinking of only what he wanted. Izzy had no intention of ever getting caught in a one-way relationship ever again.

The man smiled, which was almost as striking as his eyes. "Thanks. You must think I'm a rubbish dad."

"You're welcome," Izzy said with a smile, "and no, I didn't. Anyone can have a bad day."

She started toward her car, glancing back at the man. She would likely never see him again.

* * *

Dr. Chad McCain pulled out his phone. He was needed in the ER. "I've got to go."

He left the hospital conference room without a backward look. After all, he'd gone to school to help children, not sit in meetings. He'd been on holiday for a week and was ready to return to work. He pushed through the double doors.

A nurse stepped beside him. "It's a boy with internal injuries from an automobile accident. He's in trauma one."

Chad didn't slow down. Yet everything in him wanted to turn around and go the other way. Instead he put his head down and forged forward. After Henry had been injured in the car accident that had killed Nan, his wife and Henry's mother, vehicle cases were hard for Chad to face. All he could see was his injured son, pale as death, laying on a too-large gurney.

His staff knew his history and always tried to warn him of what was coming. With a fortitude that came from who knows where, other than knowing a child needed him and that he had the skills to help, Chad strode into the trauma examination room. He prepared to go to work by pulling his stethoscope out of the pocket of his lab coat. The space was already filled with nurses and EMTs.

"We have a ten-year-old white male with a compound fracture to the left femur, a head laceration, problems breathing and possible internal injuries."

The voice came from the side and just behind him. It wasn't one he recognized as one of the usual nurses, yet it wasn't unfamiliar. He didn't have time to look and see who it was. With everyone having a mask on, he might not recognize her anyway. "Let me see what's going on here."

A space opened for him to move in next to the patient. With easy practice, he placed the ear tips of the stethoscope in his ears and the bell on the boy's chest. The patient's heartbeat was fast. Chad glanced at the monitor. And missing beats. He positioned the bell on the boy's side. His breathes were shallow. Chad moved the stethoscope down to the boy's midsection. The gurgling sounds indicated internal injuries.

"Call the OR. This child needs abdominal surgery ASAP. The Ortho will have to wait. Let's get a set of X-rays."

"They're on the way."

There was that voice again. He just couldn't place it. "I want a blood panel, antibiotics and fluid running. Vitals?"

One of the nurses called out the numbers.

Beep, beep, beep…

The high-pitched sound originated from the monitor. The noise shocked everyone around him into action.

"The patient isn't breathing," Chad stated. "Start CPR." He placed his hands on the child's chest as a nurse placed a mask with a breathing balloon attached over his month. She squeezed in a rhythm.

"BP thirty over ten," someone in the group called.

"Crash cart!" Chad snapped without missing a beat.

"Here," the nurse whose voice he didn't know announced.

"Paddles?" He turned. His look met those of the nurse holding them. *Her!* He tensed. The woman from the store who'd helped him with the apples. What was she doing in his department? He felt mortified that she should have seen him at his worst, dealing with one of Henry's tantrums.

The nurse's eyes widened over the top of her mask. She recognized him as well. Chad took the paddles without hesitation, prepared to shock the boy back to life. Hovering them over the child's bare chest, he called, "Clear."

Everyone took a step back before Chad placed a paddle beside the heart and the other on the boy's side. "One, two, three."

With a beep from the machine, the boy's body came off the bed. As quickly as he turned to give the paddles back to the "apple" nurse, another nurse closed in to check the patient's vitals.

Chad glanced at the monitor, apprehension making his muscles tight. "Let's go again." The "apple" nurse had the paddles ready when he turned to her. He followed the same procedure. This time the monitor issued a steady beat. With a heaving sigh, he gave the paddles back.

"Okay, people." Relief sounded in his words. "We have him back. Now let's keep him alive long enough to get him to surgery. Let the OR know we're on the way. Then notify Ortho they're going to need to take care of the leg."

"Already done," the voice that belonged to the "apple" nurse said.

Chad nodded. Whoever she was, the woman was an efficient nurse. One he'd be glad to work with any day. He just cringed at the thought of how she must see him.

He checked the monitor. The boy's blood pressure remained low. "He's still in trouble. Give him two liters of oxygen. Let's get that blood work drawn, X-rays done and fluids in so this boy can be off to surgery ASAP. We don't have time to waste here."

Chad again listened to the boy's chest. He pursed his lips. His breathing remained shallow. It would be his guess that he'd broken some ribs as well.

The "apple" nurse said, "They're ready for him in the OR."

Relief washed over him. He accepted death could be a part of his job, but he didn't like letting it win any more than he had to. Between almost losing his son and the death of Nan, he knew well how special each day was. It made him a better doctor and father. He was determined to keep death at bay as often as humanly possible.

He remained with the patient until the surgery nurses came to get him. With that done, Chad started out of the trauma room, with one thought in his mind: Who was this new nurse?

Izzy felt more than saw the doctor follow her to the circular unit desk. Never in a million years would she have guessed he'd show up in the ER. She'd been as surprised and mortified to see "grocery" doc as his eyes indicated he'd been to see her. This was the last place she'd expected to see him.

"Imagine my surprise when you turned up in my ER today." His deep graveled voice came from behind her.

Izzy turned to face him. "No more than mine."

His brow rose. "At least here you won't have to pick up my apples."

She grinned. "I hope not."

"Henry and I didn't make a very good first impression. I'm sorry about that."

His expression reminded her of a sheepish little boy's. "Not a problem."

He waited to speak for a moment. "You ever have one of those days when things just don't go your way?"

Like the day she came home to find Richard in their bed with another woman. "More often than I'd like to admit."

"That day in the grocery was one of those days. Anyway, it's a small world. By the way, I'm Dr. Chad McCain. Lead ER doc."

"I'm Elizabeth Lane. New head staff nurse."

He gave her a wry grin. "You won't hold my grocery-buying skills against me, will you? I assure you, my medical skill are far superior."

She made a noise in her throat. "I'm glad to hear it."

Izzy watched him walk away toward an exam room. Taking a seat behind the curved unit desk, she logged into the computer and pulled up a chart. A tech and a nurse sat not far away.

"I see you finally met our Dr. McCain. He was in rare form this morning," the tech said.

"I guess he was." Izzy wouldn't make any comment that might get back to the doctor.

"Yep." The nurse clicked a key. "He's great, isn't he?"

Another nurse shrugged. "He's one of our favorites around here."

"It must be hard on him, handling these types of cases." The clerk passed the nurse a piece of paper.

"I'm sure seeing a boy injured in a car wreck reminds him of almost losing his own son in one. But he remains professional no matter what the case looks like. He holds it together somehow."

Izzy wouldn't ask what they meant. What had or hadn't happened with Dr. McCain wasn't her business. She wouldn't want anybody to share her history as gossip. Thankfully she could keep her gullibility where Richard had been concerned to herself. She'd made a change to a new town, a new hospital and a new job. She wanted a clean start. Not to see the look of pity on everyone's faces because they knew what Richard had done to her.

One patient after another kept the ER busy right through the afternoon. It wasn't until then that the patient care slowed enough for her to go to her shoebox-sized office down a short hall off the main part of the department. She had a meeting the next morning to prepare for.

As head staff nurse, she'd spent most of her time the past week reviewing how the department operated. Part of her job was to see that the Emergency Department ran smoothly and the doctors had what they needed when they needed it.

As a pediatric nurse, her duties also included assisting during acute injuries or when a member of the nursing staff was out, otherwise she handled the scheduling of nurses and reporting of data to the administration. She liked the patient-care aspect far more than the paper pushing.

Two days later, while Izzy was deep into material she had been busy building into a presentation one evening, there was a sharp knock at her office door. Her head popped up in surprise.

Dr. McCain stood in her doorway. He cocked his head toward the main part of the department. "I need your help. We have a burn patient coming in. I want someone with me who has experience."

Izzy pushed back her chair and followed him out the door. "How do you know I have burn experience?"

"Checked up on you."

"Do you check up on all the new nurses?" She wasn't sure how she felt about that.

"No, but I made an exception with you."

He must have read on her vita she had worked six months in a burn unit. Apparently she measured up. She hadn't felt lately as if she did. At least not in her personal life. "What do we have coming in?"

"A six-year-old with a full-thickness burn to his back, arm and hand." His words were tight, surrounded by anger.

"Do I want to know how it happened?"

He glanced at her, his mouth in a straight line. "No, you don't."

Izzy winced. She hated these cases. They stayed with her too long.

As they passed the unit desk, the tech said, "ETA three

minutes," and handed them each a mask. Controlling infection with a burn was paramount.

Dr. McCain's stride lengthened, and Izzy hurried to keep pace. They reached the large automatic glass doors to the sound of the ambulance siren. It abruptly went off, indicating the ambulance was turning into the hospital. Once it was backing up to the door, Izzy and Dr. McCain hurried out to meet it.

She could smell burnt skin before she saw the boy. The EMT lifted the gurney out of the ambulance. The boy lay on his stomach with his face turned to the side. He was pale as the sheet that lay over him. It was held up by a towel rolled at his side so his skin wasn't touched.

Dr. McCain already had his stethoscope off and on the uninjured side of the boy's chest as they walked inside the unit.

"Trauma room three," Izzy told the EMTs.

An EMT started his report. "Six-year-old white male. Unresponsive. He has morphine on board to manage the pain. He passed out halfway here. The cause of the burn was boiling water down the right back, right arm and hand. Full-thickness burns. Injury happened forty-five minutes ago. Respirations are slow and heart rate low but steady."

Izzy swallowed hard. Nothing about the report sounded positive except it wasn't a grease burn, where the cleaning became more difficult. Still the boy would carry the scars from this day forever.

"This area needs to be a sterile as possible." Dr. McCain stopped outside the room and quickly pulled on a paper gown and plastic gloves. Izzy followed suit.

In the room Izzy hooked the boy up to monitors. Other staff entered, gowned and gloved, going to work beside her and Dr. McCain. Each knew their assigned job. Izzy relinquished the monitor setup to the other nurses and techs. Instead she turned to help Dr. McCain remove the ice packs placed on the burnt areas, then picked up the sheet covering the skin and handed it over to him, both of them careful not to touch the boy's skin.

Izzy winced at the red angry burn.

Dr. McCain didn't slow down his orders. "I need a CBC and full panel here. Also an electrolyte level. Temp?"

"Ninety-six," Izzy reported.

"Turn on the heater. People, it's going to get warm in here. Nurse Lane, let's put a catheter in, check fluid outflow. We also need a good central line in place with fluids and antibiotics running."

Over the next few minutes, she worked with Dr. McCain to get the catheter placed by rolling the boy toward her while Dr. McCain worked at his front. She placed the central line in the boy's unburnt arm. Another nurse saw to hanging and starting the fluids.

Despite all the movement of him and around him, the boy remained comatose.

Dr. McCain spoke to her. "It's time to get him bandaged and up to ICU. We'll leave the rolled towels where they are and let the saline run into them."

Izzy spoke to a tech. "We're going to need more towels in here. Lay them under the bed to catch the runoff."

A nurse pushed a cart with bottles of saline on it beside Izzy. She opened and handed Dr. McCain a bottle. He slowly pored the sterile water over the burn site. The blistered area made Izzy cringe. She lifted the boy's hand and arm with her palm, being careful not to touch any injured area.

Dr. McCain continued to go through bottles of saline, making sure the areas were all clean. In several places, he removed the dead skin, making sure the pink skin below showed. "Now for the silver sulfadiazine."

Izzy handed him a large scrub with a sponge on the end filled with medicine.

His eyes met hers over the mask as he nodded. When that one sponge had been used, he handed it to Izzy and she gave him another. Slowly and meticulously Dr. Cain applied the medicine. She couldn't help but be impressed. He worked efficiently, carefully and compassionately as he gently spread the ointment.

"You ready to start bandaging?" He looked at her.

"I am." She picked up a large roll of gauze and moved around beside him.

Dr. McCain wrapped the gauze while she saw to it that he had what he needed. A few times she held it in places as he positioned the next swathe.

"Talk to me, people. I need to know temp, heart rate, respirations, urine output. Someone needs to notify ICU we're sending them a patient. Also get Dr. Huff on the phone. I need to talk to him about this boy."

In an organized order, different staff members reported to Chad as he and she continued wrapping.

With bandages in place, Chad said, "Let's get this boy upstairs."

A couple of techs and a nurse pushed the patient out to the elevator.

"You did good work in there, Dr. McCain." Izzy gathered up supplies.

"Make it Chad. You weren't half bad yourself." He smiled.

Izzy's stomach dipped. The man had an extra nice smile. "You can call me Izzy."

"Izzy Lane." He looked off as if in serious thought. "It makes me think of the Beatles song 'Penny Lane.'" He hummed a few lines and grinned.

She quirked one side of her mouth. "Yeah, I've heard that before."

His face straightened and he looked at the clock. "Got to go. Henry's waiting. By the way, thanks again. Great job." He headed toward the exit, notes from the song "Penny Lane" following him.

They washed over her like a gentle breeze. She and Chad had apparently formed an unlikely team.

On Friday evening after work, Izzy stopped by a local restaurant for supper before she went home to her lonely hotel room. All she wanted tonight was to sit down to a meal and have a peaceful weekend. It had been an interesting couple of weeks.

Her first one had involved more paperwork and study of policy and procedure and meetings than actual administrating in the ER. The second week had been busy, exciting and challenging. Just learning people's names and personalities had been a full-time job. Most of the staff had been welcoming and helpful. Best of all, they showed her no pity.

She entered the local burger restaurant a nurse had recommended. Looking around, she winced. There wasn't an empty table in the room. So much for her meal out. Apparently fast food would be her only option this time of day.

A large hand waving in the air drew her attention. It was Chad with Henry sitting in a booth along the side wall. Her eyes widened when he waved her his way.

She approached the table. Going through a drive-through and eating in her hotel room alone had no appeal.

Chad asked as he stood, "Would you like to sit with us?"

She and Chad had tentatively found their way working with patients, but she wasn't quite sure they were ready for social situations. Izzy looked past him to Henry who had a fork and a knife in his hand and beat the ends on the table.

This wasn't her plan for a restful evening, but how could she politely excuse herself?

"Thank you. That would be nice." Izzy slid into the booth.

Chad sat next to Henry, who was in a booster seat on his side of the booth. "Henry, sit down please. This is Ms. Lane. We met her at the grocery store. She works with me."

"Hi, Henry." Izzy settled on her seat. "Your wife won't mind me being here?"

"I'm a widower." Chad's tone came out flat with no sadness, but a note of being resigned to the status.

"Oh, I'm sorry I didn't know." How sad he had no one and Henry didn't have his mother. Still, relief washed through Izzy. She'd never do to another woman what had been done to her, and felt relieved she wasn't keeping him from a partner. Being faithful and loyal were important in a committed relationship. She took them seriously.

With a wide-eyed look, Henry watched her, then went back to waving the silverware around.

Chad caught Henry's arms. "Henry. It's time to settle down."

Henry did so but began to beat the utensils on the table again. Chad removed them from his hands and Henry yelled a protest.

Everyone in the restaurant stopped and turned toward them.

"Henry!" Chad hissed. "Shh." He placed his hand on the boy's shoulder.

Henry grabbed for the fork and knife, but Chad took them away, placing them out of his reach.

Henry squealed.

"Henry, would you like to draw me a picture?" Izzy picked up the coloring sheet and crayons that were on the table. She pushed the sheet toward Henry, then handed him one crayon.

The boy scribbled wildly.

Izzy placed her hand over his. "There's not another page so you need to make this one last."

Henry's eyes widened in surprise. She removed her hand. He went back to coloring but more like he should for his age.

Chad gave her an appreciative smile and relaxed in his seat. "You've done that more than once."

"Yeah, a few times. I have nieces and nephews. A little redirection almost always works." Izzy wished she could say she'd done the same with her own children.

"Kids take a lot of energy," Chad said.

"They do, especially after a long day at work." But she'd have liked to have that feeling of exhaustion.

A server came to their table. He handed Chad and her menus.

Izzy ordered her drink.

Henry's voice rose. Chad placed his hand on the boy's arm.

Chad was trying with his son. It must be difficult to discipline when he thought about almost losing his child in a wreck. Izzy leaned across the table. "You're being so good, Henry, that I'm going to give you another crayon."

Henry's attention remained on her as he took the crayon.

Chad shook his head and looked at her in wonder. "Miracle worker. Your children must be the best-behaved around."

Izzy cringed. A band tightened around her chest. She'd wanted children. Had even missed some of her best years waiting to have them. "I don't have any children."

"Well, you've missed your calling." Chad grinned, making him more handsome.

That band eased some. "I hope to have some one day."

Concern filled his eyes. "I didn't see anything about a Mr. Lane on your vita. Is there one somewhere?"

"No."

The waiter returned with her drink and asked to take their order. Chad ordered a hamburger plate for him and a child-size for Henry. She requested a large salad.

"You need to try the burgers," Chad suggested.

"I'm afraid I couldn't eat all of it." Her appetite hadn't been the same since she'd left Richard.

"I still recommend a burger. You can always take the leftovers home. I promise it's great."

Izzy looked at the server. "I'll have the burger plate then."

Chad grinned. "I don't think you'll be disappointed."

"I'm not as afraid of being disappointed as I am of not being able to get in my clothes tomorrow."

He studied her a moment. "From what I've seen, you don't have anything to worry about that."

Thought failed her. Was he flirting with her? She looked at Henry. He had stopped coloring. She covered her embarrassment by asking, "May I see your picture?"

Henry pushed the paper toward her.

"This is so pretty. You're doing such a good job." She returned the page to him. Henry went back to his coloring.

Chad looked at her in wonder. "You make it look so easy."

"It's not. I just happen to be lucky that it's working."

"I'm ashamed to say I was too busy building my career to be around as much as I should have been. You know what kind of hours we keep in the ER. I didn't spend as much time with him as his mother. If I had, maybe he'd be better for me."

Guilt at perhaps having judged him washed over Izzy. Now some of his actions with Henry made more sense.

"Even months later we're still learning to live together. We aren't doing a great job of it at the grocery store I'm afraid, but we're surviving."

"It can't be easy. It'll just take time. You have it. Henry is young. You'll both catch on. How long has it been since your wife died?"

"Nan's been gone thirteen months." He mussed Henry's hair. "We're slowly learning to adjust. Most of Henry's behavior can be blamed on me. I indulge him. I realized after Nan was gone she'd done more than her share of parenting. Henry and I have had a major learning curve."

Izzy reached across the table and laid her hand over his for a moment. "I'm sure you've just been doing what you need to do to survive."

"Yeah, something like that." He didn't sound too sure.

The server returned with their meals.

Izzy's brows and voice rose. "Oh, my gosh, look at all this food." She glanced at Chad and found him grinning. "You actually thought I could eat all of this?"

He added ketchup to his plate. "Maybe you'll have to have a take-out container, but I think you'll like the burger." Chad cut Henry's sandwich into four pieces. He asked Henry, "Do you want ketchup to go with your fries?"

Henry nodded.

Chad looked directly at the boy. "I want you to be careful with the ketchup. If you're not, you can't have any more."

Henry eyes turned serious, and he nodded again.

With Henry settled, Chad's attention returned to her. "What brought you to Atlanta? I saw you had been living in Nashville."

Why she'd moved to Atlanta wasn't something she wished to discuss. She had to keep it simple and keep her secrets. "I just needed a change, and the staff nurse job was open. I've been wanting to move up."

"I bet they weren't happy when you left." Chad took a large bite of his burger.

"They weren't." She gave him a weak smile. "It's always nice to be wanted."

Chad could tell Izzy's smile didn't reach her eyes. He knew well what it was to have someone look at him like that. Before the accident that took her from him, Nan had done the same. She had been as saddened by the slowly deteriorating relationship as he. For years she'd felt neglected. He was sorry for that. It hadn't been his intention.

She'd understood the idea of a doctor keeping long hours but hadn't liked the reality. He hadn't either but that was part of the profession. She'd covered her anxiety well until the last few years of her life. They had talked about a divorce at one point but soon learned she was pregnant.

Chad believed children should have both their mother and father together. By that time, he'd seen too many fights between divorced parents when emotions were running high over an injured child. He'd wanted better for Henry. Had wanted the marriage to work. He'd tried harder at the end, but it was too little too late. He hadn't succeeded. It wasn't long before Nan died that he'd learned she was having an affair. Anger and guilt fought to overtake each other, which soon turned to bitterness.

Henry could be a handful. The problem was Chad couldn't bring himself to be tougher on him. He and Nan might have had their issues, but he loved Henry dearly. He'd almost lost Henry in the accident.

Izzy praising Henry brought Chad out of his gloomy thoughts. "You've been doing such a good job. What a big boy you are."

She was great with Henry. He responded to her. She encouraged him to behave and gave him affirmation for doing so. Izzy worked magic as far as he was concerned. "Had you always lived in Nashville?"

Izzy's gaze met his. Intelligence swam in her eyes along with a flicker of weariness and pain. What had happened to put that there?

"I'm Nashville born and raised."

"That must have made it hard to leave." He watched her.

"Yes and no."

"That sounds like a story." One he really wanted to hear for some reason.

"It was just time."

She wasn't going to give him the reason why, and he wouldn't ask directly. It wasn't his business. "I guess you worked at Vanderbilt University Hospital?"

"Actually, I was at St. Vincent out on the west side."

He popped a fry in his mouth. "I know that hospital. It's a good one."

She brightened with pride. "I like to think so."

Izzy wasn't freely giving information. "Then the opportunity opened down here, and you decided to take it?"

"Yes." Izzy sounded as if she was finished with this line of questioning. "It was a good opportunity to make a positive step in my career. This burger really is good by the way."

Her embarrassed look made him smile.

She opened her mouth wide to take a bite. "I'm glad you insisted on me getting it. I can't believe I ate almost all of it."

"I knew you wouldn't be disappointed." He picked up the bill the server left.

When Izzy reached for her purse, Chad said, "I'll get this."

"I don't want you to do that. I barged in on you and Henry. I'm the one who should be paying."

"We were happy to have the company. Weren't we, buddy?" Chad looked at Henry, who had returned to coloring.

Izzy scooted out of the booth. "I'll agree if you promise that next time you'll let me pay."

"Okay." Would there be a next time? Chad hoped there would be. He'd enjoyed his time with Izzy, found her interesting. "Consider it my thanks for helping make me and all the others around us have a peaceful meal."

Izzy chuckled. "You're welcome but I don't think I did anything miraculous."

"It depends on who you ask." He left money on the table, took Henry's hand and their group made their way to the door. He placed his hand at her back to guide her toward it. Izzy stiffened and glanced over her shoulder. Seconds later she relaxed as they stepped through the crowd waiting for seats.

Outside on the sidewalk, Izzy turned to him. "Thank you for the meal." She looked down at Henry. "I enjoyed being with you."

Chad liked the way she included Henry in her thanks.

Henry wrapped his arms around one of Izzy's legs. "I like you."

Izzy went down on a knee and hugged Henry. "I like you too."

For some reason Chad felt jealous of his son. Chad could use a hug as well. He wasn't going to let that happen. "Can we walk you to your car?"

"I'm just over there." She pointed a few cars down. "Have a nice weekend, guys." Izzy waved a hand over her shoulder.

Chad watched Izzy until she was safely in her car. For them having had a slightly awkward start, he had learned to appreciate Izzy's skills in the ER, and now as a friend.

CHAPTER TWO

A WEEK LATER while Izzy sat at the unit desk, one of the nurses asked, "Have you found an apartment yet?"

"I've been looking but I can't find anything that I can afford or is what I want."

Another nurse asked, "Have you tried Garden Greens?"

Izzy nodded. "I called them yesterday. There's nothing until after the university semester ends. Staying in a hotel room is getting old and expensive. I'd really like to find an apartment above someone's garage. Somewhere I could have a little something that's really my own."

"Maybe you could look in Virginia Highlands," the first nurse offered. "Those are older homes with nice yards. A family-type area. A number of them have garages with a room above."

The unit tech swiveled in her chair to face Izzy. "Have you been looking through the ads? Or going online?"

Izzy pushed at her hair. "I've done it all. I just can't seem to find what I want."

The tech picked up the ringing phone. Her face turned serious. "Near-drowning on the way in."

Everyone sobered. Izzy groaned. Those cases were some of the worst. They were never good. The recovery, if there was one, was long and discouraging. They almost always resulted in brain damage.

"I heard," Chad said from right behind them. "Which exam room?"

She watched Chad head toward the double doors to the ambulance bay with the nursing team assigned to him for the day following.

He had made the last week interesting. Any time he passed her in the unit or went by her office door, she heard the tune "Penny Lane." Her immediate impression had been of someone serious, but it turned out he had a sense of humor. Mostly at her expense. More amazing was she didn't mind. It had been a long time since someone had noticed her enough to tease. She'd lived with a man for years who never bothered to tease her or give her a sweet nickname. She and Chad didn't know each other well but he still had her smiling. It was a salve to her battered self-esteem.

Later that afternoon Izzy still had her head buried in paperwork and forms she'd been working on most of the day. A knock at her office door made her look up to see Chad leaning against the door, looking unsure.

"Hey. Am I needed?"

Chad waved her back into her seat.

He moved over to the single metal chair in front of her desk and slumped into it. His knees knocked against her desk, and he sat straighter.

"I have something like one of those rooms above the garage that I heard you were talking about. Except mine is behind the garage."

She wasn't sure how to react to that statement. Was he offering it to her? "You do?"

"I do. It needs some work. I'd have to move a few things around but if you'd like to look at it, you're welcome to."

"Are you offering to let me rent it?"

His eyes met hers. "Yes, isn't that what I said?"

It hadn't been but she had no intention of debating that.

"I suppose it was. If you've been using it, then why would you let me move in?"

"Because you need a place to stay, and I have one."

Did she want to live so close to someone she worked with? Or was it living so close to him? What would the others in the department think if she lived in his backyard? "I don't know."

He rose. "Come look or don't. I just thought I'd offer. You can always be looking for another place. It's better than a hotel room. That I can promise."

Uncertainty filled her but Chad did make the place sound appealing. She needed a home and he had one. What could go wrong? "I can't promise anything, but I'll come check it out."

"I know what you're thinking."

She couldn't imagine he did.

"That you'll have to put up with the noise of a kid. I promise you won't. Ms. Weber will see that he stays out of your hair when I'm not there. I promise we'll respect your privacy."

"That wasn't at all what I was thinking." She grinned, giving him a teasing look. "A little sensitive about Henry's noise level? I like Henry. Who's Ms. Weber?"

"She's an older neighbor who acts as my nanny. And maybe I'm the one who's a little sensitive about Henry." A contrite expression came over his face, giving him a boyish air. He looked away.

"You shouldn't be. He's a nice kid. If you haven't noticed, I work in a children's hospital so therefore I like children. Henry wouldn't be my reason for not taking the apartment, I assure you."

"Just come see the apartment. Then you can decide. Deal?" He put out his hand.

She looked at it for a moment before slipping hers into it.

His larger one enveloped hers. Electricity shot through her all the way to her toes. She mumbled, "Deal," and pulled her hand away.

What was that reaction to Chad? A man she'd only known for a few weeks. One she worked with. It was unnerving at the least. There was no space in her life for those types of feelings. They couldn't be trusted.

On Saturday afternoon Chad watched Izzy pull into his drive. He'd trimmed the grass between the double cement lanes that morning. She parked behind his SUV sitting in front of the garage.

"Come on, Henry. Ms. Izzy is here." Chad smiled as Henry dropped the truck he'd been playing with and started toward the back door.

Izzy climbed out of her car. She drove one of those mini cars his legs wouldn't fit in. Yet it suited her petite body. When had he started noticing her height? Wearing a simple green T-shirt, jeans and sport shoes, she looked more like a college student than the woman in charge at the hospital. Izzy had seamlessly blended in with the staff and quickly become invaluable to the department. And him. He found himself wanting her at his side during the most difficult cases.

Chad went down his back steps. Reaching the yard, he turned to find Henry pushing the screen door as far as he could before he let it go. Chad winced when it slammed shut. "Henry, I've asked you a thousand times not to slam the door."

The boy ran past him straight to Izzy and wrapped his arms around her leg.

Chad hurried after him, fearing Henry might knock Izzy down.

She rocked on her heels and gave him a hug. "Hi, Henry."

Chad grabbed her elbow, steadying her. A shot of aware-ness went through him before he let her go. Izzy's gaze met his as she patted Henry's back.

"Play with me?" Henry asked, looking at Izzy with ad-oration.

"I can't right now. Maybe later. You dad needs to show me something. I'm going to see if I'd like to live here."

Henry looked at Chad with an expression that reminded him of Nan. Pain, quickly followed by anger of what had been and what was not shot through Chad.

"Ms. Izzy live with us?"

A stricken expression came over Izzy's face as she let go of Henry.

Chad hurried to correct his son. He placed a hand on Henry's shoulder. "No, she'll live in the apartment. Let's show it to her?"

Henry straightened his shoulders and took Izzy's hand. He marched along the stone path around the back of the garage.

Chad followed. "I don't think I got to say hello. I'll try to control Henry's exuberance in the future."

She smiled. "Hi. It's nice to have someone glad to see me."

Chad had been looking forward to Izzy's visit as well for some reason. He just hadn't shown it as clearly as Henry. The question was why? He enjoyed being around her. Teas-ing her. He'd dated some since Nan but none of the women had captured his attention as Izzy did. She was attractive, but others were equally so—there was just something about Izzy that appealed to him. Not that he would act on it. That wouldn't be fair to her. He would never make prom-ises again.

Henry let go of Izzy's hand. He waited on her to open

the door before he stomped into the room. Soon she and Chad joined him.

Chad looked around the area, seeing it as she must. It was large with a partition built in one corner that created privacy for the bathroom. The kitchenette was stationed in the front corner. The rest was open space with a bed on one wall and an old leather couch and chair facing a large picture window that looked out to the backyard. The place looked neglected and worn.

He cringed. It really wasn't inviting. He'd be shocked if Izzy agreed to stay. "I'm afraid it's nothing fancy. If you do want to rent, you're welcome to do anything you wish with it. I haven't been back here in a long time. I'd forgotten how rough it looked."

She laughed. "You really shouldn't go into selling real estate."

He quirked one corner of his mouth. "You'd be welcome to share the yard. First come, first serve on the garage. I can also promise you privacy. Am I doing better?"

"Those are selling points." Izzy grinned and stepped over to the kitchen area. She stood beside the L-shaped counter with the sink on one side, the stove on the other.

He joined her but stayed on his side of the counter. "I'm afraid there's not a dishwasher."

"That's not a problem. There're only a few dishes when there's just one person."

"If you want to do any gourmet cooking, you're welcome to use my kitchen." He loved to share a homemade meal. It had been too long since he'd eaten something he hadn't heated up in a microwave.

"What you have here should be fine for anything I cook." She wandered over to the other corner and peeked into the bathroom.

"I know the couch and chair aren't much. Of course,

you're welcome to bring any of your own furniture. I can get rid of this—" he touched the top of the sofa "—if you'd rather have something else." Nan had hated his college furniture so much she'd banished it to the apartment as soon as she could. He'd always liked the set.

Izzy continued to walk around the room. "I love leather furniture. The chair looks perfect to curl up in." She went to stand in front of the picture window. "This view is wonderful. The big oak tree is perfect. It's like living in a treehouse. Swiss Family Robinson's house at Disney World has always been my favorite."

"That's what you'll think until the nuts start falling. And the sun streaming in wakes you in the morning."

"I'll just put up some blinds or curtains." She looked at him with a crease lining her forehead. "If that's okay with you?"

"Sure. Do anything you want to with the place." Noticing a dirty spot on the wall, he said, "I should have given it a coat of paint before I offered it to you."

"I can do that. Is egg-white okay with you?" She studied the space.

"I don't want you have to do that." The woman was a dynamo in a small package.

"I don't mind. I like fixing places up." Her eyes shined brightly as if she were already making plans.

He opened his hands palms up. "Then help yourself."

She continued to circle the space. "There are even shelves for books. This is much nicer than a hotel room. Thank you for offering it to me. I'll take it."

Chad was aware he had no business being so excited about her agreement to live there. What was he doing? He was going to be her landlord and she was going to be his tenant. They were colleagues. That was it. Still, she was a breath of fresh air in his stale world.

Her sad eyes got to him. He wanted to know what she was thinking when she looked at Henry the way she did. There was just something about Izzy that made him want to get to know her better. Discover the secrets he suspected she hid behind those large dark eyes. He couldn't—wouldn't—let his thoughts or actions go beyond friendship. "Henry and I promise not to intrude on you."

She waved that idea away. "How much is the rent?"

He told her a figure. Her eyes narrowed. "That sounds like too little, but I'll take it."

"Good."

"When's a good time for me to move in?"

He grinned as he stopped Henry from jumping on the sofa. "Whenever you're ready."

"Then I'll go to the hotel and get my belongings now. I'll be back in an hour or so. Is the water running and electricity on?" She'd morphed into the business mode he recognized from working with her at the hospital.

"The water is, and by the time you get back, I'll have flipped the switch for the electricity."

She started toward the door. "Good. I'd prefer not to start my time here living by candlelight."

Chad could only imagine how lovely she would look by candlelight. An image he shouldn't be picturing. These thoughts couldn't continue. Why were they there anyway? After Nan, he'd closed his heart off. He wouldn't allow a woman to crush him like she had done. Life was too short to live in misery. After all, he'd learned pretty harshly that he wasn't good at relationships.

"Come on, Henry," he called. The boy had found one of his old toys near the sofa. "We've got a new tenant and we should go and let her be." Chad picked up his son.

"Izzy?" Henry's arms went out to her.

Chad chuckled and ruffled his hair. "No, you don't. You're going with me."

"I tell you what, Henry. Maybe we can play one day this week. Okay?" Izzy offered.

The boy nodded.

She took his hand. "Then we have a date."

"We're going," Chad said to Izzy. "Do whatever you want with the place. Holler if you have any questions." He headed out the door. Why did he have a feeling his life might have just taken a right turn?

Izzy rolled into Chad's drive for the second time that day. She'd fallen in love with the area, his home and the apartment on sight. The neighborhood was exactly what she had been looking for. Completely different from the chrome and cement she'd lived in for so long. The simple, beautiful setting made her feel like she'd found home. The big oak tree sealed the deal.

Chad's house had charmed her as well. It had a porch across the front with columns that were larger at the bottom than they were at the top. Ceiling fans hung on each side of the porch with groups of chairs. Painted a light butter yellow, the house looked like a true 1920s bungalow.

A small bike with training wheels lay on its side on the rock sidewalk and a ball sat in the grass.

There was no doubt a child lived here.

Moving into Chad's backyard might not be the best emotional decision she could make, but she did love the setting. She would be living close to the hospital, in a neighborhood instead of a cold apartment building five stories up. It was the change she was looking for. In fact his house was everything she had ever wanted.

Izzy parked behind Chad's SUV. She'd hardly stopped the car when Chad was at her door.

"What can I help you carry?"

"Me too," Henry eagerly said.

She had retrieved her clothes from the hotel, then stopped at the local home supply store. There she'd bought cleaning supplies and other needs she'd made a note of. "Yeah. Anything you see in the car goes in. Thanks for the help."

"I should have gone with you to the hotel. I didn't think about it until you left. As soon as we get you unloaded, I need to put your number in my phone."

Something about being in Chad's phone seemed too personal. Yet necessary.

"You stopped to do a little shopping, I see." His voice held a note of humor.

The easiness of being comfortable enough with each other felt right. Richard had been so serious all the time. Why hadn't she seen that? Why hadn't she seen a lot of things? "Yes. I got that paint we talked about."

"I'll pay you for that," Chad insisted.

"That's not necessary."

He opened the passenger side door. "We'll argue about that later." Chad looked at the darkening sky. "We should get your stuff in before it rains." He picked up the two gallons of paint.

She gathered an armload of clothes.

"What about me?" Henry demanded.

Izzy handed him a bag.

"What else did you get?" Chad looked inside the car.

"Some towel racks for the bathroom. General cleaning supplies. When I moved, I didn't bring much with me. I have a few things in storage at my parents'. I'll go get them my next full weekend off."

"Where do they live?"

"They're still in Nashville."

Chad put down a can and pushed open the door of the apartment.

Izzy draped her load over the top of the couch. "Just put the stuff in the middle of the floor. I'll sort it all later."

They continued to make trips to the car until everything laid around her new home.

"Henry and I'll leave you alone to get settled. We'll be in the house if you need us." Chad hesitated at the door.

Did he want her to ask him to stay? "Thanks for your help."

"No problem. Come on, Henry." Chad reached out a hand. "We need to hurry if we don't want to get wet."

"I stay here," the boy wailed.

"Henry," Izzy said softly. "You can come visit tomorrow."

The boy quieted, his eyes wide.

"I promise." Henry needed a woman's attention. Izzy's heart went out to him. He missed his mother.

"See ya later." Chad and Henry left.

Why did she suddenly feel lonelier than ever?

Chad saw the flash of headlights from the kitchen window as Izzy pulled into the drive later that evening. He figured she'd gone for food. More than once he'd talked himself out of asking her if she'd like to come to his house to eat. Even Henry asked about Izzy.

A buzz filled the air having someone nearby. Or was it because it was Izzy? More than once he'd wondered how her settling in was going, but he stopped himself from disturbing her. He'd put Henry to bed and was taking out the trash when Chad saw her.

She stood in the yard with her arms in the damp air twisting one way and then the other stretching.

He walked toward her. "Hey."

Izzy jumped. "I didn't hear you out here."

"I promise I wasn't skulking around. I brought the trash out." He pointed around the corner of the garage. "How's it going?"

She brushed a lock of hair away with the back of her hand. "Pretty good. I'm probably going to be sore in the morning, but I've gotten some things done. I even managed to paint one wall."

"I should've been helping you with that." He would've if he hadn't had Henry to see to, or if she had acted as if she wanted his help.

"I didn't mind. It was the easy one. I'll do a little more over the next couple of weeks. It'll get done. Would you like to see?"

"Sure." Chad wasn't sure he should be entering her domain. Yet he was a landlord. He needed to check out the apartment every so often.

Inside, Izzy spread her arms wide. "A clean kitchen and a painted wall."

The wall behind the bed did look crisper and the kitchen gleamed. "You have been busy."

Chad stepped up to the chair and picked up one of a couple of packages containing bathroom towel rods. "You shouldn't have to do all these. I should have put them up before I told you about the place."

"I'll take care of installing them tomorrow."

"I'll can take care of them right now. Then maybe I won't feel so guilty about letting you do all the work in here." He skimmed the instructions.

Izzy sagged as a look of relief formed on her face. "Would you mind? Putting those up is really not in my skill set. I never get them tight enough."

"Here I was thinking you didn't have a deficiency in your skill set. I thought you could do anything."

She chuckled. "Boy, do I have you fooled."

Izzy did seem pretty perfect. "Let me get my tools and check on Henry. He should be asleep." Chad put the towel bars back where he'd found them.

Returning with his toolbox and a baby monitor, Chad picked up the holders and headed for the bath. "Izzy, come show me where you think these should go."

She came to stand in the doorway of the tiny room. "One needs to go on that wall and the other near the sink."

"I'm not going to put them up unless you show me exactly where you want them. Otherwise, I won't get them right." He tore open a package and handed a rod to her. "Show me."

He backed up so she could squeeze in front of him. Her back brushed his chest. Heat shot through him. It had been too long since he'd had a woman. Especially one that appealed to him as much as Izzy. She smelled of something sweet and healthy. Her hair felt like silk beneath his chin. What would she do if he kissed that bare spot between her hairline and the edge of her T-shirt? That was not something he would let happen.

She placed the holder on the wall. "Do you have something to mark this with?"

"Uh?"

"Pencil. Pen. Caulk?" She glanced over her shoulder.

Chad shook his head. "Yeah. Right here." He twisted and pulled a carpenter's pencil out of his toolbox. Reaching around her, his forearm brushed her breast as he marked the spot.

He felt more than saw Izzy tremble. "You get in the shower."

"What?" His body caught fire at the possibilities. Those thoughts had to stop.

"That way I have enough room to turn around to mark the other holder. Hand me that one."

He picked up the shorter bar and gave it to her.

Izzy took it and the pencil from him. She held it to the wall. After marking the spot, she said, "There, you should be all set. I'll leave you to it."

Chad watched the enticing swing of her hips as she walked out of the bathroom. How silly would he look fully dressed and soaking wet from a cold shower? He'd made a friendly offer to rent this place and now he was having these lusty ideas about his tenant. He must do better.

Forty-five minutes later he stepped out of the small space in firm control of his emotions. "All done."

"Great," Izzy said from where she made the bed.

Izzy and a bed Chad refused to think about. "I've got them as snug as I can. You shouldn't have any problem with them falling."

"I'm impressed. Good in an emergency and good with your hands." She fluffed a pillow and propped it against another on the bed.

Was Izzy flirting with him or just unaware of the innuendos she kept making? "You've no idea."

She looked at him with wide eyes and a quizzical expression, then blinked before her face turned beet red. "I... uh, didn't mean it the way it sounded."

Chad grinned. "I know what you meant. Thank you for the compliment. I'll reimburse you for the holders. I'll take it off your first month's rent."

"Thanks. If you keep this up, I won't have to pay any rent."

He stepped toward the door. Izzy joined him. Without thinking, he reached out and touched her cheek. "You've got a spot of paint right here."

Her gaze met his, held. "I imagine I have it all over me. A good shower should get rid of it."

She rubbed at the spot, her fingers touching his. Chad didn't even want to think about her taking a shower. The more he was around Izzy, the more all sorts of "wrong ideas" kept coming to mind. He wasn't looking for a serious relationship, which was something he suspected Izzy was after. So why was he so interested in her?

It had been a while since Nan's death, but the melancholy nature of their relationship hadn't faded. Or his part in the failure of the marriage. That wasn't a place he felt capable of going again. Lessons learned. Izzy didn't strike him as a woman who would be satisfied with anything less than commitment. Something he couldn't take a chance on giving again. Or carrying the guilt for. What if the marriage failed again? He wouldn't do that to Henry. Or himself. "See you later then."

"Thanks for offering me this place. This is so much better than a hotel room."

He needed to get back to the house. See about Henry. Think less about Izzy. "You're welcome. Have a good night."

Chad left before he was tempted to do anything more. Such as kiss her.

CHAPTER THREE

AT THE HOSPITAL five days later, Izzy was sitting behind her desk when one of the unit nurses came to stand at the door. "Izzy."

She glanced up. "Yes."

"We need your help. We're swamped with the two nurses out."

Izzy looked at the pile of papers on her desk. She'd just have to stay late and catch up. "Yeah. Where do I need to go?"

"Dr. McCain has a patient in exam room one. Suspected meningitis." The nurse hurried off.

After tugging her scrub top into order and pulling her hair back into a band, Izzy headed out the door. She arrived at the exam room as Chad walked up. He didn't pause, his face wearing a no-nonsense expression. After only a few weeks, Izzy recognized he was in doctor mode. He liked to tease but when it came to his patients, he turned serious.

They hadn't seen much of each other even in the last few days despite her living in his backyard. They weren't on the same schedule. A couple of times they had waved at each other as one of them came or went. Once she'd been pulling in as he backed out of the drive. She waited to let him out before she turned in.

Now he looked at the electronic charting pad as he spoke

to the parents. "Hello. I'm Dr. McCain. I'm the ER doctor. I need to ask you some questions."

Izzy went to work recording the comatose ten-year-old girl's vital signs.

"Can you tell me what's going on?" Chad voice had gone low.

The mother spoke up. "Jeanie was playing in the backyard with a friend. She was fine, then she came in the house and said she wasn't feeling good. The next thing I knew she was throwing up. I touched her and she was burning up. She seemed confused when I ask her where it hurt." The pain and fear rang clear in the woman's voice.

Chad moved to stand across the bed from Izzy. The girl lay with her eyes closed, showing no reaction. As he pulled his stethoscope from his pocket, he spoke to Izzy, "Let's get a CBC and total protein panel along with a procalcitonin draw."

"Right away," Izzy told him. She picked up the electronic pad he'd set at the end of the bed. She punched in the order. She then watched as Chad checked the girl's eyes, gently pressed along the child's neck. Chad's tenderness of touch always amazed her.

He looked at her and said quietly, "We'll need to do a spinal tap."

Izzy stepped out of the room and returned with the prepared kit. Chad sat on a stool in front of the parents, and the father held the mother's hand.

Chad spoke in a grave tone. "Your daughter's very sick. I believe she has meningitis. Which is an infection in the brain and spinal cord. I can't be sure if it's a viral infection or fungal until tests are done. The neurologist will decide on the course of treatment when all the tests are in. Jeanie will be going to ICU."

The mother sobbed.

Chad's shoulders stiffened but he continued talking. "Jeanie's in the right place and will get the best of care here. I'll be peforming a spinal tap to remove enough fluid for testing in a few minutes. I'm going to ask you to wait in the waiting room until someone comes to get you. They'll show you where to go."

"We understand." The father stood and helped the mother up.

Chad patted the woman on the shoulder. "We'll do everything we can to help your daughter."

The parents stepped to the bedside and kissed their child. With tears in their eyes, they reluctantly left the room.

Izzy couldn't help but admire Chad's understanding bedside manner. Making sure to call the child by her name. That meant a lot to the parents. He had a way with people. He'd certainly charmed her in a short time.

"Izzy, let's get this spinal tap done and the sample to the lab."

They put on gowns, masks and gloves. Another nurse joined them.

"Roll her to her side," Chad said.

Izzy and the other nurse went to the other side of the bed from Chad. The assisting nurse stood at the girl's feet while Izzy went to her head. They rolled the girl, giving Chad a clear view of her back. He prepared a sterile area along the girl's spine, pressing his finger to find the spot between the vertebrae.

"Needle," Chad requested, and Izzy handed it to him.

Chad inserted a thin needle into the spinal cord and suctioned out fluid.

"See this gets to the lab right away." He packaged it in a sterile package and handed it to the nurse.

Izzy cleaned up the tap area and put a bandage over the entry wound before throwing away the leftover supplies.

Chad said, "I'll send techs in to take her up to ICU. I have more patients to see. Thanks for the help, Izzy." With that, he was gone.

Hours later Izzy was back behind her desk, inputting the next week's schedule, when there was a rap on her door.

Chad stood there. "You're here late."

She sighed. "Yeah. Doing some actual nursing put my paper-pushing behind today."

He gave her a wry smile. "That happens. I finally have a break. You look like you could use one too. Would you like to join me in our lustrous cafeteria for dinner?"

Izzy grinned at his formal invitation. Looking at the papers on her desk, she shouldn't take Chad up on his offer for more than one reason. Yet she was hungry and did need a break. She'd missed their banter during the week. Pushing back from the desk, she said, "Thanks for asking. I'd love to."

"How've you been?" Chad asked as they strolled down the long hallway toward the elevators. "Your new home working out?"

"Yeah, it is." She grinned and teased, "Questionable landlord but otherwise great. I've been busy here. I'm still learning the ropes." Izzy looked at his profile. It was a nice one. For years she paid little attention to other men since she was committed to Richard. Yet she could say without a doubt that Chad was an extremely handsome man.

She couldn't remember the last time a man had asked her to dinner. Even to a hospital cafeteria. Richard had always expected her to have dinner waiting on her days off. He'd often asked her to pick something up on her way home from work. She'd been raised in a world where the wife took care of the meals. It was her mom's way of showing love.

When she started helping fund Richard's schooling, she'd hesitated for a moment but he had convinced her she'd be doing it for them. For their future. "Wasn't that what love was all about?" he would say. But his love was one-sided; she hadn't seen it.

"It's hard to believe you live fifty paces from me and I haven't seen you all week except in the driveway." Chad matched his pace with hers, seeming not to expect her to keep up with his long stride. Another difference between Chad and Richard. She needed to stop comparing them. It wasn't like one was going to replace the other.

"Yeah, our schedules have been opposites this week."

"Have you met Ms. Weber yet?"

"No. I've seen her coming and going a couple of times." Izzy pulled the shirt of her scrub into place.

"Then I'll make sure you meet her when we're all there at the same time. She walks over from her house to see to Henry. He often goes to her house as well."

Izzy had been working during the day and at night painting her apartment. "That sounds like a nice setup for you and Henry."

"It's working for now. As he gets older, I'll have to make adjustments." They stopped at the elevator bank. Chad pushed the down button.

The elevator dinged and the doors opened. They stepped inside. Just before the doors closed a group joined them, pushing Izzy and Chad toward a corner. His large frame warmed her all the way down her back. Izzy's body hummed with awareness of Chad standing near. She didn't dare speak for fear her nervousness would show. Neither did she move a muscle as they went down one floor.

Izzy felt dainty next to Chad's bulk. She released the breath she'd held when the doors opened, and they moved out. They continued behind the others to the cafeteria.

"I've only been down here one other time." Izzy looked around the space with tables and large glass windows.

"Where do you normally eat?" Chad looked at her.

"I bring my meals and eat at my desk or in the break room if I'm asked." She turned toward the serving lines.

His brows rose. "Asked?"

"The staff deserves to have some time when they can be themselves without the boss around. And to vent without being heard."

"That's considerate of you." Chad's admiration showed in his eyes.

She shrugged. "I know how it is. I've been in their position before."

"Still, you don't have to be so nice. Henry has good taste in women."

"Thanks." But did he feel the same way about her as Henry did? Why should it matter if he did?

Chad gave his lips a resigned twisted. "I hate to admit it, but I eat here most days. I'm not much of a cook. This is easy and convenient. It gives me a chance to get out of the unit. Sometimes I just really need to get away."

"So this is where you bring all your dates?"

His head swivel around.

Izzy winced. "I'm sorry. That was just a figure of speech."

He placed his hand over his heart. "Ouch. That hurt."

"That wasn't my intention. I just got out of a bad relationship. I'm not interested in dating anyone."

His gaze met hers. Reassuring and demanding at the same time. "What can be simpler than supper in a hospital cafeteria as a non-date?"

Izzy had no doubt her face had turned beet red. "I'm sorry that wasn't very nice and very presumptuous."

"I think I need to hear more about this life-changing event but first let's get our food."

Izzy went through one of the three serving lines to get

her food. She didn't want to go into her past over a meal with Chad. Yet she'd opened the door. Her aim had been to make it clear there wouldn't be anything more than friendship between them. She had to learn to believe in herself again.

They met again at the cash register. Chad let her go ahead of him. She stepped to the cashier.

Chad told the woman checking them out, "I'll get both of these."

Izzy narrowed her eyes at him. "I told you—"

"I know what you said but I asked you to keep me company." He handed some bills to the woman who watched the interaction between them too closely.

As they walked toward an empty table for four, Izzy said over her shoulder, "I thought I made it clear this wasn't a date."

"Then next time you can pay. Will that make you happy?" Chad walked close behind her.

"That's what you said last time. I already owe you for one meal." She stopped at a table near a group of windows where she could see the outside.

"So now you're keeping score." Chad settled into a metal chair as if he were looking forward to the world's best meal.

Somehow he'd managed to make her sound petty. She sat in the chair across the table from him.

Chad took a large bite out of his grilled cheese sandwich. Finished chewing, he then drank his drink through a straw. "Now tell me what brought on your attitude about dating."

"It's no real attitude. It's just as I said. I've come out of a bad relationship, and I don't wish to step into another one."

"And you think eating dinner with me would be going back into a bad relationship?" He looked serious but there was a teasing note to his tone.

Izzy huffed. "That's not what I meant."

"I know. Is that bad relationship why you decided to move to Atlanta?"

"Let's just say I needed a change." If she'd known this would be the line of conversation when he'd asked her to dinner, she might have said no.

"That sounds ominous."

She had to put a stop to his interrogation. Shame washed through her. Admitting she'd been used by Richard wasn't something she wanted to share with Chad. With anyone for that matter. "I really don't wanna talk about this."

"Okay. What would you like to talk about?" He continued to eat.

"How about you telling me what's your favorite place in town?"

He leaned back in his chair and studied her a moment. "You really are avoiding the subject. But I'll go along. There're a lot of things about Atlanta I like. I think there's something for everyone. Certainly, the sports are nice. There's the art and natural history museums. The Fox Theatre brings in plays. Of course, Henry's favorite place is the zoo. I don't get to do as many things as I would like. Henry and my work keep me pretty busy."

"Maybe you could change that."

"I don't know. We only have so much time in a day, a week…"

Izzy pushed a piece of lettuce away. She'd wasted too many of her days, she thought. "Yeah, but Henry will only be young for a short while."

Izzy wasn't sure where this conversation was headed but she did appreciate learning more about Atlanta. She couldn't resist trying to figure out why Chad, who had a nice home, a good job and a precious child, wasn't in a serious relationship. What was wrong with him that wasn't obvious?

"Since we seem to be touching on the personal, would you tell me in more detail what happened to your wife?"

"She was killed in an automobile accident." A sadness came to his eyes before he said, "Henry was with her."

"That must have been awful." Chad's actions made more sense now.

He put his sandwich on the plate and wiped his mouth. "Worst day of my life. I don't know what I would have done if I had lost them both."

"I know yours and Henry's worlds must have been turned upside down." She placed her hand on his for a moment.

"It was, but we're figuring it out. Mostly Henry is." Chad grinned. "I just do what he tells me to."

Izzy laughed. Something she hadn't really done in months. She liked Chad. Henry as well. Too much.

Three days later Chad hurried out the back door toward Izzy's apartment. He knew she was there because her car sat in front of his in the drive.

"Izzy," he called through the screen door.

"Yes?" Her voice came from somewhere near the kitchen.

"I need your help."

She opened the door with a worried look on her face. "Is Henry all right?"

"Yeah. I'm needed at the hospital for a few hours. They're short a doctor. Just a half shift. This is Ms. Weber's day off. Would you mind watching Henry for a few hours?"

"It's no problem. Give me five minutes and I'll come to your house."

He grinned. "I'll make this up to you. I promise. I really appreciate it."

"Not a problem. I had promised Henry a playdate and this will give me a chance to do that."

He'd promised himself he'd stop working so many hours before Nan died but he couldn't tell the hospital no when they needed him. Work also helped him cope with the changes in his life after Nan. Even now with just Henry, Chad was making the same mistake. Izzy was right about time. It would pass quickly. But what could he do when he was needed?

Chad returned home just before dark to sounds he'd not heard in a long time, if ever. The noise of a child playing happily in the yard. Female laughter flowed over him like the sweet sound of a brook. He walked around the apartment to the backyard, where he found Henry swinging as Izzy pushed him. His son smiled as Izzy returned it. Chad wished he were included in that glow of happiness.

Izzy seemed to create that. As hard as he worked to keep her at arm's length, there was a greater tug to get closer to her so he could bask in the warmth. She'd radiated hurt when she'd talked about her past relationship. His heart had gone out to her. For a moment he had a fleeting idea that he could show her what a relationship should be like. The thought was laughable. Based on his marriage, he knew nothing about making a woman happy. What made him think he could do that for Izzy? Or that she would be interested in him doing so.

"Higher," Henry squealed.

"Like this?" Izzy gave him a push.

Henry's giggles filled the air.

Chad hadn't seen Henry this happy in a long time. He missed his mom. Needed a mother figure in this life.

"Daddy," Henry called.

"Hey, buddy. It looks like you're having a good time."

"I go high."

The smile Izzy offered was like bright sunshine on a cold winter day. His chest tightened. When was the last time someone had been truly glad to see him? Nan had gotten to the point where she hadn't even made the effort.

Henry slowed to a steady swing.

"Have you been having fun?" Chad stepped in front of Henry but not close enough to get hit.

He nodded four times. "We make cookies."

"That does sound like fun." He looked at Izzy. "I hope you didn't ruin your dinner."

She smiled. "Eating cookies for dinner isn't that big of a deal every once in a while. Isn't that right, Henry?"

The boy smiled.

Izzy gaze remained on Chad. "How did it go at the hospital? Super busy?"

"Busy enough." He moved to lean up against the tree. "Sounds and looks like y'all been having more fun here though."

"Henry, I think it's time for you to play in the sandbox. I'm gonna talk to your dad for a few minutes." Izzy slowed the swing and lifted Henry out of the child swing.

"Push me," Henry whined.

Izzy bent to look at Henry at eye level. "What did we talk about earlier?"

"I not whine?"

She smiled and cupped his cheek. "That's right."

Henry went to the sandbox nearby.

"Let's sit down. I know you must be tired." Izzy walked over to the two retro metal chairs sitting under the oak tree.

"I don't recognize these." He fingered the top of one of the yellow chairs.

"I found them at a yard sale just down the road. I thought they'd look nice here. Give me a good place to read."

"I like them." He appreciated most things Izzy had a hand in.

Satisfaction filled her smile. She took a seat.

Chad sank into the other chair. He rested his head back and closed his eyes. The last of the day's sunshine warmed his face. A breeze rustled the leaves. A sweet smell of something floral tickled his nose. Izzy's scent. He could enjoy that smell forever. "I really appreciate you watching Henry. I'm sure you're tired too."

She yawned "It's a good tired, I have to admit. Anything exciting happen in the unit?"

"Mostly the usual stuff. Small injuries, strep throats and a couple of rashes. I only had one admit." He paused. "Oh, and one aggressive mother making a pass."

"Oh, wow, you did have a big evening."

He huffed. "That's a nice way of putting it."

Izzy voice held humor. "The trials of being a handsome doctor. Not your type?"

"Nope. You think I'm handsome?" He raised a brow and grinned.

She huffed. "Don't even pretend you don't know you are a catch."

"Nan thought so until she didn't. She thought being married to a doctor would be wonderful. It wasn't. She ran around on me in the hope of finding some happiness because I couldn't give it to her." He couldn't look at Izzy. Instead he watched Henry, who had left the sandbox to swing a stick.

Izzy sucked in a shocked breath. "That is awful."

A shadow of sadness filled his eyes. "My marriage was already on the rocks when Nan died. I'd asked for a divorce a few days before the accident."

She reached across the space between them and took his hand. "Chad, I'm so sorry."

"I am too. Marriage is supposed to be forever. My parents have been married for forty-five years. My grandparents for sixty-five. I thought Nan and I would be the same."

Pushing with his foot, he made the chair rock. "Nan had been unhappy for years. My work hours can be hard to live with. In hindsight we shouldn't have married. She needed more attention than I had time to give. Between finishing school and starting my career, there wasn't much time left. For that, I'm really sorry. We talked of divorce but then she found out she was pregnant. We decided to try to make it work."

He sighed. "But then I found out she was cheating on me. I had already seen a lawyer about filing for divorce when the police came to the hospital to tell me about the accident. I hated the idea of getting a divorce for Henry's sake, but he also needed parents who were happy together. I've often wondered if Nan drove off the road on purpose. I wouldn't have put it past her, but I'd like to think she wouldn't have taken that chance with Henry. So you can see you're not the only one with a screwed up relationship in your history."

Izzy squeezed his hand. "You didn't deserve that. You didn't do anything wrong."

He raised a shoulder and let it drop. "Maybe not, but it does still make me wonder what I could've done or should've done to make our marriage better. If there was a difference I could've made. Or worse would I have been willing to make? Apparently, I'm just not cut out for marriage. But I am determined to be a good father despite the hours I work. Henry is my complete focus when I'm not at work. That leaves little time for dating or romance."

Izzy moved her hand to her lap. "We always have people in our lives we aren't enough for no matter how hard we try. I'm not much better. I gave nine years of my life and my money to a guy to come home and find him in bed with another woman. I have no interest in making that mistake again."

"At least you knew when to get out." He wished she were still holding his hand. Somehow it made the pain of this discussion easier.

"I did, but it was hard. To have devoted that much time to someone who I felt cared about me as much as I did him and to learn he had been using me was devastating." Izzy looked at Henry. "You at least got something wonderful out of a bad situation."

"I did, didn't I?" He smiled fondly at Henry.

Izzy's voice took on a soft note. "It's obvious that you love Henry dearly. All the love and care you've given matters. It's never too late for that to make a difference."

"I hope it does. He's had a hard young life. How did we get on this unpleasant subject?"

She gave him a thin-lipped smile. "Apparently, we both needed to talk. I'm glad you felt you could tell me."

Which wasn't like him. He was working hard to put what he could in the past. "I think that's because you're easy to talk to."

"I'll take that compliment." She stood.

It was time for him and Henry to go to the house. What had him speaking so plainly to Izzy? He'd kept his distance from women. There had been a few dates but never any real involvement outside of the physical. Why did Izzy have him confessing to her?

Chad got to his feet as well. "It was meant that way." He reached out a hand. "Henry, it's time to go in."

The boy came to him.

Chad took Izzy's hand, playing with her fingers as he looked in her eyes. "You do know it was his loss, don't you?"

Her eyes glistened. "That might be the nicest thing anyone has ever said to me." She gave him a quick kiss on the cheek. "Thank you."

CHAPTER FOUR

IZZY SAT UNDER the oak tree the next morning, enjoying the cool before the heat of the day set in. She had been rethinking her conversation with Chad. What he'd said swam in her head. He had endured too much. Her heart went out to him. The idea his wife had treated him the way she had was incomprehensible. He hadn't deserved what happened to him, yet he'd been reassuring her.

Then he'd said something nice, and she'd kissed him. Even though it was on the cheek, it made it personal. He'd looked as surprised as she'd felt. They were both mature adults so surely he would have seen the kiss for the impulsive action was. She did. So why could she still remember the briny taste of his skin.

She must protect herself from the growing feelings she had for Chad. The more she was around the McCain males, the more she liked them. Sharing the evening with Henry had been like being a mother. She'd enjoyed every minute. What she didn't need to do was get used to it. Her living situation was temporary. Right now she was vulnerable emotionally. A rebound relationship would be fatal. She didn't trust her judgment where men were concerned, and she couldn't afford to make a mistake again. Love had blinded her once. She wouldn't let history repeat itself.

A good friendship, with boundaries was what she

needed. She'd maintain distance, not become involved except on a superficial level. People did that all the time. Why couldn't she? All she had to do was keep her guard up. Being around Chad and Henry had helped her to start breathing again. To put her life together. She would always be grateful for that.

"Do you have anything planned outside of sitting under this big oak tree this weekend?" Chad asked as he walked up behind her.

"I have to work tomorrow but other than that I plan to read a book. I'm not even doing any painting. Why?"

"The people in the neighborhood are having a block party this afternoon. Ms. Weber is insisting that Henry and I come. You're a member of the neighborhood now. How about going with us?"

"I don't know." She paused a moment. Why shouldn't she go? "If I went, what would I need to bring?"

Chad took the other chair, leaning forward, putting his elbows on his knees. "I don't know. It's covered dish, whatever that is. Henry and I were planning to carry rolls."

She laughed. "I think we can do better than that."

"*We.* I like the sound of that. But heavier on the *you* where cooking is concerned."

Izzy stood with her hands on her hips and glared down at him "Then *we* need to go to the grocery store."

"Back to the scene of the crime. Couldn't you just go and leave Henry and me here?" He gave her a pleading look.

She shook her head. "No. I think it'd be a good trip for you both. Henry could use some practice in that department."

He groaned. "There's is no mercy with you, is there?"

She shook her head, giving him her sternest look.

"Okay, if you insist." Chad stood.

"I do."

His shoulders sagged. "I'll get Henry and meet you at the car."

Izzy smiled at Chad's disgusted look. "I'll see you in a few minutes."

He started away.

"Uh, Chad, about that kiss last night. I shouldn't have gotten so personal."

He came to stand close, his gaze holding hers. "Not a problem. We both were talking about some heavy stuff. I appreciate you listening to mine."

When he turned and walked away, Izzy let out her breath. Why had disappointment filled her? Had she wanted him to kiss her?

Twenty minutes later she road to the store in Chad's SUV with him driving and Henry in the middle seat.

"Izzy?"

"Huh?" She sat in the front seat with her hands clasped in her lap.

"Do you plan to ever look at me again?" Chad's voice held humor.

"I'm not *not* looking at you." Her focus went to his hands on the steering wheel. They were capable hands—she'd seen them help children, lift Henry and touch her.

"In the eyes."

She glanced at him.

Chad grinned. "You can't avoid me forever."

She glared at him. "I can try."

A full-bodied laugh filled the SUV. "I'd like to see you try."

A few minutes later, he pulled into the grocery store parking lot. Henry squealed as she helped him out of the car seat. She bent to Henry's level. "You can't scream in the grocery store. You're going to be a good boy. If you're not, you'll have to come back out here and sit in the car. Do you understand?"

The boy nodded, his look fixed on her.

"Good. Then inside we go."

Chad pushed the cart with Henry in the seat as Izzy walked along beside them. She patted Henry's arm. "Remember, quiet voice."

Chad stopped the cart, looking back and forth as if deciding which aisle he needed to go down. "What're we going to fix?"

"I thought we'd make my mom's macaroni and cheese. How does that sound to you, Henry?" She leaned in close to him.

The boy smiled. "Mac and cheese."

She returned it. "I think Henry agrees. How about you, Chad?"

"Sound good to me."

She liked this too much. It felt as if they were a family. The pleasure of that idea was becoming fixed in her head. Couldn't she just enjoy it for a little while? It would only be temporary.

They continued around the store, gathering the supplies needed. At one point Henry became louder than necessary. She raised a brow in Chad's direction and he placed his hand on Henry's arm. "Don't be so loud."

The boy quieted down. Chad gave her a self-satisfied smirk as if he'd accomplished a life-saving procedure. She nodded her encouragement.

They kept moving around the store. It wasn't until they were in the checkout line that Henry started acting up again. His demands for candy rose to a yell. When Chad told Henry he couldn't have any, the scene escalated.

Izzy spoke to Henry, but it did no good. To Chad she

said, "Why don't you take Henry to the car? I'll finish checking out."

Chad opened his mouth to argue.

Before he could say anything, she said, "I don't mind." Henry needed to learn a lesson. An immediate one given by Chad. She wouldn't always be around. That idea had her pausing for a moment, made her sad.

With Henry kicking and screaming, Chad carried him toward the parking lot. By the time she joined them, they were both sulking in their seats. She suppressed a smile as she opened the rear of the SUV.

Chad got out and helped her put the grocery bags inside. "How's it goin'?"

"Let's just say I'm ready to go home." He looked as if he had worked a long tough twelve-hour shift.

She chuckled and patted him on the arm. "It's still a win."

He started the SUV. "Yeah, but that doesn't mean I'm taking a victory lap."

A few hours later, Izzy glanced at Chad as they made the short walk to the neighborhood park. He carried the casserole dish with the macaroni and cheese in it while she pushed the stroller with Henry strapped in the seat. She brushed a few strands of her hair away from her face as she carried on a conversation with Henry.

A group of Chad's neighbors greeted them with smiles and calls, each giving her inquiring looks. What must they think? That she was Chad's girlfriend? For some reason that idea didn't bother her when it should have.

Henry twisted around to look at Chad. "I swing?"

Chad looked at the group of children playing nearby. He nodded. "In a few minutes." Chad directed her toward a table loaded with food.

Izzy walked beside him. "I've not been to something like this in years."

"They didn't have these where you used to live?"

"We had them, but Richard didn't ever want to go. No matter how many times I asked, nothing made him change his mind." She should have seen the signs. Maybe she just hadn't wanted to. It had always been a battle to get Richard to go with her anywhere. Why hadn't she stood up for what she wanted?

Chad pursed his lips. "I have to admit, this isn't my usual thing either. A couple of neighbors pretty much forced me to get out and come last year. I was glad I did and Henry enjoys the other children."

"Thanks for encouraging me to attend. I need to meet all the people I can." Izzy took the food from him and arranged the bowl on the table among the others.

"Your mac and cheese really looks good. I'm looking forward to eating some."

Warmth flowed through her. This time she met his look. He returned it and her heart did a little jump for joy.

They mingled with the others there. Chad introduced her to those he knew. A number they both met for the first time. As they moved around to different groups, Izzy spoke to Henry, keeping him happy. When it was time to eat, Izzy stood in the food line with Henry and Chad. She held Henry's plate while Chad placed food on it and filled his own plate at the same time. She managed to put food on hers as well. Chad spooned a double helping of her mac and cheese on his plate. He made sure he had her attention and winked as he scooped the second large spoonful.

She grinned like a girl whose crush had just proved he felt the same way as she did. Tomorrow she would worry about how tangled in Chad's charm she had become. Today she was going to enjoy having a handsome, smart, caring and funny man trying to impress her. It was an ointment to her burned self-esteem.

They were sharing a private moment. The spot in the center of her chest warmed. She liked Chad too much. With him, she recognized what she had missed in her life while being with Richard. It was nice to share humor and laughter again. Sadly she'd not had that for so long she'd failed to miss it. Chad had a very serious profession and being a single father had its challenges. Still, he could find joy in life. It was contagious.

With their plates filled, Chad's to overflowing, they found an empty park table. Henry sat between her and Chad. Izzy scooted in beside the boy and put an arm around him so he wouldn't fall backward off the picnic table bench. Chad settled Henry's plate in front of him and then took his spot close on the other side, sitting on the tips of her fingers. Heat ran up her neck. She quickly moved her hand.

Chad gave her a grin as his eyes twinkled. He leaned close. "Are you trying to touch my butt?"

"No!"

He grinned. "I wouldn't have minded."

She huffed and focused on her food.

Soon, an older couple took the bench across the table from them. Two children a few years older than Henry were with them.

"Hello," the woman said. "May we join you?"

"Sure," Chad agreed.

"I'm John Cartwright." The man offered his hand to Chad. "This is my wife, Elenore, and a couple of our grandchildren. We live over on Maple Street."

"It's nice to meet you. I'm Chad McCain. This is Izzy Lane and Henry." Chad placed his hand on Henry's head briefly. "We live over off of Lemon Drive."

"Hello," Izzy offered before Henry drew her attention away when he needed help.

"This is our first neighborhood get-together. We just moved here a few months ago," Mrs. Cartwright said.

"Welcome to the neighborhood," Chad offered.

"This is a nice idea." Mr. Cartwright nodded toward the food table. "Brings the neighborhood closer. That doesn't happen enough."

Over the next few minutes, their table settled into eating their meal.

Mrs. Cartwright smiled at Izzy. "We sat at the right table. You're such a lovely family."

"We're—" Izzy and Chad said at the same time.

The Cartwrights looked from Chad to Izzy and back again with confusion on their faces.

Chad cleared his throat. "Izzy is a coworker and rents an apartment from me. We're not married."

The Cartwrights faces cleared with understanding.

The man said, "We thought by the way you interacted with each other you were married. Sorry for the misunderstanding."

It shouldn't have bothered Izzy that they weren't a couple, but she couldn't deny the niggling feeling that it might be nice if they were. When had she started thinking like that? Before she met Chad, she'd been so determined to keep to herself, not share her history. Then the next thing she knew she was telling Chad the whole ugly story. What was happening to her?

A commotion at a table nearby drew her attention away from the uncomfortable moment.

A woman stood beside a small boy with a frantic look on her face. "Johnny, what's wrong?"

"I can't breathe," he gasped.

"Someone call 911." Chad climbed off the bench and loped toward them.

Izzy grabbed her phone. She explained where they were and what was happening.

In the background she heard Chad say, "I'm a doctor. Can I help?"

"He was just eating dessert and now he's got this rash and says he can't breathe." Panic filled the woman's voice.

Izzy said to the Cartwrights, "Can you watch Henry for me?"

They nodded.

She went around the table and handed Henry to Mrs. Cartwright. "Do you have an EpiPen?" Izzy asked the Cartwrights.

"I do." Mrs. Cartwright handed Henry back to Izzy before searching her purse. "One of the girls is allergic to everything."

Just before Izzy reached Chad he called, "Does anyone have an EpiPen?"

"Here's one." Izzy handed it over his shoulder.

Chad looked at her with surprise and appreciation. He took the pin. "That was quick."

"Hi, I'm Izzy," she said to the boy, directing his attention away from what Chad was about to do. "I'm a nurse and I can promise you'll feel better in a few minutes. Dr. McCain is going to make a quick prick and you'll be breathing easier."

Moving the boy's shorts to expose his thigh, Chad pushed the pin into his thigh.

Slowly the boy's color improved and his breathing eased. Izzy stood with the mother as Chad took the boy's vitals.

At the sound of an ambulance drawing near, Izzy said, "I'll go meet them."

Chad nodded.

Moments later she directed the EMTs to where the boy sat on the picnic table bench. As the EMTs went to work, Izzy and Chad joined the mother, who watched.

Chad spoke to her. "He needs to go to the hospital to be checked out. He's had an allergic reaction to something. Peanuts are the usual culprits, but it can be other things."

Fifteen minutes later the EMTs loaded the boy in the ambulance as Chad and Izzy stood nearby.

"Thank you," the mother called over her shoulder as she headed for her car.

"Where's Henry?" Chad made a frantic glance around as if he had just remembered him.

Izzy touched his arm. "He's with the Cartwrights. He's fine."

Chad relaxed. "Where did you come up with an EpiPen that quick?"

"Mrs. Cartwright. I figured there was a good chance that it would be needed."

They started back to their table.

"I'm impressed. I knew you were good but not how good." He put his arm around her shoulders and gave her a hug.

Chad's praise warmed her through and through like a roaring fire on a cold winter day. Another thing she hadn't known she needed until he came along. Someone to appreciate her.

Returning home at dusk with Izzy beside him and Henry asleep in the stroller had a rightness to it. Chad had never experienced that peace even during the best part of his marriage. In an odd way he had started thinking of the three of them as a family today. Something that he shouldn't continue to do.

He had no desire to lead Izzy on. He had accepted long

ago that he hadn't been a good husband to Nan. That married life wasn't for him. Izzy wasn't a good-time girl who would expect nothing from a man. If anything, she would demand and deserve his best. He hadn't been able to give that before and wasn't confident he could do it now. Yet something about Izzy pulled at him. Challenged him. Made him want to tease her. Kiss her.

He couldn't believe how quickly Izzy had slipped into his life and fit. It should've scared him how much they looked like a family as they joined the others at the gathering earlier. For the first time in a long time, he'd felt positive about life. Chad had no intention of going into a serious relationship again, but if he had, Izzy would be the type of woman he'd choose to do it with. Still, his fear of not measuring up held him back.

Chad suspected he might be putting off his need for companionship on Izzy. She was nice and convenient. But also he couldn't ignore the sparks between them. Ones he'd never felt before.

"Well, thanks for inviting me. I have to say it was more exciting than I'd expected," Izzy said when they reached his drive.

"Yeah, not all of it was what I had expected either. I had planned on it being a little more low-key."

She shifted the empty bowl from one hand to the other. She grinned. "That's hard to imagine. There's nothing low-key about you."

"I'm not sure if that's a compliment or not." Chad smiled like a guy who had been noticed by the prettiest girl in class.

The back porch light burned warm and inviting as they walked up the drive. Izzy had flipped it on as they went out his back door before going to the party. She'd said, "I hate coming home in the dark."

He was used to doing that. Even when Nan had been alive, she hadn't anticipated him coming home by doing something as simple as turning a light on.

Henry woke. "Izzy tuck me in?" His looked questioned her.

Izzy hesitated a moment. "Sure, I can do that."

She held the door for Chad to carry Henry into the house. He continued down the hall. A few moments later, she joined him in Henry's room minus the dirty dish.

In the process of removing Henry's clothes, Chad quickly slipped pajamas on the boy with the ease of practice. Henry laid in his bed and Chad pulled the covers up.

"I want Izzy," Henry whined.

Chad stood and Izzy came to sit on the bed beside Henry. She adjusted the blanket across his chest and kissed him on the forehead. "Night, sweet boy. Sleep tight. Now close your eyes."

Henry did as she asked.

Izzy stayed for a few minutes, then slipped out of the room. Had her eyes been glassy with moisture?

Chad returned to the kitchen to find Izzy sitting at the table with a mug of tea in front of her. Her eyes were clear. Maybe he had imagined those tears. "Hey there. Is Henry asleep?"

"Yeah. I appreciate you coming to tuck him in. I think he misses the female touch."

"I'm sure he does, but you're a great father. He loves you. I hope you don't mind, but I made myself at home. I needed a cup of tea."

Maybe she had been upset. "You're welcome anytime..." Chad paused. "I just don't know that I'm enough for him."

"I'm sure there are many parents who feel like that. That's how life works."

Chad pulled a drink out of the refrigerator. "You make it all sound okay."

She twisted her mug. "I didn't mean to belittle your troubles."

"I didn't think you were." He took a seat beside her at the table.

"I think we were the talk of the picnic in more ways than one today."

Chad groaned. She giggled. He studied her a moment.

"What?" Her brows rose.

"I like that sound."

"Sound?" Izzy looked around the room.

"You giggling. It's like windchimes ringing."

She shyly dipped her head. "Thank you. You keep saying such nice things. Flattery will get you everywhere."

He raised one eyebrow in suggestion. "Everywhere? I like the idea of that."

She offered him a smirky grin. "You know what I meant. By the way, I've been meaning to tell you that I won't be here next weekend. I need to go to my parents' and pick up the furniture stored there. They're ready to get it out of their way and I could use it."

"What're your plans to haul it here?" Chad stretched out his legs, getting comfortable.

"I'm still thinking about that. I'm either going to rent a truck or drive my father's back down. I hate to do that though. He uses it almost daily. It'll put him in a bind to have to ride around in my tiny car."

Chad winced. "I can imagine that would be uncomfortable."

She looked him up and down, "I guess you could."

It gave him a particular feeling in his lower half to have her study him as if she missed nothing. "It's small."

She laughed. "You'd look like one of those clowns in a circus car getting out of mine."

He chuckled. "But it's just the right size and looks good on you."

Izzy's face went a pretty shade of pink. Had she never been told how attractive she was? That guy she'd given so much of her life to had been a real jerk.

"Instead of renting or borrowing a truck, why don't Henry and I just go with you? I could rent a trailer up there and tow your stuff back. Get it all in one trip. How does that sound?"

She fiddled with her mug as if unsure of that idea. "Let me think about it."

"What's there to think about? I have the weekend off and you do too. If I'm out of town, I can get all my time. You told me I need to make the most of my time."

"Yeah, but I didn't mean by driving up and down the road for me."

"Henry and I, plus you, will get to spend some quality time together." He took a swallow of his drink.

She moved her head from one side to the other in thought. "I guess we could. It would be nice to get it all in one trip. But I hate to ask you for such a big favor."

"But you didn't ask. I offered." For some reason he really wanted to do this for her. To spend time getting to know her better. Going down the road would certainly give him a chance to do that.

"Let me talk to my parents and get back to you." She stood. "I better go. I have to be in early in the morning."

"I'm on the night shift." He picked up her mug and put it in the sink.

Izzy stepped to the door. "That's always fun."

"At least when we're busy, time goes by fast." He stepped toward her. "I'll walk you home."

"Not necessary. I'm just out back. I think I can make it." She waved a hand for him to stay there.

Chad's gaze filled with heat captured hers. "I know right where you are, and I'd still like to make sure you get home."

They made their way along the path to her door. Chad placed a hand on her upper arm, stopping her before she went inside. "Izzy, I know it might not be a good idea but I'd very much like to kiss you. But you can tell me no. Stop me if you don't want it."

Chad waited. She said nothing, then took a small step toward him. His heart picked up speed as his hands circled both her upper arms, holding her with a light touch. He looked into her eyes as his lips touched hers. Her mouth was warm and responsive as he teased her plump bottom lip. Izzy tasted so inviting. She returned his actions sending his heart rate into overdrive. The blood roared in his ears as his desire grew.

Letting his fingers travel down her arms to her waist, he nudged her against him. Her arms slid up his chest to wrap around his neck. He deepened the kiss and she joined him, a moan slipping from her lips. He ran the tip of his tongue along the seam of her mouth, asking for entrance.

To his delight, she opened for him. Her hands went to his shoulders, gripping them. Chad held himself in check with an effort not to crush her against him. He could overwhelm her, cause her to bolt. His desire could get out of hand. He eased back.

Izzy moved against him as if wanting all he could give. He had plenty to share. His arm tightened around her waist as his other hand ran along her rib cage. His thumb brushed the curve of her breast. The mewing sounds from Izzy heightened his need. He demanded more. She gave it.

The neighbor's back porch light blinked on. Izzy jerked away from him, and he said a sharp word under his breath

She looked everywhere but at him. This wasn't what he wanted. Not at all.

"I'm sorry. I shouldn't have let you do that. Please forget it happened." With that, she went inside and didn't look back.

Hell would freeze over before he forgot that red-hot kiss.

CHAPTER FIVE

EARLY THE NEXT Saturday morning, Izzy sat in the front passenger seat of Chad's SUV while he drove. Henry was securely strapped in his car seat behind them, chatting happily about everything he saw out the windows. Izzy joined him in looking through the windshield into the bright sunshine.

Chad had spoken to her again in the middle of the week while they were at work and convinced her he and Henry should drive her to her parents'. Regardless of her serious reservation about agreeing, she couldn't disagree with his logic. To her dismay but not surprise, her parents had insisted Chad and Henry spend the night with them. Izzy's middle fluttered with nerves. It looked like there was more to her and Chad's relationship than she'd intended. Her intention had been to pick up the furniture she had stored and return the next day. Not give her parents ideas.

After Chad's kiss, it was difficult not to have ideas of her own. She'd spent most of the week trying to forget about it. Unsuccessfully. About how it made her feel. How she had clung to him. How she had wanted him to do it again.

Then the denial came. She couldn't let it happen again. It was too important she protect herself. Think rationally. To not be naive. For self-preservation's sake, she couldn't get into another relationship. She couldn't afford emotionally to misjudge a man again. What she wanted and needed had to matter as much to the man as it did to her.

When Henry settled down and then slept, Chad said, "It's nice of your mom and dad to invite Henry and me to spend the night at their house."

Izzy lips tightened. "That's the kind of people they are. They'll welcome anybody." Izzy's eyes widened, realizing how callous she'd just sounded. "I'm sorry. I didn't mean for that to sound the way it did. I should have said they're very hospitable."

"If you'd be more comfortable, I'll get Henry and me a hotel room."

"No, no." She shook her head. "Don't do that. Mom wouldn't be happy if you did. I appreciate you going to this much trouble for me. I'm sure this isn't the way you wanted to spend your weekend off."

"Hey, I'm glad to get out of town. It's been a while since I've had an entire weekend off and I want every minute of it."

"The life of a doctor," she quipped.

Chad glanced at her with a shadow of gloom in his eyes. Had he thought of his wife's attitude about his job? "Glamorous, isn't it?"

They both laughed, which broke the tension she'd been feeling. Those simple moments let her slip back into the easy way between them.

"Why did you become a doctor?" Izzy suddenly wanted to know what made him who he was.

"I wished I could say it was an earth-shattering moment, a lightning bolt from the sky or some tragedy. But it was more like I was good at math and science and my teachers encouraged me to think about being a doctor. I decided to go to med school and found my home. I love the science of the job but most of all I love the patients. They come to me needing help and I give it to them. I help make lives different in the middle of heartbreak. There's little in the world more rewarding than that."

Wow. Izzy studied him a moment. She wasn't supposed to let him draw her further under his spell, but somehow he'd managed to make it happen.

"I don't think just being good in math and science was the only reason you went into medicine. I've seen you in action. You have the smarts and the capacity for empathy. Don't deny it. I've seen you talk to parents. They feel you care. That's what makes you one of the best doctors I've ever worked with."

Chad moved his hand as if fanning himself. He grinned. "Stop. You're embarrassing me." He glanced at her. "Not much different than the life of a nurse I would imagine."

"Not much." She checked on Henry, who still slept. "Aw, but the life of a child."

"You're welcome to take a nap. You don't have to entertain me." Chad had them moving down the road at a steady speed.

Izzy looked at his strong profile. This morning he hadn't shaved. Dark stubble covered his jaw, giving him a ruggish look she found appealing. "I'll be glad to drive as well. Let you nap if you want."

He changed lanes. "I'm a little old-school when it comes to driving."

She couldn't decide if she was impressed or not. "It comes with the macho-man image, doesn't it?"

Chad's brows drew together. "I've never considered myself a macho man."

"You qualify in my book." She sucked in a breath. That she shouldn't have said. It was too telling about how she felt about him. Truthfully nothing between them could be called just friendly any longer. The air around them sizzled when they were together. Like now, in this small space, sparks popped as if embers from a fire floating into a night sky.

She had to accept that. What simmered between them was desire. Two adults who wanted each other in the most basic way. There wasn't anything wrong with that. Would it be so bad to act on their attraction? If she held her heart in check.

A big goofy grin spread across Chad's lips. "Thank you, ma'am."

"Don't get any ideas," she huffed. "That sort of slipped out."

"Doesn't matter how it got out. I'll take it as a compliment." He smiled.

She looked out the side window and said flatly, "Maybe it isn't. It all depends on how you define macho man."

The grin left his face and his eyes turned serious. "And how would you define it?"

Confident she didn't want to go into all the positive attributes she saw in him, she had to redirect his question. "You know this conversation isn't going in a direction that I'm completely comfortable with."

His silvery eyes twinkled. "I was rather enjoying it."

"I can tell. It was all about you."

He chuckled. "Of course, we could discuss you."

"I don't particularly like that subject either." Chad had to already think she was pitiful after she'd told him how she let a man walk all over her.

"Tell me about your family then. Your mom and dad. What to expect."

Izzy leaned back in the seat, turning her back to the door slightly so she could see him more clearly. "I guess they're like anybody else's parents. They raised three children. They live in a subdivision in a brick ranch house like the others around them."

"And in this idyllic life, did you have a dog?" A humorous note filled his question along with a seriousness. He really sounded like he wanted to know.

"Yep. Leon. I named him after my first boyfriend."

"Interesting." Chad nodded as if he were a sociologist learning something important about her. "Makes me worry about your next dog's name."

She laughed, something she did a lot around Chad. "I thought it fit. Anyway, Dad is retired. Mom still teaches school. She is thinking about retirement next year."

"And how about your siblings?"

"You are full of questions. I have one sister. She lives in Memphis with her husband and three children. My brother lives in Nashville and has a wife and son and a baby on the way. You may meet him tonight. He usually makes an appearance when I come home."

Her plans had been to have the same thing as the rest of her family. A happy marriage, children and a life with someone special. But she'd failed. Instead she helped put Richard through school, which now made her sick to her stomach to think about. All that time and money and emotion wasted. She had fallen for Richard's promises of tomorrow that had turned into years of nothing—used and betrayed.

"What're you thinking?"

"How do you know I'm thinking anything? Aren't your eyes supposed to be on the road?"

"You got quiet, and your mouth pursed." He stated this with confidence.

Chad already knew her better than Richard ever had. Oddly that comforted her. She relaxed her facial muscles. "I don't purse."

He gave her a quick speculative glance. "If you say so but it sure looked as if you did. Regardless of that, what's bothering you?"

"I was just thinking about how happy my brother and sister are." She wasn't lying.

"And you wish you had what they do, don't you?"

Apparently she was completely transparent where Chad was concerned.

"Look, we all make mistakes. Heaven knows, I certainly have." He glanced over his shoulder to Henry. "But sometimes we have to go through the muck to come out on the other side on dry land and for the better. Along the way we must remember we're worthy of happiness."

She wiped her cheek. "Why, Dr. McCain, I had no idea you were so philosophical."

"Not philosophical so much as a man who saw his life turning out differently. You had a jerk for a boyfriend. Now you don't. It's time to leave that all behind you and live again."

"Like you are?"

"I'm trying. Some days are easier than others. Other days I have my boots stuck in the muck just like everyone else. But I do try to keep pulling them out."

Chad feared he'd gone too deep with Izzy. Been too hard on her. Had stepped too far into her personal life. But he wanted to know more about her. She said nothing after his little speech. A few minutes later, he'd looked over to find her eyes closed. Maybe he had added to her issues.

She'd told him to forget about their kiss. Like that was going to happen. Instead of forgetting it, he relived it over and over. It had been different than any kiss he'd ever experienced. It could only be because it was with Izzy. But that didn't mean he should pursue her further.

Hadn't he promised himself it would remain Henry and him against the world? Chad had thought about it and decided that was the best way not to have either one of their hearts broken. He knew well what a bad relationship could do to their lives, and he didn't intend to enter into another one again.

He wasn't going to offer Izzy any more than what they had now. Marriage would never enter his plans. He'd been poor at it the first time and he wouldn't take a chance on being in that situation again. Izzy deserved the best and he had proved he wasn't. What he needed to do was step carefully and not mislead Izzy into believing he could give more than he could.

Izzy woke as they approached the outskirts of Nashville. He'd had to work to concentrate on not going off the road as she stretched in the seat. "Sorry, I didn't mean to go to sleep on you."

Chad wished she had gone to sleep on him. Literally. Those visions did nothing to help him remain loyal to his vow to stay uninvolved with her.

Twisting, she looked between the seats and said to Henry, "Hey there. We're both sleepyheads."

Chad watched through the rearview mirror as Henry returned Izzy's grin. She was so good with him. Chad shook his head. She should be, after all she was a pediatric nurse.

"I need some directions, Izzy." She told him which exit he needed to take off the interstate. As he pulled into the quaint suburban town outside of Nashville, he scanned the area. "This must have been a nice place to grow up."

"Yeah, it was. Most people who live here commute into Nashville or are part of the music industry."

"What did your dad do before he retired?"

"He was an executive with an insurance company. Nashville's one of the biggest insurance centers in the nation."

"I had no idea. With an executive and a teacher as parents, what made you decide to become a nurse?"

"I always like helping people. My dolls, my dog, the girl down the street. It was a natural progression. I volunteered in the local hospital. One of the older nurses took me under her wing and encouraged me to go to nursing school. I worked and went to school at the same time. Richard just went to school." She didn't try to keep the bitterness out of her voice.

"You mean you supported him and went to school at the same time?" What would it be like to have that type of devotion in his life? The more he knew about Izzy, the more he admired her.

"I did. Sort of stupid, wasn't I?"

"I was thinking you were pretty amazing. I wish my wife had shown that amount of love and support." A sadness surrounded his words.

"That's nice of you to say, but I should have recognized when I was being taken for a ride. Being used."

"Love makes us put on blinders sometimes. I knew Nan wasn't happy, but I wanted to keep it together for Henry."

"Yeah, but that's different. I worked while Richard went to school. First his undergraduate degree, then his master's. All the time we talked about getting married. Or come to think of it, I talked about marriage. He would say *let me get through school and get the right job*. Then it was *until I get this or that promotion*. What type of person keeps believing that?"

Chad took her hand. He liked that she didn't pull away. "The type that believes in people. Wants to see the best in them. The kind of person who has a big heart and wants to help people. There's nothing wrong with you. All that was on him. You have nothing to beat yourself up over."

"You sure know how to make a person feel better." She offered him a wry smile.

"Just part of my charm. Or more like been there, done that."

She laughed. He returned it. At least Izzy didn't look as sad as she had earlier.

Izzy grew tense the closer they came to her parents' house. When Chad's hand returned to the steering wheel, she placed hers in her lap. She began clasping and unclasping her hands. "You need to take the next right into that subdivision."

Chad followed her directions. "Are you nervous about seeing your parents? Or about them meeting Henry and me?"

"You would notice." Izzy looked out the side window.

"It's pretty hard to miss."

She sighed and looked at him. "Let's just say my mom and dad will make more of you being with me than they should."

"Why is that?" He slowly drove down the street.

"They never liked Richard and they'll see you as a nice replacement."

His brows rose. "They don't even know me."

"You're not Richard." She paused. Chad was so much better. In so many ways. "And I might have told them a few things about you."

"Like how well my son behaves in the grocery store?" He grinned.

Izzy laughed. She liked that Chad could laugh at himself. "I might have left that out. Even if I never said anything, it wouldn't have mattered because they'd like any kind of replacement."

"That doesn't sound like a ringing endorsement. They disliked Richard that much?"

Her mouth tightened. She had said things she didn't want to. "They saw through him far earlier than I did."

Chad continued to drive along the tree-lined streets filled with large older homes. It reminded her of the area she now lived in but hillier. No wonder she was pleased with her apartment. She clasped her hands once more.

He placed his hand over hers. "Hey, everything's going to be fine."

"You'll think that until you get tangled up in whatever my parents will say and do."

"What'll they do or say?" Chad's face screwed up in confusion.

"Ask personal questions. Make embarrassing suggestions. Assumptions." Her words came out in a flood. She didn't want Chad embarrassed. Or worse to feel pressured to feel something for her.

"I think I can handle anything they come up with. Don't worry."

"Just remember you've been warned." She looked ahead. "It's the house down on the right with the two big oaks in the front yard."

"I see it." He swung the SUV into the paved drive.

Her parents exited the front door the second Chad stopped the car. Had they been looking out the window for them?

Despite Izzy's concerns, she hopped out of the SUV and hurried toward them. She loved them dearly. They just wanted her to be happy.

Chad was in the process of lifting Henry out of the car seat when Izzy and her parents came to stand on the lawn nearby. He closed the door, turned to the group with a smile. He held Henry in his arms.

"Mom and Dad—" Izzy moved to stand between him and her parents "—this is Chad McCain and his son, Henry. Chad is my landlord and coworker." She gave Henry a reassuring smile.

"It's a pleasure to meet you, sir." Chad extended a hand to Izzy's father. He took it with a firm grip.

Izzy moaned inwardly when her mother pulled Chad into a hug with Henry between them.

"It's nice to meet you as well." Her mother let Chad go and stepped back. "I understand you've been very good to Izzy."

This time Izzy's groan was loud enough that Chad looked at her with a grin. "I've tried but I have to admit she's done more for Henry and me than we have for her."

Izzy's mom looked at Henry. "Hi, Henry. I'm Martha. I just made a batch of cookies and I wondered if you'd help me eat them."

Henry's eyes opened wide. He looked at Chad, who smiled. "You can have some."

Izzy was impressed with how Chad and Henry interacted, and without Henry screaming a demand.

Her mother put out her hands. "Why don't you come with me? We'll go get a big glass of milk and have a few cookies. You can call me Mama Lane. That's what my grandchildren call me."

"What about me?" Izzy's father asked. "I like cookies too."

Henry had willingly gone with her mother. They started toward the front door. Over her shoulder her mother said, "Izzy, you show Chad where to put his bags. He and Henry will be staying in the back room with the twin beds. You take your old room."

Izzy and Chad stood watching the older couple completely engrossed in what Henry was telling them. They shared a laugh.

She nudged Chad. "You probably don't know it but that'll be the last you see Henry until we leave if they give him back then."

Chad chuckled. "I figured that might be the case. How're you holding up so far?"

Heat went to her cheeks. "I'm okay. I'll get through it. By the way, you and Henry did great a minute ago about the cookies. I was impressed."

"I can't take all the credit. It was from your good example. Even Ms. Weber has commented on the difference. She's been telling me for months I should do something."

Izzy couldn't help but be proud. "I'm glad you think I've helped."

"I want you to know that I won't take anything your parents say to heart." He removed their bags from the SUV and started toward the house.

She joined him. "I'm counting on that."

Izzy led the way inside, then to the bedrooms. She took her bag and placed it in her room across the hall from where Chad and Henry would be staying. Then they followed the sound of Henry's laughter to the kitchen. He was obviously entertaining her parents. She and Chad found them all sitting around a kitchen bar, eating cookies.

"Any chance I could get one of those?" Chad asked.

Izzy's mother quickly gathered a plate and a cup of coffee. She placed them in front of him at the bar.

"Thank you, Mrs. Lane. Please don't feel like you must wait on us while we're here."

"I promise I'm not doing for you any more than I would for anybody else." She glanced toward Izzy.

"She's not kidding." Izzy took a cookie and bit into it. "These are great as usual, Mom. I hate to run out just as soon as we got here but I made arrangements to rent a trailer. We're gonna need to go get it before the place closes. I want to have time to load things ahead of when it gets dark. We must be headed back first thing in the morning."

"Can't you stay longer?" her mother whined.

"Not this time. It'll be longer next, I promise, Mom."

"Why don't you let Henry stay here with us while y'all go and pick up the trailer? We'll find something fun to do," her mother offered.

"That's fine with me. If you're sure?" Chad looked from her mother to her father, who nodded.

Chad turned to Henry. "Would you like to stay here and play with toys until I get back in a little while?"

"Toys?" Henry gave an eager nod.

They all laughed.

"I'll expect you to behave." Chad's look turned stern.

"We better go," Izzy said, touching Chad's shoulder.

Izzy noticed her mother watching them closely.

"I'm ready." Chad stood.

Mr. Lane did as well. "I appreciate you helping Izzy out this way. She's got that tiny car that doesn't hold anything to speak of."

Izzy put her arm around her father's waist and hugged him. "Tell the truth. What you're glad of is not having to give up your pickup truck for a couple of weeks."

"That too." Her father pulled her tighter.

Later that evening Izzy sat back in her chair at her parents' dining room table, listening as Chad kept up a running conversation with her parents. Her brother, Steve, and his wife, Laura, who had come for dinner, joined in the discussion. Chad fit into her family perfectly. Even Henry enjoyed playing with her nephew, Ross, despite being younger.

Richard had never melded with her family during the few times he had visited her parents. In fact he struggled with any kind of relationship with her parents as well as her siblings. As the years went by, Richard joined her less and less when she came home. He always found excuses to stay behind. In contrast, Chad, who barely knew them, acted like an old friend.

"Martha, I can certainly tell where Izzy got her culinary skills." Chad sighed with satisfaction. "That might be one of the best meals I've ever had."

Izzy watched her mother preen under his praise. Even if Chad laid it on a little thick, Izzy appreciated his efforts. It was important to her mom for people to appreciate her cooking.

"Thank you, Chad. Feel free to flatter me anytime." Her mother smiled brightly.

Chad laughed and so did the rest at the table. "May I help you clean up?"

"My goodness, no. My guests don't help clean the table. Instead, why don't you young folks go into Nashville and see what's going on."

Steve and Laura looked at each other and shook their heads. Laura said, "I'm sorry. I wish we could but it's already past bedtime for Ross." She grinned and patted her rounded middle. "And for me and this new little one on the way."

"We'll watch Henry," her mom stated as she looked at Izzy, then Chad. "So that you can go."

Izzy narrowed her eyes at her mother. "Mom, I don't think Chad wants to do that. He's driven up here and then loaded the trailer. He may be too tired to go out."

She'd helped as much as she could with the loading of her belongings onto the trailer, but Chad with her father's help had done the bulk of the work. A couple of times she'd caught herself watching Chad's muscles ripple beneath his shirt as he lifted the furniture. Heat had flashed up her neck to her cheeks when he caught her doing so. He'd grinned and winked as if he knew she'd been ogling him. She'd quickly made herself busy, directing her father to the next piece of furniture to load. Chad was far too perceptive for the stability of her nerves.

"I can't impose by leaving Henry here. It wasn't my intent to come and put him off on you."

"We wouldn't mind. You two go enjoy yourselves. If you've never been to Broadway or by the Parthenon at night, you should. You can drive my car since the SUV has the trailer on it."

Izzy sighed. Her mother had thought of everything. Pulling out all the stops to let her and Chad have some time alone. Without making too much of a scene, Izzy didn't know how to stop the forward motion of her mother in train-engine mode.

"Go on." Her mother waved a hand. "Chad said he's never been to Nashville except passing through."

Izzy gave Chad a questioning look. He quirked his lip as he shrugged. "Sounds like fun if your parents are sure they don't mind watching Henry."

"We don't mind at all," her mother jumped to answer. "Why don't we get Henry ready for bed and settled before you go. Then you won't have to be worried about him being any trouble."

"He's had a big day so he should go right to sleep." Chad pushed back from the table.

"While you do that, I'll help Mom with the dishes and cleaning up." Izzy gathered the dirty plates within reach.

"All right. I'll meet you at the front door in twenty minutes." Chad went in search of Henry, who was playing with Ross in the den. Steve and Laura gathered their things to leave.

Steve gave Izzy a hug. "Chad's a nice guy. Way better than that other one."

Izzy shook her head. "There's nothing between us. He's just my landlord."

"I've never seen a landlord look at someone the way he does you." Her brother's eyes twinkled.

Laura joined him. "Come to think of it, I never have either."

Her brother put his arm around Izzy's shoulders and squeezed. "Nope, he likes you."

Izzy swatted at his chest. "Enough of that."

"It's great to see you. We miss you around here, but I understand why you felt you needed to move." Steve put his arm around her shoulder.

"I'll come home when I can. You guys can always come visit me." Izzy hugged him, then Laura.

"We'll try to do that soon," Laura assured Izzy while rubbing her stomach. "Give us time to get this girl here."

They hustled out of the house, taking Ross with them as he complained about having to leave.

Izzy joined her mom in the kitchen. She shooed Izzy out. "Why don't you go freshen up your face? Maybe change your shirt for something sweeter before y'all head out."

"Mom, I've told you more than once that Chad and I are just friends."

"Okay, so you don't think you need to look nice even for a friend. Or anybody else you might meet?" She gave Izzy a nudge. "Go on and do what your mother says. You'll be glad you did."

Knowing she wouldn't win the argument, Izzy took her mother's advice. Izzy pulled on a ruffled blouse and let her hair down, giving it a good brushing. She then checked on Chad and Henry.

"Izzy tuck in?"

"Sure, honey," she answered before Chad could say anything.

Sitting on the side of the bed, she kissed Henry on the forehead. "Good night. Sleep tight. See you in the morning."

She stood. Chad took her spot. "I'll be there in a few minutes."

Chad soon joined her in the living room.

Izzy wasn't comfortable having her parents force Chad to spend time with her. "You know we don't have to go out. We don't have to do this just because my mother insisted."

His look held hers. "I'm a grown man. I know I can make my own decisions. I'd like to go if you would."

Izzy plastered a smile on her face. If he wanted to do this, then so did she. "Come on then. Let's go see what Nashville has to offer."

An hour later Izzy strolled beside Chad as they moved down Broadway. "This is the older section of Nashville. The area known for honky-tonks and music cafés. Many of the country music singers got their start here. I'm sure you've heard Nashville is the capital of country music."

"Yes. That much I do know." Chad took her hand as the crowd grew larger around them.

She left her hand there, not wanting them to get separated. At least that's what she told herself. It felt natural to have Chad's hand surrounding hers.

"Go on. I'm enjoying having my own personal tour guide."

Izzy appreciated how effortlessly Chad built up her ego. It had been so damaged by Richard it was wonderful to have someone who treated her with respect. "The Bluebird Café, just around the corner, is known for launching many famous performers. They still host up-and-comers today. I don't know if we can get in, but we can try."

"That's all right. Country music isn't my favorite, but I certainly listen to a lot of crossover artists."

"We could go to the Wild Horse Saloon and have a drink. It's just over there." She pointed across the street. "How're you at line dancing?"

"We can if you want to."

For once Chad sounded unsure. "That sounded less than enthusiastic."

"Ah, come on. I'll try anything once." He gave her hand a tug.

She smiled. "Anything?"

An intensity filled his eyes. "Almost anything."

A shiver went through her. She had the idea they might not be talking about the same thing.

They entered a large two-story room that was filled with people. The dance floor was already busy. They found a small table along the back wall and ordered a drink.

"So." Chad gave the dance floor a doubtful look. "Have you done much line dancing?"

"I've done my share. Few people live in Nashville and don't line dance or listen to country music. I even own a pair of cowboy boots. They're tucked away in the back of my closet."

He wiggled his brows. "I like a girl in boots."

Izzy grinned. "Are you flirting with me?"

"Maybe a little bit." He grinned. "Do you mind?"

She dipped her head, aware of the warmth coursing through her. "Not really."

They sipped their drinks through a couple songs.

Izzy was interested to see what skills Chad had in the dancing department. He seemed flawless in all she'd ever seen him do. "You ready to give it a try?"

Chad held out a hand, palm up. "If you promise not to make fun of me."

His boyish look of worry pulled at her heartstrings. She placed her hand in his. "I'll be there right beside you. Just follow what the others are doing."

They went to the dance floor, forming a straight line along with everybody else. Just as she suspected, Chad caught on quickly and was quite a good dancer. She watched him move to the music, his actions lithe and sure. His dips were particularly nice because she had a chance to appreciate the grip of his jeans across his butt. Best of all, he acted as if he was having fun. The fact he had been willing to try something new was refreshing. She appreciated that he didn't take himself too seriously. Something Richard couldn't do.

They danced for another half hour before Chad said close to her ear. "It's time for me to sit down. I haven't had this type of physical activity in a long time."

Izzy led the way back to their table, but it had been cleaned and taken by another couple. "What do you say to slowing the music down? There's a piano bar farther down the street that I've heard is really good."

Chad again spoke next to her ear, the brush of his words going across her cheek like a caress. She shivered. "It sounds like a good plan."

They soon found the small dark club that looked like little more than a dive. A female voice sang a Patsy Cline song as they found a table in the dark room with a piano located in the middle. A few couples circled a small dance floor off to the side.

Izzy leaned across the table. "It's still pretty early so there aren't a lot of people here yet."

A girl came to take their drink order and they settled in to listen.

"She really has a good voice." Chad nodded toward the piano player.

Izzy smiled. "She is good."

The piano player started to sing a slow sultry song.

Chad stood and offered his hand. "This is more my speed. Would you care to dance?"

Izzy wasn't sure she should be so close to Chad, but she couldn't pass up the opportunity either. The idea of him holding her made her nerves quiver. She placed her fingers in his. He led her to the floor and confidently pulled her into his arms. Chad led her with poise and grace to the beat of the music. As they swayed, he placed his cheek against the top of her head. Slowly, he moved them around the floor.

Her hand stroked his shoulder. Could she stay here forever? Not an idea she should be entertaining.

"I'm glad your mom insisted we come down here," Chad whispered against her ear.

Izzy couldn't disagree.

They danced seamlessly into the next song. When that one ended, Chad said, "Wait right here." He went to the piano player and spoke to her before dropping some bills in a jar.

The lady glanced at them, then the notes of "Penny Lane" began to fill the room.

Izzy smiled and shook her head as Chad took her in his arms again, moving her into a faster step.

His lips brushed her temple on the way to her ear. "I couldn't resist."

"You know you've ruined this song for me forever. Every time I hear it, I'll think of you."

He held her gaze with those all-knowing eyes. "And that's a bad thing?"

It could be a heartbreaking one. She needed to change the subject.

Chad took her through a pattern of fancy steps.

"I thought you couldn't dance?" she panted, a little breathless.

"Never said I couldn't. Just that I've not done much line dancing."

Izzy smiled. "I think I've been had."

He grinned. "I like holding you much better than standing beside you."

She couldn't disagree with him. Finally left no choice, Izzy said, "It's getting late. You've had a long day. I better get you home."

Chad's gaze held hers. "Too bad. I was enjoying holding you."

Heat filled her. Could they have an uncomplicated relationship? She did enjoy his company. They headed toward the entrance. She felt Chad close behind her. As she exited to the sidewalk, Izzy bumped into someone.

"Hey!"

Her heart went to her throat. She knew that voice.

"I'm sorry," she murmured. The dreamy world she'd been in with Chad dissipated in a flash. She didn't need this now.

"Izzy."

Her hands trembled. Of all the people in the world she could run into, it had to be Richard!

She said his name as dry as a dessert plain. "Richard."

She felt more than saw Chad step close. Izzy appreciated his support. She straightened her shoulders, looking Richard in the eye. After all, she'd done nothing wrong. She refused to act as if she had. He's the one who should be ashamed.

"How're you?" Richard asked.

He acted as if they were old friends with nothing negative between them. "I'm fine."

An obviously pregnant woman came to stand next to Richard. Her hand curled around his arm, a wedding ring glimmering in the light. Izzy's heart tightened with disappointment, grief and resentment. This other woman had all that Richard had promised her. A marriage and a soon-to-be family. Izzy's supper turned in her stomach.

"I heard you moved to Atlanta."

"Yes. I'm home collecting the rest of my furniture." Why was she explaining herself to him?

Richard glanced at Chad.

Izzy felt no compunction to introduce the two men. She had no desire to contaminate Chad with someone like Richard. All she wanted was to get out of there. "We have to be going. Goodbye, Richard."

Chad wrapped a reassuring arm around her waist and led her away. "I guess that was Richard, the ex?"

"Yes."

Chad kept a hand at her waist as they headed to the parking lot. "Enough said."

Chad couldn't help but be impressed with Izzy's civil reaction to meeting her ex again after what he had done to her. If it had been him seeing Nan again, Chad wasn't sure he could have done as well. In fact, he was tempted to turn around and punch Richard for how he'd treated Izzy. What he was still doing to her. Their relationship had completely colored Izzy's view of the world.

Izzy said nothing on the way to the car. He kept his arm around her waist as they made their way down the crowded sidewalk. He didn't press her for more information. Instead he held her close even when he didn't need to. Her body remained ridged.

Inside the car she gave him directions in a subdued

voice. It wasn't until they were close to her parents' house that Izzy said, "I'm sorry you had to witness that."

"You have nothing to be sorry about."

"We were having a nice evening, then my ugly baggage comes out of hiding." The words hissed through her clinched teeth.

"You had no control over that." He pulled over into the parking lot of a small park and turned off the car. "Do you want to talk about it? It might make you feel better."

Izzy stared out the windshield with her hands clasped in her lap. "We were together for nine years. We talked about getting married and starting a family. He acted as if he wanted it as much as I did. But there was always something in the way. Needing to finish school, finding a good enough job, him getting a certain promotion so we'd have the money. There was always an excuse. Then one day eight months ago I come home to find him in bed with that woman." She all but spit out the word *that*. "Now she's pregnant. Having the baby that should have been mine. She has everything that Richard kept promising me." Izzy let out a little sob.

Chad's chest tightened, wanting to absorb her pain. "There'll be another man—a better man—and a houseful of children, I'm sure." Chad kept his voice low and reassuring. Who wouldn't want a woman as lovely as Izzy? The guy must be an idiot.

"I hope so. I just wish I hadn't wasted so much time on him. My sister and brother already have families. Then there's me, the odd man out."

"We all know I'm not a shining example of how to have the perfect relationship." That's why he didn't trust himself to ever consider marriage again. He couldn't afford to get it wrong again. He and Henry deserved the right person.

"Yeah, but I feel so stupid."

Chad smiled wryly. "I've been there and done that too." He took one of her hands and played with her fingers.

She looked at him. "What do we do about our bad choices?"

"It has been my experience you live and learn." Chad pulled her into a reassuring hug.

Izzy returned it. Her lips brushed his cheek and traveled toward his mouth. "You're a nice man," she whispered. "Not only did I drag you up here to get my furniture, but you put up with my parents' not-so-subtle matchmaking, then I involve you in my emotional baggage."

He chuckled. "You do know how to entertain a man."

"I know other ways to entertain." Her mouth found his.

Izzy's lips were plump, reminding him of berries warm from the summer sun. She opened in invitation, causing his blood to pulse through his veins. Her tongue searched for his. She sighed and pressed into him. Chad took over the kiss, applying more pressure as his hand traveled along her side and slipped under her satiny blouse to the silk of her skin. Izzy whimpered and rubbed against him.

He pulled her across the console dividing them until she sat in his lap. Her hip pressed into his stiff manhood. "Izzy."

She kissed along his jaw to nip at his earlobe.

The flash of headlights going by brought him back to reality. "I'm sure I'll hate myself for this later, but we need to think about what we're doing. As much as I'd enjoy having you right here and now, it's not the time or the place. I won't have you in the back seat of your mother's car. More importantly, I've no interest in being your rebound guy. I'd rather you not regret being with me."

Izzy went stock-still. Even in the dim light he could see her stricken look. As if she'd just realized what she was doing. He found that flattering.

"I'm, uh…sorry." With jerky movements, she pushed

away from him. When she had difficulty getting over the console, he helped her. She scrambled the rest of the way into her seat.

"You have nothing to be sorry for."

Izzy said no more as he started the car and drove to her parents'. In the time it took him to climbed out of the car, Izzy was almost to the front door of the house. "Izzy."

She stopped and waited for him.

He joined her and his hands cupped her shoulders before he placed a kiss on her forehead. "Things will look better in the morning. I promise."

CHAPTER SIX

Izzy HAD TO force herself to face Chad the next morning at the breakfast table. She'd embarrassed herself on a level that was unprecedented. Had she actually thrown herself at him? She groaned. Was she really that desperate?

"Are you okay, honey?" her mother asked.

"I'm fine." She chanced a glance at Chad to find him giving her a reassuring smile. It eased some of her pain. Marginally. When had she become so desperate for attention that she would throw herself at a man?

Regardless of Chad's silent encouragement, she kept her eyes averted from his as much as possible. She could feel Chad watching her as she interacted with her parents and Henry.

Chad's rejection still stung even though he had a good reason for doing so. In an indescribable way, Chad's actions pained her more than Richard's had. She hadn't intended to put herself in that position again. After last night she intended to keep that distance she had originally believed she needed to have from Chad. Even a hint of not being wanted hurt. She had had enough of that in her life.

They left her parents' home with them smiling and chit-chatting with Chad and Henry nonstop. They even had Chad agreeing to return for a visit soon. Just as she feared, her parents had become too friendly with Chad for her comfort. They wanted something between her and Chad that wasn't there. What had happened had to stop before it got further out of hand.

Out on the interstate, Chad drove in the steady stream of traffic headed south. "Izzy, are you ever going to look or speak to me again?"

Her heart thumped. She didn't want to have this discussion. She filled her voice with innocence. "I don't know what you mean."

"You know exactly what I'm talking about."

She looked back at the napping Henry. Anything not to have this discussion.

"The last thing you are is stupid." Chad's tone remained smooth and reassuring.

"Do we have to talk about it?" she asked softly but with a bite to the words.

"Apparently we do."

That got her attention. It wasn't like Chad to use that tone with her except at work during an intense case.

"You need to let me know what you're thinking." He stopped at a light and his look bore into her despite his eyes being behind sunglasses.

She huffed. "Look, I embarrassed myself. And you last night. I appreciate you being a gentleman. That's all. Now it's been said."

"You might think so, but I think you're imagining something that's just not true."

Izzy turned to face him. Anger filled her. She recognized rejection. Knew it intimately. "Oh, no. I think I have a good handle on the situation."

"And I think you don't." His voice had turned tight. "I believe you're under the impression that I don't want you." He paused. "That's the furthest thing from the truth."

Some of the ice around her heart melted.

"In fact, I don't think I've ever wanted somebody more. What I don't want is you using me to get back at your ex. Or using me as your way to forget your ex. He still clouds your world far too much."

The air in the SUV hung thick with the weight of what Chad had just said. She saw the intensity of his feelings by the lift of his chin and the tightness of his jaw.

"Now that we've settled that. I want you to look at me and talk to me. Tell me something you'd like to do someday. Anything."

For the first time that morning, Izzy truly smiled. "You're a strange man, Chad McCain."

He grinned. "You're not the first person who has said that. I want to know. What would you like to do more than anything in the world? Someplace you'd like to go. Something you'd like to learn."

She didn't have to think about it. "I'd like to visit all the state capitals in the United States."

He looked at her long enough that Izzy said, "The road."

Chad's attention returned to his driving. "Sorry. I just hadn't expected that answer. Have you ever been to the capital in Atlanta?"

"Nope. It's on my list for my next day off."

"Then I'd like to be the one to show it to you." He glanced at her, wearing a smile.

"All right." Izzy returned his grin. "I answered your question. Now it's your turn. What would you like to do?"

His attention never left the road. "I have a long list of wants but right now most of all I'd like to kiss you again."

At that idea, heat flowed through Izzy and her smile grew larger.

Two days later Izzy passed Chad in the hallway of the ER unit. The notes of "Penny Lane" never failed to come across his lips. Izzy grinned. That tingly feeling he always created in her appeared. She shouldn't be so giddy about the personal attention he showed her, but she couldn't help but like it.

They hadn't seen each other except at work since their trip to Nashville. It was just as well. She needed some distance from him. Needed time to sort her feelings. Izzy wasn't sure there would ever be enough time for her to figure those out. She went between accepting the feelings that were growing in her and convincing herself she should stay as far away from him as possible. The problem was she lived in his backyard and worked with him. That wouldn't be easy.

Recently her saving grace had been they were on different shifts until today. Even now the ER had been so busy they hadn't had a chance to talk to each other. She'd deny it if asked but she missed him.

Izzy walked up to the unit desk. The unit tech said, "Dr. McCain has a fall patient coming into trauma one. You want to help him out?"

She couldn't say no. They made a great team in an emergency. "I'm on my way."

Izzy entered the room. The patient had just arrived. The EMTs were still giving Chad the report.

The girl had a four-by-four bandage lying over the right side of her forehead.

"Hi, I'm Izzy, one of the nurses. What's your name?"

"Judy."

"Judy, may I take a look at your injury?" Izzy smiled. The girl nodded.

A two-inch laceration marred her young face. A red line of dried blood went over her eye and down her cheek.

"Can you tell me what happened?" Izzy asked.

Chad joined them then.

"I hit the street curb hard," the girl said.

Izzy said, "This is Dr. McCain. He's going to take care of you. He's nice and you'll like him."

Chad's look met hers for a second. His eyes twinkled.

"Judy, can you tell me what happened?"

"I was walking along. I just fell." She sounded perplexed.

Izzy looked to Chad. "I'll get her vitals."

Chad said to Judy, "I'm going to need to check your eyes. I'm afraid you might have a concussion." He pulled down on her bottom eyelid.

"I don't want to be here," Judy groaned.

Izzy spoke close to her ear. "I hate to say it but I'm afraid you're gonna have to stay. You need stitches and you need to be watched for a while. You took a hard hit to the head."

Chad spoke to Judy. "Can you follow my finger?" He moved his finger back and forth in front of her face. "What made you fall?"

"I don't know," the girl muttered.

"She just went down." A man who stood in the corner responded, adding, "I'm Judy's dad."

Chad asked Judy, "Does anything hurt? Other than your head."

"It was hurting before I fell."

Izzy's gaze met Chad's. That didn't sound good.

He nodded. Chad asked his next question in an unemotional voice, but Izzy recognized a note of concern. "Can you show me where?"

The girl pointed to the top right side of her head.

"Judy, I'm afraid you're going to have to join us here at hotel Atlanta Children's. You need to have some more tests run. I can promise you all the Jell-O you want and a visit to see an amazing fish aquarium. But before you have a chance at those amazing things, I'm going to need to put in some very eye-catching stitches in your head."

The girl gave Chad a half smile.

"It's that bad?" the father asked.

Chad nodded. "I suspect there's more going on than needing stitches. Izzy, I'm going to need a suture kit."

Izzy pulled a rolling tray over next to the bed with the kit already on it. She removed the bandage, then cleaned and sterilized the area around the laceration while Chad pulled on a gown and gloves.

"Judy, I'm not going to lie to you. This is going to hurt but soon it won't. Just hang in there with me. Izzy is going to hold your head steady. I need you to be very still. Dad, if you want, you can come hold her hand."

The father stepped to the other side of the bed and took Judy's hand.

"Are we all good?" He checked the group for nods. "Now, Judy, remember you can't move. Dad, why don't you tell us all about Judy's first Christmas?"

Chad was doing a good job of distracting the girl while he used a needle to numb the area around the wound. "It's going to take a few minutes for that medicine to work. While that's happening, Izzy and I are going to step out and find you a nice room for the night. We won't be gone long."

Izzy followed him out. Chad turned to her as soon as they were out in the hall with the door closed between them and the patient. "Will you call admissions and get her a room. I'm going to call neurology and get them on this case right away. One of her eyes is dilated. My best guess is a tumor."

"I'm on it."

"You always are." Chad smiled.

Ten minutes later they were back in the room stitching Judy's head. Izzy applied a bandage over the area.

"You're all done here. I understand they're blowing up

the balloons and pulling out the party hats on the third floor to welcome you."

"No, they are not," Judy said with a dry tone and a hint of a smile.

Chad smiled. "You never know."

"Thanks, Doctor," Judy's father said.

"Not a problem." Chad looked at Judy. "I'll be checking on you. A tech will take you upstairs."

Izzy cleaned up the area while Chad moved on to his next case. Just when she thought he had been at his best, he went and moved the bar higher. He was wonderful with a girl who had to have been terrified. Chad made it hard for Izzy to stick to her plans to stay away from him.

Later that evening Chad leaned against the door facing Izzy's office as if he didn't have a care in the world. He was so handsome and wearing her favorite grin. Izzy's heart quivered. "Can I help you, Doctor?"

His cheeky grin turned wolfish. "Yes, you can. But I don't think you'll agree to it."

Heat built inside her, settling in her chest. He might be surprised. "Why're you hanging around at my door then?"

"I was going up to check on Judy and wondered if you'd like to go along?"

"I would like that. Thanks for asking." She closed the laptop she'd been working on.

They had started toward the elevators when Chad said, "I need to stop by the gift shop for a sec before we go up."

"Okay." She hadn't known him to frequent the store.

Five minutes later they were in the elevator going up. Chad held a large helium balloon in bright colors.

Izzy looked at him and smiled. Few people would have thought to do something so nice for a child he really didn't know. "You're a special man, Dr. McCain."

"Thank you. Coming from you, that's high praise."

They walked to the third-floor desk and stopped. There all the female staff looked at Chad and smiled as if he might be their choice piece of candy.

"I'm Dr. McCain from the ER. Will you tell me what room Judy Reynolds is in?"

"Three twelve," a women said.

Walking toward the room and away from the desk, Izzy said in a low voice, "Well, you made an impression."

"How's that?" He sounded innocent as if he had no idea what she was talking about.

She looked at him with disbelief. "You didn't notice how all those women acted at seeing you holding a balloon. All their mouths dropped open, and they started to drool."

His gaze met hers, a grin on his lips. "Nope, I didn't notice. Did you drool too?"

Thankfully she didn't have to answer that because they had arrived at Judy's room. Chad knocked and pushed open the door. Judy lay in the bed, watching TV.

"Since you didn't believe me about the party, I thought Izzy and I would bring it to you."

The girl gave them both a genuine smile. She took the balloon from Chad.

Izzy suspected it but now it had been confirmed. Chad could charm the young and the old. She wasn't the only one who'd fallen under his spell. She might have been fighting tooth and nail not to have feelings for him but the man had a way about him. She couldn't keep pretending differently. Would it be so bad to explore what there was between them? Just see what happened?

They visited with Judy for a few minutes, then started back to the elevator.

"Henry's going to his grandparents' in the morning and will be gone until Sunday afternoon. Dr. Ricks gave me two tickets to see the Braves play tomorrow evening. I was wondering if you'd like to go?"

Izzy pursed her lips. She should say no but she didn't want to. "I don't know…" She paused. "But I do want to go. I love professional baseball. However, I have to work tomorrow until three. Will that be a problem?"

"Shouldn't be. The game starts at seven. We'll have plenty of time to get there."

Chad followed her back to her office. He stepped inside and closed the door.

"You need something else?" Izzy turned to him.

"I do. It's been too long." His arm reached around her waist, bringing her closer.

Izzy didn't have the willpower to stop him. She needed his kiss too.

Chad's lips found hers with a tender touch that was both stimulating and brief. He let her go and stepped back. "Sadly, again not the place or the time. But soon." He kissed her hard and fast. "Very soon."

He stepped to the door.

"Chad."

"Yeah?"

"I drooled too."

He grinned as he headed out the door. "Penny Lane" drifted back to her.

As determined as Chad was to keep his emotions in check where Izzy was concerned, he couldn't seem to resist her. It had become impossible for him to not think about her. He spent his nights arguing with himself over what was right for him, her and Henry. But the answers conflicted with his desires. She was a great nurse, a wonderful person, loving with Henry and made him want to kiss her senseless every time he saw her. The woman had him twisted up in a knot. One that he couldn't undo.

A prickle went through him when he took her hand while they walked to the baseball stadium, and she didn't resist. He craved her touch, enjoyed holding her hand. The problem was the more he was around Izzy, the more difficult it became to act unaffected by her.

"Are you really into baseball?" He knew few women who would have been as eager as her to go to a baseball game.

"I have been all my life." Her face alighted with pleasure as she looked around.

"You don't think it's kind of a slow game?" He guided her toward their entrance gate.

"Not for me. I like all of the tactical stuff. Which ball to throw. What goes into the coaching. There's nothing better than bases being loaded, a man up to bat with two outs and three balls count. You can't beat the drama. Anticipation. Then with a crack of the bat, he hits a home run."

Chad chuckled. "Yeah, you really are into it. So how do you feel about a stadium hot dog?"

She smiled. "Nothing better in the world."

"Then I guess that's what we'll be having. Unless you want to wait until we get home."

"A hot dog sounds perfect to me." Izzy beamed.

The desire to take her behind the stadium and kiss her almost got the better of him.

"It's not the only thing that's perfect."

Izzy's gaze met his. Chad's attention focused on her mouth. Unable to go without any longer, he kissed her. She leaned into him. The call of someone broke them apart. She looked shy and rattled. So sweet he wanted to kiss her again. "Come on. We don't want to miss the first throw."

As they continued toward the ballpark, a crowd gathered around them. They entered the stadium and found their seats.

"Wow, these are great seats. I'm impressed," Izzy said as they found their places five rows behind the Braves' dugout. "I'm going to be spoiled for my next game."

"You should be spoiled often but I can't take credit for the seats. Remember I was given the tickets."

"Still, you asked me to come along." She gave him a long meaningful look.

He cleared his throat. "I'll go get our food and be right back."

The national anthem had been sung and the first ball thrown out by the time he returned. Chad grinned as he handed her the food. "You do know that you can sit back and still see."

"Yeah, but I like to be as close to the field as I can be." She took her drink and slipped it into the holder. "This is a truly amazing place and experience. Thank you for giving this to me."

"You're welcome." Chad settled in his seat and propped his foot up on the empty seat in front of him. Izzy looked cute dressed in blue jean shorts and a red T-shirt with a Braves logo on the sleeve. Her hair had been tucked up inside a ball cap.

With her food finished, Izzy moved back to the edge of her seat. He couldn't stop himself from running his hand across her back and could have sworn he heard her purring. Her focus remained on the field, but he sensed her awareness of his touch. He could keep it up for as long as she let him.

Hours later they walked out of the stadium hand in hand. This time Izzy had slipped hers into his. He smiled as if he were a kid who'd won a prize. They worked their way toward his car along with the mass of humanity.

As they walked in the early darkness, Izzy snuggled to him. "You must be cool." He wrapped an arm around her and pulled her close. At the SUV he ushered her into it.

"Thanks for today." She touched his arm. "I had a wonderful time."

"I noticed that. And I'm glad you did."

"A little intense, was I?"

"Just a little." He pulled out into the traffic.

She giggled.

The sound rippled through him. There was something relaxing about Izzy's laugh. As if it could sooth any hurt. "Would you like to stop for something to eat?"

"I'm fine. I ate way too much at the game. If you want something, stop. I don't mind."

When had he rethought his stance on getting involved with Izzy? That's just it. He hadn't. She'd just happened. He'd thought he could resist her. With time he'd come to find out he couldn't. "I'm good too but I did have one more thing planned for the evening."

"What?"

Her eager look had him reconsidering it for going home and hopefully to his bed. With her. "I wanted to show you something. I think you would really like it. But it can wait until another time."

"No, let's do it now."

"Okay, if you really want to." He maneuvered the SUV out onto the interstate.

"I do."

He drove past the turn off to his house and continued downtown.

"Where're we going?" Izzy demanded.

Her curiosity was one of many things he liked about her. "Wait and see. I want it to be a surprise." Chad turned off onto a drive with few lights. He came out of the tree-lined street and pulled into a large empty parking lot.

"Oh, my goodness. It's beautiful." Awe filled Izzy's voice as she looked at the grand building with a bright gold dome glowing in the floodlights. "Can we get out?"

"Sure."

They met each other at the front of the car. Chad leaned back against the grill, and she did the same beside him.

"I thought you might appreciate seeing the Georgia Capitol Building after dark. Or have you already seen it?"

"No, I haven't. I've only really gone between the hospital and home and back again." She grinned. "With the exception of trips to the grocery store."

He gave her a nudge with his shoulder. "You're not going to let me forget that, are you?"

"I doubt it." Her focus remained on the Capitol. "It's magnificent. Thank you for bringing me here."

"On our next day off, we'll tour the inside." Before Izzy, he would have never had an interest in doing so. He wanted to show her everything.

Her head went back so she could look at the tip-top of the dome. "What makes the gold paint glow so?"

"That's real gold. From Dahlonega, a small town in north Georgia. The gold was brought down here in wagons pulled by mules. The dome is gold leaf." He might sound like a history teacher but Izzy hung on every word. His ego grew.

"That's amazing," she said in admiration. "So beautiful."

He watched Izzy. Not unlike her.

"Thank you for showing me this." She kissed his cheek.

Heat shot through him. "I think you can do better than that."

Chad brought her around to stand between his spread legs as he continued to lean against the SUV. His mouth found hers. Izzy came up on her toes and met his kiss. His hands went to her waist and slipped under her T-shirt to find warm silky skin. She wiggled against him. His manhood shot to rock-hard. Her mouth opened. Chad entered, wanting to devour her.

He needed her gentle ways. Her steadfastness. The serenity she brought to those around her. The peace she somehow brought to his life. He needed to inhale it, surround himself in it, hold on to it.

He eased away from the kiss. "I think we should take this somewhere else."

CHAPTER SEVEN

HALF AN HOUR later Chad pulled into his driveway and stopped the SUV behind Izzy's car.

Their relationship had grown to something he didn't want to define. He should leave her alone, couldn't make promises about tomorrow. Yet there was something between them, something he'd never had with another woman. No matter how hard he pushed it away, the desire to explore it remained. As undefined as it was, there was still a rightness to it. They fit. For right now at least.

Not wanting to scare Izzy away, he had to be careful, but he also didn't want the evening to end. He had so few nights that were all to himself. Henry would return tomorrow. "Since there's a nice breeze, why don't we sit in the backyard for a while? I'll get us both a drink."

"That sounds nice. Why don't you let me get the drinks since my kitchen is closer? Would you like iced tea or water or something stronger?"

To his immense pleasure, she'd agreed. He hadn't been confident she would. "A cold beer?"

"I should be able to fill that order." She headed toward her door.

Chad settled into the metal chair. Leaning his head back, he closed his eyes. He listened as Izzy open and closed her door. A few minutes later, her soft steps came toward him. He knew the moment she stood in front of him without looking because the scent that was hers alone filled the air. He smiled. What a lovely smell. Chad opened his eyes.

"I thought you might have gone to sleep." She looked down on him.

"Nope. Just listening to the night sounds." And for her. He found Izzy as peaceful as a quiet night. He reached for the beer bottle she held, taking a long swallow as Izzy settled into the empty chair beside his.

"It's been a nice evening." Her words were so soft he almost missed them. "I had fun at the ball game. I loved seeing the Capitol. Thanks for sharing that with me."

Chad hadn't felt this content in a long time. He wished it could stay that way. Izzy made his busy, stressful single-parent life easier by just being around. He would worry about tomorrow then. Right now, all he wanted to do was pull Izzy into his lap and kiss her senseless. Then take her to bed and love her to the point she was too weak to get out of bed.

He inhaled deeply and released it slowly. What was happening to him? Izzy. He didn't say anything for a few minutes.

"What were you thinking?" Izzy asked.

Did he dare tell her? "Do you really want to know?"

She didn't immediately answer as if she knew her response would change everything between them. "Yeah, I do."

"I think there's something special between us. I'm not sure what it is or where it can go, but I know it's special enough that it would be a shame not to act on it." Izzy didn't say anything. His throat tightened. Had he misjudged the situation?

He glanced at Izzy. She smiled. Even in the darkness,

he could tell. "I'd be lying to you if I didn't tell you I'd like to have you in my bed."

Her intake of breath had him watching her. He took another gulp of his drink. When she stood, his heart sank. She was going in and leaving him to wallow in his need.

"Mine's closer."

Heat shot through him. "Are you saying what I hope you're saying?"

Izzy offered him her hand. "For a very intelligent man, you can be awful slow sometimes."

He put his bottle on the ground, got to his feet and took her hand. She led him to her door. Opening it, she stepped inside. He followed.

She turned. Her hands went to his chest, traveled up to his shoulders, across them, then returned to wrap around his neck. She nipped at his bottom lip, then pressed her lush mouth on his. With her chest against his, she kissed him deeply. His already-thick manhood twitched. His hands trembled as they cupped her butt and brought her against him.

"Not that I'm complaining but what made you agree?"

"I trust you. You make me feel special. Make love to me, Chad."

"Sweetheart, I promise you can always trust me, and you are unique." He would show Izzy just how special he thought she was. "Izzy, you need to know that I'm not looking for anything permanent. All I can offer is tonight."

"That's enough. I'm good with just tonight. I just needed to feel wanted."

"You are wanted, have no doubt of that."

Izzy moved toward the bed. He reached for her pulling her back to him. He brought her into the circle of his arms and tenderly kissed her. She melted into him. His manhood throbbed. Izzy opened for him when he teased the seam of her lips. She deepened the kiss as if she needed reassurance of her desirability. He intended to show her she was that and so much more.

What he wouldn't do was pounce on her like a starving man.

Chad brushed his fingers along her arms until his tangled with hers. He continued to give her gentle kisses along her neck. Izzy made little noises of pleasure that fed his desire. His hands moved to her waist, where he slowly gathered her T-shirt in search of bare skin, making circles at her waist and back with his thumb.

Izzy purred in appreciation.

His manhood tightened. Chad reminded himself to go slow and easy. He hadn't expected Izzy's easy acceptance or aggressiveness. Not that he minded. In fact, it turned him on more. His marriage had been so lackluster in the sex department. He enjoyed having someone who acted excited about being with him.

This wasn't the practical and cautious Izzy. He suspected he was seeing the real Izzy, open wide and alive. His heart raced at the thought of experiencing that passion. Yet he wanted to savor her. He needed her to feel treasured.

"I think we need to slow this down a little. I'd like to make it last."

Her hands stilled. She stepped back, looking away.

This was the last thing he wanted. Using a curled finger, he lifted her chin until she met his gaze. "Hey, nobody's complaining here. To the contrary. Don't turn away from me now."

"I wondered if you thought I was coming on too strong. I've been accused of that before."

"Stop thinking such garbage. Whatever *he* said, he was wrong. On every level. As far as I'm concerned, you're perfect."

A genuine smile formed on her lips. "Thanks for thinking so. You're pretty perfect as well."

"Now where were we?" He lowered his head. "Somewhere right about here." His lips tenderly found hers as he lifted her T-shirt. Chad pulled it over her head, dropping it to the floor.

Izzy didn't move. She watched him as he cupped a breast. Full, ripe, he judged its weight before he brushed the pad of his thumb over the skin along the line of her bra. She felt warm and smooth beneath his finger. "So beautiful."

She trembled. Her heart raced beneath his hand. He couldn't remember ever being so well rewarded from a touch. Leaning down, he kissed the top curve of her breast where his thumb caressed. "I love how responsive you are."

Her hand slipped into his hair, holding him to her as his lips traveled over her skin, finding her nipple beneath her bra. The other hand pulled at his shirt until she touched the skin of his back. Her fingers kneaded his muscles, encouraging his attention. He pushed at her bra until both her breasts were visible.

Lifting one, Chad placed a kiss on the tip of her nipple. "So beautiful." His gaze captured her dazed one. "May I see how delicious it tastes?"

Izzy mouth parted slightly but no sound came out. Her eyes filled with the foggy look of delight and anticipation. Her breath hitched as his mouth surrounded her nipple. He tugged, then circled it with his tongue. Izzy moaned. Her hands on each side of his head held him to her. With a flick of his fingers, he released the back clasp of her bra and removed it, letting it go the way of her shirt. As he did, Izzy pushed at his shirt. He jerked it off. The cloth floated to the floor.

When he would have brought her against him, she held him away with her palms against his chest. "It's my turn to admire you."

Izzy had promised herself she wouldn't step off into deep water where Chad was concerned. That had changed quickly. She found him impossible to avoid. It looked as if she needed a rowboat if her heart was to survive the onslaught of Chad's lovemaking. Her mind had stopped working. All she could do was feel. Chad's desire for her showed in his every touch. It empowered her. She'd felt weak for so long.

Chad stood, his hands featherlight as they glided up and down her arms while she explored his chest. She ran her fingers through the dusting of hair in the center. Teased his nipples with her teeth before she kissed them. All the time her hands were moving across his skin. She marveled at the flex and pull of the muscles beneath their warm covering. Everything about Chad felt right. Strong, steady and secure. She was safe with him.

She heard the hiss of his breath when her distended nipples brushed his chest. She went up on her toes to kiss his chin. He was as sensitive to her touch as she was to his. Her lips traveled along his jaw as her hands worked the button of his khaki shorts.

"I think it's time I got involved here." Chad's words were a low growl that rumbled through her. His mouth covered hers in a hot wet kiss as he crushed her tightly against him.

She wanted more and more of Chad. Her hands returned to the clasp of his shorts. She found the zipper. Below it lay his length, thick and hard, waiting for her. Her center had gone wet in anticipation. This need growing in her hungered for appeasement. By this man.

Chad's mouth remained on hers as his hands came to her waist, then up to tease the outer curves of her breasts.

She returned his kisses while she slowly lowered his zipper. Her fingers brushed his length with the back of her hand. She wished his underwear were gone.

Chad's kiss gentled as she pushed his pants to the floor. When she would have gone after his underwear, his hand stopped her. "I think you have some catching up to do."

She pressed against him, appreciating the heat of his skin in the air-conditioned room. As his hands moved down her sides, goose bumps that had nothing to do with the temperature rose along her skin.

Chad led her to the bed. He sat and brought her between his legs, facing him. She rested her hands on his shoulders. "I want to see all of you." His hands traveled to the waistband of her shorts. He worked the button open and the zipper. With hands on her hips, he tugged, letting the fabric drop to her feet.

Izzy toed off her tennis shoes and stepped out of her shorts.

Chad wasted no time in sending her panties to the floor. She stood bare and exposed in front of him. Chad inhaled sharply.

He held her at arm's length. Izzy watched as he studied her. She moved to cover herself, but his hand circled her wrist and held it. "Izzy, you're amazing. Breathtaking. Magnificent."

Each adjective made her heart swell. Izzy's body grew hotter.

"Come here. I want to touch you." He brought her closer. His hand rested on one hip while the other brushed along her thigh, down to her knee, then up again to her hip.

She shivered, shaking with longing.

Chad's fingers went down to her knee again. He teased

the hollow place in the back. He used her inner thigh as the pathway up. Her body reacted as if it were an instrument humming to only a tune Chad could play. Her center tingled in anticipation of his touch, drummed with need. Instead of giving her relief, his fingers moved to her other thigh. Again, going to her knee. That patience and thoroughness he was known for in the ER might drive her crazy.

Izzy's fingers bit into his shoulders. Her body swamped with aching need, making it difficult to stand.

Chad's gaze captured hers as his touch moved upward again. "Tell me what you want, Izzy. Let me give it to you."

"Touch me." The words were a soft beg.

He brushed her curls. Her legs widened. She wanted more. His finger ran across her heated center. Her knees wobbled.

"Steady." Chad's hand tightened on her hip. "I'm just getting started with loving you."

Izzy wasn't sure she could stand much more.

His damp finger ran along her thigh but soon returned to the arch of her legs. This time he found her center and entered.

Izzy whimpered. Chad pulled his finger away and returned. His mouth found her breast. He mimicked with his tongue what he did with his finger. Izzy held onto him for dear life as her body twitched and jerked while her center tightened and curled in on itself. She pushed down on Chad's hand, asking, then grasping, for that supreme relief. It came as a blast of pleasure that made her throw back her head, close her eyes and moan. Her entire body shook and sank against Chad.

He lifted her to the bed. Looking down on her, he smiled. "Heavens, you're beautiful."

With her eyes still glazed with bliss, her body sedated,

she said, "I can assure you that you may take all the credit for it."

Chad chuckled. "You do know how to build a man's ego."

She cupped his cheek. "And you know how to give a woman an experience of a lifetime."

A wicked look formed on his face as his eyes gleamed. "I'm not done yet."

Izzy sighed. "I sure hope not."

Chad stood and removed his underwear. Finding his shorts, he took out his wallet and pulled a condom from it.

Izzy watched his movements with fascination. "I can appreciate a prepared doctor."

"More like a hopeful one." He started to open the package.

Izzy curled a finger and called him forward. "Come here first. Let me admire you."

He hesitated a moment. "I don't know if I can stand much admiration at this point."

"Let's just see." She offered him her best pleading look while moving to sit on the side of the bed.

Chad stepped to her. Izzy's hand circled his aching manhood. His breath hissed on its way in. Her hand stroked him. His jaw tightened. This couldn't go on much longer. She met his gaze as she pumped her hand as far down as possible and back again.

"That's it." He growled and removed Izzy's hand. Taking the foil package, he said, "Move to the center of the bed." Seconds later he was covered and joined her. His lips found hers as he positioned himself between her legs. She wrapped them around his waist pulled him to her. Unable to wait any longer, he entered Izzy.

She took all of him, nudging him closer with her heels.

Encouraging him. Her arms came around his neck, and she clung as he pumped into her. She was everything he'd dreamed of at night and imagined during the day. Warm, welcoming and responsive.

Too quickly he climbed the peak. Seconds later Izzy pulled her mouth from his, stiffened and eased as a soft sigh of her release whispered by his ear. He made one final plunge and exploded into oblivion that could only be described as extraordinary.

He was in trouble. If he only had one night with Izzy, he better make the most of it.

When he could catch his breath, he rolled to her, gathering her to him, and kissed her temple. "Izzy, I don't know what to say but thank you."

"Mmm..."

Her eyes were closed. She slept. Standing on shaky knees, he moved the covers back and placed her under them. He then climbed in beside her, pulling her against his chest. She snuggled in close. This was what made a perfect moment. He listened to her gentle breathing for a few minutes before he joined her in rest.

Sunlight was just beginning to show through the large picture window the next morning as Chad came out of the bathroom to find Izzy still sprawled naked on her stomach in the bed. She reminded him of a golden goddess in a Renaissance painting. His manhood instantly hardened. He wanted her again. In the most basic way. To mark her as his. Standing at the edge of the bed, he grabbed her ankles and pulled her toward him.

"Huh?" She looked back with hooded eyes.

His hands ran up her legs to her waist. He pulled her hips up to him. When she would have turned, he kissed her shoulder. "Stay on your knees."

She stilled.

His finger found her center and teased until she was ready. His other hand fondled a breast. Izzy wiggled her butt against his thick length, almost sending him over the edge.

He groaned. His manhood throbbed. "I can't wait any longer." Seconds later, after grabbing a condom, he pressed into her.

Izzy moaned. She raised her hips, giving him better access. He thrust into her. She took him without complaint. The pleasure of having her was almost more than his control would allow.

"Join me, Izzy."

She raised her hips higher. Her body shuttered. She drew his name out as her orgasm washed over her. Moments later his body shook with the force of his release, one that blinded him to nothing else but the sweetness of Izzy.

She lay on her stomach, panting. He fell half on her and half on the bed. He kissed her shoulder blade as his hand ran along her waist and over the rise of her behind. "Sweetheart, that was amazing. I'm sorry I took you like a barbarian. When I saw your sweet bottom, I had to have you."

Izzy rolled to face him. "I'm not complaining." She kissed him. "Now, hush so I can get some sleep so we can do it again."

A chuckle rippled through him. "Sounds like a plan."

His arm lay over her waist. What was to become of them? After last night he didn't know if he could give up Izzy. She would never accept half measures and he couldn't offer her more. She wanted marriage and children. He'd been down that road before. He didn't know if he could do it again, even to keep Izzy.

She shifted and snuggled into him. Her hair smelled

of flowers as it tickled his chin. His chest had a knot in it. The more painful question would be how could he ever let her go?

Izzy woke to a warm male next to her. It took her a few moments to realize where she was and who was with her. A Mona Lisa smile crept to her lips. She had a secret. It was Chad McCain. Right now he was all hers.

She hated to leave him and his warmth, but hadn't they agreed this would be temporary? She shouldn't get used to having him close. She made a trip to the bathroom. Chad still slept. Izzy resisted the temptation to slide back into bed. Instead she went to the kitchen. He would be hungry when he woke.

Quietly she prepared omelets and toast. It was almost time to call him for breakfast when she heard the low rumble of, "Good morning."

Chad sat on the edge of the bed with his chest bare and a sheet across his hips. His tussled hair and morning stubble covering his chin gave him a sexy look.

Maybe she should forget about breakfast until later. The grumble of Chad's belly ended that idea. He stood and she turned away. She couldn't take anymore. The man spoke to her on a physical level as well as an emotional one. For however long it lasted, she intended to enjoy it. She'd figure out the rest later.

Chad pulled on his jeans not bothering to button them. What was his plan? Torture her?

She returned her attention to the omelet. Chad reached around her and moved the pan off the heat. He kissed the back of her neck, then turned her to face him. "Every morning should start with breakfast and a little sugar. Not necessarily in that order."

His lips found hers. Izzy's arms, with a spatula still in

one hand, went around his neck. She leaned into him, accepting all he'd give. This she would take for as long as she could get it. However short that might be.

The sound of his stomach complaining again broke them apart.

"I think I better get some food into you."

He grinned, then gave her a quick kiss on the cheek. "I'm going to the bathroom, and I'll be right back."

He was as good as his word and soon returned. Izzy had their places set on the bar. Their food waited.

"This smells good and looks wonderful. You could spoil me with your cooking." Chad dug in with gusto.

He could spoil her by just being there. Izzy spent most of her meal watching Chad. He looked perfectly at home here with her. She studied the way his shoulder muscles moved as he forked food into his mouth. Last night she'd enjoyed every ridge and dip to her heart's content.

His look met hers with a raised brow. "You're not eating."

"No."

"You better eat. I have some physical activity planned for you today." His look of desire made her middle flutter with want.

"I thought we only had last night." Izzy needed to slow herself down.

His lips turned teasing. "I thought we might extend it until this afternoon unless you have an objection."

She bit into her toast. "What do you have planned?"

Chad's gaze caught and held hers, his eyes having taken on a predatory look. "I want to take you back to bed and make slow love to you. Then I'm going to take you downtown to a nice hotel for lunch. I don't have to pick up Henry until four, so I think I'll bring you back here and love you a little more."

Izzy put her finger on her bottom lip and tapped. "It sounds doable."

"So you don't have a problem with my plans?" Heat flickered in his eyes.

Warmth streamed through her, pooling at her center. "Not at all."

The next few days Izzy lived in a cloud of blissful memories and sadness. Thoughts of her and Chad's time together heated her while at the same time disappointment cooled her, knowing they wouldn't be together again. Unfortunately it was the way it must be. That's what they had agreed to.

In such a brief time, Chad had captured her heart. She'd tried and failed not to let him and Henry draw her in. Staying emotionally uninvolved had been impossible. Especially after the passionate lovemaking Chad and she had shared over the weekend.

He'd said nothing about his feelings or wanting anything more before he left to pick up Henry. Instead he'd given her a long hot kiss that curled her toes.

The worst thing was having to see Chad at the hospital. She had to force herself not to react when his hand accidently brushed hers. Or let it show when her hands trembled if he stepped too close. Still, she couldn't help but grin like a silly schoolgirl when she heard the notes of "Penny Lane" when he walked by her or passed her office.

It did help they were on opposite schedules, but it hurt as well. On the days she wasn't working, she eagerly waited for the sound of the SUV pulling up the drive. With great restraint she kept from going to him. She refused to let on how much she wanted him back in her bed. Somehow she had to put a stop to this needed that gnawed at her.

They had agreed to keep what had happened between

them just that—between them. She feared she wasn't that good of an actress, but she gave it her best effort. Even Ms. Weber, who Izzy was beginning to call a true friend, gave her a speculative look when Chad was mentioned.

On the Thursday evening after their weekend, there was a knock at her apartment door. She looked up from the book she'd been trying to read.

"Hey, can I come in?" Chad asked from outside the screen door.

Izzy stood, cramming her hands into the back pockets of her jean shorts. "Sure."

"How are you doing?"

"I'm fine." Great. They were back to acting like strangers.

"Uh, about this past weekend. I haven't had a chance to say how much I enjoyed spending time with you. I should have said that before now."

Was he feeling as unsure around her as she was around him? "I thought it was nice also."

"So we're still good?"

"Yeah, we're good."

He shifted on his feet for a moment. "I noticed you have the day off tomorrow, and I don't have to be in until seven for the evening shift. I promised to take you to the Capitol. I like to keep my promises. If you want to go, I'll see if Ms. Weber will come a little earlier to watch Henry."

For her own sake, she should decline but she didn't want to. The problem was she loved doing anything if she was with Chad. How easily she'd fallen back into the pattern she'd had with Richard. Making her world revolve around a man. But Chad wasn't just any man. "I'd like to go."

"Then I'll check with Ms. Weber. We'll do tourist things for a while. Maybe sneak a kiss or two in a dark corner." He winked.

Izzy's blood zipped. She had no idea how much she'd missed a man flirting with her. Chad did it so well. "We'll see."

"Okay. I understand. I like spending time with you, and I'll accept that."

Izzy smiled, one she meant. "Good because your friendship is important to me."

"I feel the same." He returned her smile.

The next day Chad found a parking place close to the Capitol and they entered through a side entrance. Soon they stood in the rotunda looking up at the beautiful artwork.

"This is truly amazing," Izzy said in awe.

She glanced at Chad to find him watching her. Her cheeks turned warm. "I must sound like a silly girl."

"Not at all. I'm glad you're enjoying yourself."

He sounded as if it was important to him that she was happy. "Isn't this where they stand on the steps when giving a press conference?" She pointed to the large marble stairs in the center of the Capitol building.

"Yep. At least I know you keep up with the local news. Come this way. I want to show you what a fifth-grade boy liked most when he visited the Capitol a long time ago." He took her hand.

With a feeling of rightness, she let him.

"I hope it's still here."

They went around a couple of corners.

"There it is." Chad proudly put out a hand.

"Ooh." She squished up her nose. "It's a two-headed calf."

A sheepish look came over Chad's face. "I guess it's wasted on a girl."

She gave him a teasing slap on his arm. "You do need to work on you dating skills."

His eyes took on a wicked look. "I don't have to when I have other skills."

Izzy flushed. On that they could agree.

He studied her a moment. "Hungry? I know a burger dive a couple of blocks from here."

"Sounds good. It won't have any two-headed animals, will it?"

Chad chuckled. "Nope. They'd already be hamburger anyway."

They walked toward the exit door.

Izzy stopped to look through the window of the senate meeting room. "Thanks for bringing me here. It's very impressive."

As they continued down the marble hallway, they passed three men, one walking ahead of the others. The one in front smiled and said, "Hello."

Chad answered, "Hello, Governor."

When they were outside, Izzy turned to Chad. "Was that really the governor?"

"Yes." Chad wore a huge grin.

"You spoke to the governor." She looked back at the door in amazement.

Chad chuckled and led her toward the SUV. "Come on. Let's go eat."

They entered the diner that look like it belonged in the 1950s, complete with metal tables and chairs with red plastic seats. Chad settled her at a table. A few minutes later the waiter took their order. Soon their burger plates were place in front of them.

"This place is something." Izzy wrestled with her lettuce, tomato and onion that continued to slip out from the bun.

Chad grinned. "I can tell you're enjoying it. You've got ketchup on the tip of your nose."

Izzy giggled.

"Don't do that." Chad's voice turned tight.

"You don't like my laugh?" Hurt filled her chest. She looked at Chad, finding him watching her with a flame of want in his eyes.

His heated gaze remained on her. "The problem is I like it too much. If you don't want to miss out on that burger because I've taken you out to the car and had my way with you, I'd be careful."

"Chad, we agreed to one night. I can't keep my distance if you talk like that."

"Izzy, I can't promise you tomorrow, or all the things you want. But I can promise we can have a good time together. Enjoy each other's company. Do things together. We're good together. Great in fact. I don't want to give that up and I hope you don't either." He looked deep into her eyes. "I ache for you. One night isn't going to be enough for me."

At least Chad was being upfront where Richard hadn't been. Chad wasn't making promises he couldn't or wouldn't keep. He wasn't planning to use her. She ached for him too. More than she ever dreamed she could. She'd go into this relationship with her eyes open. "Then we can agree to a fling?"

"As long as if works for both of us." A wolfish gleam came to his eyes. "Henry and Ms. Weber should be napping by the time we get home. Maybe we could put that time to good use."

She smiled. "I'd like that. A lot."

Saturday a week later Chad knocked on Izzy's door. She greeted him dressed in a large T-shirt that just hit the top of her thighs and a smile. He swallowed hard. "I hope you don't open the door dressed like that for everyone."

"No, I save this outfit for special people."

He grinned. What had he done to deserve being this happy? The only thing that would have improved the moment was if it had taken place in his bed when he woke that morning. It was killing him to keep Izzy at a distance when he only wanted to have her next to him. His attraction to Izzy he'd fought from the beginning. Even at the grocery store before he'd even known her, there had been something. She made his emotions whirl. He was waiting on his brain to catch up.

The last week had been nice. She'd shared a few meals with him and Henry. Had stayed after to watch some TV. He'd not realized how lonely he had become. It was nice to have someone around. It was especially nice to have Izzy close. To share a laugh. Sneak a kiss. Have someone whom he looked forward to seeing at the end of the day.

Like now he couldn't resist pulling her to him and giving her a quick kiss on the lips. "Henry wants to go to the zoo. Would you like to go with us?"

"That sounds like fun."

Chad remained in the doorway, afraid if he went inside it might be a while before he came out. If only Henry could be left alone... It had been days since they'd had sex. Instead of physical activity, Chad had made a point to make Izzy feel wanted out of bed by spending time talking to her while they watched Henry play, or by inviting her to dinner at his house or just small touches. "We'll go to Piedmont Park afterward for a picnic."

She pushed her hair back out of her eyes. "Sounds good to me. Do I need to fix anything?"

"Nope. Henry and I'll take care of everything. Today you just get to enjoy." He pulled her to him again. This time he allowed her to return his kiss. "See you in twenty minutes."

With a lightened step Chad strolled to the house, looking forward to spending the day with his two favorite people. That feeling he could only describe as euphoric. It had been so long since he'd felt that way it took him a moment to recognize it for what it was. He hummed "Penny Lane" as he entered the house.

Yet something niggled at the back of his mind. How long could things stay the way they were before he or she wanted more? Or less? He'd long ago decided he wasn't husband material and that's want Izzy wanted. Chad winced. How could he ever let her walk away?

They were in the SUV on the way to the Zoo Atlanta when Izzy asked Henry, "What's your favorite animal?"

"Lions."

"Do you think you'll see one today?"

Henry nodded.

"What's your favorite?" Chad asked her.

"I like the giraffes." She looked a Henry. "They have those long necks."

"How about you?" Izzy touched Chad's arm.

"I'm a polar bear guy." A few minutes later, he pulled into the parking lot of the zoo. There he strapped Henry into his stroller. "Let's go see if we can find all our favorite animals."

As they walked toward the entrance, Izzy said, "I'm impressed with how you handled that stroller."

At her approval, his chest expanded. "I can't say it didn't take time to learn."

"Most things worth learning do. You're a good father, Chad. The way you treat Henry, your patients and me, I think you must have been a better husband than you give yourself credit for. You have nothing to feel guilty about."

"Thanks. Coming from you that means a lot."

She stopped, gave him a long look, then a smile. One of those that he felt in his chest. "I meant it."

"Go, Daddy." Henry wiggled all over, shaking the stroller. "See lions."

Chad and Izzy laughed, then Chad said, "Let's go see some lions."

They found the lions first. Henry and Izzy spent a long time talking about what they were doing and what they ate. Chad enjoyed the interaction between the two. The excitement on their faces was infectious. Izzy would make a wonderful mother. And wife.

For some reason that didn't strike fear in his heart. His mind was going places he had closed off. Could he or Henry stand it emotionally to open that door? Was he ready to make that step?

They stopped to see the polar bears as they worked their way around the zoo. When they came to the snake habitat, Izzy said, "I believe I'll just wait out here."

"You sure you don't want to go in?" Chad teased.

She pursed her lips in the cutest way. "I'll be fine right here."

Chad whispered in her ear, brushing his lips across her cheek. "And I thought you were fearless."

He and Henry went inside the dark room. When they returned, Izzy waited for them in the bright sunlight. Ironically that's how he thought of her. As a shining light in his life. Chad shook his head. He had it bad. If he weren't careful, he'd break out in song. Seconds later he caught himself humming "Penny Lane."

"I've been looking at the map. It looks like the giraffes are just around the next turn," Izzy said.

"Giraffes," Henry squeaked.

Chad raised his brow at her.

She grinned. "It's just as important to know when you can scream as it is to know when to be quiet."

Chad leaned close, making sure no one else could hear. "I like it when you scream."

Izzy's eye twinkled as her cheeks pinked.

He watched with a feeling of rightness settling in his chest as Izzy and Henry enjoyed talking about the giraffes. Henry was fearful at first but soon warmed up to the large animals with Izzy's encouragement.

From there they started making their way back to the car. Ahead of them was a family of five. One child was in a stroller and the other two held the hands of a parent. At one time he'd wanted that. Maybe it wouldn't be so horrible to want that again. To have more babies. Brothers and sisters for Henry. A wife for him.

But could he be the right husband and father for them? He couldn't and wouldn't give up his medicine. He'd not been enough for Nan. What made him think he could be enough for someone else? Today he and Izzy and Henry were just playing family. What happened when life got hard?

He looked at Izzy. Still, she had his mind wandering places he'd once said he'd never travel again.

CHAPTER EIGHT

THREE DAYS LATER a staff member stood at her door. "Izzy, Chad asked for your help in trauma two. We have a go-cart accident patient."

Izzy hated that. They were the worst. Mangled children were tough cases. "Tell him I'm on my way."

Izzy closed the laptop, pulled her hair back in a band and headed out the door. When she arrived, the boy lay on the gurney with his eyes closed. Izzy had no doubt Chad had given him medicine to help him rest and relieve his pain.

Chad was already busy issuing orders. "I need X-rays, full routine lab work, vitals and IV antibodies going. Use the uninjured arm for those. We need to cut the clothes off. Izzy, I need you with me. While I check for internal injuries can you start cleaning him up?" He looked up and down the bloody body of the eight-year-old boy. "We're going to need at least six suture kits to start. I'd like you to assist."

Izzy went to the storage cabinet and pulled out the kits, setting them on a movable tray. "I'm going next door to get two more. Anything else we need?"

"More saline and plenty of four-by-fours. This boy didn't win against the tree."

Izzy hurried to gather the supplies. When she returned, the X-ray techs were there. As soon as they finished, she and Chad moved in again along with the other staff to do their jobs.

"The plastic surgeon on call needs to be notified," Chad said to no one in particular.

"Done," a nurse called.

Izzy smiled. Her staff knew their jobs. "Sherry, help me clean up this boy so Dr. McCain can go to work."

Chad jerked off his plastic gloves. "I'm going out to talk to the parents a moment while you're getting him ready for stitches. They must be worried."

Izzy and the nurse went to work removing the blood from around the wounds. Chad quickly returned. He pulled on fresh plastic gloves. Izzy put on a fresh pair as well.

Chad's chin when to his chest. His eyes closed and he took a deep breath.

"Chad?" Izzy looked at him with concern.

His shadowed gaze met hers. He looked like his mind had gone somewhere else.

"You okay?"

"Yeah." His eyes cleared. "Let's do the laceration on his leg first. It looks like the deepest and longest. I suspect the X-ray is going to show that the left arm is broken. We'll wait on that one. The one on his shoulder we'll do next and work our way down to the smallest. When Plastic gets here, they'll handle those on his face."

Izzy popped the top on the saline bottle and poured it over the long wound. Had Chad been thinking about how Henry had looked after the accident?

"Watch for any debris." Chad adjusted the large light above them. He was back with her now. They leaned over until their heads were almost touching.

"There's something." Izzy pointed to a spot inside the wound.

Chad picked up long tweezers and pulled out a piece of bark. "Well done."

They continued to search as Izzy poured. Satisfied they had found everything, Chad opened a suture kit and went to work.

Izzy said to Sherry, "Start cleaning the other wounds while I help Chad."

He made small stitches inside the wound. She dabbed the gauze in the wound, making sure Chad could see. As he finished knotting each stitch, she cut the thread.

Izzy glanced up at Chad, whose look remained on the stitches he was placing in the boy's arm. He methodically went about his work. His hand remained steady as he made the hoops and twists.

For hours they worked, getting the boy's injuries closed. Izzy's shoulders ached. Just as they finished, a plastic surgeon walked into the room.

"Glad to see you, Pete." Chad removed his gloves and threw them in the trash. "The patient is all yours. You'll pass him off to Orth to set his arm."

"I hate to see these go-cart injuries. They sure can mess up a kid." The tall thin man wearing green scrubs studied the boy's face.

"I couldn't agree more." Chad turned to her. "Good work." He looked to Sherry. "Nice job." Chad rolled his shoulders.

Izzy wished she could massage them but that would be noticed and commented on.

He dropped the gown and mask in the garbage bin on the way out the door.

Minutes after she returned to her office, Chad entered without bothering to knock. He flopped into a chair and ran his hands over his face, then through his hair. "I hate those cases. It's almost more than I can do to get though them. Children mangled in accidents. The auto ones are always the worst, but go-carts are up there."

Izzy came around the desk, closing the door as she moved toward him. She stood close beside him. Chad reached around her waist, bringing her close. She returned his hug, pressing his head into her chest as she ran her fingers through his hair.

"I know they must be difficult with your history. But Henry is safe."

"It's just that I see him in every one of those cases. It drags up all those horrible memories. If I hadn't upset Nan, she might not have had the accident."

"You're just guessing that. You'll never know exactly what happened. You can't keep blaming yourself for everything."

"Easier said than done. You made it better today by being beside me. And now. Somehow you make it all easier." He gave her a gentle squeeze.

"That's nice to hear." Izzy looked at him, giving him a weak smile. "I'm here for you."

"I never doubted it."

"Good."

He looked at her. "You're strong, passionate, bighearted and dependable. I can count on you. You don't know how much that means to me."

She kissed him on the forehead. "It means a lot to me to hear you say that."

"I mean every word."

His phone rang. He answered. "I'm needed in the ER."

She gave him a quick kiss on the lips. "I'll tell you what, why don't you and Henry come to my place tonight for supper. We can all watch a movie together. Have a slow easy evening. Decompress."

He stood. "Thanks. I don't know what we did before you came into our lives."

That evening Chad entered Izzy's apartment to the smell of something hot and fresh. Home cooking. Better than that, Izzy stood at the stove. Her face flushed from the heat.

She came to him and took Henry, who received a big kiss. "Hello, handsome."

"Down." Henry wiggled. She put him down to go play with toys from a basket she kept for him near the sofa.

"Hey." Izzy looked at Chad when he stepped forward. Interest showed in her eyes. She gave him another look, this one from head to toe. Heat shot through him. "I like that look on you. A tight T-shirt and jeans. You're rocking the sexy doc look."

He walked up behind her, pushed her hair to the side and kissed her behind the ear.

"Mmm… I like you. So sweet."

"I like you too." Why did he feel better just being in Izzy's presence? She drew him to her like a bee to a flower. Then didn't let go.

"I've tried a new recipe. I hope you like it," she quickly added.

"Smells wonderful." He stepped back from her, afraid he couldn't keep his hands off her. "I bet you taste better."

She fidgeted with a spoon. He'd gotten away with her. Chad liked that idea.

"How were things at the hospital when you left?" She filled the glasses with iced tea.

"Let's just say I'm glad to be here."

Izzy moved around the small kitchen, and everything about her said home. His chest tightened. He mustn't get used to this. Despite coming out of a bad relationship, Izzy still believed there was a happily-ever-after out there for her. He'd been kicked in the teeth too hard to even think it was possible for him. Would their playing house come back to haunt him?

She turned back to the stove. "We have about ten minutes before dinner. Sit down and talk to me while I finish up."

Chad took one of the two stools at the bar. He checked on Henry, who happily played on the floor. Izzy had already set two places at the bar and brought Henry's high chair over from his house. She thought of everything.

She pulled a casserole out of the oven and placed it on a hot pad between the two plates. Going to the refrigerator, she brought out a bowl of salad and put it on the bar.

"This looks great. I probably wouldn't have eaten and just fallen into bed after a shower if you hadn't invited us over. This is far better."

"I want to see what you think about the chicken recipe." She picked up Henry and put him in the high chair like she'd been doing it forever.

Chad spooned a steaming amount of casserole onto her plate and placed it in her spot, then did the same for his plate.

"I fixed something special for you, Henry." Izzy went to the refrigerator again and brought out a plate with a peanut butter and jelly sandwich on it and a cup of milk.

If he didn't already care for Izzy, she would've grabbed his heart then. "You're amazing, Izzy."

Chad waited to eat until she joined him with Henry in the chair between them. He ate a fork full of food. "This is so good."

He finished his whole plate. "That was wonderful."

"I'll clean up." Izzy moved to stand.

Chad placed a hand on her arm. "Sit. I'll clean up. It's only fair. You cooked."

Half an hour later he sat on the couch with Henry asleep with his head on Izzy's lap. Chad took a seat beside her. He lay his arm across the back of the sofa as he played with Izzy's hair. He couldn't remember a more restful evening. Just what he needed after his day. He had almost let his emotions get away with him over the go-cart patient.

Izzy made the atmosphere easy and comfortable. It felt like a family sharing time together. Everything he had sworn he never wanted again. Even watching a children's movie with Henry asleep had a rightness to it. His fingers teased the circle of Izzy's ear and she shivered. She leaned her head back and smiled at him. Yes, life did feel right. Too much so for his comfort.

The next morning Chad had just finished with a patient and returned to the nurses' desk to do his charting. It was one of the rare times no one was around. He settled in a chair and went to work on his iPad. Something brushed his shoulder. A faint floral scent that could only be Izzy pushed the ever-present smell of antiseptic away.

"How are you doing this morning?" he asked as she came to stand beside him.

Closer than either one of them dared while at work. He'd always been the protector in a relationship. Now Izzy seemed to shield him. "I'm good. You just getting here?"

"Yep. I'm not wild about these half shifts but knowing I'll be seeing you does help."

"What are you up to?"

"I'm just finishing up some charting and thinking about Henry's birthday as it's coming up in a few weeks."

"Do you have any plans?"

He made a face at Izzy as if she'd lost her mind.

She laughed. "Are you confused by the word *plan* or the idea that you should have some?"

Chad quirked the corner of his mouth. "Both?"

Izzy's laugh was that one he loved so much. His thoughts turned to other needs. "If Ms. Weber will take Henry for the night, do you think I could convince you to spend it with me?"

She gave him a coy look. "I don't know. What's in it for me?"

A wicked look filled his eyes. "I'll make it special. I promise."

She looked around, then brushed her hand through his hair. "I'll hold you to that."

It felt good to have someone to tease and laugh with. He'd missed that in his life. Needed it.

With excitement putting an eager step in his walk, Chad went to Izzy's apartment. He'd gotten Henry all settled at Ms. Weber's house already. She'd given him a knowing look and smile, stopping him with a hand on his arm before he left. "Don't you hurt that girl. She's had enough pain and didn't deserve it."

"I don't intend to." Why did he sound so defensive? Was he being unfair to Izzy? Leading her on? Making her believe there could be more between them?

"I know but sometimes we don't think things through like we should. Don't see what we have because we fear a repeat of the past. I'm old enough to know we can change the direction of our lives. Now go and have a good time."

Was he letting his past control his future? Could he make changes in his life?

Not soon enough for him, he finally stood in front of Izzy's door. She took his hand and pulled him inside. Her arms circled his neck. Izzy kissed him as if she had missed him as much as he had her.

"I've missed you."

Izzy caressed his hair as he nuzzled her neck. "I've missed you more." He walked her back toward the bed. It only took minutes for him to remove her clothes and even less time to remove his own. Their lovemaking was wild and needy. She found her bliss seconds before he howled his release. Wrapping his arms around her, he held her close.

Sometime later he kissed one of her breasts as he sat up. "Next time we'll go slower."

"I didn't hear anyone complaining."

He chuckled. "You do know how to make a man feel good."

"You do the same for this woman."

Chad gave her a tender kiss on the lips. "Mmm… I like that."

He smiled. "I thought we might go out to eat but I like being here just the two of us better. Would you mind if I just order a pizza?"

She kissed his chest just above his heart. "Sounds wonderful to me."

Chad found his pants, pulled them on, then sat on the side of the bed next to her. He placed the call for pizza.

He looked at Izzy, who lay with her head propped on her hand, watching him. The sheet wrapped her body, not revealing anything but everything at the same time. When had he become such a romantic?

His heated gaze met hers as he traced the ridge of her shoulder. "The pizza won't be here for another half an hour." He tugged on the sheet. "I have some ideas about what we can do while we wait. I promise it'll be all about you."

After the pizza arrived, they moved to the bar to eat it. Izzy wore his T-shirt, which looked super sexy on her. It rode up her thighs, leaving a seductive expanse of skin to tease him. Izzy had become a drug he needed. He couldn't get enough of her.

"Chad, can I ask you something?"

His eyes came up. "Sure. You can ask me anything."

"Do Nan's parents know she cheated on you?"

This was one he hadn't expected. "I'm sure they do. She told her mother everything, but we've never discussed it though. With anybody. I don't want Henry to hear negative talk about his mother. I've been careful not to drag Henry's mom's name through the mud. I care about Henry's happiness and his memory of Nan."

"That's admirable of you." Izzy looked at him as if he were the most amazing person she knew.

"Please don't ever say anything to anyone about it."

She laid her hand on his knee. "I would never."

Izzy woke to the sun shining through the large window of her apartment. She reached over to find Chad wasn't in bed, his side of the sheets cool. Opening her eyes, she saw him sitting at the bar with his pants on. His elbows were on his knees and he was holding a mug of steaming liquid in his hands.

Something about him being there seemed so right it made her chest hurt. "Morning. How long have you been up?"

"Just long enough to make us some coffee. I was enjoying watching you."

"You're embarrassing me." She moved to sit on the edge of the bed, bringing the sheet with her. "You are looking rather pensive over there. What's on your mind?"

"I was thinking about Henry's birthday party. That's not really my field of expertise. We didn't do one last year because he was so small and Nan hadn't been gone long.

The in-laws keep pushing for one. They want to have it at their place."

She pulled the sheet up under her arms. "If they want to do it, why not let them?"

"Because they keep trying to barge in more and more. I don't think that's what I should be doing. His friends are around here." Chad took another sip of his drink.

"Then plan one. I'm sure Ms. Weber will help. I can help."

Anticipation filled his voice. "Would you?"

"Sure. We could do something here in the backyard. At Henry's age, they're happy with running, swinging and the sandbox. You have all that here. We can add a few games and you have a party."

"You make it sound so easy." A doubtful note hung around his words.

"It's not as difficult as you think. When is his birthday?"

"Two weeks from now."

"Then we better get started." She moved to get off the bed.

Chad put the coffee mug down. "I think it can wait a few more minutes. I don't have you to myself for too much longer."

"You're suggesting—"

"I'm not suggesting." Chad approached the bed, wearing a wicked grin. He captured her as she tried to scramble off the other side, taking her down with him. She giggled as his lips found hers.

The weeks passed quickly as they planned the party. Chad had had no idea he would enjoy preparing for a child's birthday. Izzy managed to make that fun as well, despite her treating it as if it were a battle and she was the general.

When the day arrived, he had no doubt everything would be just right.

They had recruited Ms. Weber, who would prepare the food. He and Izzy had joined her in organizing a menu that would suit the children as well as the adults. Izzy had seen to the ordering of a cake from a bakery that Ms. Weber recommended. The games were all prepared.

Izzy had even spent time filling tiny favor bags even though Chad had questioned if they were necessary. By her look of disdain, he knew he'd gone too far. He'd settled for being the banker and keeping his mouth shut.

By the Saturday of Henry's birthday party, everything was in place. Izzy had him up early, placing tables near her apartment. She and Ms. Weber had decided that Izzy's place would be easiest to work out of for the food. He'd been told to put the grill close by where he would be cooking the hot dogs. The tables all had bright cloths on them. All the chairs in her place and his house had been brought outside. Colorful banners were strung to whatever would hold them.

Henry's plastic pool had been turned into a place to fill up water guns, while another area was roped off for a balloon game. Izzy had thought of everything. He'd never seen her happier. Except for when she'd come for him.

There hadn't been much opportunity for any alone time, but he'd enjoyed every minute they spent together getting ready for the party. Even now as he looked over the transformation of his backyard and Henry running from one spot to the other, Chad couldn't help but take in the changes Izzy had made in their lives.

Izzy came up to stand beside him. "So what do you think?"

He put an arm around her waist and gave her a squeeze. "It's perfect like you."

She returned the hug. "Let's just hope the kids have a good time."

"I'm sure they will. How can they not?" He smiled down at her. "Any chance we can have our own party tonight? The in-laws are coming to the party and taking Henry home with them for the night."

Izzy grinned. "I'll bring the leftover cake."

"I like a woman with an imagination." He moved his brows up and down.

"Then I'll be thinking about what part of your body I want to lick the icing off."

That thought stirred his manhood. "You better behave. I have a children's party to attend, and I might not be presentable."

She giggled. "Got to go. Ms. Weber needs some help."

He grabbed her hand as she stepped away. "Hey, I don't know if I've said thank you for this, but I really appreciate you helping out."

She went up on her toes and kissed his cheek. "You're welcome."

Izzy placed a tray of grilled hot dogs on the serving table near her apartment. She turned toward the drive to see a middle-aged couple in their mid-fifties walking up it. They were fashionably dressed and of medium height.

Were they Nan's parents? Izzy had been looking out for the couple and they were just as Ms. Weber had described them, even down to Mrs. Pritchett having recently lost some weight. They meant nothing to Izzy, but she was still nervous about meeting them. What did they know about her? Had Ms. Weber said something?

As Izzy watched the couple headed straight for Henry. She smiled when they both wrapped Henry in big hugs. Izzy returned to her kitchen and picked up a bowl of chips. To Ms. Weber, Izzy said, "I believe the Pritchetts have arrived."

"Watch out for her. She can be difficult. She doesn't think much of Chad, but he maintains a relationship for Henry's sake."

Half an hour later Izzy helped Chad with the balloon game. The entire time she was aware of Mrs. Pritchett watching her. An air of uneasiness hung around the older woman. Nothing about her looked as if she would be open to talking to Izzy or any other woman Chad might be interested in. If Izzy were in the woman's position, she'd want to know who was having an influence on her grandson.

While the children played, Chad manned the grill. With the help of the other parents, she, Chad and Ms. Weber soon had the children fed. Izzy cut the cake while Chad served ice cream and helped Henry. Izzy led another game, then Henry opened his gifts.

With that done, Chad and Henry told their guests goodbye. Izzy started cleaning up.

"It was a very nice party. I wasn't sure that Chad could pull it off." Mrs. Pritchett stood in front of the table.

Izzy's ears roared with nervousness. "I thought it went well. The children acted as if they had fun."

"They did. By the way, I'm Rona Pritchett. Henry's grandmother. His mother's mother."

"I thought so. I'm sorry I haven't had time to say hello. I'm also sorry to hear about your loss."

It took a few seconds for the woman to speak. "You've been busy. I told Chad we could have this at our house but that's not want he wanted."

It took Izzy a moment to register the venom in her voice. Izzy continued to clean up the table, but her hands trembled. Izzy cleared her throat. "By the way, I'm Elizabeth Lane. It's nice to meet you."

Mrs. Pritchett's eyes narrowed. "So, you are her?"

"I'm not sure who the *her* is you are referring to, but I'm Izzy."

"You're the one Henry talks about all the time." Suspicion filled the older woman's eyes.

Izzy threw some paper plates in the trash. "I hope he says good things."

Mrs. Pritchett's lips pursed. "Exactly how're you involved with Chad?"

"We're coworkers at Atlanta Children's Hospital. He's my landlord and friend." The woman didn't need to know that their relationship had gone beyond that.

Izzy picked up the cake tray, preparing to take it to her kitchen.

"Let me help you." Mrs. Pritchett stepped up to the screen door and held it open.

"Thank you." Izzy moved passed her and into the dim cool area of her home.

Mrs. Pritchett followed her. "I'm asking these questions, because I love Henry. You can understand that I am concerned about the people he is around."

"I've come to know Henry over the last few months, and he's a sweet boy who loves his father and whose father loves him."

"I'm concerned about how you might affect Henry's future. He's lost his mother and may see any woman Chad brings home as his mother."

Izzy sucked in a breath and started for the door. She didn't want to have this conversation with Nan's mother. "Excuse me, I need to see about the food before it goes bad."

"Do you know what Chad has told Henry about Nan?" Mrs. Pritchett glared.

"Nothing but good things to my knowledge. In fact, he wants Henry to remember his mother in a positive light.

Chad is concerned about how his and his mother's history might affect Henry in the long run."

Izzy headed out the door. Mrs. Pritchett said, "Chad drove her to have an affair."

One of the nurses from the unit who had a child Henry's age stood nearby. Had she heard? Chad wouldn't like it if she had.

Izzy quickly gathered the hot dog platter and returned inside. None of this discussion should be public.

Mrs. Pritchett followed her. "You can't trust him."

Izzy put the platter down. "Chad wants Henry to know only love and security. Love from you and from him. I know you're hurting, missing your daughter. But saying hateful things about Henry's father isn't going to gain you anything in the long run."

Tears filled Mrs. Pritchett's eyes.

"I know what you're feeling is part of the grieving process. I'm sure Chad does things in his parenting that you wouldn't do but that doesn't make it wrong. It just makes it different."

A stricken look came over Mrs. Pritchett's face. Minutes went by before she spoke again. "You're in love with Chad, aren't you?"

"How I feel about Chad isn't important. What's important is that Henry feels loved."

"You answered my question. You need to know what you are getting into."

"I already know the type of man Chad is. I've seen him in action at the hospital. He's a compassionate man who cares about others. I've watched him with Henry. He's a devoted father. He has been a good friend to me."

"What do you think she's getting into Rona?" Chad's low tight tone made Izzy jump.

She hadn't noticed him coming up.

"Izzy rents my apartment. She's a capable nurse in my ER and a good friend who's great with Henry. That's it. Nothing more. That's more explanation than you deserve."

"I have the right to question the woman that might take my Nan's place."

Izzy flinched. She didn't want to replace any woman. She would be her own person.

"That's not going to happen. So you can stop worrying about it. H.G. and Henry are waiting on you. I'll walk you to them."

Over his shoulder Chad gave Izzy a tight smile and took Rona's elbow.

Izzy felt sick. There it was. Chad had said it loud and clear. He had no intention of marrying her. She'd started to hope, to think he might change his mind. They'd been so much like a family over the last few weeks. Chad had seemed happy. She knew she had been.

It was time for that dream to end. She needed to wake up.

CHAPTER NINE

CHAD SHOWERED AND changed before heading to Izzy's. Henry's party had been a success. Thanks to Izzy. The only blight on the day had been Rona. He could see now how much Nan was like her mother.

He'd seen clearly the hurt look on Izzy's face when he had led Rona away. Hopefully he could help Izzy forget what Rona had said. More than once he'd thought about Izzy and icing during the party.

The backyard had been cleared of all things party-related. He'd insisted Ms. Weber go home, telling her that he and Izzy would finish the rest of the cleanup. They had done it without much communication, both focused on what must be done.

Chad knocked before walking into Izzy's place. "Hey, are you as tired as I am?"

"Yeah. But it was a nice party." Izzy sat in the large leather chair.

He walked around her to sit on the sofa. "Thanks to you." He patted the cushion. "You want to come over here and sit by me?"

She looked at him with sad eyes. "I'd better stay here."

His throat tightened. Was this about what Rona had said? "Look, Izzy, you can't pay any attention to Rona.

She's always stepping where she shouldn't. I'll have a talk with her."

"Don't do that. It wasn't just her."

"Then what's wrong?" Chad put his hands on his knees. He wanted to pull her into his lap but stopped because something about Izzy's body language said she wouldn't want that.

"It's time for us to call a halt to whatever this is between us."

That was the last thing he'd expected to hear this evening. "Why?"

"I just realized today that I've started to play a game of family and I like it too much. That I would like for it to last but you still don't want that. I've played pretend before. I can't do it again. I'll be moving out as soon as I can find another place to live. I should have known better."

"Why all of a sudden? I thought we had a great day. What happened? Please tell me. Maybe I can fix it."

"I'll tell you, but I don't think you can fix it." She took a deep breath. "You told Rona that we'd never marry." When he started to speak, she raised a hand. "I've known all along that's how you feel, but I had hoped over the last few weeks you might have started to change your mind. I should have known better. That hadn't worked in my last relationship so there's no reason to believe it should in this one. I had just hoped. It's time to cut it off before it's more painful for all concerned."

"I thought you were happy with the way things are. We agreed to a fling."

"Now the fling is over."

"You don't have to move." The moisture filling her eyes told him this was as difficult for her as it was for him.

"Do you think that I could live out here?" She pointed to the floor. "And watch you and Henry coming and going and pretend there hadn't been something between us. You give me more credit than I deserve."

Panic filled Chad's chest. How had this gone so wrong? He jerked to his feet. "Izzy, you're overreacting. Can't we talk this through?"

"I think we're past that. You need to figure out what you want your life to look like. You must let your guilt go. It takes two to make a relationship. You didn't drive Nan to have an affair. She made a choice. You made choices. I must make one now. I know what I want my life to look like and I won't settle for less. I had dared to think you might change your mind. Now I know that will never happen. Maybe in time we can be friends."

Chad couldn't push off the hundred-pound weight that had settled on his chest. He snorted. "That's what everyone says, then they never speak to each other again."

Izzy just looked at him.

"I can't change your mind?"

She shook her head.

He headed for the door. "If you decide differently, you know where I am."

A few hours later Chad watched through the kitchen window as Izzy loaded her car with as much as it would hold. A few words thrown out without thought had blown up his entire world.

More than once he started out to ask Izzy not to go. Then he thought to help her load, but he couldn't bring himself to encourage it. He'd hoped she'd get tired and quit. Where was she going anyway? Back to the hotel? Concern tightened his middle.

He sat at the kitchen table, staring at a spot on the wall when there was a knock at the back door.

"Hey." Izzy stepped back so he had to come out of the house. Was she afraid of him? Feared being alone with him in a small space? "I wanted to see if it was all right to keep the key until I get my furniture. Also, I wanted to know if I can stop by tomorrow after work and talk to Henry. It isn't fair to him for me to just disappear. That's scary for a child."

Chad could hardly breathe at the idea of her leaving. With her big heart, she was concerned about how Henry would feel. "Both of those are fine." He paused a moment. "Where're you going? I need to know you're safe."

Izzy was looking at a spot over his shoulder, not meeting his eyes. "Amanda, one of the nurses from the sixth floor asked me the other day if I was still looking for a place. Her roommate moved out for the summer. I'm going there."

"I wish you'd stay here."

"That wouldn't be wise for me or you, and certainly not Henry. Take care of yourself, Chad." She walked toward her car with a stiff back and didn't look back.

He stood in the yard, watching until her little car disappeared. Maybe Izzy was right. He needed to figure out what he wanted. Then he could approach her. And tell her what?

That he wanted to marry her? That he loved her? What? He wasn't sure anymore.

A long agonizing week later Izzy sat at the unit desk, reviewing charts. She'd lived in a fog of despair since leaving Chad's. Richard had hurt her, but it felt nothing like this bone-deep pain she had over Chad. She'd done the right thing by leaving but that didn't hold her tight in the middle of the night. Or make her laugh. Or make her feel as if she was enough.

She wouldn't be used just because she loved someone. Her head would do the thinking this time, not only her heart. No matter how much it hurt, she would stand up for herself. She wanted, needed more. Yet she couldn't see a happy future without Chad.

During the week she'd stayed out of Chad's way on the days they both worked. Hiding out in her office was really what she'd done. When he passed her, there was no more whistling of "Penny Lane" and only the briefest of eye contact. They were strangers again. Not much better than when they had met at the grocery store. Sadness filled her but she didn't know how to fix their stalemate. The best she could do was plow through each day.

Three loud beeps came over the emergency system radio. "School bus accident," the radio squawked. "Expect major injuries."

Seconds later the ER was like a beehive in full work mode.

Chad came to stand beside her. "What types of injuries are we expecting?"

It was the closest she'd been to him in days. His scent surrounded her. "Broken legs and arms. Head injuries. Possible internal injuries on two."

"I want the internal injuries in exam one and two. I want you with me, Izzy."

She could do this. There were patients to save. She could and would be professional, focused on what she needed to do. Chad and she made a good team. They trusted each other's instincts in an emergency at least. "I understand. I'll go check the rooms and make sure everything is ready." She asked for his ears only. "You going to be okay?"

Chad gave her a curt nod. He didn't look up from the paper he held. "We also need to get another portable X-ray machine down here."

"Already taken care of." She went around the unit desk.

His head rose, his eyes meeting hers. "Thanks, Izzy. I can always depend on you."

She blinked, her chest squeezing.

Fifteen minutes later, under the squeal of the sirens, everybody went into action. The first gurney came though the double doors. Izzy was there ready to show the EMTs where to go. The first patients in were the possible internal injuries.

Izzy pointed to exam one, grabbed the gurney a dark-haired boy of thirteen lay on. She pulled it inside. Chad joined her seconds later. She started gathering vital signs, checking for heart rate and respirations. Chad had whipped off his stethoscope from his neck and was listening to the patient's abdominal sounds. While they did this, other nurses and techs hooked the patient up to monitors.

"We need to get an IV in. Start fluids," Chad ordered. "Along with a full blood panel."

Izzy watched as Chad palpated the child's abdomen.

"Let's get an abdominal X-ray."

Minutes later Chad looked at his tech pad. "Call the OR. Let them know we're sending up a patient with spleen damage. Also, call the blood bank. They need to have A blood standing by."

"I'll take care of it," Izzy said. With that done, she checked on the other nurses, making sure they were handling all the pre-operation orders. "The OR will be ready in ten minutes."

"Come with me," Chad said to Izzy. "Let's check on the other internal injury patient before we start working through the other cases."

Before she left, she instructed the nurses to monitor the patient until the OR staff arrived to get him, then she followed Chad out. They moved into the next exam room where a blonde girl of seventeen waited. They went through the same procedure.

"I need an IV started," Chad stated.

Izzy said, "I'll take care of it." She took the IV starter

kit from the tech. After preparing the sight, she efficiently placed the needle. Soon she had the fluids flowing.

Chad continued to examine the girl, pushing on her stomach, checking lower. "We need an X-ray here. The liver is distended. We need to check for damage."

With that patient seen, they went to the next one. Izzy said, "This is a laceration in the hairline."

"I'll need a suture kit." Chad pulled on plastic gloves.

"Already set up for you."

Chad's eyes met hers. "Thanks."

Izzy nodded. They worked seamlessly together. In bed they were perfect, yet an emotional gap as wide as the ocean stood between them.

Working as quickly and flawlessly as they could, they got the most critical patients the care they needed before turning their attention to the less dire ones.

Izzy stayed by Chad's side as they moved from one exam room to the next. The patients went from broken bones down to sprained wrists and knots on the foreheads. Slowly they saw all those injured in the bus crash.

Three hours after they'd started, Chad sank into a chair. He looked exhausted.

Izzy's heart went out to him. She certainly hadn't slept all night since leaving him. "Can I get you something?"

Chad put his head in his hands. "I'm just worn out. I hate auto accidents. And to get a bus load..." He looked at her. "And I haven't been sleeping well."

The sharp edge of being responsible nicked her. Was he implying it was because of her? Yet the knowledge gave her a warm feeling to think he missed her.

"You did a good job today." She wanted to massage his shoulders. Help him somehow. Just to touch him. But she wouldn't. She couldn't open that door. What if she couldn't close it again?

"You did too. We make a good team." He held her gaze with his eyes.

"In an emergency medical situation, we do," she said firmly.

His eyes turned sad. "We're good at more than that. I miss you, Izzy."

She couldn't let Chad sweet-talk her back into his arms. Isn't that what Richard had done? Wanted and needed her for all those things in life where a woman was useful but for what really mattered, she wasn't good enough. Izzy wasn't going down that path again no matter how much her heart ached.

"Chad—"

A nurse stuck her head inside the room. "I hate to say it, Dr. McCain, but you're needed in exam room six."

Chad pushed himself out of the chair. "I got this one, Izzy. If I'm not mistaken, you were supposed to go home hours ago."

He'd kept up with her schedule? In that small way he'd shown he cared. She fought the urge to hug him. Instead she watched him walk down the hall to his next patient.

Chad leaned back in his desk chair. He didn't know how much longer he could take not having Izzy in his life. Not just at work but in his home, at his table, in his bed. He missed her desperately. Just seeing her at the hospital was painful. He ached for her. He'd let his need for her slip two evenings ago when he'd told her how much he missed her. For a moment he'd been prepared to beg her to come back. In the short amount of time she'd been in his and Henry's lives, she'd become important. Vital to their happiness.

Izzy had visited Henry the day after she left just as she had promised. She'd hugged Henry with tears in her eyes. When she explained she had to move and would no longer be in the apartment, one of those tears rolled down her cheek. Henry and Izzy had already created a bond. The boy would recover from Izzy leaving. Chad wasn't sure he would fare as well. Henry asked about Izzy, almost daily. That didn't help ease Chad's pain.

Ms. Weber questioned Izzy's quick departure as well. She'd asked more questions than Chad had been comfortable answering. When her questions ended, she'd started to give lectures on a man who didn't recognize a good woman when he saw one. As the weeks crawled by, they turned into longer lectures. Ms. Weber went on about him taking care of himself so he could take care of others. As subtle or unsubtle as she might have been, the point being he shouldn't have let Izzy go. Chad never offered into the discussion that Izzy had been the one to leave.

The two women had become fast friends while Izzy had been in the apartment, spending time together and having tea while Chad was at the hospital. Izzy had a way of doing that. Making friends quickly.

He pushed his fingers through his hair, then sat up in the chair. Somehow he had to get control of his life. Make a step forward.

Chad's mouth went dry. Sex with Izzy was amazing. Outstanding in fact, but that didn't make marrying her a wise decision. He'd had no intention of ever marrying again until Izzy came along. She had made him wonder what if? Before he wouldn't even entertain the thought of marriage. Now, he cared about Izzy, but marriage?

He ran his hand through his hair. Did he even deserve a second chance? He'd hurt Izzy. Could he be all she deserved? Could he close the door on the ugliness of his past and dare to love again?

He'd messed up big time with Izzy. Had hurt her deeply. If he wanted her back in his life, he would have to prove his love, but he didn't know how to do that. More difficult than that could, he trust Izzy completely?

Enough of those thoughts. He needed to go to the nursing station and sign off on a chart. He pushed out of the chair. As he approached the desk, he could see Izzy on the front side focused on the electronic pad, punching keys occasionally.

Three nurses were huddled close to each other, looking at a picture on the computer screen where they sat behind the desk.

One said, "I can't imagine running around on somebody as gorgeous and nice as he is."

"Yeah, I've always considered him a real catch," another nurse agreed.

Chad smirked. The hospital was a hive of gossip. That's why he didn't want his business known.

"If he was my man, I wouldn't think about having an affair."

The first nurse said, "Yeah, Dr. McCain's all that and a box of chocolates. Imagine his wife running around on him, then he has to deal with her being killed in an automobile accident. How sad it that."

Chad jerked to a stop. His stomach roiled while his jaw tightened and mouth thinned. Those nurses were talking about him. About Nan. His look bore into Izzy's. She'd promised not to tell. Had she been so angry she'd betray him? As Nan had?

Izzy's eyes went wide. Her skin paled as shock covered her face. She shook her head, denying she was the one who had said something. Who else could have? Izzy was the only person he'd told so it must have come from her.

The nurses continued to talk but it was just a buzz in his ears.

Izzy's eyes begged him to believe her.

His heart wanted to believe she hadn't done this to him. His past, the fear and the guilt had him questioning that idea. He'd been lied to before, betrayed. His heart was breaking. He'd thought Izzy was different. Badly he wanted to believe she cared enough about him that she wouldn't take revenge.

He turned and walked back down the hall. Thankfully the nurses hadn't noticed him. How humiliating would that have been? Could Izzy have put an end to their relationship any more efficiently?

He heard Izzy snap, "Don't you ladies have something more useful to be doing besides gossiping?"

That evening in the bedroom of her new apartment, Izzy still felt sickened by what had happened that day. Chad hadn't believed her. He thought she had shared his secret. The look on his face haunted her. She loved him deeply and hated to see him hurt. She couldn't stand the idea she was the cause of his pain.

Apparently the nurse had heard what Rona had said and spread the information. She hadn't missed the accusing look in Chad's eyes. How could Izzy ever convince him she hadn't said anything?

She'd gone looking for him, but he'd been busy with cases. After that, she left a message on his phone, but he'd not returned her call.

Sorrow overwhelmed her. Izzy needed to talk to someone. Her mother. She always made problems seem smaller and answers clearer. Picking up the phone, Izzy punched in her mother's number.

"Mom. It's Izzy."

"What's wrong, honey?"

Izzy hadn't spoken to her parents since she'd move away from Chad's. They had been on a cruise. She hadn't wanted to go into what had happened between her and Chad then, and like now her mother would have known something was wrong just from hearing Izzy's voice.

Izzy had feared completely breaking down then as well as now. She gathered her willpower to hold her emotions in check. She's never been very good at keeping things from her parents, especially her mom.

"Mom, you know I wasn't telling you the truth about how I feel about Chad when we came up to get my furniture."

"Yeah, I know, honey. But after what you've been through, I understood why you spent so much time denying your attraction to him."

Izzy told her what had happened between them. That she had moved out of the apartment and that Chad believed she'd given away his confidence. "Any chance I might have had with him is gone now."

"How do you know? Did he say so?"

"No, but I could tell by the look on his face. He also said he'd never marry me. And after what happened today..." Izzy barely contained a sob.

"He loves you. He may not realize it yet or maybe he's not able to say it. He'll come around. Don't give up on him."

"I don't know."

"Even your dad thinks so. We saw the way he looked at you. Richard never looked at you the way Chad does. You glow when you're around him."

Izzy never thought of herself as someone who glowed. But being around Chad did make her feel warm all over even when they were angry with each other. "I'm not glowing now. I'm miserable. Mom, I don't know how I'm going to go on. I can't keep changing jobs and moving. I have to see him almost every day. But I won't accept less than I deserve ever again. I promised myself I wouldn't settle."

"I'm not disagreeing with that at all, honey. You're a smart woman, Izzy. You'll figure something out. Get him to listen to you. Explain. It could be as simple as just telling him how you feel. Does he know you love him?"

"That's not what he wants to hear. I can't get him to talk to me."

"Keep trying. You have the biggest heart of anybody I know. I think that's what makes you such a good nurse. Chad has that same quality. I'm sure that makes him a good doctor. A good dad, a good man. I don't think I could've ever said that about Richard. I bet Chad's heart is big enough for you too."

"That's not the problem. It's that he's scared to love again. To trust. That won't get better after what happened today."

"You know sometimes when we come out of a bad re-lationship, we put that relationship off on the next person. I don't think there's much about Chad, if anything, that's like Richard. I doubt there's little or anything about you that's like his ex-wife. Maybe you need to point that out to him, then give him time to figure that out. Think about it."

"Mom, you always put everything into perspective. I love you for it."

"One day you'll have a chance to do the same for your children. You just wait and see. I love you too, honey. Let me know how things go."

Izzy loved Chad as well as Henry. She couldn't think of anything she wanted more than to be a part of their lives. But she needed Chad to want that too. He would have to figure that out. Right now she wanted him to know she hadn't been disloyal. That he could trust her. With his back-ground, he valued those traits above all others. He had to know she wasn't anything like Nan.

Izzy dropped her phone to the bed. Despite loving Chad

as she did, she needed him to feel the same about her. Wanted him to say he loved her. What would it take to make that happen?

Chad walked up to the unit desk the next morning. Everyone was talking at once. He feared it might be about him. Even so he had to face them sometime.

He'd finished his shift in humiliation the day before, then gone home. There he checked his messages and listened to Izzy explain how she hadn't divulged his past. She'd explained about the nurse standing nearby when Rona blurted the affair information out. That Izzy would have never shared his secret.

Minutes after he'd walked away, he'd come to that conclusion. Izzy was nothing like his ex or any other woman for that matter. Loyalty, honor, goodness was ingrained in her. If she cared about a person, she stood by them. She cared about him and Henry. Never would she hurt them.

He tried to call her to apologize but her phone was busy. He didn't leave a message, intending to call her later. Then Henry had a stomachache and that took up the rest of the evening.

The tech looked up. "Dr. McCain, did you hear? Izzy was in an accident on the way to work this morning."

Chad's heart dropped to his feet. He broke into a sweat. This couldn't be happening, not again. His heart clinched with fear. Was Izzy seriously injured or worse? He couldn't lose Izzy. He loved her.

"Get someone to cover for me. What hospital?"

The tech stammered. "Uh, okay. Downtown Medical."

Five minutes later Chad was in his SUV, driving toward the adult hospital. It was only five miles away, but it might as well have been on the moon for as fast as traffic let him travel. He slammed his hand on the steering wheel when he was caught by another red light.

He'd fought it. Didn't want to believe it. But now when it might be too late to tell her, he could see it clearly. He loved Izzy. He just hoped he had a chance to tell her. To say he wanted her forever.

Chad had convinced himself he and Henry only needed each other, then along came Izzy. She had climbed over the fence around his heart, and under as well, and made herself necessary. Now the stabilizer in his life might be gone. He couldn't live without her.

He'd seen the love between Izzy's parents and what her brother had with his wife. Izzy needed that in her life, deserved it. He couldn't offer her less than all his heart. If he took that chance, it would open the door to being hurt again but Izzy was worth taking the chance.

She was right he hadn't been the only one wrong in his marriage. Nan had shared a part in the failure. With Izzy at his side, he could get beyond his past failures to find a life-long happiness. He knew that as surely as he knew how to help a patient in an emergency. Izzy wasn't Nan. It wasn't fair to put her inadequacies off on Izzy.

If he lost Izzy, he didn't know what he would do. He loved her more than he could describe. As soon as the light changed, he pushed the gas pedal and roared up the street. A couple of people honked at him as he sped around them.

No wonder she had compared him to the jerk she'd given years of her life to. Chad hadn't offered her any more than Richard had. Their relationship had all been one-sided— in his favor. He couldn't blame her for washing her hands of him. But he intended to change that.

He whipped into the first parking spot he came to, jumped out and ran for the ER entrance. Sliding up to the desk, he huffed out, "I'm Dr. Chad McCain. Is Izzy—Elizabeth Lane here?"

The tech took his painful time checking the computer. "Yes, she's in exam room thirteen."

Chad started toward the double doors.

The tech half stood. "Sir, you can't go back there."

"I'm her personal doctor."

The tech looked bewildered. "Okay."

Chad pushed through the doors. He searched the room numbers until he came to Izzy's. He opened the door. There was no one there. His chest tightened as if a car lay on it. Where was she? Had she died?

He returned to the hall, looking both ways. As he headed toward the nurses' desk, he saw Izzy on a gurney being pushed his way. He hurried to her, taking her hand. "Izzy, where're you hurt?"

"Chad." Izzy gave him a weak smile before her eyes fluttered closed again.

"Thank heavens, you are alive."

"Sir, you need to wait in the waiting room," one of the nurses said.

"I'm Dr. McCain. I'm Ms. Lane's personal physician."

The woman looked down at their hands, then nodded. "Okay, but you need to stay out of the way."

His look didn't leave Izzy when he asked, "How injured is she?"

As they continued to Izzy's room, the nurse said, "Bruised good in several places. The worse is a broken fibula where the other car hit her. That tiny car of hers took the blunt of it, I heard. She has been to X-Ray and should be on her way to the OR in about thirty minutes."

The office staff settled Izzy in the room and left with, "Someone will be in to get her in a few minutes. You can stay until then."

Chad gave Izzy a kiss on the lips. "You scared the life out of me."

Izzy's eyes opened. "I didn't tell them."

"I know, honey. I know."

Soon a couple of people from the OR arrived.

"Izzy, I'll be here when you get back." He squeezed her hand.

"I love you," she muttered.

He kissed her tenderly. "I love you too."

CHAPTER TEN

IZZY'S EYELIDS FLICKERED. She blinked at the blur of something or someone moving back and forth. Where was she? As her vision cleared, she recognized a hospital area. The blur turned into a man. *Chad.*

"Chad, stop. You're making me dizzy."

He came to a jolting halt in his pacing, then moved to the chair situated beside the bed and sank into it. "How're you feeling? Do you hurt anywhere?"

"I'm fine."

He brushed the hair off her forehead. "I'm sorry this happened to you."

She tried to touch his face, but the IV line stopped her. "How do I look?"

"Beautiful."

She smiled weakly. "No, really."

Chad cupped her cheek. "You took a pretty good beating. You're bruised."

Izzy looked around the stark room. "I'm in recovery?"

"Yes."

"They let you back here?" She couldn't believe that.

He dipped his chin and gave her a sheepish grin. "They really didn't have a choice. I called in a few favors."

Chad was really that concerned about her. "You did?"

"Yes." He took her hand, bringing it to his lips. He kissed the back of it. "You scared the hell out of me."

She tried to move.

Chad stood, hovering over her. "Easy. They have your leg all trussed up."

"I can't believe I broke my leg." She looked down at her now-chunky leg.

The worry in her eyes he hadn't expected. "That's much better than I feared."

A nurse approached. "I see you're awake. Are you ready to go to your room?"

"I guess so."

"Let me get one more set of vitals and then I'll send you off." She looked at Chad. "Since you have your own personal physician, you'll be in good hands."

"Yeah, but he works with children and I'm a little bigger than that."

Chad smiled. "I do but the principles are the same."

The next morning Izzy sat in a chair as Chad moved around the room, packing the few belongings she had to take home. The day before he had ordered her nightgowns delivered so she would have something besides a hospital gown to wear. Embarrassing as it was, he'd also helped her during the night to the bathroom. He'd even brought her a large arrangement of flowers when he left for his supper. She couldn't have asked for anyone to be more aware of her needs. He'd called her parents as well and reassured them.

"You know you didn't have to go out and buy me something to wear." She pulled at the full-leg knit pants.

Chad looked at her. "What was the plan? Get those skinny jeans on over that cast?"

She lifted her nose. "Maybe, but I admit there might have been a degree of difficulty." She looked down at her broken leg. "I don't know how I'm going to manage the stairs at my apartment."

"You're not going to. You're coming home with me."

She opened her mouth and Chad held his hand up to stop her. "Listen, then you can argue. Your apartment doesn't have anyone around all the time like my house does. If it's not me, then Ms. Weber is there. If you get in trouble, there's somebody to help you. Come and stay until you're cleared by the doctor and then you can leave. As long as you need a place with no steps, the garage apartment is perfect."

Izzy didn't really have a choice. Chad was right. The apartment would be a better situation if she took it. "I guess so."

Chad's grin was one of a winner. "Don't forget I can offer a tree with a chair under it. With the weather being pretty for another month or so, you'll have a lot of time to enjoy it."

Izzy couldn't deny the appeal. "I do like that idea. But I leave as soon as the leg has healed."

"Good, then it's settled."

Chad drove her to his house and carefully helped her to her apartment, which sparkled with cleanliness.

"I see Ms. Weber has been busy."

"How did you know I didn't do the cleaning?" Chad settled her in the chair and put a pillow under her leg.

"Because as good as you are at most things, cleaning isn't your thing."

His gaze caught hers. "You know me so well. I'm going to get you situated, then go to the house. I'll get our lunch and Henry. He's dying to see you. If you feel up to it."

"I would love to see him. I've missed him." Chad walked to the door. "Chad." He looked at her. "Thanks. You didn't have to do this."

His gaze bored into hers. "Yes, I did. I'm glad I had the chance." He hurried out the door.

What had he meant? *Had the chance?*

Ms. Weber joined them for their meal. When it was over, Izzy yawned. Chad lifted her into his arms while Ms. Weber pulled the bed covers back. Lying her gently down, Chad propped up her leg on a pillow and covered her.

The sun was lowering when she woke.

"Hey there. You want something to eat or drink?" Chad sat on the sofa, reading a book.

"Drink, please." She pushed into a sitting position.

Chad brought her a glass and a couple of pills sitting on the mattress near her.

"Have you been here all the time I was sleeping?" She took the pills and drank all the water.

"I have."

"You don't have to nurse me." She couldn't make more out of that then there was. Chad was a good guy who cared for people naturally.

"I know that. I want to." He moved to stand. She stopped him with a hand on his arm. "I forgot to tell you. I want you to know I didn't tell anyone about what Nan did."

"I know. You told me at the hospital."

"I did?"

"Yes, just before you went into surgery." Chad looked as if he expected her to say more.

"I don't remember anything after the accident until I woke up in the hospital room yesterday afternoon with you pacing."

"Hey, don't make fun of your medical care personnel. He was worried about you." Chad took the glass to the sink. "Hungry?"

"No, thanks. You know you don't have to entertain me."

"I don't mind. Would you like to go outside and watch the sunset?" He came to stand at the end of the bed.

"That does sound nice." Chad scooped her up. "Hey, I can walk."

"Yeah, but I enjoy having a reason to carry you."

Despite the thrill of being cradled against him, she didn't need to think this made things different between them. "Chad, you know this doesn't change anything."

"You need help for a while and I'm providing it, that's all."

For some reason that saddened her.

They watched the sun set and the fireflies come out.

"I think it's time to get you inside and fed." Again, Chad lifted her.

This time she gave no complaint. He sat her at the bar, then warmed a bowl of soup for them.

"Please tell Ms. Weber thank you when you see her."

"Will do."

After their meal, she said, "I think I'll go back to bed. The anesthesia must still be in my system. Plus the pain pills." She started toward the bath with her gown in hand but when she toppled to the side, Chad hurried to support her. He helped her to the bath.

From inside the bath she said, "Dang it."

"What's wrong? Are you okay?" Chad sounded like he was right outside the door.

"I can't get these pants off." She was trying to seat on the commode but there wasn't enough space to straighten her leg.

"Then come out here. I'll help you."

"I'm not going to let you do that."

"Open up or I'll come in. It's not like I haven't seen you before."

Izzy swallowed hard. He had and she'd liked it. Every

minute of it. She slipped the gown over her head, then opened the door with her pants still on. Chad assisted her over to the bed, where she laid down. His hand slipped under her gown and pulled on the waistband of her pants. She helped all she could, shimming one way, then the other.

"Izzy," Chad growled. "That's enough of that."

She looked down at him. His eyes burned with desire. He blinked and they returned to all business. Minutes later he had her tucked in bed and all the lights off but a lamp. "Call me if you need me."

"You aren't staying here tonight."

"I am. But don't panic, Izzy. I'm sleeping on the sofa." His words had a tight note to them.

The next four days she was back at home, as Izzy thought of it, went much as the first. Chad took a few days off despite her telling him that wasn't necessary.

"I need to learn to take time off and now is a good opportunity to start."

Izzy looked at him in amazement. Chad really was making some changes.

He and Henry spent most of those days off entertaining her between her naps. Ms. Weber came in the evenings with their meal and joined them.

Her parents made a quick overnight visit. Chad was nice enough to let them stay at his house.

Her mother asked as they sat under the tree, "How're things going?"

"Nothing has changed." Izzy couldn't keep the sadness from her voice.

"But he's taking care of you. He insisted on his call to us he would do it just after the accident. Someone doesn't do that if they don't care."

"That's only because he has a good heart."

Her mother gave her a speculative look, raising her brows. "That's a really big heart. I think it's more."

"He hasn't said anything."

"He will and you need to be ready to listen when he does."

It had been five days since the accident when Chad announced, "I'm going back to work tomorrow. Ms. Weber will check in on you."

"I'll be fine. You've been a great nurse. I appreciate it." Chad had been wonderful to her. Almost as if he did love her. Yet he'd said nothing. The panic on his face in the hospital and the way he stayed beside her as if she were a newborn incapable of anything showed he cared. Still, he didn't mention the future.

Chad moved in a supply of books and puzzles to give her something to do. He'd bought her a learn-to-paint set that he set up in front of the large picture window.

"I thought you could try your hand at painting to pass the time. Maybe do a painting of the oak tree. Since you love it so much."

"You do have high hopes for me." She was touched by the thought Chad had put into keeping her from getting bored.

On the days he was off, he spent a lot of time with her along with Henry. They often sat outside, watching Henry play. Chad had surprised her with a lounge so she could put her leg up.

"You do know you're spoiling me." She had no doubt her heart was in her eyes.

"Which is as it should be." He settled in the chair next to her but didn't look her way.

Was Chad afraid she might see something he didn't want her to?

Soon she could move around the apartment on crutches

with little trouble and life formed a pattern. Chad and Henry spent the time they could with her. Their group acted more like a family each day. She looked forward to seeing them. Chad said nothing about the days ahead and neither did she. One afternoon she was asleep on the lounger when the soft touch of lips woke her. She could've sworn she heard Chad say *I love you*, but when she opened her eyes, he wasn't there. Once again she'd imagined it.

She'd been at Chad's three weeks when one of the nurses from the unit asked her if she'd like to get out for lunch and a chick flick. It was time for Izzy to start pulling away from Chad, become less dependent on him. So she accepted.

Chad looked out the kitchen window for the fourth time in five minutes. It was still early for Izzy to return from the movie. He'd made all the plans for their dinner and for Ms. Weber to have Henry at her house. Now all he had to do was hope.

Chad couldn't take it much longer. He'd stayed away from Izzy, waiting on her to recover from the accident enough to listen to him. More than that, he wanted to show her how he felt about her as well as tell her. He'd spent the last three weeks trying to get to know her better, to make her feel cherished, but it was time to move forward.

He wanted to kiss her, hold her, love her. Tell her how he felt about her.

When had he last been this nervous? Not even when he'd been the head attending for the first time in the Emergency Room. His nerves rattled like a skeleton in the breeze. Tonight had to go well. It just had to.

He wanted a lifetime with Izzy. He needed to persuade her of that. Convince her he could be what she needed. The man, the lover, the partner she desired and wished for. He had no doubt Izzy was what he needed. The light he'd found when she was near had gone out of his life when she had left. He wanted her warmth forever.

Henry was clean and dressed in his newest pajamas. He and Ms. Weber sat in the living room with her reading to him. Earlier that evening she had helped Chad prepare the meal. He wanted to say he had cooked it. Izzy must feel special. Now the food warmed in the oven in Izzy's apartment.

The backyard was ready. Chad had spent most of the time Izzy had been gone stringing small white icicles lights from the large oak. Under those he'd placed a table for two, then covered it with a white cloth. He'd set the table with Izzy's dishes, not wanting to use the ones he and Nan had shared. He'd added glasses and silverware. Wine waited in a cooler. As a special touch he had bought flowers at the grocery.

He checked the drive one more time. A flash of headlights let him know she had arrived. His heart raced in anticipation as he headed toward the back door. He called to Ms. Weber, "She's here."

Chad groaned. He'd heard the excitement in his voice. He wouldn't let himself think about Izzy no longer wanting him. His heart thumped as he hurried to meet her, helping her out of the car.

He leaned down to speak to Sara, the nurse from the unit. "Hey. Thanks for taking her. I know she's getting tired of my company."

Sara smiled and looked at Izzy. "I doubt that."

Izzy couldn't prevent the blush running up her neck. "He's not too bad to be around. Thanks for thinking of me."

"Not a problem. I enjoyed the movie. Well, got to go."

He and Izzy stood together, watching Sara back out of the drive. Izzy's scent filled his nostrils. She wore a silky blouse and dress pants. Her hair hung free and brushed her shoulders. His fingers twitched to touch it, but he resisted.

She looked soft, sweet, feminine and completely desirable. "I didn't expect this welcome." She looked at him up and down. "You look nice."

He'd taken special pains in his dressing even changing shirts three times. He'd settled on a collared fine blue-striped dress shirt, navy slacks and dress shoes. The evening was too important not to look his best.

"Her eyes turned worried. "You got a date?"

"I hope so."

Her eyes widened, filled with fear.

"I wondered if you might join me for dinner. We need to talk."

Her eyes brightened and she smiled.

Chad offered his arm. "Please come this way." He led her toward the back door. "Henry wants to say hi before we have dinner."

"I thought he would be having dinner with us."

Chad shifted from one foot to the other. "He decided to accept another invitation. I'm sorry but you'll have to settle for just me."

Her smile made his heart leap. "I don't mind."

"Izzy." Henry came running out the back door with Ms. Weber behind him.

Izzy gathered Henry in her arms, her nose buried in his neck. Chad picked him up, so he was eye level with Izzy.

"Hi, Izzy," Ms. Weber said.

"Hello, Ms. Weber. I wasn't expecting to see you."

"I just stopped by to pick up Henry." She gave Izzy a sly smile. "I better get this one home to bed. Come on, Henry."

Izzy kissed Henry on the cheek. Chad hugged and kissed him as well. "You be a good boy for Ms. Weber." Chad lowered him to the ground.

Ms. Weber reached out a hand. Henry put his in it. "He'll

be fine." She gave each of them a knowing look. "Enjoy your evening."

He and Izzy watched until Ms. Weber and Henry went around the corner of the house.

Chad put out an elbow. "Where were we?"

Izzy looped her hand around his arm, leading her toward her apartment. Her warmth seeped into him. He'd missed her touch.

As they approached the tree, she stopped. Her lips separated in a gasp. "This is beautiful, Chad. Just breathtaking. You did all of this while I was gone? You've been busy."

"I thought you might like it." He led her to the lounger.

She looked around in wonder. "What's this all about?"

"I can't do something nice for you?"

"You've been doing that for weeks, but this is the loveliest of all your ideas."

His chest filled. Izzy liked his efforts. "May I offer you a glass of wine?"

"Yes, please." She settled on the lounge. "This has always been one of my favorite places. It's truly magical now."

Chad opened the wine and poured them both a glass. He handed one to her with a less than steady hand, then took the chair beside her. A light breeze blew. "You're not too cool, are you?"

"I'm perfect." Izzy looked at him as if memorizing every detail of his face. Her words were soft. "Thanks for all you have done since the accident. I don't know what I would've done without you. You gave me a place to stay and took care of me."

"My pleasure." And it had been.

A gentle smile formed on her lips. Her gaze held his. "You really are a nice guy. You've made me feel very special."

"That's because you are." He cleared his throat. "Are you hungry? Dinner's ready."

She continued to focus on him. "Do you mind if we just sit here for a few minutes?"

He didn't mind anything if he was with her. "Not at all. You just tell me when you're ready."

Izzy took in a fortifying breath. She had to say this. Clear the air. "Chad, I'm sorry I tried to make you be someone you're not. To expect something that you had already said you couldn't give. My only excuse was that I was trying to protect myself. It wasn't fair to you. I'll always regret that."

Chad set his glass down beside his chair, then moved to sit at the foot of the lounger. He took her drink and placed it beside his. His gaze held hers as he took one of her hands. "I'm sorry too. You had made it clear what you wanted out of life. I listened but I didn't take it into consideration. You deserved better from me. You were right. I needed to quit hiding behind my guilt and my bad marriage. Neither have anything to do with the type of person you are."

"But it wasn't my place to try to make you change."

"You are right. It takes two in a relationship. I might not have been the best husband to Nan, but she made mistakes too. I've been carrying around the idea I'd fail again because I did once without considering things could be different because you're different. Also, I was afraid I couldn't be who you wanted me to be, so I just wasn't going to try. I'm truly sorry for putting the past off on you."

"Chad—"

"Please let me finish." Chad's fingers tightened briefly on hers. "Izzy, we're good together. As partners at work, as friends, as lovers." A note of pain and longing circled his words. "I've never felt as close to anyone. We fit like a lock and key. I don't work without you."

Izzy sat up, trying to get as close to him as she could. Her eyes still held his. "I care about you, appreciate all you have done for me, but I don't see how anything between us can go anywhere." She lifted and dropped a shoulder. "We don't want the same things. I haven't changed my mind about marriage and children. You had that and want no part of that again. I understand. I just think we're setting ourselves up for pain."

Chad straightened. "I think you'd be surprised at what I want. I've thought about what you said. You've changed me, Izzy. Because of you I'm willing to take a chance. I'm trying to set boundaries at work. I now believe that I can be the husband and father that I want to be, or at least I can try if you're beside me. You've shown me what it's like to have someone truly care. For me. About Henry. To be loyal and supportive."

Izzy chest filled with hope.

"When I learned of your accident, I thought I might die." He put her hand over his heart. "I couldn't lose you. You're my life. My heart. My home. I love you."

Izzy stared at Chad. She'd never dared to believe she might hear him talk this way. Her heart swelled. It was almost more than she could take in.

"I told you so at the hospital when you were headed for surgery."

"You did?" She watched him in amazement.

"I did, but apparently the meds had kicked in and you were already out of it."

She sighed. "That I should have remembered. I wish I had. Why haven't you said anything since then?"

"Because I wanted to show you how much I care. I wanted you to feel my love. To see how much I enjoyed us being a family. How much I wanted us to make a life together."

He cupped her face, looking into her eyes. She leaned

into his palm. "What I want you to know is that I love you. Deeply and completely. I have for a long time. I just couldn't admit it to myself and certainly not to you. I didn't expect you to come into my life, but you took it like a storm, turning me around and dropping me on my butt.

"You're the best thing that's ever happened to me and Henry. I should've told you that weeks ago, but I was scared. Can you forgive me for hurting you? Will you give me another chance?"

Izzy's heart was almost to the bursting point with joy. She shifted closer. Chad's arm came around her waist as her lips tenderly met his. Chad took over the kiss, taking it deeper. Her fingers ran through his hair. He pulled her into his lap.

"Mmm…" Izzy pulled her lips away from his. "By the way, in case you're wondering, I love you too."

His mouth found hers again. Sometime later he broke the long hot kiss that had her tingling in anticipation of more.

"By the way, the other day, did you kiss me and tell me while I was sleeping that you loved me?"

Chad smiled. "Which day? I've told you every day for the last three weeks."

Izzy's heart swelled as her eyes turned misty. "Then I need to catch up. I love you with all my heart."

His eyes darkened. "Do you mind if we push dinner back a little while longer?"

"No." She pressed her lips against his brow. Her voice went low and husky. "Why? You have something else you'd rather be doing?"

Chad nudged her off his lap. Standing, he picked her up. "I sure do. If you feel you can handle some activity with that cast on."

"I can if we're careful."

"You don't have to worry about that. I'll always take care of you."

"That sounds perfect to me." She grinned on the way to the apartment when Chad whistled "Penny Lane."

At midnight Chad sat at the table under the oak with Izzy across from him, having finished their warm but dry meal. Earlier they had made love slow and easy, whispering their devotion until they had fallen into blissful sleep.

When they woke up, Izzy had insisted they have their romantic meal. After all, she'd said, Chad had gone to a great deal of trouble to cook for her. Chad had pulled on his pants and she his shirt, then they'd gone outside. He'd seated her at the table, returning inside with a fanfare to fill their plates, while Izzy had refilled their glasses.

"This is excellent." She pointed to the plate.

"Ms. Weber helped me." He filled his fork.

"She helped you plan this, didn't she?"

Izzy rubbed her bare foot over his, sending a stream of desire through him. He wanted to forget about their meal and go back inside. Would she always create this instant need in him? He planned to find out. "Just the meal. The rest was me."

"I've loved it all. I love you." She leaned over to kiss him. "I feel very special."

"You are. I can't promise this all the time. But I can promise to try to make you feel special and loved in some way every day."

Her pleasure at his words glowed in her eyes.

"Would you like to dance?" He stood and offered his hand.

"There's no music." Yet she took his hand.

"I'll hum something." Chad pulled her into his arms. The notes to "Penny Lane" filled the air.

Izzy patted him on the chest. "You and that song."

"You're in my ears and my eyes just like in the song but also in my heart and mind. I love you."

She kissed him as if he were her world. "Back at you."

They swayed a few more minutes before Chad stopped. "There's one more thing I had planned."

"More?" What could be more perfect than tonight?

"Look what I found." He reached behind her.

Izzy turned. Her breath caught. "Chad—"

He went down on a knee. "Izzy, will you marry me? Have children with me? Make my life happy?"

She squealed like Henry in the grocery store and threw her arms around Chad's neck. "Yes, yes, yes. Forever. Yes."

* * * * *

COMING SOON!

We really hope you enjoyed reading this book.
If you're looking for more romance, be sure to
head to the shops when new books are
available on

Thursday 29th September

To see which titles are coming soon, please visit

millsandboon.co.uk/nextmonth

MILLS & BOON ®

Coming next month

A FAMILY MADE IN PARADISE
Tina Beckett

The elevator doors opened, and he was dumped onto the fourth floor. Rounding the corner, he pushed through the glass door to Neves's waiting area. He frowned when he spied Rachel in one of the chairs. He glanced around. No one else was here.

Hell, he hoped this wasn't about what had happened between them last year. In all honesty, he'd been waiting for that to catch up with him. But after a year?

You're being paranoid, Seb.

They'd both been consenting adults who'd agreed to remain mum about the night they'd shared. Not that the hospital really had any rules against colleagues sleeping together, although the unspoken consensus was that it could be a sticky situation. But it evidently worked for some. There was at least one pair of surgeons at Centre Hospitalier who were married. And his and Rachel's encounter had only been one night long.

Rachel didn't even look at him. Dressed in a gauzy white skirt and a blouse that was as blue as the ocean, she looked almost as inviting as the warm currents a short distance away. And when she crossed her legs—that slow slide of calf over calf was reminiscent of… He swallowed. Okay, don't go there.

But at odds with his thoughts were the tense lines in

her face and her refusal to glance his way. It couldn't be a coincidence that she was here. Did she know why they'd been summoned? Was this about the girl at the beach yesterday?

He glanced at Neves's administrative assistant, who must have guessed his thoughts, because she nodded. "He hoped you were in the building so he could meet with you both together."

His eyes went back to Rachel before returning to the desk. "About?"

"Hey, I just work here." Cécile raised her hands, palms out, in a way that said she had no idea why they were here. And he couldn't very well ask Rachel if she knew. Not in front of Neves's assistant.

Cécile picked up her office phone and murmured something into it. Then she looked up. "You can go on in."

When no one moved, she grinned. "Both of you."

Continue reading
A FAMILY MADE IN PARADISE
Tina Beckett

Available next month
www.millsandboon.co.uk